THE BYSTANDER

THE GAME AT
CAROUSEL

BOOK 1 — THE BYSTANDER

ROB M. LASTREL

Podium

Published in 2024 by Podium Publishing
www.podiumaudio.com

THE BYSTANDER

CHAPTER ONE

SILAS THE MECHANICAL SHOWMAN

My friends and I are going to die here, but I'll die more times than them, I think.

This trip was supposed to be a chance for me to turn over a new leaf. My first real road trip after three years in college.

The car ride here seemed normal enough at first. I was in the back with the luggage on one of those tiny extra seats that large SUVs sometimes have. There was no legroom, but I couldn't complain. I never got invited to things like this. I was happy to tag along. They could have strapped me to the roof for all I cared.

Antoine sat quietly in the driver's seat, his shoulders tense, his eyes hyper-focused on the road. He was usually talkative, always ready to provide his opinion on any given topic, but as we neared our destination, he had gone silent. I hadn't known him for very long, but I could still tell he was uncharacteristically nervous.

In the front passenger seat, his girlfriend Kimberly reached a hand over to him and gently grasped the crook of his elbow. "Everything will be okay," she said softly. "We're here for you. You know that, right?" Most guys in our graduating class had a crush on Kimberly. She had long blonde hair and natural poise.

Antoine shrugged his broad shoulders and nodded his head. "I know," he said with practiced confidence. "I'm just excited. That's all. That's to be expected."

Kimberly ran her hand up his bicep and onto his shoulder affectionately.

Antoine looked worried to me, but none of us really knew what Antoine was feeling. How could we?

Eight years earlier, his older brother Christian had decided to start over. He left behind his family, his college education, and an all-but-guaranteed career in professional football after graduation. No one knew why he had done it, and what sparse communication he had made with his family afterward had left more questions than it had answers.

My first thought was that Chris had joined a cult, but even I knew not to suggest that to Antoine.

Chris had gotten back in touch with Antoine a few months earlier. Antoine said it was like answering a phone call from a ghost. Eight years with no contact, and then suddenly he was Facetiming with his brother every night.

That phone call was what led to the road trip.

We were on our way out to Chris's lake house in some exclusive resort town in the Ozark Mountains.

When I was invited on the trip, I took the chance to look up Christian Stone. When he took off, he was being talked about on SportsCenter and in blogs on college football. From the sound of it, the guy would have been a millionaire if he had kept at it. He had huge prospects. I couldn't imagine why he had left it all behind. Then again, if he had a lake house, he couldn't have been doing too poorly.

The radio went out about twenty minutes before we got to our destination. Antoine flicked the scan button on the steering wheel to try to find a station. The radio searched and searched for a broadcast but only found one.

"It's RUN 41.1 Carousel Public Radio. We've had a beautiful day here in Carousel. The city council has begun setting up for the Centennial Celebration, so stay away from town square unless you like traffic. Our correspondent, Jeffrey Tethers, is at Lake Dyer with the fishing report, and we have Coach Boom in the studio to talk about Friday night's game. All after this commerc—"

Antoine clicked the radio off. "I'm going to pass them on the next straight-away," he said. He had been growing frustrated at the small car in front of us. They were creeping along the road at a measly thirty miles an hour. We had been behind them for twenty minutes, but with the winding, heavily forested roads, there was no safe place to get around them.

"Just be patient," Anna said from the backseat. "We can't be too far off."

As she spoke, a green VW van approached us from behind. It had to slow down considerably upon reaching us. Its horn began honking almost immediately.

"Great, now we have a car behind us," Antoine said.

As if to change the subject, Kimberly interjected, "I have no signal. Does anyone have a signal?" She raised her phone up toward the sunroof to no avail.

I checked my phone. I had no signal either. I had one new message.

Camden, my oldest friend, had just sent a picture of a sign advertising a bed and breakfast that had the phrase "closed fur renovations." He had taken the picture some miles back when we stopped for gas. I chuckled at the typo. We must have lost signal right after that.

It had been a long time since I had been a part of a group chat with Camden. Not since sophomore year in high school. Camden and I had been best friends in middle school, but not as much afterward. He had somehow managed to thread the needle of being smart *and* popular. I barely managed to accomplish the first part.

At some point in time, the geeks and the nerds go their separate ways. There was no animosity between us. It was just hard talking about the good old days when the good old days were from before you finished puberty. We had grown up so much since then. I spent my time watching scary movies and puttering about online between classes. He spent his time with competitive internships and scholastic competitions.

Honestly, when I got the invite to the lake house, I was surprised. I hadn't heard from him in over a year.

As we crept around another corner, the VW van gunned its engine and quickly passed by Antoine's SUV and the little car in front of us. That must have emboldened Antoine because he followed suit and left the slow car in the dust.

Ten minutes later, after zooming around tight, forested corners, the small backwoods road gave way to a large parking lot. It was so big I thought we must have been near an airport or a sports arena. There was no airport though. No football stadium either, nothing to justify the huge empty lot.

There were maybe a few dozen vehicles scattered about, but they were few and far between. What's more, there were no people anywhere. It was completely abandoned. Except for us and the VW van, which had been parked in the shade. The driver, a dark-haired woman in her mid-thirties, carried a large, overstuffed backpack along with a sports duffel. She wore a brown leather jacket and distressed blue jeans.

Antoine parked next to her van in the shade.

"Carousel," I read aloud off of a large sign at the front of the parking lot.

"Yeah," Antoine said as he opened the back of his SUV. "Paradise, USA."

There was only one road leading from the parking lot to Carousel, and it had been blocked off. It had those removable metal poles that you might see on a college campus designed to keep cars from driving down the wrong street. They were locked into place with padlocks. We would have to go the rest of the way on foot.

When we were invited, Antoine's brother Chris had warned us of this. It was because of the Centennial Celebration Carousel was having. No traffic allowed in. It made enough sense to me. It didn't matter; we were there to bask in the sun at his brother's lake house. We would stay out of town for the most part.

I had the least luggage of anyone in the group, just one duffel. As they were retrieving their things from the car, I went ahead toward the road leading to Carousel. The path was decorated on both sides with advertisements for the Centennial Celebration—apparently, this was a big deal for the town.

The woman in the brown leather jacket had slowed her pace and was taking in her surroundings. We weren't in town yet. There were no street signs here, no people. Just off the road was a single wooden building that had little signage except for a door that read "EMPLOYEES ONLY." It also had a covered porch on the front and what looked to be a town map hanging against the side of the building.

I debated whether I should try to speak to the woman. She didn't look like she wanted to talk to me or anyone else. She was all business. The way that she scanned the building led me to believe that she hadn't been here before either.

I turned and waited for my friends to catch up. Antoine and Kimberly quickly joined me, but Anna and Camden were lagging behind staring at the cars in the parking lot. I walked down to them to see what they were so interested in.

"These cars have been here a long time," Camden said. "The tires have dry-rotted."

He was right. Every vehicle in the parking lot but ours had flat tires. Their windshields were covered in dust. Their paint jobs were faded. I didn't know what to think of it.

"That's strange, right?" I asked.

"Yep," Camden said. "Maybe this is long-term parking, and the other cars were moved for the Centennial."

"That makes sense, I guess."

"Look," Anna said, "we're here to support Antoine. Worst-case scenario, we'll just get the hell out of dodge. Don't go acting weird. He has enough to worry about."

Just as we turned to walk up the road, the little compact car that we had passed on the way here finally pulled into the huge parking lot. We watched as it slowly drove its way to the front of the lot and parked beside Antoine's SUV. Two people exited the vehicle along with luggage. They were arguing.

Well, the woman was arguing. The man was just kind of taking it.

"I just don't understand why they would hold an event all the way out here in the middle of nowhere. Don't they know it's more sensible to hold it in a bigger city?" The woman spoke with a waver and a voice like a mouse whose tail had been stepped on.

I wouldn't say they became part of our group, but they definitely started moving with us as if they thought we were all supposed to be grouped together.

"You all here for the convention?" the man said. "Name's Bobby Gill."

He held out his hand. I extended mine for a handshake. "Riley Lawrence," I said.

"They don't need to know your name," the woman said to Bobby Gill. "This place gives me the creeps. Let's just go."

"It's just polite, Janet," Bobby Gill said. He looked over at us expectantly. "So how about this convention, huh? I can hardly think I'm so excited."

Camden responded, "We're not here for that. We're just going to the lake."

"Ah," Bobby said. "Carousel is holding a horror convention you may know. Carousel Horror Nights. They have for nearly three decades." He could barely contain his excitement. "I've been asked to be a guest speaker. I moderate one of the top horror boards on the internet. Arterial Oasis. If you've heard of that."

I *had* heard of it. I didn't say so because his wife Janet looked annoyed at my presence.

I got an easy out when we heard a loud *bang* up ahead.

We moved closer to investigate.

"Were you trying to break it off its hinges?" Camden asked.

The door that read "employees only" was now open.

"I just knocked on it," Antoine said. "I heard someone in there."

"I don't see anyone," Anna said.

The woman who drove the van was peeking her head in as Antoine and Kimberly watched.

The inside of the building was dark. Little light managed to seep in and even the open door didn't illuminate the shadows within. I couldn't imagine anyone was in there. My heart started to beat quickly though. I couldn't say why.

Then music started to play. It was old-fashioned carnival music that came out too slow, like it was coming from an old wind-up music player in need of a tune-up.

Next were the lights. Yellow-white light bulbs illuminated the inside of the room. The lights weren't hanging from the ceiling. No, they were all affixed to a machine that was about the size of an ATM. As my eyes adjusted to the light, I saw what the machine was: one of those old animatronic fortune tellers. The kind that might be seen at carnivals or on boardwalks. Every circus has at least one, and they could even be found in an arcade.

Normally, the animatronics would give you a rolled-up fortune in exchange for a quarter. It might even be programmed to tell your future out loud. Often, they were dressed like psychics or traveling palm readers. This one was different.

The base was a red square box, and above that, a glass box contained the upper torso of a smiling figure. He was dressed like an old-fashioned usher that you might see at a movie theater. He wore a red jacket with brass buttons and a round usher's cap with a chin strap, and in his hand, he held a flashlight that flicked on and off along with all the other light bulbs attached to the machine.

Across the top of the machine was a sign that read "Carousel's own Silas the Mechanical Showman."

In the middle of the machine, right below the glass case, was a red button with a receptacle underneath.

For a moment, no one in the group said anything as the fortune-telling machine began whirring to life. I think Antoine might have cursed under his breath, and Kimberly gasped. Beside me, the woman, Janet, was pulling on her husband's arm.

After the carnival tune ended, the dummy in the glass case began to speak. His little wooden mouth moved up and down with a slight clack of yellow teeth.

"Welcome to Carousel, the town where movies come to life. The show's about to start, and you're in the front row!" he said in a slightly warped mechanical voice.

"What the heck," I said.

"Come on up and get your tickets. The Centennial Celebration awaits."

No one moved.

"Are we supposed to get a ticket?" Anna asked, looking at Antoine. After all, he was the one who invited us.

"I have no idea. Chris didn't say anything about this," he responded.

As if to answer the question, Silas the Mechanical Showman said, "No admittance without a ticket. You don't want to miss the show!"

Antoine shrugged his shoulders and approached the machine. He pushed the red button and the gears inside the mechanism turned, releasing three large tickets into the receptacle underneath. Antoine retrieved them and began to read through them. He didn't say anything as he read, but a puzzled look appeared on his face.

Before I could ask what the ticket said, Kimberly had also pushed the red button and retrieved her tickets. Then the woman in the brown jacket, followed by Anna and Camden. The couple who had arrived in the small car each pressed the button after each other, though the woman absolutely did not want to, from the look on her face. Finally, it was my turn.

I pressed the button and three tickets slid out. As I picked them up, I noted how heavy they were, how thick. They were printed on high-quality stock, and each was cool to the touch. Each of the tickets had a title, an illustration, an elaborate graphic design, and a text description.

"These are awesome!" Bobby said. "They really go all out with this convention."

I don't know what I had expected to be on the tickets, but I certainly didn't expect what I ended up seeing.

One of my tickets was blue, another green, and the one that interested me the most at first, for whatever reason, was silver.

Still, no one said anything as we each reviewed our tickets.

My silver ticket read:

<table>
<tr><td colspan="2">The Film Buff
Minor Archetype
You are the Film Buff. The master of the unwritten rules of horror movies. You've seen every slasher, spine-tingler, and creature feature; now we will see if you can survive them in real life! With your help, your allies may stand a chance against the nightmarish beings that lurk in the shadows of the silver screen.
That is, if you can get them to listen to you before it's too late . . .</td></tr>
<tr><td colspan="2">Base Stats</td></tr>
<tr><td>Mettle – For Feats of Strength and Offensive ability</td><td>1</td></tr>
<tr><td>Moxie – To make your performance convincing</td><td>3</td></tr>
<tr><td>Hustle – To be Quick, Nimble, Evasive, and to always hit your Mark</td><td>1</td></tr>
<tr><td>Savvy – For Perception, Planning, and Deduction</td><td>5</td></tr>
<tr><td>Grit – For Willpower, Toughness, and Endurance</td><td>1</td></tr>
<tr><td>Plot Armor – Conquering all five aspects of Plot Armor will make you a Master of Horror.</td><td>11 (total of all stats)</td></tr>
</table>

Was this some strange roleplaying event? Were my friends and I even supposed to get tickets?

My curiosity was piqued. I read further.

My green ticket read:

<table>
<tr><td>Cinema Seer
Type: Buff
Archetype: Film Buff
Aspect: ---
Stat Used: Savvy</td></tr>
<tr><td>The Film Buff has seen every horror movie and can guess every twist and turn. When the Film Buff makes a clever prediction about an important and impactful plot event, all allies who hear it will obtain a boost in Grit and Savvy if that prediction is proven true.
Beware, the more predictions the player makes, the less powerful they will become. Predictions must be made On-Screen. Multiple buffs in a single storyline are difficult to perform at the lower levels.
You may not want someone calling out a plot twist in your theater, but you would kill to have someone do it in Carousel.</td></tr>
</table>

On-Screen? What could that mean?
The blue ticket read:

<table>
<tr><td>

Trope Master
Type: Insight
Archetype: Film Buff
Aspect: ---
Stat Used: Savvy

</td></tr>
<tr><td>

The signature ability of the Film Buff is their ability to understand how monsters and slashers operate within a story. With this ticket, the Film Buff will have insight into which tropes enemies have equipped. This trope works best with high Savvy and close proximity to the enemy.
Enemy tropes have generic descriptions. The clever player will figure out how their tropes will be expressed in each specific storyline.
With great power comes great balancing: during storylines where this trope is equipped, the Film Buff's Plot Armor will be reduced by half. Hopefully, that's all that will be cut in half.

</td></tr>
</table>

The curtains were up.
The show was starting.
The Game at Carousel had begun.

CHAPTER TWO

THE UNANSWERED PLEA

Hello," the voice called. It was a woman. "Are you all looking for Carousel?"

I looked down toward the road. Three people stood there expectantly. I had to blink a few times. The lights from the animatronics display had left bright impressions on my eyes.

The person talking was a slender woman with black hair. She might have been in her late twenties. Two men accompanied her. One was a tall twig of a guy who wore a jester's grin around the same age.

The other guy was older—forty-five or so—and he did not look nearly as entertained to be there. He wore a gruff beard and tamed his slightly overgrown hair with a ballcap. He said nothing, but slowly smoked away at the cigar in his mouth.

Antoine spoke first. He cleared his throat. "We're here to visit my brother. Carousel is just down this road, right?"

"It sure is," the tall skinny man said.

The woman said, "My name is Valerie. These are Todd and Arthur." She gestured toward the tall man and then the gruff man respectively. "We're here to guide newcomers to town and help you get all set up. Things are a little diff—"

She was cut off by the taller man, Todd. "Is your brother Christian Stone?" he asked with a bemused smile.

His two companions seemed taken aback by his question. They looked intently at Antoine.

". . . Yes," Antoine said. "Do you know him?"

Valerie, Arthur, and Todd looked at each other.

"Yeah, we know him," Valerie said, not missing a beat. "Have known him for years now. That would make you Antoine?"

"That's me," Antoine said. "We're supposed to be heading to Lake Dyer. He has a lake house over there," Antoine said. "Is that down this way?"

Todd started to laugh. "He invited you out to the lake house?" he asked. "Sounds like you have a fun time ahead of you."

"We'll take you to him," Valerie said cheerfully. "Are all of you here to visit Chris? There's a Centennial event; we're expecting guests to start coming in soon."

"The two of us are going to the horror convention in town," Bobby said, putting his arm around his wife. "Is that this way too?"

"Yes," Valerie said softly. "You must be Bobby Gill?"

"That's me," Bobby said.

She turned to my friends and me. "We have to give the guests a little tour as we go before we can take you to Chris. Do you mind just following along?"

Antoine took a moment to consider what he was being asked and said, "Sure. Were we supposed to take these?" He held up the three tickets he had gotten from Silas the Mechanical Showman.

"Those are for participating in the events," Todd said, "if you decide you want to do that. We have some really cool stuff this year. I'm sure Chris told you all about it."

"There's a trivia contest at a bar, right?" Antoine asked. "Scary movie trivia?"

"There is," Todd said. "But you're not going to win if there's anything I can do about it."

As a matter of fact, the movie trivia contest is why I was invited. They needed a ringer.

"Great," Valerie said. "If we can get the guests of the convention to come to the front, please."

Bobby Gill and his wife Janet shuffled forward hauling their luggage.

The woman in the brown jacket stayed behind with the rest of us, never saying a word, carrying her meager luggage.

"Kind of a strange time to be visiting the place, right?" Camden whispered to me as we grabbed our luggage and began following the three guides.

I nodded.

"What kind of place is Carousel?" Anna asked Antoine as we took to the road.

"Dude, I have no idea," he answered. He must have been as confused as we were. Apparently, his brother didn't tell him about the welcome committee.

Anna moved closer to me and Camden and asked me, "What are you doing after graduation?"

"Traveling the world," I said as we marched down the road. "I'll move from place to place, staying one step ahead of my student loan provider."

Anna laughed. "I've considered that," she said. "I think they'd find me."

"Realistically, grad school," I said. "I don't know what I would study, but at least it would put off the real world for a few years."

"They should put that on their brochures," Camden said.

"What about you two?" I asked. I looked at Camden. "You still going the medical school route?"

"No," Camden said. "I'm sticking with engineering. The allure of acquiring knowledge has faded. I just want to graduate and make enough money to take care of my family, then I'm retiring early."

"No surfing doctor?" I asked. It had been a joke when we were kids. Camden said he wanted to open a medical practice near a beach.

"Surfing engineer," he said. "The hours are better."

Camden and I managed to pick up where we left off. Lame jokes were like a secret handshake for us when we were kids. I was happy to see we were still in lockstep.

"What did you decide on?" I asked Anna.

"Antoine says he's going to make me the Secretary of the Interior when he wins the presidency, so I have that job lined up," she said. "I think I'll do some volunteer work until then."

I laughed. "He made a good choice."

As we walked, my curiosity turned back to those strange tickets we had been supplied so generously by the creepy animatronic figure. I took mine from my pocket and examined them. My friends may not have been too interested in whatever role-playing game the town at Carousel was putting on, but it looked interesting to me. Was Carousel a fancy LARPer colony or something?

"What did you get?" I asked Camden, showing him my tickets.

He showed me his.

He had a silver ticket:

The Scholar
Major Archetype
You are the Scholar. You were always the smartest, cleverest, and most knowledgeable. Let's put it all to the test. When danger lurks at your door, will you be able to outthink evil, plan for success, or solve the mystery?
Study up! This will be the hardest test you have ever taken.

Base Stats	
Mettle – For Feats of Strength and Offensive ability	1
Moxie – To make your performance convincing	2
Hustle – To be Quick, Nimble, Evasive, and to always hit your Mark	2
Savvy – For Perception, Planning, and Deduction	5
Grit – For Willpower, Toughness, and Endurance	1
Plot Armor – Conquering all five aspects of Plot Armor will make you a Master of Horror.	11 (total of all stats)

His stats were almost the same as mine.

He had also received a green ticket:

<table>
<tr><td>

Right Tool for the Job
Type: Buff
Archetype: Scholar
Aspect: ---
Stat Used: Savvy

</td></tr>
<tr><td>

Every monster has its weakness. The Scholar must work to find it. When formulating a plan that incorporates the enemy's mortal weakness, receive a bonus to Savvy. When fighting an enemy and attacking it with its mortal weakness, receive a bonus to Mettle.
Werewolf, meet silver bullet.

</td></tr>
</table>

His third and final ticket was blue:

<table>
<tr><td>

Eureka!
Type: Insight
Archetype: Scholar
Aspect: Researcher
Stat Used: Savvy

</td></tr>
<tr><td>

In the movies, a character is often able to find the one line of text in a book that will help them solve the mystery or defeat the monster. It never takes more than a few moments of looking. When this ticket is equipped, the player will be given guidance on the red wallpaper to assist in searching through volumes of text for needed information. You will be drawn to it quickly.
This trope may help you find the information you need, but it's up to you to figure out how to use it.

</td></tr>
</table>

"What the heck are these things?" I asked under my breath as I handed the tickets back to him. What had the ticket meant when it said the player would receive guidance on the red wallpaper?

That would probably be explained to people who were actually playing the game, I figured. I found myself letting the issue go.

"Fitting archetype," Camden said, pointing to my Film Buff ticket.

"Yours too, Scholar," I said.

I wanted to take a look at everyone else's tickets, but before I could even begin to ask, the three guides had stopped in the road and turned to look at us.

* * *

"We have to wait here for a few minutes. There is something that newcomers need to see," Valerie said in a slow calm manner. The way a zookeeper speaks to a lion.

There was something strange going on. I couldn't put my finger on it. Even stranger, I felt myself overcome with a warm, fuzzy feeling. I wasn't worried a bit.

On the left side of the road at the place we had stopped was a wrought-iron fence. The gate farther down the road had a sign on it. The top part of the sign was broken off. All that remained was the slogan, "The Jewel of Carousel." The gate was padlocked, and the entire fence was covered in those decorative spikes that can often be seen on fences surrounding expensive homes. It was a step up from barbed wire, at least.

"I can't wait," Bobby said. "I knew this was supposed to be a fancy convention, but I have a feeling this is going to be great." He looked at his wife and squeezed her tight. "I have a good feeling about this, honey."

It was like he was trying to will her into enjoying herself.

His wife didn't look so enthused. She looked worried.

The guides continued looking at their watches. I checked my phone, but the time was way off. It said it was five in the afternoon, but the encroaching darkness told me it was much later in the evening. Almost sunset.

Whatever time they were waiting for must have come because they suddenly stopped looking at their watches.

"You need to listen to us with what is about to happen. It is vitally important to do what we say," Valerie said.

There was that calm, zookeeper tone again.

Her eyes were scanning through the wrought-iron fence. I couldn't see much on the other side, what with the overgrown grass and thickets. Todd, the tall guide, wasn't looking at the fence. He was watching us, watching our reactions. The third guide, Arthur, hadn't said a thing. His eyes were on the tip of his cigar as if nothing about this situation interested him in the least.

I heard something coming in the distance.

Footsteps.

Heavy breathing.

Whimpering.

A woman burst through a thicket right next to us and ran directly into the fence at full speed. She was young, around my age, with dark skin, long, curly, flowing hair—and a look of absolute terror in her eyes.

Kimberly and Janet screamed.

The woman hit the fence with such force that a wound opened up on her forehead. Blood began gushing down her face.

"Help!" she screamed as she saw us. "Please! Please!"

She shook the fence, but it held solid.

Valerie spoke loudly and calmly to us. "Don't do anything," she said. "Don't even speak to her."

We were freaking out. Antoine was cursing repeatedly; Kimberly was pulling at his arm, looking for some reassurance.

Yet, no one did anything. We were frightened, but we were also . . . subdued. It was like we were watching a movie and not real life. We weren't reacting like normal.

"Help me," the woman screamed again. She looked directly in my eyes, pleading with me. "Please. They're coming."

I started to point toward the gate down the road, but Valerie must have seen the thought forming in my mind and reached forward and grabbed my arm.

"Do not speak to her," she said. "Look at her. Focus on her. Do you see something strange?"

Of course I see something strange, I thought. *There is a terrified woman bleeding all over the place.* I still did what Valerie commanded. Sure enough, I caught a glimpse of something I had never seen before. It was the first time I saw the red wallpaper. I couldn't make out what was on it, but it was the first makings of a movie poster. I saw the word NPC too, but I didn't believe it. I felt sick to my stomach.

Yelling could be heard behind the woman. Men were chasing her down. I heard the baying of a hound.

"Please," she said. "They have another guy in the basement. Please help us."

No one said or did anything. Everyone had a terrified look on their faces. Everyone except the three guides, whose expressions were something closer to shame or, perhaps, resignation.

Then the woman began attempting to squeeze through the bars. She was too big. The bars were too tight and their barbs too sharp. They stuck into her like fishhooks, but still she pushed desperately for freedom.

"All right, let's go," Arthur said, speaking for the first time. "You don't want to see the next part."

I believed him.

He turned to leave. Everyone followed him at a quick pace as we left the woman.

Samantha. Her name was Samantha. I wasn't sure how I knew that, but I did.

We passed by the gate and were soon beyond the property altogether. The last thing we heard of her was a scream that echoed from far behind us. I refused to even think about it.

"What kind of place is this?" Janet demanded. She was in between tears and fury.

"Honey," her husband said, "it's just part of the show. It's for the convention."

God, I hoped he was right, but the three guides ignored the question.

After they had gotten us away from the bleeding woman, we came to a section of the road dominated by farmland. There was corn as far as the eye could see.

Valerie coughed to get everyone's attention. "We're sorry you had to see that," she said. "But we hoped that by showing you that, it might make the next part easier."

She looked back at Arthur. He nodded to her, encouraging her to continue.

"Carousel is not what you think. There is no horror convention. Your brother Chris did not invite you. It was all a trick."

"What the hell are you talking about?" Antoine said. "I spoke to Chris. You said you knew him."

Valerie looked genuinely sad when he asked that.

Arthur took over. "How long has it been since you've physically seen your brother?"

Antoine hesitated to answer.

"Years, right?" Arthur continued. "What was it, eight or nine years?" He looked back at Todd.

"Eight years," Todd said.

Valerie nodded.

Antoine didn't answer for a moment. "I've been Facetiming him," he said.

"I don't know what that is, but I can tell you it was not your brother you were talking to," Arthur said.

"What are you talking about?" Antoine said defiantly.

"Let me guess. Your brother disappeared one day. Probably left a note or a phone message, so the police weren't called. You haven't seen him since then, not until he called you out of the blue years later?"

Antoine didn't respond. Arthur's guess was on the money.

"He asked you about your life and your friends. Of those two things, he always seemed more interested in your friends. Wanted to know a lot of specific details. Got to know their names, their personalities, their hobbies?"

Antoine's eyes widened.

"And when he finally invited you to come out to his lake house—"

Todd chuckled.

"—he told you which of your friends he wanted you to bring along. Not your buddies on the basketball team. He wanted you to bring your smartest friend," he gestured toward Camden, "and your prettiest lady friend," he pointed at Kimberly. "He even must have asked if you knew anyone who was obsessed with scary movies, didn't he?"

He pointed at me.

How did he know?

"He said 'bring these specific friends and come out to my place,' right?"

Antoine didn't answer. Kimberly implored him, "Antoine, is he right?"

Antoine nodded. "It wasn't like that though. Chris was just—"

"You weren't speaking to Chris," Arthur said. "Chris has been trapped here with us the whole time. If I'm not mistaken, he came here with Val and Todd, right?"

Todd nodded.

"You weren't talking to Chris. You were talking to Carousel. And now that it's got you here, it'll never let you leave."

CHAPTER THREE

THE FINAL STRAW II

As I was trying to deal with the revelation that Arthur had laid on us, I heard footsteps behind me and turned to see Janet rushing back toward the parking lot, her husband in tow. He was trying to get her to stay, but she wasn't having it.

"Wow," Todd said. "Normally it takes a bit longer to convince people we're telling the truth. I see this as a win."

"I thought you were keeping them calm," Arthur said sharply to Valerie.

"I tried. I am," Valerie said. "She must have gotten a high roll."

A high roll?

Like in a roleplaying game? If that meant what I thought it meant, then Valerie was somehow keeping us from panicking and running away like Janet had.

A thought entered my mind: *Should we be runni—*

"No worries, you all," Valerie said. "Everything will be fine."

There she went with that zookeeper's voice.

And it worked. The spark of panic that had risen in me was extinguished.

I felt like everything would be all right. We just needed to get to the bottom of things.

"Go get the strays," Arthur said to Todd.

Todd nodded and followed behind them, his jester's grin never fading.

As we waited, Arthur and Valerie spoke to each other in hushed tones. I thought I heard them call Janet a "hysteric." A little extreme. Heck, I had half a mind to follow behind and hitch a ride out of here.

I didn't expect to see them come back. Janet looked determined to be rid of this whole mess. After I heard some tire screeching in the distance, I figured they had hightailed it, but ten minutes later they reappeared on the road. Janet looked terrified. Bobby looked puzzled. Todd was laughing up a storm.

"The exit is gone," Bobby said in a low tone. "The road we came on . . . was just gone. This convention is . . . something else."

He was still clinging to the theory that all of this was part of some elaborate interactive horror convention. In a small way, so was I.

As the couple slowly made their way back to the group, Arthur continued to explain the malevolent entity known as Carousel.

"You have to be careful around town," he said. "There are a thousand different ways to get killed here, and some of them are really hard to see coming."

Valerie took over. "Carousel is a terrifying place, but it operates under predictable rules. One of those rules is that when you get here, you have to complete a storyline."

She pointed back toward the wrought-iron fence where we had seen the terrified woman. "That woman is named Samantha. She is a non-player character for a storyline called *Permanent Vacancy*. It's a medium-level storyline, so we didn't want you to interact with her, or else you might get stuck in the story. The fact remains: you do have to complete a storyline soon. Carousel is going to keep trying to push you into one. So, we picked one out for you—one that we think we can help you complete without much trouble."

The three guides waved us farther down the road.

And we followed, shell-shocked and numb.

As we walked, we passed by a patchwork of crops.

"This is the wrong time of year for this stuff," Camden whispered to me and Anna as we walked. Antoine and Kimberly walked farther behind us.

I looked around. He was right. Corn, wheat, pumpkins, and sunflowers. Those are not something you would see at the beginning of summer. Those were fall crops.

The crops weren't the only thing that was wrong. The weather was too cool. Even the sun and the sky didn't look right for summer.

I was working full time trying to rationalize everything I was seeing. This wasn't helping.

Could this be real?

I thought about what we had been told about storylines. I pulled out my tickets. My "Plot Armor" was eleven, but it would be reduced by half when I entered a storyline.

In a movie, "Plot Armor" is a term that is used to explain away improbable plot points. The masked killer takes out the ex-marine like he's made of cardboard, but the high school cheerleader manages to fight him off—that's Plot Armor.

One character dies from getting tapped in the head; another survives three explosions and four stabbings. Plot Armor.

The bad guy is unkillable by a minor character, but the protagonist manages to get the better of them with ease? Two words. Plot. Armor.

I don't know how it functioned in Carousel, but if it meant what it sounded like—and all of this was actually real—it could only mean one thing: that I was screwed.

We walked for so long that we started to see buildings. Eventually, we came upon a large gate that read "Patcher's Family Farm." I was almost shocked to see that, unlike the rest of Carousel that we had seen so far, this place had people—in fact, it had kids running around screaming and having fun.

Patcher's Family Farm was an agritourism destination. You know, one of those places with hayrides, pumpkin chunking, and farm-themed carnival games.

None of the people on the farm paid us any mind. I got a very strange feeling from them. This is where my visions of the red wallpaper really started to flare up. I saw words that I couldn't quite read, but I knew something was unusual about them. I suspected that, like the bloody woman Samantha, these people were NPCs.

They also wore an aggressive amount of denim.

I don't know which of those things made me more uncomfortable.

We were led to the back of the farm where there were no NPCs. A huge display of pumpkins was set up on hay bales. Next to them was a booth that read "Corn Maze $5." A sign on the booth said "Open."

As I was reading, the words "The Final Straw II" flashed into my mind.

"Where's the attendant?" Janet asked. She had woken up from her fearful hibernation.

She was right; it was clear that there was supposed to be an attendant here. There was a chair behind the booth that had been knocked over, and the cash box was sitting open and untouched where anyone could just take from it. I looked around, but we were alone.

"You have a good eye. Hysterics are very good at this part," Valerie said. "It is quite strange that the attendant is missing and the chair is knocked over, and yet the cashbox is right here, open. Try to look at this booth and really focus on it. What do you see?"

I did as she instructed. Truth be told, I didn't see anything but red wallpaper, but it's true, something was screaming out to me from within my mind. There was something there to see, but I couldn't quite make it out. What was my mind trying to tell me? Suddenly, I got a flash: an image that appeared to be one of those old-fashioned elevator indicators you might see in a fancy hotel, with a needle that would point to what floor the elevator was on while you were waiting.

But the indicator in my mind didn't have floor numbers. Instead, it had words. And while I couldn't read all of those words, I could read one: "Omen."

"It takes a while to be able to see things clearly," Valerie said. "But this is an Omen. It's an ominous sign that something is about to happen. This is a storyline called *The Final Straw II*, and you know it's a storyline because it has an Omen right here—a sign of bad things to come.

"Sometimes Omens are subtle, like an attendant being missing mysteriously. Other times they're obvious, like a bleeding woman running up to you asking for help. But whenever you see an Omen, the next thing you have to look out for is the 'Choice.'"

Todd took over. "In this case, the Choice is pretty simple. You either enter the maze or leave. You also have the option of investigating the farmhouse over there," he said, pointing around the side of the corn maze. "But we want you to ignore that for now."

Now Arthur spoke up. "The corn maze is simple. Get to the end. That's it. That's the entire storyline as far as you're concerned. The three of us will take care of the actual plot. All you have to do is walk from the entrance of the corn maze to the exit. That's it. It's virtually impossible to get killed permanently in a storyline like this."

I thought it was strange that he said, "get killed permanently." Does that suggest that you could be killed temporarily?

Anna thought it was strange too. "What do you mean killed permanently?" she asked.

Arthur took a deep breath. "As long as one person survives to the end of the story, you'll all come out without a scratch on you. Simple."

"I want you to look at this sign," he said, pointing to the sign above the booth. "There is a simple rule on it. You see that?" he asked.

Painted in red paint, the booth said, "Enter one at a time—do not cut through the corn."

"Carousel operates by rules. You see a rule, you follow it. So stick to the paths. We always tell people that, and we always get ignored. Don't be the person that ignores us this time."

They started to wave us through one at a time. I positioned myself so that I could go in last. After everyone else had walked or run into the corn maze, I walked in.

The word "Choice" appeared in my head. I ignored it.

After entering the maze and taking a few turns, I was well and truly lost. So much so that even when I turned around and tried to find the entrance I had just come through, I couldn't find it.

I tried thinking back to the picture of the maze that I had seen at the booth, trying to remember its turns and twists. It didn't look this complicated, but it was useless.

I won't lie; I was thoroughly spooked. Whatever calming effect Valerie was able to cast over us disappeared the instant I entered the maze.

I stuck to the middle of the pathways as best I could and didn't take a turn unless I was certain that it was an actual path and not just a place where the corn had been planted thinly. If the rule says don't cut through the corn, then I'm not going to cut through the corn.

As I walked forward, I heard footsteps all around me, but try as I might, I couldn't see anyone else. I caught a glimpse of something orange and decided to go check it out. Whatever it might be, it was better than being lost in a sea of corn.

It took me five minutes to wind my way around until eventually I stumbled back on the orange thing I had seen. It was a pumpkin display, a smaller version of what had been on the outside of the corn maze. Nothing more than six hay bales and a dozen or so pumpkins of various sizes—some of them had even been carved into faces like a jack-o'-lantern.

The red wallpaper overtook my vision. This was the first clear image it had given me. I saw a movie poster of this exact scene, but it was different. In the painting, the pumpkins were all smashed. The poster's title was simply "Territorial."

As much as I desired to look away, I had to keep reading further. Beneath the poster was a brass plate, like those that might be beneath a painting at a museum. It read:

Territorial	This killer will punish those who harm its domain.

As strange as it is, I knew exactly what it was talking about. Sometimes in horror movies, characters that destroy a monster's domain are killed off instantly. This usually happens in the first few scenes. Cut down a sacred tree, build on an Indian burial ground, or even smash a pumpkin, and you're dead.

I grabbed the tickets in my pocket. I flipped to the one that said Trope Master. This was my ability; I could see the rules the monsters played by. That's what this was.

If some punk kid were to come along to this display and mess with it, the monster of this storyline would appear and punish them. I considered screaming out to my friends that they shouldn't destroy the pumpkin displays. That was my job as the Film Buff, right?

As I was considering this, I heard a twig snap behind me. I nearly jumped out of my skin as I turned and saw the woman in the brown leather jacket.

I saw a movie poster in my head. A woman walks through an alley where an axe murderer waits behind a dumpster. "Dina Cano is *The Outsider*."

"Dina?" I asked. This vision was really throwing evidence onto the pile that I wasn't the target of the most elaborate prank ever.

She nodded slowly with a shade of distrust. "You run into any trouble?" she asked. That was the first time I had heard her speak.

"No," I said. "I am freaked out though. Are . . . are you seeing stuff in your head?"

"A red wall," she said. She was taking it better than I was.

"I'm seeing words," I said. "They're telling me that this display is linked to whatever monster is here. If someone harms it, they get punished."

"Film Buff," she said. She must have been able to see the movie posters in her head too.

"Do you think they drugged us?" I asked. "To make us think that we were seeing things? To scare us?"

I really wanted her to say that she knew it was fake. Maybe she could explain what was going on. I prefer my horror stories on the silver screen.

She paused for a moment and then grew a diabolical grin on her face. She walked closer to me, near the pumpkin display, looked me in the eye, and said, "There's only one way to find out."

She reached out and grabbed one of the pumpkins. After a moment's contemplation, she lifted it over her head and slammed it back down to the ground, shattering it.

CHAPTER FOUR

BENNY

I heard myself screaming, "Why would you do that?" and not in a manly way either.

I backed away from the pumpkin display. The shattered gourd and its spewed innards lay at her feet, but Dina had her head on a swivel, watching and waiting for something to appear, for some evidence that all of this was real.

It came from the sky.

It looked like a man in a costume at first, but only at first. I became a believer as the creature floated—yes, floated—over the corn. It was slow and deliberate. I was close enough to see that there were no wires. There was nothing that could be supporting this thing except for the impossible.

It was a scarecrow—not the most famous of horror monsters, but off the top of my head, I could think of three or four movies that featured this creature.

As it grew close, I could see that it wore gray-blue coveralls, like a mechanic might wear. In fact, it had a little red-and-white name tag on the chest that read "Benny." For its head, it had stuffed sackcloth with a little straw hat. For eyes, it had buttons. Each was a different size and color. Its mouth was sewn in, stitched in dark colors into an ironic smile. Its hands were gardener's gloves. All of this—the coveralls, the sackcloth head, the hat, and the gloves—were apparently sewn together into one unit and stuffed with straw. The legs of the coveralls were tied at the ends into knots and were so full of straw that little sticks poked through holes in the uniform.

The way it flew reminded me of how Peter Pan was always depicted as flying: belly down, legs folded upward, head up, arms out.

In its right hand, it held a rusty sickle.

I continued to back away from Dina as I watched the terrifying creature bear down upon her. It could simply stab her and that would be the end of it, but it stopped in the air, paused, and appeared to be looking deep into her soul.

My vision went red. I saw a movie poster of the scarecrow. "Benny the Haunted Scarecrow in *The Final Straw II*."

Its brass plate said, "Plot Armor: 42."

My Plot Armor was currently rounded down to a meager five. This wasn't even fair.

Other posters were hung on the red wall. I quickly recognized that these represented the tropes that were equipped for this monster. My Trope Master ability was working overtime, allowing me to decipher the rules that this creature lived and killed by.

BENNY THE HAUNTED SCARECROW IN THE FINAL STRAW II	
PLOT ARMOR: 42	
TROPES	
JUDGMENT CALL	This creature only kills those who it has deemed unworthy or immoral by its own sense of justice.
IT PLAYS WITH ITS FOOD	This creature spends time to toy with its victims. Often, it enjoys the playing more than the killing.
TERRITORIAL	This killer will punish those who harm its domain.
MINION MAKER	This monster is able to summon or create monsters to do its bidding.
Six Additional Tropes not Perceptible	

The words soon disappeared from the red wallpaper as I ran away. Trope Master was proximity-based, and it appeared that the red wallpaper required you to physically look at the thing you wanted to see on the red wallpaper.

I heard Dina yelling.

"Do it!" she yelled. "What are you waiting for? If it's all real, just do it."

I cursed in surprise. What in the world was wrong with her? Why would she ask this creature to kill her? Whatever the reason, Benny the Haunted Scarecrow quickly obliged.

I saw it move its rusty sickle toward her, and my instinct to run took over. I heard a sickening *thud* behind me as I ran away. In my mind's eye, I saw the Plot Cycle indicator move its needle to the words "First Blood."

I could see the Plot Cycle begin to fill out. Omen > Choice > Party > First Blood.

I don't know when the "party" was supposed to be. I must have missed it.

I ran for what felt like a mile through the twists and turns of the corn maze. I had no luck in finding an exit. Though I was running at my highest speed, there was this thought in the back of my mind that I was running too slowly, that I could never outrun this creature.

In my head, I saw the word "Hustle" with the number "1" beside it. My Hustle stat, which determined my speed, was literally a one—tied with my lowest stats. I didn't know how it worked, but I suspected that I could never outrun that scarecrow with that score. Its Plot Armor was forty-two. If more than one of those points was attributed to Hustle, I was a goner.

Not only could it fly but—I can't explain it—I didn't feel like I was making any progress.

I sure felt like an Olympic athlete, passing by ears of corn at top speed, jumping over roots that had grown out of the ground, and making quick turns at every opportunity. Before long, I figured I must have been on the opposite side of the maze, but then I saw something up ahead. It was another display.

Finally relieved to see something other than corn, I ran toward it. From a distance, I could see someone standing in front of it, and I saw no sign of Benny the Scarecrow. I booked it all the way to the display, but as I grew closer, I realized to my horror that there was a broken pumpkin on the ground: the same one that Dina had thrown there earlier.

Somehow, I had gone in a complete circle. It made no sense. This was the exact same pumpkin display I had just left. In all my turns and twists, I had ended up right back here. I refused to believe it.

In my head, I saw the red wallpaper and a blank painting with a bronze placard beneath it that had no writing on it. It was as if there was a monster trope relevant to what was happening, but I couldn't see it.

The person standing in front of this display wore a light-brown leather jacket and distressed jeans, but on their head was a round, orange pumpkin. I was so unprepared to see this sight that I didn't comprehend what I was looking at until I got close.

These were Dina's clothes. This was her body.

On the haystack next to the remaining pumpkins was her head.

I screamed.

Her headless body, which had ignored me until then, suddenly turned as if to look at me, but it had no eyes. This wasn't a jack-o'-lantern; it was just an ordinary pumpkin. It lunged at me clumsily.

In my head, upon the red wallpaper, I saw a poster of one of these headless creatures, but not this one.

HARVEST CREEP THE FINAL STRAW II	
PLOT ARMOR: 7	
TROPES	
SINGLE TRACK MIND	This creature will follow a simple command until it is killed.
TOO DUMB TO DIE	This creature is virtually impossible to destroy by ordinary means, as it has no brain or relevant vital organs.
HOW DO THEY NOT NOTICE THAT?	This creature's unnatural visage will not alarm players until they are very close, regardless of how obviously abnormal it is.

The creature ran toward me, but I easily dodged out of the way, and it continued running down the path far away from me. If it weren't for the abject horror of what I had just seen, I would almost have thought that this creature was funny. It walked as if it had never walked before in its life. I suppose it hadn't.

I wanted to run away from this place, but what was the point? Somehow, I had run in circles. It made no sense. As I considered this, I saw the blank poster and a blank bronze placard beneath it again, and it dawned on me what had happened.

The way I figured, I could see a monster's tropes if I was near the monster or near something related to the trope. I saw the Territorial trope when I was near the display. Then, as I walked through the corn, I saw this blank poster. At the time I was completely flummoxed.

Now I got why it was blank.

My Savvy stat was too low.

This was one of the additional tropes that wasn't perceptible to me.

I was certain that whatever the blank poster was, it was some sort of trope that allowed Benny the Haunted Scarecrow to change the layout of the maze. There really was no running. You either went exactly where he wanted, or you cut through the corn and got killed anyway.

So, did I want to die right then, or sometime later?

CHAPTER FIVE

WILL SOMEONE SHUT THEM UP?

I continued to run, not because I thought it would help, but because that's what you do in a haunted corn maze. It's human nature.

I expected to see the floating scarecrow appear to behead me, but so far, I had gotten lucky. My mind got stuck on the question of what my low Plot Armor would mean for my survival. Truthfully, I didn't put my odds very high.

A scream echoed through the corn.

It wasn't far away; it was a woman's scream. Not Anna's or Kimberly's, and it certainly wasn't Dina's. She had . . . er . . . lost the ability.

No, it belonged to Janet. I could tell she was nearby.

"Hello!" I cried out.

"Hello!" a terrified response rang to me.

I could hear that she was nearby, but I couldn't see her. "Don't cut through the corn," I said. "We'll make our way to each other."

Turns out she was only a couple of rows away from me, but it still took five minutes of moving back and forth to find paths that allowed me to meet up with her. When I came upon her, she was in a terrible state. Terror had transformed her face, but otherwise she was uninjured.

"What did you see?" I asked.

"I got lost," she said.

Strangely, I was *annoyed* that she was screaming. Having not seen what I had just seen, how dare she?

I wanted to tell her that we would be fine and that we would find our way out of the corn maze, but I didn't know if that was true. Now, as I looked at her, it was easy for me to see why the guides had called her a hysteric. That was her literal archetype. In my mind's eye, I saw it: a poster of Janet screaming at an axe came into my mind. Her face distorted, exaggerated. "Janet Gill is *The Hysteric*!"

Plot Armor: 8.

Surprisingly low but still higher than mine.

We began walking together as I attempted to soothe her with kind words. I don't know that many kind words. So I just said, "It's all right" over and over.

She asked me to get on my tiptoes and try to see my way out of the maze. She was pretty short. Must have thought I was a giant. I explained to her that all I could see was corn, and she didn't believe me. She would say, "No, beyond that." But there was nothing beyond that. No buildings or landforms. Darkness surrounded the corn maze. There was no cheating Benny the Haunted Scarecrow.

"Let's find your husband," I said. In my mind, I added, *and then you can be his problem.*

It turned out that finding Bobby Gill was easier than I expected. It didn't take us ten minutes to find him.

I saw a movie poster in my head: a lonely man leaned up against a support pillar at a house party; an axe murderer staring in from the window. "Bobby Gill is *The Wallflower.*"

Plot Armor: 10.

If I understood this correctly, this guy's archetype was literally "Background Character."

"Janet," he said, "I heard you screaming. Are you okay?"

"Please come here," she said. He was on the other side of a row of corn. She reached out to him.

"Don't cut through the corn maze," I warned harshly. "It'll make the creature come for you."

Bobby didn't listen to me. "This is serious," he said. "She's really upset. They'll have to understand. We didn't know this would be part of it."

The idiot still thought that this was all part of some horror convention. He clearly hadn't seen the flying scarecrow or the headless woman running around.

I don't know what the abilities of a Wallflower were, but clearly, he hadn't seen much of the red wallpaper yet—or if he had, he chalked it up to high blood pressure or something. Who knows?

I protested again, "Just wait. We can find an opening between us." But Janet cried again, and Bobby ignored me. He stepped through the corn, pushing aside two stalks.

I knew what was coming immediately. I distanced myself from the couple and began scanning the skies. Sure enough, Benny the Scarecrow was never far off. He floated over the corn walls with ease and slowly made his way to Bobby.

To his credit, Bobby did figure out that there was something very strange about this scarecrow floating in front of him, but still, he tried to talk it down.

"I had to cross over. My wife was scared. I hope you understand we didn't know the rules when we signed on for this."

Benny said nothing. He let his sickle do the talking. With a quick slash, the front half of Bobby's throat was severed; the sickle moved back, severing the rest. His head hit the ground while his body was still standing—something that could only happen in a movie. His body just sort of stood there, perhaps waiting for a pumpkin to turn it into a Harvest Creep as had been done to Dina.

As I backed away, I felt something brush up against the back of my head. A corn stalk. The path that I was on hadn't been a dead end before, but now it sure was. No doubt thanks to that hidden trope that Benny apparently had.

I knew what was coming next. Benny turned and looked at me.

Strangely, I was resigned to my fate; that, or I was so scared that the concept of running away wasn't even available to my mind. I watched the scarecrow as it flew closer and closer to me, never in any hurry.

The night would be silent if not for the screams of Janet. She was drawing big, deep breaths and letting out screams that would last, I swear, for ten seconds apiece. Though I cannot explain it, my fear of dying was actually overcome by my annoyance with her screams. I swear I'm not like this, but I could feel the annoyance with the way she screamed building up inside of me. I almost wanted to tell her to shut up. And then I saw something in my head: her Plot Armor was now seven.

Wait, hadn't her Plot Armor been eight earlier? I looked across the red wallpaper and saw two additional posters. These were the tropes that she must have received from Silas the Showman. One of the tropes depicted a close-up of a woman's neck showing the hair standing on end.

<table>
<tr><td>

I Don't Like It Here . . .
Type: Insight
Archetype: Hysteric
Aspect: Craven
Stat Used: Savvy

</td></tr>
<tr><td>

The Hysteric has a keen sense of the ominous and strong self-preservation instincts. Using these abilities, they can ferret out Omens and help guide their group out of potentially tricky situations.
Beware, the power of fear comes at a cost.
If you knew everything that was out to get you in Carousel, you would never be able to sleep.

</td></tr>
</table>

The other trope painting was of a woman screaming at the top of her lungs as a knife hung over her head.

<table>
<tr><td>

Will Someone Shut Them Up?
Type: Action
Archetype: Hysteric
Aspect: Craven
Stat Used: Moxie

</td></tr>
<tr><td>

Nothing can frustrate a horrifying situation like someone with an annoying scream. Characters with this quality are often regarded as irritating, and their deaths are usually applauded. But one thing is for sure: when this character starts screaming, it feels like it lasts forever.

When using this trope, a character's scream will make them temporarily invulnerable to direct attack, but it will agitate all those nearby and lower the user's Plot Armor.

With a scream like that, the bad guy might not be the one who kills you.

</td></tr>
</table>

Of course, lots of horror movies have characters who react with annoying screams that never seem to stop. Screaming often ruins the entire scene, much to the ire of the moviegoing audience.

Janet screamed again; her Plot Armor dropped down to six as annoyance washed over me. *God, could she stop screaming? She isn't helping anything!*

Or was she? She was unknowingly lowering her Plot Armor with every scream.

Benny the Scarecrow appeared completely unfazed by her screams; his slow deliberate movement never ceased. He studied me and completely ignored her.

Janet screamed again; her Plot Armor dropped to five. Now it was tied with mine.

Benny was right on me. As he grew close, I started to get the smell of him. I must say it wasn't as bad as I expected. He smelled like hay and car grease, but that was probably just the pair of coveralls that had been used to make up his body.

He lifted his sickle over my head. He didn't strike at first. No, I remembered that one of his tropes was called Judgment. He must have been judging me. Or was this the trope that made him toy with his victims? I had no idea.

Janet screamed again.

Plot Armor: 4.

Benny turned around, his back to me, and started to fly away. At first, I didn't understand what had happened. I thought perhaps he had just judged me worthy of living and was going to let me go.

He was much faster getting back to Janet. He held his blade over her as he had done with me.

I really wanted to do something. To rush him. To attack him. To run. To help.

I did none of those things. I just stood there. I'll never be able to justify that.

Benny must not have liked Janet because he quickly slashed at her. By the time the screaming stopped, her Plot Armor was down to zero.

I saw a little light turn on in my mind. Her status switched from Unscathed to Dead.

I don't know why I did nothing. Benny's Plot Armor was eight times mine; what could I really do?

So that's one of the things that Plot Armor does. Monsters pursue the player with the lowest Plot Armor. That's why Benny had been messing with me all night, having me run in circles, contemplating killing me: I had the lowest Plot Armor.

Until I didn't.

But he was moving back toward me.

As he floated back over to me, I realized that this pattern was going to keep playing repeatedly. Unlike Janet, my Plot Armor would always be incredibly low, and I would always be one of the first targeted by every monster we came across in this horrifying place.

The guides had stated that death isn't the end, that you can still survive if someone in your party does. What does that mean? That I was condemned to the fate of dying over and over again, trying my best to help my friends survive, but never getting to survive myself?

Benny got close. I closed my eyes. I'm not proud of it—it probably wasn't the bravest thing I could have done—but I couldn't run from him. I was at a dead end, and even if I wasn't, he could just change the maze and have me running right back to him. All I could hope was that Anna and the others would make it to the end of the maze and that whatever happened to me here wouldn't last.

With my eyes closed, all I could see was the red wallpaper and Benny's poster. I noticed his tropes again. His first trope, Judgment. Was that my final chance to live?

If I understood it correctly, that should mean that Benny won't kill me if he judges me good by whatever metric a haunted scarecrow might use for such a decision.

What *were* a scarecrow's values? Crows bad? Crops good?

Was I a crow or a crop?

Soon enough, I would be fumbling around with a pumpkin on my shoulders. I just knew it.

I waited for his decision.

CHAPTER SIX

THE OBLIVIOUS BYSTANDER

I don't know how long I stood there with my eyes closed, expecting to die. I must not have breathed the entire time, because when I eventually opened my eyes and saw the figure before me, I didn't have any air in my lungs to scream.

"Step right up," a voice proclaimed with a broken, staticky sound. "You've won a ticket!"

The figure before me was not a scarecrow, no. It was Silas the Showman, the creepy animatronic fortune teller we had gotten our tickets from.

His lights had lit up, his arms were moving, and I could hear the whirs of motors making his mouth move. His flashlight clicked on and off, and the red button flashed.

I fell backward, almost falling through the row of corn behind me. I scooted forward in a rush, hoping not to accidentally break the wall of corn and get myself killed.

Benny had judged me worthy of living, but I still think he would have killed me for breaking the rules.

I stood up and stared at the machine before me. Surely it couldn't hurt to push the button and get another ticket, but my entire body was numb, and my brain wasn't processing as quickly as I would like.

I reached out my hand, trembling, and pressed the button. A ticket dropped down into the receptacle, much like the original three had earlier that day. I reached and grabbed it. It was a player trope. This one was purple. I don't remember any of my friends getting a purple ticket. It glowed brightly at first as I held it in my hand and read it.

<table>
<tr><td>

Oblivious Bystander
Type: Rule
Archetype: Any Minor Archetype
Aspect: ---
Stat Used: Moxie

</td></tr>
<tr><td>

Often played up for comedy, the Oblivious Bystander survives not because of their wit or bravery, but because they simply did not perceive the danger at hand. They weren't looking; they were busy on their phones or smoking a cigarette while their compatriots were silently murdered in the background. If you can convincingly portray the Oblivious Bystander, monsters will not attack you. However, the moment you reveal that you've seen them, they will have no mercy.

</td></tr>
</table>

The illustration on the card was of a man with his eyes closed and his hands over his ears as a cloaked killer lurks in the background with an axe.

Silas the Showman let out a laugh and then said,

"You could have fought,

you could have ran,

but you stood by,

so, by you'll stand."

Then his electronics shut off, and he went dark. As his lights faded out, I blinked, and he was gone.

I was being shamed for not intervening when Benny killed Janet. I guess I deserved it.

I tucked the Oblivious Bystander ticket into my pocket. I would have to process what it meant later.

The bodies of Janet and Bobby were gone. They were probably running around chasing after people clumsily, just as Dina's had.

I didn't know where I was going or if I'd ever get to leave the maze. I didn't even bother running; there was no point. Then the punchline came: I found the exit within two minutes.

I suppose that whatever motive Benny had for keeping me there was now gone. He had judged me and decided to spare me and had no further use keeping me. I found the exit without trying. In fact, I was the first person out of the maze.

I don't know if I'll ever get over what I saw in the maze, but there was one silver lining. I now had a very good view of everything on the red wallpaper, including the Plot Cycle indicator at the top.

Previously, I had only seen the words Omen, Choice, Party, and First Blood. Now I saw the whole thing:

Omen	Choice	Party	First Blood	Rebirth	Second Blood	Finale	The End

The words were spread out with uneven spacing. I suppose that Party, Rebirth, and Finale were supposed to last longer than the rest.

It didn't take long for me to realize what the Plot Cycle was. This was the structure of a horror movie.

The Omen comes first, warning the main characters of what's to come. They make the wrong choice and end up angering some scary creature or putting themselves in a terrifying situation. Things are quiet for a while during the Party. The story progresses. The first person dies or gets hurt, and then there's a cycle of back and forth until eventually somebody wins and somebody loses—the end.

I had seen this cycle play out over hundreds of cheap slashers.

Now I was seeing it play out in real life.

The needle on the Plot Cycle was inching its way toward The End.

Of course, I had no idea what this storyline was actually about. Arthur, Todd, and Valerie were handling the actual plot. My friends and I were just side characters dying in the background.

As I exited the maze, I contemplated walking around to the old farmhouse where the rest of the story must have been taking place. I looked in that direction and saw that the farmhouse was on fire. I decided to stay put. The sidelines were safer.

It didn't take long for my friends to start filtering out of the maze. Kimberly was first. She had been crying; her whole body was shaking. Her right hand was clenched tightly around something, but I couldn't see what.

In my mind, I saw her poster. It depicted Kimberly staring in the mirror with a terrified expression as a man with an axe stood behind her: "Kimberly Madison is *The Eye Candy*."

She immediately came in for a hug.

The maze must have really got to her because we weren't that close really. Still, I hugged her back.

"There was a scarecrow," she said. She looked up at me like she wanted me to tell her she wasn't crazy.

"I know," I said. "I saw it too."

She wiped a tear from her eye. Her mascara had already been running. Now it smeared even worse. "He just stared at me for a long time."

"Yeah, me too," I said.

"He gave me these," she said, holding out her right hand and unclenching it to reveal an assortment of seeds. Pumpkin and sunflower, among others.

I didn't know what to make of it. I'm pretty sure that a handful of seeds is how Amish people propose marriage, but I didn't want to tell her that.

"He only kills bad people," I said. It was true enough. "He must have thought you were good."

She must have been even better than me. I didn't get any seeds.

We spent a few minutes talking about school. Her major, classes, the homecoming game. Anything to distract us from Carousel.

Antoine, Camden, and Anna had found each other in the maze. They exited at the same time.

I looked them over on the red wallpaper.

A poster depicting Anna running with a flashlight from the hooded axe murderer was titled "Anna Reed is *The Final Girl*."

Another showed Antoine playing basketball being stalked by the same figure as he jumped for a layup: "Antoine Stone is *The Athlete*."

Finally, Camden's poster depicted him reading through a stack of books as a hooded figure with an axe loomed behind him. The poster was titled "Camden Tran is *The Scholar.*"

"What do you mean there was a flying scarecrow?" Camden asked. "I didn't see that."

In fact, Camden hadn't seen anything supernatural other than the inescapable maze.

"Next time stick with me; I saw too much of him," I said.

Antoine was lost in thought.

"This dude with a jack-o'-lantern on his head . . . he wouldn't leave us alone," Anna explained. "Antoine punched him, and his head came off. His body just kept . . . walking around."

"Those were the other people that were with us," I explained.

Antoine wasn't as psyched to hear that.

"I think he was the booth attendant," Anna said. She was a little ruffled but wore a brave face.

We talked for a little bit about what the plot of *The Final Straw II* must have been about. Truthfully, we didn't have much to go on.

"Are you guys seeing red wallpaper with movie posters and stuff on it?" Camden asked.

Apparently, everyone had. We nodded.

"I thought I was going crazy," Kimberly said.

As we began sharing our visions, the needle on the Plot Cycle hit The End.

At that moment, we all took a deep breath. There was a reset. We were still pretty banged up psychologically, but physically, we were back to our factory settings, so to speak. Kimberly's makeup was fixed, her golden hair feathered and beautiful, and our shoes were clean. No more maze dirt. Even the rind of sweat I had built up from running through the maze was gone. The story was over.

I saw myself on the red wallpaper. I took a moment to review my status. The list of statuses looked like the buttons on a fancy elevator. The only button lit was Unscathed. I had seen glimpses of this panel, but now was the first time I really got to look at it.

Unscathed (Lit)	Hobbled	Mutilated	Dead	Written Off	Chase Scene	Planning
Unconscious	Infected	Incapacitated	Captured	Off Screen	Fight Scene	Exploring

Valerie, Arthur, and Todd walked around the maze from the smoldering farmhouse. They took stock of us.

"Only three shy," Todd said. "That's a good crop."

I saw a poster in my mind. It was of Todd, dressed as a clown leaning against a train. The familiar axe murderer was hidden underneath the train waiting to strike. "Todd Corrigan is *The Comedian*." That made sense.

Plot Armor: 57.

I looked from Arthur to Valerie. Once I could see the red wallpaper clearly, I was eager to learn as much as I could.

Arthur's poster was of him with a crossbow facing off against the axe murderer. "Arthur Clayton is *The Monster Hunter*."

Plot Armor: 64.

Valerie's poster was similar to Anna's. It was her with a flashlight, and the axe was dropping into frame. "Valerie Choi is *The Final Girl*."

Plot Armor: 58.

The first repeat archetype. I figured there must have been other Scholars, Athletes, Eye Candy, and Film Buffs out there somewhere.

"How do we get the other three back?" Anna asked.

"They'll come around," Arthur said.

Sure enough, a few minutes later, three very rattled formerly dead people walked out of the maze, heads intact. Bobby and his wife, Janet, were hardly speaking. He wrapped his arm around her to comfort her, but it looked like he needed just as much comfort.

I suppose this wasn't what he expected from the horror convention that he thought he was going to.

Dina, I swear, had the trace of a smile on her lips. Was she some sort of thrill seeker? Intentionally getting herself killed was beyond my understanding.

As soon as everyone had gathered together, Silas the Showman made an appearance beneath a tree next to the corn maze. It's weird to say, but I was almost getting used to him.

"Step right up and claim your prize!" he said.

"Everybody take turns," Valerie said.

We lined up and each pressed the button. Most of us didn't get a ticket. We just pressed the button, and nothing came out.

"Maybe next time!" Silas said.

Most of us didn't get anything, but something strange happened when I pressed it. Four little gold stars appeared on a plaque on the red wallpaper.

Talking with my friends later, it would turn out that all of them got stars. We didn't know what they meant.

I looked up at the three guides and almost asked them but decided against it. I was tired, scared, and floating in a sea of confusion. I really didn't care enough at the time.

The only people who got tickets were Kimberly, Bobby, and Dina.

I didn't see Bobby's or Dina's, but Kimberly showed me hers. It was colored orange:

Looks Don't Last
Type: Rule
Archetype: Eye Candy
Aspect: Beauty
Stat Used: ---
Some killers in scary movies fixate on a pretty woman. With this ticket equipped, all of them will. When using this trope, the player will always be attacked during First Blood unless the script says otherwise. The longer the player survives, the weaker the enemy becomes, losing 1% of their Total Stats per minute (up to 15%). After all, if a killer struggles with the cheerleader, how tough can they be?

I was worried that my low Plot Armor would get me killed early in every storyline. If I understood this trope correctly, Kimberly was now in the same boat.

Silas signed off with a lame joke. "I hope you didn't get lost in the plot; I hear it was a real maze. Hehehe."

The guides led us around the outside of the maze to collect our luggage.

Then they told us it was time to make the long trek across town. Apparently, we had to dodge a lot of Omens on the way, so it would be a couple-hour walk. I didn't mind.

Arthur shepherded us forward. "Let's go, it's time to go meet the others."

CHAPTER SEVEN

DYER'S LODGE

The trek across town was uneventful by design. My estimate is that we probably walked about seven miles the way the crow flies. We purposefully avoided most neighborhoods, the downtown square, and the local college campus. It was immediately clear that Carousel was not some tiny resort town. Most of what I saw was ordinary-looking buildings from afar. If you had seen the way that Arthur marched us forward, you would think that we were walking through a war zone. In a way, we were.

On the journey, the needle on the Plot Cycle jumped to Omen a dozen times on the trip. I could never see why. Every time it did, Arthur would make us run in a different direction or hide in a ditch.

Patcher's Family Farm was on the east side of town. We were headed to Lake Dyer on the west side. By the time we arrived, there was no trace of daylight, and even the stars had not come out.

I finally got the joke. When Todd laughed at the description of Chris's house as being a lake house, I figured out why.

Our destination was the faculty lodge at a children's summer camp next to the lake. Not quite the lake house that we had been sold on, but not too far off. The summer camp was right out of a dozen different scary movies from throughout the decades.

Its name? Camp Dyer.

Wonderful.

The first thing I saw when we arrived at camp was a paper flyer. I managed to grab a peek at one on our way in.

WELCOME TO CAMP DYER
Summer Adventures Await!

Camp Dyer is the perfect place to make memories that will last a life-time. This summer, we have a range of exciting activities for you to enjoy, including:
- Swimming in Lake Dyer
- Boating
- Fishing
- Hiking
- Horseback Riding
- Arts & Crafts
- Campfires & S'mores

Come explore and have fun at Camp Dyer this summer!

Counselors, please report to Dyer's Lodge.

Safety Note: At the end of the season, Lake Dyer will be closed down and drained in order to repair the Carousel Dam. Please observe caution in the proximity of the dam, and obey all posted warnings.

It just dawned on me that this part of Carousel was warm. Like, summer-time warm. It had been autumn on Patcher's Family Farm, but here it was summer.

As we approached an area with lots of cabins and recreational buildings, I heard giggles that seemed to have been coming from the bushes. Arthur cursed under his breath.

Further down the forest trail, there was a wooden arrow pointing left with the words "Dyer's Lodge" written on it.

As we walked, the giggles followed us along with little footsteps. Janet began freaking out. "We need to leave now."

"We're fine," Arthur said.

After he said that, a choir of high-pitched voices began singing:

> "Suzy Snyder, six foot five,
> haunts Camp Dyer, still alive.
> She went missing long ago,
> leaving campers in—"

Arthur raised his voice. "Go to bed!" he screamed.

He brandished a revolver that had been concealed on his person and fired it into the air three times.

Bang!

Bang!

Bang!

Suddenly, half a dozen young girls dressed in pajamas jumped out of the bushes and from behind the trees screaming in terror. They took off running back down the path toward the cabins we had passed.

"The campers should not be out at night. I hate those little . . . ," Arthur said. He stomped up ahead the rest of the way to Dyer's Lodge and entered without us. He slammed the door behind him.

Todd turned to us. "Arthur doesn't do well around creepy children. It's his thing. And that sucks because there are a boatload of creepy children in Carousel."

Of course there were.

The lodge was big. The walls were made of giant logs. It had dozens of rooms, and the entire west side was made of glass to give a good view of the lake. When we entered, I saw that there was a huge common room in the center with couches and tables and a fireplace. Twin staircases led up to a second level that had more couches and bookshelves and the like.

And around six dozen people.

All of them were players. For some reason the number of people trapped here really made it hit home how much trouble we were in. If all these people couldn't find a way out . . . what hope was there?

Walking through the door was like a cloudburst. The people began clapping and cheering the moment we entered. Someone handed me a beer. The atmosphere here was far different than we had seen so far in Carousel. These were normal people. There was no danger here.

I think I breathed out for the first time in hours.

"How did ol' Benny treat you?" someone in the crowd called out with a laugh.

"They got a Film Buff," another said. In fact, several people stared at me.

A woman stood in the center of the lounge. She was in her early forties, and from the way everyone looked at her, I knew she was in charge. I looked at her poster.

"Adeline Winter is *The Final Girl.*"

Plot Armor: 64.

How many Final Girls were there?

After we had all made our way in and closed the door behind us, Adeline began speaking. "Welcome to Dyer's Lodge. As you probably already know, my name is Adeline. I wish that we could have met under different circumstances, but that is not a luxury that fate has afforded us. I want you to know that every single player in Dyer's Lodge will be completely devoted to helping you grow to your potential and make a home here, as best as poss—"

"No!" a voice rang out. It was from upstairs. "Please, no!"

The room went silent. Confusion grew on the faces of the crowd as they looked for the source of the scream.

A man began running down the stairs. A man that looked like an older version of Antoine.

"Christian Stone is *The Athlete*."

Plot Armor: 58.

An Athlete. Just like his brother.

Antoine dropped his luggage. Chris ran to him and embraced him.

"Not my brother. Not my brother."

Both of them were crying. Kimberly and Anna were getting teary-eyed. I was too.

"Not you too!" Chris howled.

The rage and sorrow that I saw in that moment were more sobering than anything I had seen so far. We were tricked. Was Carousel going to start calling Camden's siblings now, tempting them to come? How about Anna's parents? I'm pretty sure Kimberly had an army of Instagram followers that would be here in a few hours if asked.

This was insidious.

In a way, I was lucky. The only people I cared about were already here with me. My parents died when I was little. I had no one to worry about and no one to worry about me.

"We're going to find a way out," Antoine promised Chris. "We'll figure it out."

All of the players who heard him say that dropped their gaze. Antoine's optimism was difficult to watch.

After Chris let go of Antoine, Valerie took us over to a circle of couches to talk. Many of the other players dispersed. Some went to bed. Some groups stayed up planning their next storyline quests. They hunched over maps and thumbed through binders of tickets, deciding which builds they would need for which strategies. The tables were covered with weapons and items that must have been usable in storylines.

A group of four went out into the night to "hunt," and I didn't think they meant for food.

The conversation was light. Valerie told us that we should stick around the lodge for a few days. Then we needed to start leveling up. It was that quick. "Hello, you're stuck in Carousel. Now get to work."

"You can't really go into town with your current Plot Armor. There are some good starter storylines we can show you. Relatively safe ones."

Kimberly, who had been quiet since we got here, said, "I saw a sign for a mall on the way—"

"Don't go to the mall," Valerie blurted out.

Several players heard Valerie's warning and then agreed with her.

"Stay away from the mall."

"Mall's dangerous."

"Don't step foot in there."

They said it in such a comically serious tone.

It really sounded like they didn't want us to go to the mall. Kimberly looked deflated.

Camden, Anna, and I sat on a couch watching the players at Dyer's Lodge as they casually celebrated the new arrivals. Such a macabre thing to be cheering for, but I got the sense that the celebration was to try to lift our spirits.

Every few minutes a new player would come by and introduce themselves. Then they would list out the positives of Carousel. Things like good food, exciting adventure, and not paying rent.

Once the well-wishers had stopped trickling in, Camden leaned over to me and asked, "Did you catch the thing about Valerie keeping us calm?"

"Yep," I answered.

"You thinking mind control?" Camden asked.

Anna interjected, "Maybe we shouldn't be talking about this with so many people around."

"Look at Valerie's tropes," I said.

Both Camden and Anna glanced over at Valerie. She was drinking some punch out of a plastic cup and laughing at someone's joke.

"Oh," Camden said.

The thing that Camden finally noticed was that Valerie had two very peculiar tropes equipped. One was called the Good Shepherd. It was a Final Girl trope with the Team Leader aspect, whatever that meant. It helped her calm people when she was leading them away from danger.

Her other trope was called An Honest Reputation. It was also a Final Girl trope, but its aspect was Girl Next Door. It helped convince people of what you were saying as long as you were telling the truth, but it would backfire if you ever lied.

"We were shepherded," Camden said.

I nodded my head.

Noticing those tropes did shed light on how we were able to be moved all the way to camp without panicking or trying to make a run for it. The second one also implied that Valerie had been telling the truth about everything she told us. If the trope itself told the truth, that is.

Across the room, Janet had snapped out of her comatose state and was loudly asking to speak to whoever was in charge. She did not seem satisfied when she was pointed toward Adeline.

"I want to talk to whoever can let me leave. Can you let me leave?" she asked. Adeline did her best to try to calm her down. Bobby was right behind them, unsure of what to do.

"It didn't work on her," Anna noted. "She still ran away."

"Some people can't be shepherded," I said. Valerie had described it as Janet getting a high roll, like you might get while playing a role-playing game. She had avoided getting manipulated.

I wondered if it was more than that. One glance into Janet's eyes and I got the distinct impression that she did not trust anyone.

Eventually, Kimberly came to join us. She was quiet. Her makeup had run again after the emotional reunion of Antoine and Chris.

She sat on a chair alone.

"You all right?" Anna asked.

Kimberly did not seem to register the question for a few seconds, but then answered, "I don't know."

I felt similarly.

Her eyes were still red and puffy. She moved her fingers through her hair and looked around the room. She spotted something on the counter that captured her attention.

For the next few minutes, she would periodically look back over her shoulder at the counter.

Then, after building up some courage, she stood from her chair and walked toward whatever thing it was she had been looking at.

I craned my neck to see what it was. Sitting against a log post, which ran from floor to ceiling and abutted the countertop between the common room and the kitchen, was an old landline telephone.

Kimberly picked up the phone and brought it to her ear. She was about to start dialing when her hand froze, and her eyes widened.

Suddenly, a woman emerged from among the crowd of people and took the phone from her hand. She slammed the receiver back down, hanging up the call.

"No, no, no, girl," the woman said. On the red wallpaper, her name was Roxy. She was a Femme Fatale archetype.

Roxy pointed to a sign on the post that said, "DO NOT ANSWER. DO NOT LISTEN IN."

Kimberly, who had not noticed the sign—or perhaps had not cared—looked thoroughly freaked out.

Roxy led her back to the chair she was sitting in.

"What happened, Kimberly?" Anna asked, holding her hand.

"There were men on the phone," Kimberly said through tears. "They were talking about hiding a body."

"Why would you have a phone like that?" Anna asked, but Roxy had already left us to rejoin her group.

It was a good question. It almost sounded like the phone itself was an Omen.

As time passed, the conversation shifted, and a new player joined us on the couches. His name was Travis. He wore a white T-shirt and a crooked smile.

"Well, there has to be a way out, right?" Camden asked.

"Does there?" Travis asked with a smirk. "What part of Carousel seems fair to you?"

We had been trying to come up with a way to leave. We covered all the basics. Backpacking through the woods, getting in an airplane, you name it. Travis shot down every single one. The players had tried everything over the years.

"Carousel isn't in the real world. You can't just walk to the next town and go back home," Travis explained. "You're screwed, just like us."

Adeline, the woman who greeted us when we entered, was standing behind him as he said that.

"Travis," Adeline said sternly. "What did we talk about earlier today?"

Travis grabbed his cup off the side table, stood up, and said in a mocking tone, "We calm new players. We reassure new players. We remember what it was like when we first got here, and we draw upon those feelings to empathize with what the new players are going through. We manage their expectations by focusing on achievable, realistic, and productive goals." He backed away from us while saying, "When they ask about escape, we firmly and gently address their inquiries, leaving no room for ambiguity. We tell them we have tried everything. We tell them they need to focus on resting and getting their minds right so that they can adjust to their new lives."

He then made his exit with a mischievous grin directed at Adeline.

"I'm sorry about that," Adeline said. "Travis has his own way of coping with the situation. We put a lot of effort into helping new players adjust. I hope you understand."

It sounded like we were being handled again. Earlier, it was through the effects of a trope. This time, it was through a careful orientation designed to keep our minds off how hopeless our situation really was.

As it got later, more and more players headed off to bed.

Eventually, Todd came to us with our room assignments. Camden and I were bunkmates. Literally. We shared a bunk bed.

Our room was about the size of a large closet. It was on the west side of the lodge; the side that faced the lake was entirely made of glass.

Luckily, we did have a half bath right in our room.

Being right next to the window left me feeling exposed. This place was in a magical horror world, so that was to be expected.

Camp Dyer was an ideal place for the players to call home. A secluded area with great lodgings.

I understood that, really.

But there was something that no one said out loud. When those little girls started singing their nursery rhyme, the needle on the Plot Cycle flipped to Omen. It had settled down by the time we got to the lodge, but I got the sense that we weren't truly safe.

But as I would learn, you were never truly safe in Carousel.

CHAPTER EIGHT

CORDONED COVE

I awoke to the sound of tapping on glass.

As I opened my eyes, I was met by a beam of light from the sunrise that managed to poke through the branches of some trees to the east that grew tall on a small finger of land, which jutted out into the water of the lake. At first, I didn't know where the sound was coming from, and then I remembered where I was—inside that small closet-sized room that felt like a fishbowl.

As my eyes adjusted, I could see directly outside my window. I was greeted by the faces of three smiling campers. They were wearing their camp T-shirts, pigtails, and their braided bracelets that they had made in arts and crafts.

As soon as I saw them, they started giggling and running off into the distance, drawing my eyeline back to the finger of land to the east. Nestled in the trees was a cabin. It was off-limits and boarded up, but it only sat two hundred yards from my window.

Covered in its little hiding spot—in one of the only places at camp that close to the water—it was premium real estate. Except for the fact that the cabin was tied to whatever storyline this camp was designed for. Those campers weren't just teasing me; their job was to force me to look at that cabin. The eerie black aura that emitted from the building tried its best to cancel out the sunshine and the splendor of the surrounding woods. It didn't succeed.

I could hear the birds chirping and children laughing. For a moment I almost forgot where I was.

As I got up, I immediately checked to see if Camden was still asleep on the bunk bed above me. He wasn't there; he must have gotten up earlier and managed to get down without waking me.

That was courteous of him.

Luckily, I had our half bath to myself, so I was able to brush my teeth and get somewhat presentable before I went out to the common room to greet the others.

They had all found a spot and were sitting down with plates filled with scrambled eggs and bacon.

I looked in the kitchen area and found that there was a big platter filled with breakfast foods, supplied by Grace, a player who had missed her calling as a caterer when she got lured to Carousel.

I approached the counter and fixed myself a plate, cautiously eyeing the strange phone that Kimberly had messed with the night before.

The veterans mostly ignored me, but I could see their eyes as they glanced at me, saw the name of my archetype on the red wallpaper, and then quickly looked back at whatever they were doing. I could see that they were curious for some reason; me being a Film Buff really intrigued them, but no one had said why that was yet. I added that to the thousand other questions I needed to ask. I was beginning to lose track.

A group of veterans had brought their breakfast to a large table in the corner of the room and were looking at maps and charting something on a paper I couldn't see in front of them.

They had a large book that appeared to have been cobbled together from scraps of paper, almost like a photo album. I didn't know what it contained, but as they looked through it, it looked like they were looking through an ancient tome. I had a few different guesses at what might be inside the book, each as likely as the last.

As I went to join my friends, I saw that they weren't really touching their food. It was difficult to be hungry in a place like this—a place where you couldn't trust anything not to kill you.

Kimberly had barely gotten any food on her plate to begin with, and she still hadn't eaten any of it. The only person who seemed to have any sort of appetite was Antoine, who ate spoonful after spoonful of oatmeal and scrambled eggs.

"It's good," Antoine said. "Don't worry about it."

Maybe he thought that if he ate like it was a normal place, it might feel like one, but he gave up on even that after his appeals failed to work.

As I took my place, I said aloud, "Guess I wasn't just dreaming after all, huh?" That didn't get the laugh I was hoping for, but Camden kind of gave me a charitable smile.

Kimberly sat on the couch in between Antoine and Anna, almost as if they were protecting her.

Camden had his own folding camp chair, and I ended up sitting in the center of an abandoned couch across from Anna, Kimberly, and Antoine.

I was hungry, but it felt odd to eat. After all, I didn't know if these chicken eggs had been found on a farm with zombie chickens or some other unappealing origin.

There's nothing appetizing about being told you were eating food found on the set of a horror movie.

"We're supposed to get a tour of the place today," Antoine said. "You know, I think we should really pay attention. The faster we get up to speed, the sooner we get out of here, all right?"

I grunted in response. *How dare he have a good attitude about this place.*

"Chris told me that there's a lot to do at camp," Antoine said. "And they know places around town that are safe and good for training."

Sir, yes sir, I thought.

We sat and poked at our food for a while before our tour guide arrived. We didn't have much to talk about.

That wasn't true. We had too much to talk about. It just all felt useless. More than that, none of us had gotten a restful night's sleep.

Eventually, as we sat there, we were greeted by our tour guide.

It was the woman named Roxy who had taken the phone from Kimberly the night before. She was an older, sassier version of Kimberly, but she had a certain crazed devil-may-care twinge to her as she said, "Come on, follow me if you want to live." It seemed that joking around with the new players wasn't just something that Travis liked to do.

First, she showed us out the back door onto a large deck filled with patio furniture and BBQ grills. The view of the lake really was nice from out there, and there were lots of shaded areas that you could sit back and relax in.

On its surface, it really did just look like a day camp or some sort of retreat, like we were out doing team-building exercises with the rest of our coworkers.

As we climbed down the stairs off the deck, Roxy pointed to a small building with the word "Chaplain" labeled on it with wooden letters.

"Over there is where Lara is," she said. "She is one of our best Psychics—a Seer, specifically. If you ever need to know something about a storyline before you go into it, you'll be able to talk to her about it. She may not tell you everything you want to know, but she'll be able to help you out without causing any problems with spoilers." Roxy leaned in and whispered loudly, "That means you need to get on her good side."

I thought about the irony of a psychic having taken up residence in a building reserved for a chaplain, but I didn't say anything.

The next thing we came across was an arts and crafts cabin. Except it had been stripped of all its arts and crafts and turned into living quarters for one of the veteran groups who grew tired of living in the lodge. Outside of it, children played on little tables, doing their arts and crafts under the shade of a tree instead of in the building.

It looked like NPCs were adaptable in that way.

Roxy told us not to go in there unless we had permission; some groups really liked their privacy.

"Privacy can be very hard to find in a place like this," she said. "I know at least two teams that purposefully find storylines that last multiple nights so that they can get a place to stay away from the lodge. I'm not saying I would do it, but I understand. Carousel does have some really nice haunted hotels."

The next place we came across was the nurses' cabin, which had been appropriately taken up by Doctor archetypes.

"Doctor archetypes," Roxy said, "are very important and they know it, so you have to treat them with respect. Some higher-level stories just are not possible without them."

She went on to say that once we had leveled up a bit, we might be able to take a Doctor out in the field to see why they were so useful. As if that were something we would doubt.

I could imagine if you had a bunch of monsters trying to put holes in you, it would make sense to have someone around who was good at putting those holes back together. It would certainly make finishing the story easier.

Roxy pointed at a set of equipment in the distance, a ropes course with those big thick ropes that were tied off and at abrupt angles meant to be climbed by shirtless men wearing sunglasses.

"That's the challenge course where the Athlete and the Soldier archetypes go to show off. They say that they need it in order to perform in the storylines, but really, I think they just do it so that the rest of us will watch them. You're welcome over there, but don't slow anybody down, or they will act like you kicked their dog."

I watched as a few Athletes, a Soldier, a Bruiser, and a few other types of players went through the exercise course. I figured it was part of their morning routine.

"Over there is Arthur, who I think you've already met," Roxy said, pointing to a man holding an axe chopping wood over by one of the cabins. He was standing there with a man whose name was listed as "Sam" on the red wallpaper. Sam was an Adventurer archetype.

They were working together to cleave a bunch of limbs and logs down into firewood.

"As for the lake," Roxy said, pointing to the beautiful blue body of water that we had been walking around for the last thirty minutes. "This cove is called Cordoned Cove. If you ever swim out of this part of the water, you'll probably just die." As if to punctuate this statement, in the distance, I saw something slither up out of the water for a moment before slithering right back down into it.

I didn't think she needed to warn us not to get in the water. The fact that anyone would be willing to surprised me.

The rest of the day was much of the same.

We were shown around toward the horse stables, which had actual horses that you could ride. The horses themselves were NPCs, which meant that you didn't actually need to know how to ride a horse if you didn't want to. They would just walk and lead you around the trails all on their own.

According to Roxy, there were no Omens to worry about in this area as long as you stuck to the trails.

The camp was an ordinary camp on the surface in pretty much every way. The only area that she didn't show us, of course, was the abandoned cabin.

As we walked along back toward the lodge, a child popped out in front of us and whispered to me, "I dare you to go into the cabin."

I didn't do as she dared me. I guess that meant I was a chicken.

"There aren't many places around Carousel where you can feel as safe as you are here," Roxy said. "The only drawback is how far away from town we are. You have to walk that distance almost every time you want to go back to town unless you can talk Adeline into letting you take the bus, which you will never be able to."

"Why would you want to go back to town?" Kimberly asked. "Aren't we safe here?"

Roxy didn't really answer the question. Instead, she said, "You'll understand soon enough."

Kimberly must have missed the part where we were told that Carousel wanted us to run storylines. I couldn't forget it.

As we went along, Roxy would introduce us to veterans, and the vets would always say their customary jokes about the newbies, some of which I didn't get; others were whispered so that I couldn't hear them. I must have heard the words, "fresh meat" a dozen times.

Eventually, Roxy led us back to the lodge, and we spent the rest of the day just sitting around, stewing in our own curiosity and dread. We weren't allowed to leave, or at least it was strongly suggested that we not leave. I wasn't sure if they would have stopped us.

The veterans had plans for us. Plans to teach us how to survive. I was anxious to hear what they had to say; it seemed that there was a lot to learn.

The day wore on, and eventually, the sun started to set. It was then that I saw what all that firewood was for—a bonfire on the beach. It was something that the entire lodge seemed to be interested in, although most of the people didn't stick around for the entire event.

Arthur and others built the fire and got it roaring. We ate dinner, which consisted of hot dogs and other grilled items and roasted marshmallows, and for a moment, it almost felt like we were in a normal place.

That was, until the veterans started talking about their life before Carousel.

To boil it all down, most of them were college students when they arrived at Carousel. They were our age. That was scarier than any of the monsters that might be in Carousel: the fact that these people—many of whom were in their forties, thirties, or late twenties—had been there since they were our age.

It was hard to be optimistic after hearing that.

I did find it kind of funny. Back in the real world, people told scary stories when they sat around campfires late at night, but in Carousel, you told stories about your life before the scary stories, your life before you got there.

This talk did not go over well with my friends, many of whom were dreadfully fearful that they wouldn't get to see their loved ones for a long time. This was a pain that the veterans were very aware of, and they attempted to comfort them.

Kimberly cried because her affluent parents would probably spend a fortune trying to find her. Antoine and Chris both spoke sadly about how now their parents had lost both of their sons.

Camden was upset because, as the oldest child, he felt an obligation to help take care of his parents and his brothers and sisters, and now they would think that he had abandoned them, which was a thought that he couldn't stand.

Anna had parents and two sisters who would miss her dearly.

I knew her family pretty well, as we had grown up as next-door neighbors. I could only imagine what kind of distraught feelings her family would feel in the coming months.

Camden leaned over to me and said, "Riley . . . your grandparents . . . I'm sorry."

He was holding back tears. He knew my grandparents. After my parents died, they were the ones who raised me. Camden had been over to my house plenty of times. They would always ask about him after we stopped hanging out.

"Grandma and Grandpa died early last year, two months apart," I said softly.

It was hard for me to talk about something so emotional, something that still felt so raw, so recent.

Camden looked confused and said, "Why didn't you tell me?"

I didn't have a good answer for that.

"You had that internship," I said. "We hadn't spoken in a while. I didn't know how to bring it up."

I worried it would bum him out. I also worried that it wouldn't, that he might have forgotten them. We drifted apart and only saw each other on occasion; that is, until I got a random call inviting me to a place called Carousel.

Anna was on my other side, and she reached a hand over and comforted me, although personally, I kind of wished I hadn't said anything. I hated the idea of making my problem someone else's.

The discussion was interrupted as a woman's loud scream sounded in the distance, over in the area we were told not to go—the woods to the west of camp, south of the lake.

"Banshee," a veteran named Reggie said, watching to see how we would react. He was a Bruiser archetype and a big hulking guy.

Ever the optimist, trying to soothe Kimberly—who was very worried about the sound—Antoine said, "It could be a cougar. They're supposed to sound like a woman screaming sometimes."

"No, it's never something normal like a cougar," Reggie said. "It's almost always the first thing you fear it might be when you're in Carousel. Death is always in walking distance; you've got to get used to it. As long as you stay in the campgrounds instead of going into the woods to the west, it won't hurt you. Don't worry about it."

That was not as comforting as I'm sure Reggie thought it would be.

In front of the campfire, we felt safe. I wondered if someone had a trope that did that, that made the campfire feel safe. Perhaps it was simply human instinct, passed on from generations long gone.

As time passed, the fire died, and it was time to go to bed.

CHAPTER NINE

FAST TIMES AT DYER'S LODGE

The next day, Todd collected us all for what he called "Adeline's tutorial." He said it like he was telling a joke, so I was certain that wasn't the official term.

Class met out on a pavilion on one of the docks that extended far into the Cove. It sounded like a really cool setting for a class until you consider the fact that we had seen a lake monster in Lake Dyer the day before. On the pavilion, we were given chairs and desks to sit at under the shade. There was a chalkboard that had been dragged out onto the docks.

It was my friends Bobby Gill, his wife Janet Gill, and Dina Cano—the woman who had brought down the wrath of Benny the Haunted Scarecrow upon herself.

We whispered amongst ourselves, wondering what lessons might be like and what types of important information they were going to give us to help us survive in the horror movies that we were going to be asked to go survive.

"Werewolves are killed by silver bullets," Antoine listed off. "Dracula needs a stake through the heart." He was trying to make Kimberly laugh but was having a tough time.

"I was talking to some of the veterans," Anna said, "and they told me that the difference between a successful team in Carousel and an unsuccessful one is how well they understand the game itself. So, we really need to pay attention."

I leaned over and whispered to Camden, "Even in a place like this, Anna's still a teacher's pet." I didn't mean it as an insult; I had just forgotten the years when I had classes with Anna and how seriously she took every lesson.

As we waited, the conversation shifted.

"So the guy on the phone, who you think is your brother, tells you to bring your smartest friend, and the first thing you do is you go out and find the only Asian friend you have?" Camden asked.

Antoine looked offended at the accusation.

"I invited you because you *are* my smartest friend," Antoine replied. "You got an A in organic chemistry."

"You got an A in inorganic chemistry!" Camden responded.

"That's how I know you're smart," Antoine said coolly.

Of course, it was clear why he chose Kimberly. Not only was she beautiful, a literal beauty queen, but she was his girlfriend. It wouldn't have been right for him to pick anyone else.

"So why did you choose me?" Anna asked.

"Just wanted someone who was cool to hang out with, and you were friends with Kimberly," Antoine said dismissively. "Adeline's here." He pointed back in the direction of the beach.

It was a good question: How might you be able to single out a Final Girl just by asking questions? Had Carousel asked him if he knew anyone who had just survived a large-scale catastrophe unscathed?

For me, the only reason I came was because he needed someone for the horror movie trivia contest that wasn't real. He was also asked to bring his funniest friend, Derrell, but Derrell was busy and wasn't able to make it. Some people get all the luck.

When Adeline arrived, she came with Arthur, who sat at the back of the pavilion instead of the front. Adeline was carrying a box when she got to the front of the class; she produced from it a stack of books. The books were small, and she passed one around to each of us.

The book was labeled "Carousel Survivor's Field Guide" with a list of authors, the final one being Adeline Winter. The other authors' names I didn't recognize, but that might have been because I wasn't exactly going around introducing myself to all the veterans.

"This is the *Carousel Survivor's Field Guide*," Adeline explained. "This is a collection of basic knowledge passed down from player to player since before I arrived in Carousel. I added my own modifications and input, and I hope that it will be very useful for you. You're going to want to remember everything inside of it, but take into account that this is all information found by players through trial and error. There is room for mistakes, so be wise about it."

As soon as Camden picked his copy up, he started zooming through it using his Eureka! trope, which allowed him to find any information he wanted inside of a book.

I didn't have that kind of ability, but I would likely read through it a time or two within the next week or so. It was small enough that I could probably commit most of it to memory fast enough. Carousel was essentially a game, and both Camden and I had played plenty of video games.

"So, shall we begin?" Adeline asked with a smile.

"Let's do it," Anna said.

"Our first lesson will be a review of Omens because I assume you already learned a lot about Omens just by surviving your trip to Camp Dyer," Adeline said.

She wasn't wrong.

A lot of what Adeline had to say about Omens was stuff we already knew. Omens look ominous and foreboding. They make you aware that something strange is going on, something potentially dangerous. They are often found in lines of dialogue from NPCs saying something that's curious or come from something that's explicitly dangerous.

Avoiding Omens was the reason that we hid away in Camp Dyer.

Our second lesson was far more enlightening and a lot harder to understand at first.

The lesson was about stats. Stats in Carousel didn't work like they normally did in a video game.

"In Carousel, there are five stats: Mettle, Moxie, Hustle, Savvy, and Grit," Adeline explained. "Each of them accomplishes a different thing within a storyline."

She went over what they all did.

The way that stats work is different than what you might expect. All stats are directly limited by suspension of disbelief. The higher your stats, the further you could diverge from what was realistic and start to pull off things that could only happen in the movies.

As she went on to discuss Savvy, that's when the debate started.

"I don't understand," Antoine said. "You're saying that if I have an idea—and it makes sense, and it should work—that I still shouldn't say it because I don't have a high Savvy?"

"That's right," Adeline answered.

"No," Antoine said. "That can't be right. I can't just sit back and wait for my team to die because I couldn't tell them the best way to win. If I get a good idea, am I just supposed to sit on it and wait around for someone else to tell me what to do like I'm an idiot or something?"

"Savvy is not about being intelligent. I'm sure you're very intelligent," Adeline said calmly. "This has nothing to do with that. All this has to do with is making sure that the players stick to the roles that they were assigned. Every player has to play their part."

"Why do I have zero Savvy anyway?" Antoine asked. "I've been on the dean's list for three years in a row; I have made almost all A's. I got into college on a full academic scholarship while playing sports at a high level."

Adeline said, "Your Savvy and your stats when you start are not based on your actual personality or abilities. They're based on the archetype you were assigned. The Athlete is not a Savvy-based archetype; it doesn't have any Savvy in the beginning. If you would like to try to build a character that has high Savvy as an Athlete, you can try, but I would suggest that you learn to trust your teammates to come up with plans."

Antoine wasn't happy about that. The way Antoine talked made you think that he was going to try to save us himself.

Adeline continued going over the final stat on the list, Grit, which helped prevent lethal injuries and helped you fight longer without tiring.

As the lesson went on, we eventually got to a stopping point, and Adeline asked, "Does anyone have any questions?"

The first thing that anyone asked was from Dina. She had been listening intently all class and had abandoned her characteristic aloofness when the lessons started. "Can you tell us about the star ratings we got at the end of the last storyline?"

When we had completed *The Final Straw II*, each of us had received star ratings. I had personally gotten four golden stars on the red wallpaper right beneath my name poster. We had discussed them amongst each other, but we weren't sure how the system worked.

Adeline turned to the board and wrote down three words: novelty, performance, and difficulty.

"Every time you enter a storyline, you will be graded off of these three categories," she explained. "Novelty is for when you experience new storylines and new situations. Since you're new players, pretty much everything is novel, and you'll get big points every time you do a storyline.

"Performance is exactly what it sounds like. You have to play the character you're cast as and the better job you do the better rewards you'll get. Difficulty is subjective and has to do with your Plot Armor versus the Plot Armor of the enemies in the story. The more difficult a storyline is for a player, the more rewards they will receive—assuming that they contributed.

"Once you get five stars, you go up one Plot Armor and get to assign a point into one of your stats. Once you get to level forty or so, you'll find that you'll rarely get any star points at all. You'll have to do over a dozen storylines to get your score to budge. The problem is if you have less than five stars, they start to fade and you lose them—which is part of the reason we have to continue to play storylines."

She looked intently at Dina to confirm that she had sufficiently answered the question. Dina nodded.

Adeline scanned the room. We all had our hands up except for Janet.

"Janet, do you have any questions?" Adeline asked.

Janet had been sitting in the back, trying to look invisible. She shook her head; she looked very suspicious of all of us, as if we were all secretly plotting against her.

Bobby had a question. After a few seconds of not getting picked, he asked, "Can I trade archetypes with him?" He pointed at me.

Adeline paused for a moment.

"Well, you can't become a Film Buff. You're a Wallflower. You're stuck with the archetype you were assigned when you showed up, and you don't get to change it until you get to advanced archetypes like Monster Hunter or Antiquarian. But you will never be a Film Buff."

"I think that I would make a great Film Buff," Bobby said. "I used to moderate a message board about horror and horror movies."

"That doesn't seem like it was the deciding factor," Adeline said gently. "Later on, if you want to try and find an advanced archetype that you think fits your personality better, we can try to help make that happen."

Bobby looked deflated at that answer.

Antoine raised his hand and asked, "How do we escape? Is there some goal that we're working toward? What is the plan? Everyone keeps avoiding that question, no matter who I ask."

Adeline took a deep breath.

"Right now, we think it's important that you focus on growing as players and learning the ropes. Focusing on escape can drive you to do illogical things. I will tell you that we are currently working on several different strategies, trying to find the way out, but we have not made much progress lately. I don't want you to get your hopes up, but I also don't want you to be hopeless. There are lots of avenues left to check, and we will look under every stone, trying to find a way out."

"What happens if we just walk westward or eastward, north or south?" Antoine asked. "There has to be some way out; we just keep walking."

Adeline shook her head.

"We've tried everything. The entire city is surrounded by storylines that are too strong for us to beat, meant to keep us in. As you stay here, and as you get more familiar, you will learn more about our efforts and any potential escape routes that we have been able to determine. But again, right now, focus on the basics, and then later you can worry about trying to get out."

None of us were happy with that answer, but we didn't expect much. Except for a few cheeky veterans most of the players here treated us like we were teetering on the edge of sanity and that telling us too much would be like giving a sharp knife to a mental patient.

"Were you a teacher before you came to Carousel?" Kimberly asked. "You seem like you might have been a teacher."

Adeline smiled and blushed. "I would have been. That was what I was studying for. Then I accepted the wrong invitation to spring break, on a lake someplace in the middle of nowhere, and got stuck here."

That meant she had been in Carousel the better part of twenty years, if I had her age right. That was depressing.

The next person to ask a question was Anna.

"How do we avoid dying?" she asked.

Adeline started to answer, but then she looked up behind us. I turned to see that Arthur had stood up and was walking toward the front of the class.

"You don't," Arthur said. "You don't avoid dying, not strictly speaking. You avoid dying poorly."

I got the impression that he had this speech prepared.

"In storylines, you're going to be put up against incredible odds, and you're going to be tempted to put your own survival ahead of the actual task at hand. Your goal is to get to the end of the story. Your goal is not to survive; your goal is not to kill the monster. Your goal is to *portray* a horror movie. That's one of the things that new players have the hardest time wrapping their heads around." He walked around the room as he spoke, making sure he made eye contact with each of us. "You're not just going to succeed by being tough or by coming up with ways to avoid deadly situations.

"You have to think strategically. And if and when you die, you have to make it count." He had made his way back to the front of the class and leaned up against the rail that surrounded the pavilion. "The truth is that some of you will die dozens, hundreds of times before we leave Carousel. There'll be painful, horrifying, humiliating deaths."

He shook his head and looked down at the floor below, as if remembering his many deaths from the past.

"You don't need to ask yourself about how you can avoid dying; you need to ask yourself about whether your death is a good death."

He jumped forward in step with his speech. "Did you defend your teammates? Did you find out important information that you could relay back to your teammates? Did you distract the monster? Did you act as First or Second Blood so that you could push the story forward?"

He lingered on that point for a minute.

"Those are the questions you need to ask. Because you will die; there's no avoiding it. And if you die enough, and you die well, maybe one day we get to go home," he said. And then he walked off the pavilion, back toward the lodge.

After we were done with class that day, my friends and I sat around and asked each other our opinions on what Arthur had said about dying.

"It doesn't make sense," Antoine said. "We have to die? That doesn't sound right. Why would there be a game where you were destined to fail?"

"We don't know enough yet," Camden said. "Maybe death is guaranteed. Maybe it isn't."

I really liked the idea of not dying. Having seen three people die right in front of me . . . I could not wrap my head around letting myself get killed. I thought back to the trope I had gotten in the corn maze, the Oblivious Bystander. Wheels started turning in my head. A plan in its infant stages.

"Maybe if we do it right, none of us have to die," I said. I had nothing to base that on but wishful thinking.

We had been talking for so long that we hardly noticed we were not alone.

Dina was still on the pavilion with us.

"What I really want to know is how do we win the game? This whole thing is one big game, right? How do we win the game at Carousel?"

None of us knew. We hadn't been told anything about a larger plot to Carousel.

But it was a good question.

What if there was more to it than just escaping?

CHAPTER TEN

THE MUSEUM AT HALLE CASTLE

One morning, I woke up and saw that the four stars I had earned by surviving *The Final Straw II* had faded to a mere three stars. That was Carousel's subtle reminder that you were supposed to run through storylines regularly. The dread of seeing that star fade felt like a physical force in my gut.

I was certain that the next monster I faced would not look at me and decide that I was worthy to live, like Benny the Haunted Scarecrow had.

I knew that ill fate was coming, and I was going to fight it with everything I had. Unfortunately, the only things I really had were my high Savvy and my Oblivious Bystander strategy that I had been working on. The more I thought about it, the more that aching feeling in the pit of my stomach started to go away.

I had to believe in it; I had no other shot at surviving.

The truth was, for better or worse, I was getting used to Camp Dyer. I found myself looking forward to the breakfasts that Grace would make and to my peaceful strolls through camp. I enjoyed the singing birds, and sometimes, when I was caught off guard, even the children's laughter sounded angelic—until I remembered that they were only there to try and trick me into entering the forbidden cabin.

That morning, I was walking along the beach and saw that Kimberly, Anna, Camden, and Antoine were out on the pavilion where we took our classes. We didn't have a class scheduled, so I thought that it was strange and made my way out to them.

Kimberly was crying. Anna was crying. Camden and Antoine were trying not to join them. I couldn't for the life of me figure out why the sudden burst of emotion was happening right then. We had all been emotional off and on for days, but this seemed abnormally turbulent.

"What's going on?" I asked gently when I approached them.

Kimberly explained through sobs that it was the day we were officially missing because it was the day we were supposed to come back from our trip.

It was like the mourning and the pain of being separated from their loved ones hit them all over again.

I couldn't bring myself to cry; I was too numb. If anything, I felt guilty that I had no one back home waiting for me, and they had their entire lives waiting for them.

Antoine and Kimberly spent their time with Chris. I could tell that he was happy to be reunited with his long-lost brother. For him, Carousel didn't just represent being separated from his family; it also represented finding it.

Those two emotions conflicted for him, and I could see it on his face anytime the subject came up. We all expressed regret at having come, at having pressed the button, but Antoine was the quietest at those moments.

A few days later, the time came when we couldn't put it off any further; it was time for us to run another storyline. Just thinking about it was enough to turn my stomach in a twist.

It felt like all of the information we had been taught by Adeline evaporated the moment I started thinking about actually being in another horror movie; knowing that I would get hunted first terrified me.

That morning, Todd took us on a long walk out of Camp Dyer and toward Carousel proper. We were trying to find a specific Omen, but first, we had a small stop to make. There were minimal Omens on the way to our destination that I could tell. Todd didn't seem too worried.

Bobby and Dina had been assigned other teams. Wallflowers and Outsiders were both tricky archetypes to play, apparently. They wanted to get them off to a good start.

Janet refused to go on any storyline. In fact, she refused to do much of anything but hole up in her room and ask for her husband.

As we approached, Todd pointed up ahead and said, "That's it." He was pointing at one of those old-fashioned diners with the stainless-steel siding and the tubular shape. There was a sign outside that said "Diner," but the *n* and the *r* flickered off and on. That was the only sign that there was anything nefarious about this place; there were no Omens in the diner, Todd assured us.

"Before we head in, I need to show you something," he said. "I don't want this to freak you out, and honestly, I should have shown this to you days ago." He led us around until we were on the street with the diner and then brought us over to a wall across the street from it.

On the wall was a collection of notice boards—like those that might be found in any small town—but instead of notices of funerals or potlucks, these notice boards had nothing but flyers with faces and names prominently displayed on them. The word "Missing" spread across the tops of the posters.

At the sight of them, Kimberly gasped; I probably did, too. There were hundreds of missing posters spread over the boards.

"Please tell me these aren't players," Anna said. I could hear panic in her voice.

Todd was silent for a moment.

"They are," he answered. "This is what happens to you if you fail a storyline. Years ago, back before my time, they used to be able to rescue players that failed storylines, but that's not the case anymore, so they just pile up. When one board gets full, they add another."

"This isn't possible," Antoine said. "How could all of these people go missing and no one notice? Eventually someone back home would notice."

"Who says that no one noticed?" Todd asked. "We don't really know what's going on in the real world. I think you ought to know that there are real consequences to what happens inside storylines. Adeline is always telling us not to scare the new players, but I think it's important that you understand what's at stake."

I looked over the sea of missing posters.

The pictures were taken as if they were casual photos that you might take of your family members or friends.

I couldn't focus on any one of them in particular; there were too many. They blew gently in the wind as we stared.

The ones on the far left were older and crinkled; the ones on the right were bright and new, as if they had been put there recently. There were a variety of colors. I didn't know what that signified, and I didn't want to get close to find out.

It was overwhelming.

"Do you know anyone who's up there?" Anna asked.

Todd looked at the wall; I could tell from his face that he did.

"We all do," he answered.

As we walked across the street toward the diner, Camden asked Todd how players used to be rescued and why they couldn't be anymore, but Todd said that he should ask Adeline or Arthur about that because they were around when it was still possible.

We ordered burgers for lunch and ate them solemnly. It was hard to work up an appetite when we knew what was about to happen to us.

Kimberly kept eyeing Todd like she always did when she was tempted to ask a question—or to pick up a telephone, as she had the night we arrived. Eventually, she built up the courage.

"Todd," she asked, "is it possible that I don't have to bring my 'Looks Don't Last' trope?" She was afraid of being killed first.

I couldn't blame her; I had the exact same fear. Selfishly, I hoped that Todd would turn her down. As terrible as it made me feel in my heart, I really didn't want to die.

I was in luck.

"Why would you want to get rid of that?" Todd asked. "It's one of the strongest tropes in the game. Helps you control the First Blood and gives you a strong debuff against all enemies in the storyline. That one's a keeper."

I couldn't tell if he was trying to encourage Kimberly or if he really was so disconnected from the fear of death that he couldn't see why she didn't want it. It was hard to read the veterans. One day, would I be unable to understand the fear of death?

"I assure you that you all are going to do fine," Todd said. "I can't tell you what the next storyline is actually about because then we have to worry about spoilers, and you won't get any rewards for it. But I can tell you that we would not set you up to fail, as funny as that might be. You will succeed, and you'll make yourselves proud. I'm confident in that."

And with that, Todd led us out of the diner and toward something horrifying.

We were told that they were taking us to the castle. It was supposed to be an easy storyline. Recommended Plot Armor of twelve.

At first, I thought "castle" was some sort of exaggeration.

Before long, we started seeing signs for something called the Halle Museum.

"That's the castle," Todd said, pointing at the sign. "Just follow these along the road. There's nothing left to worry about along this stretch if you turn off when you get to the castle. It'll be hard to miss."

"And you're not going to tell us what's in there?" Antoine asked.

"Nope."

I felt like we were getting hazed.

He had to hurry off because if he took us too far toward the castle, he would be included in our party, and his high level would reduce the amount of experience we got from completing the storyline. That was what had happened with *The Final Straw II*.

The signs led us right to it. As we walked, the skies grew gray. I noticed that a perpetual storm cloud hovered above the mountain that we were walking toward. Just as the east side of town was perpetually in fall, and the west side of town was always summer, it looked like this mountain was always rainy.

At the base of the mountain was a road blocked off by a red gate. Behind it was a large sign that read "The Museum at Halle Castle."

As we approached, a stout woman in her fifties was attempting to lift boxes from the back of her little green station wagon. She was parked as close to the gate as she could get without bumping it.

When we got close, she turned to us and said, "Oh, there you are. You're late.

Hurry up and help me with this; we have so much to get done before tomorrow. I'm sorry I had to spring this on you last minute, but the team I hired to clean the museum in preparation for reopening has dropped off the face of the earth. They just walked off the job. Didn't even tell me. Won't answer my calls. You can't get good help these days."

On the red wallpaper in my mind, the little needle jumped to Omen.

My money said that the team she hired didn't walk off the job at all.

The five of us looked at each other. It was now or never. We would never be ready, but that didn't matter. We nodded to each other.

Antoine said, "Let me get that for you." He stepped forward and picked up the box the woman had been struggling with.

In my mind, I saw that her name was Judy. She was an NPC with a Plot Armor of three. That didn't bode well for her at all.

Who was I to say that? As we walked up the mountain, the needle on the Plot Cycle clicked over to Choice and, at some point, my Plot Armor dropped in half to five again. I was barely better off than she was.

"Are you sure you can handle that?" Judy asked Antoine.

Antoine responded, "Yeah, I work out. I play basketball at school."

Judy nodded.

Camden, Anna, and I laughed in the background. That was so awkward. Antoine looked back at us with a smile.

His Plot Armor rose by two points.

Antoine's archetype was the Athlete. Along with that he got two tropes.

One of his tropes gave him a bonus when using a sports implement as a weapon. Chris told Antoine that he can buy a baseball bat or golf club for this trope. So far, it was useless because he had neither.

His other trope, though, was pretty funny.

<table>
<tr><td>

Gym Rat
Type: Buff
Archetype: Athlete
Aspect: Sport
Stat Used: Moxie

</td></tr>
<tr><td>

In horror movies, character archetypes must be quickly established so that the audience knows what to expect. The easiest way to let the audience know you're an Athlete is to slip it into dialogue. When equipped, the Athlete gets a bonus to Mettle and Hustle when they mention that they work out or play sports. Must be used before First Blood. Repeated use will have no effect. After all, even the nerds have muscles in the movies.

</td></tr>
</table>

He got a stat buff for telling people he works out.

His Plot Armor was normally twelve. However, buffs to stats increase Plot Armor as well, so he was currently at fourteen. Plot Armor is simply all stats combined.

Compared to me, he was Hercules.

"The groundskeeper was supposed to come open things up. I don't have the key to the gate," Judy explained.

We walked up the side of the mountain in a corkscrew until, eventually, we saw it. The castle was massive. It wasn't the medieval castle I would've pictured, with large gray stones. It was one of those that you might see in Germany with a white exterior and large wooden beams making up much of the outside.

This one had a drawbridge, but there was no moat.

"You know, this castle was actually brought over from Europe after the destruction of World War Two," Judy explained. "They brought it here piece by piece, the Halle family. They knew the importance of history."

"Ten bucks says it's a Nazi castle," I whispered to Camden.

He cracked a smile.

"Why is the drawbridge already down?" Anna asked.

Judy got a puzzled look on her face and said, "It must have been left open. Unless the groundskeeper has already been here."

Outside of the castle was a parking lot. The grounds were covered with signs detailing where museum guests were supposed to go and how they were supposed to pay for tickets.

As we approached the entrance, lightning cracked above us.

"Let's get inside, dears. We have so much to get done," Judy said.

As we passed through the drawbridge, we stepped into a courtyard. It was completely enclosed by high castle walls. There were many doors in the courtyard, each with signs indicating both the historical significance of the room behind the door and what the room was currently used for. One of the rooms was used as a gift shop for instance. Another was a small cantina with a selection of food and beverages.

Judy guided us to the hold of the castle. "Luckily, I do have a key to this door," Judy said.

She fiddled with the keys in her pocket and selected one, but as she moved it close to the door, she noticed something. With her finger, she pulled the door open. It was already unlocked.

"I'm going to have to have a word with that groundskeeper."

As we entered, it started to rain. Wind howled through the castle.

The needle on the Plot Cycle flicked to Party.

CHAPTER ELEVEN

ALWAYS WATCHING

This is the second-worst party I've ever been to," Kimberly said. She had a large scrub brush in her hand and was cleaning a table so dusty that mud formed when she sprayed it with cleaner.

"I think 'party' is just a metaphor," I said. I focused on the Plot Cycle in my mind and studied the entries for each point on the cycle.

Omen	Choice	Party	First Blood	Rebirth	Second Blood	Finale	The End
Ominous foreshadowing signals the oncoming danger.	The players choose not to heed the warning.	The players explore the setting and story scenario, unaware of the peril to come.	The monster attacks either literally or figuratively.	The players undergo an epiphany that allows them to move from reacting to acting. Reveals the true nature of the story.	The monster attacks again.	The final sequence. No new information can be obtained. The players mount a final attack.	Story over.

"What party have you been to that was worse than this one?" Anna asked.

"At the homecoming after-party freshman year, I found my boyfriend in the upstairs bathroom making out with Cindy Martens," Kimberly answered.

I thought to myself, *She may change her mind when she sees how this party ends.*

We were currently cleaning the gift shop—a small room with shelves filled with books, knickknacks, and other souvenirs that the museumgoers might want to take home with them.

Judy, the NPC playing the role of our boss in this story, entered the room and asked, "Can one of you load those books up onto the shelf somewhere? The author actually used a real picture of this castle on the cover. Obviously, we needed to have some copies available."

"Sure," I said. Truthfully, I had been hopelessly dusting the top of the shelves, and I was more than happy to switch tasks. I stepped down and grabbed the box that Antoine had brought in from outside. It was definitely heavy. I opened it up and retrieved a handful of the books from within.

"*The Codebreakers' Compendium: A Comprehensive Guide to Morse Code and Other Cryptographic Techniques Used in Wartime,*" the book read.

"You know, this very castle was a site used by cryptographers during World War Two," Judy said.

I looked at the cover of the book. Sure enough, the castle was featured in an old-timey black-and-white photo. I recognized the white exterior and the strange layout of the courtyard.

When Judy wasn't looking, I handed the book to Camden and asked, "Which side used this castle in World War Two? Allies or Axis."

Camden picked up the book and flipped right to a section near the beginning and said, "Axis."

His Eureka! trope allowed him to search through books nearly instantly. I had been testing it periodically whenever I got a chance. He hadn't failed yet.

As soon as Judy left the room, I decided to try to do my best to fill my role as the Film Buff.

"I can only see two tropes right now," I said. My Trope Master ability required proximity most of the time, but right now, two of the enemy's tropes were clear as day, probably because they were related to the castle itself.

He had one called Home Lair Advantage, which meant he knew the castle inside and out, including secret passageways and trapdoors.

The other ability was called Always Watching, and it said that he would be secretly watching the players for the entirety of the storyline.

I explained this to my friends.

"I think the Always Watching trope means that the monster is either spying on us from a secret passageway or else it has some sort of clairvoyance and can keep an eye on us from wherever it is," I said.

"So, what do you think the monster is?" Anna asked.

"Well," I said, "it's a German castle, so my first instinct would be Nosferatu."

I was met with a couple of blank stares.

"Vampires," I said, and they understood. "Of course, the lightning and the castle remind me of Frankenstein—the movie, not the book. The general draftiness of the castle makes me think it might be a ghost of some kind because the wind howling is typical in haunted houses. On top of that, this is also a museum, which means it could be a cursed item or even a mummy, although I don't think that matches the decor."

"What about werewolves?" Kimberly asked.

"Maybe," I said, "but the cloud cover means no full moon, and I think it's still daytime outside unless that changed when we got here—which it could have because this is Carousel. If you see the clouds break and there's a full moon behind it, you'll know for sure. But then again, werewolves don't have clairvoyance.

"Of course, it could always be serial killers. 'Always watching' could mean that they're looking at us from a hidden place or even that they have cameras set up, so keep your eye out for those."

I wish I had more actionable information to tell them. "Might be clairvoyant" was not the most useful thing to prepare them with.

"All right, thanks," Anna said. "I think since it's the Party phase, we're supposed to spread out and explore the area. Valerie said that if you don't explore the setting of the story and find all the important things you're supposed to find, then they just won't be there when you need them to be in the Finale."

She was right, but none of us really wanted to explore a castle when we knew we could very easily die there.

"We need to stay in groups," she said. "Kimberly and Antoine, try seeing if you can look around the main hall. Camden, see what Judy is doing every time she leaves. I'm going to go check out the cantina and the main showroom. I bet one of these displays for the museum has information that we need."

Shoot, she was right. I wished I had said that. Then it could have been a prediction for my Cinema Seer ability, and everyone would have gotten a buff.

"I'll go with you," I said. Partially because I hadn't gotten to hang out with Anna all that much and also because I didn't want to stay here by myself. Sticking with the main character might increase my odds of survival.

We had spent some time getting acquainted with each other's stats and abilities. I was coming in with Trope Master, Cinema Seer, and Oblivious Bystander. These allowed me to see enemy tropes and make predictions in order to buff my allies, and of course, prevent enemies from targeting me if I acted oblivious.

As described, Antoine had a buff on top of a buff. It's Part of the Uniform buffed him when using sports equipment as weapons, and Gym Rat buffed him when he mentioned he played sports on-screen.

Anna had a trope called Last One Alive that ensured she could not be killed until every single one of her teammates was dead. She really was a Final Girl. She also had a trope called Who's with Me? that buffed allies who assisted her in the Finale.

Kimberly had an interesting trope called Convenient Backstory that allowed her to learn new skills and buff herself simply by explaining how she already had that skill because of some event in her past. Social Awareness allowed her to see characters' Moxie stats and intuit social dynamics. Looks Don't Last ensured that she would be targeted in First Blood, but the longer she lasted the weaker the enemy got.

Camden had Eureka!, which allowed him to find important text, and Right Tool for the Job, which buffed him in Savvy or Mettle if he used an enemy's mortal weakness in a plan or a fight, respectively.

We hoped it would be enough to best our enemies.

Player Stats and Tropes					
	Riley	Antoine	Anna	Kimberly	Camden
Archetype	Film Buff	Athlete	Final Girl	Eye Candy	Scholar
Plot Armor	11	12	14	10	11
Mettle	1	4	3	0	1
Moxie	3	1	2	4	2
Hustle	1	3	2	3	2
Savvy	5	0	2	1	5
Grit	1	4	5	2	1
	TROPE MASTER Type: Insight Stat: Savvy Effect: Sees enemy tropes. Lose half of PA.	IT'S PART OF THE UNIFORM Type: Buff Stat: --- Effect: Higher Mettle when attacking with sports equipment.	LAST ONE ALIVE Type: Rule Stat: --- Effect: Cannot die until the party is killed.	CONVENIENT BACKSTORY Type: Buff Stat: Moxie Effect: Can change backstory to assist with the current task.	EUREKA! Type: Insight Stat: Savvy Effect: Helps find important information within text.

	CINEMA SEER Type: Buff Stat: Savvy Effect: Buffs Savvy and Grit of allies by predicting plot elements.	GYM RAT Type: Buff Stat: Moxie Effect: Buffs Mettle and Hustle by revealing athletic backstory.	WHO'S WITH ME? Type: Buff Stat: Moxie Effect: In Finale, allies gain a buff to relevant stat when assisting the player.	SOCIAL AWARE-NESS Type: Insight Stat: Moxie Effect: Can see the Moxie stat of all char-acters and enemies. Can intuit social dynamics.	RIGHT TOOL FOR THE JOB Type: Buff Stat: Savvy Effect: Buffs Savvy and Mettle when fighting an enemy with their weakness.
	THE OBLIVIOUS BYSTANDER Type: Rule Stat: Moxie Effect: Cannot be the target while convinc-ingly acting oblivious to the enemy.			LOOKS DON'T LAST Type: Debuff Stat: Grit Effect: Is attacked at First Blood. Debuff enemy 1% PA for every minute survived, up to 15%	

When it came time to put it all to the test, I think we had a good shot of winning.

The cantina served the type of food you might get at a baseball game, but instead of hot dogs, you got bratwurst. Most of the cabinets I checked were empty. There was no food there that could spoil. In fact, the only foodstuffs that still existed were a giant can of pickled jalapenos and another can that had yellow cheese product.

"Look at this," Anna said. She was bent down, staring into the cabinet under the sink.

I peered over and saw four full bottles of absinthe. At first, I didn't think I was seeing it correctly. "The staff here must be drunk twenty-four seven."

"Is absinthe even German?" she asked.

"Good question," I said. "Should be Jägermeister instead."

She laughed.

The cantina didn't really have anything interesting. I looked around for holes in the walls that might allow whatever monster or killer in the castle to see us, but I didn't see anything. No cameras either.

As we made our way to the main hall to look at the exhibits, Anna asked, "So did you come down here to protect me?"

"Have you seen our stats?" I responded. "I came down here for you to protect me."

Another laugh.

"Well, keep up," she said. "We don't have all night."

Maybe literally.

The main hall was filled with glass cases containing everything from medieval armor and weapons to shells and firearms used in World War II. There was a replica of a German Enigma machine as well as the equipment necessary to communicate by Morse code. Nothing stood out to me as being obviously related to the plot, however.

"I'm not seeing anything," I said. "You got anything?"

She didn't answer.

I turned to see that she was transfixed by a large painting in the center of the main hall. I moved in to get a better look at it. It depicted a regal man in a proper suit standing next to a woman in a wedding dress. The woman was beautiful, but there was a frailty to her that was visible even in the painting. She was thin, and her eyes were dark, and her skin was so pale as to almost be translucent. Her smile, though, was very charming.

The way the man in the suit looked at her, you could tell that he loved her. He had a stern face; only his eyes showed emotion.

"'Doctor Simon Halle and his bride Anastasia,'" Anna said. "'Wed August 12th, 1964.'" She read off a brass plate beneath the painting, not so different from the ones that I often saw on the red wallpaper.

"'Amor Supra Omnia,'" I said, reading the next line. "Wonder what that means."

A woman's voice echoed through the hall.

It was Judy.

"'Love above all things,'" she said. "A very saccharine sentiment, don't you think?"

She moved closer to us and stared up at the painting. "I see you've met Simon Halle," she said. "He was the last heir of the Halle family. A very sad story."

"How so?" Anna asked.

"He spent his family's fortune trying to cure his wife's illness. Apparently he went broke, and that's how the castle got turned into a museum by the Historical Society."

"What was wrong with her?" I asked.

"Who's to say?" Judy said. "Cancer, perhaps, or maybe some form of resistant tuberculosis. Whatever the case, he drove himself mad trying to find a cure. Of course, they disappeared after running out of money. I reckon they ran off to die somewhere, just the two of them."

"How long ago did that happen?" I asked.

"Coming on thirty years now, just five years after they were wed," Judy said. "Now, if you could go help Camden inventory the wine in the cellar, it would be much appreciated."

"We'll get on it," Anna said.

As we walked away, I leaned over to Anna and asked, "Did she just say that 1964 was thirty-five years ago?"

"She did," Anna responded. "I guess that makes it 1999 in this storyline."

Retro.

It sounded like a lot of people had gone missing in this castle: the old cleaning crew, the groundskeeper, and now Simon and Anastasia Halle.

Wonder who's next?

CHAPTER TWELVE

FIRST BLOOD AT HALLE CASTLE

The door down to the cellar was located near the gift shop. When we got there, Camden was waiting outside.

"I wasn't going in alone," he said.

"Yeah, there's probably spiders down there," I said with a grin. Technically, Camden was third in line to be attacked after me and Kimberly, but I couldn't blame him for not pressing his luck.

Anna shook her head and pushed past us, opening the door and flicking on the light. The electricity in the castle was shaky at best. Even turning on this one light, you could almost feel the entire system straining. It had those old bulbs that you could hear warming up. Anna led us down into the cellar.

As I followed behind, I could feel the air get cooler. It was a small, square room with a wine rack that stretched across one whole wall. Like all the other rooms in the castle, the ceiling was high down here. We must have descended quite a bit. The floors were made of a cool, bluish stone that was different from the rest of the castle.

Other than that, there wasn't much to the cellar.

"Empty," Anna declared.

"Well, that was easy," Camden said. "Let's get out of here."

Camden and I feigned turning around and ascending the stairs.

"No, we have to check everything," Anna said with a smirk.

There were a few boxes laid around the basement. They had contained wine at one point, but now all we could find were a few empty bottles. It made sense to me. I imagine that the Historical Society in Carousel might have helped themselves to any valuable specimens in the Halle family collection, assuming that there were any left over after the estate sale.

Anna turned in circles in the small basement, looking for something of interest. "We need to look for any sign—"

A blood-curdling scream echoed throughout the castle. "Kimberly!" Anna said.

We all started running up the stairs and back toward the source of the scream. Antoine was supposed to always stay with her. The Athlete was the best fighting build we had, with Anna's Final Girl being the next best.

"It's too early for this," I said. "We're still in the Party phase."

The little needle wasn't quite to First Blood yet, so it made little sense for Kimberly to have been attacked already, based on my understanding of how the Plot Cycle worked.

Last we knew, Kimberly and Antoine had gone to the main hall with the task of exploring and finding anything relevant to the plot. The main hall was at one time part of the showroom, where we had seen exhibits inside glass cases, but a divider wall had been built by the Halle family.

As we ran, our footsteps echoed throughout the castle.

"Kimberly!" Anna yelled as we rounded the corner to the main hall.

When we got there, we saw Antoine and Kimberly standing near the back wall. They did not appear to have been injured. Looking at their statuses, they were both marked as Unscathed.

"What's wrong?" Anna asked.

Antoine turned his head to the wall behind them and said, "We found something."

Sure enough, they had.

What had appeared to be a solid stone wall with a simple bookcase had now opened up and revealed that a small portion of the wall was hinged and could swing on its axis. The seam was unnoticeable before. It was a secret door.

"We stumbled into it," Antoine said.

The five of us looked at the secret door and then back at each other. We couldn't see what was on the other side yet; it hadn't opened that much.

"Get ready," Anna said. She crept forward and placed her hand against the stone. She pushed.

The stone turned.

The door rotated, with the left side opening into the wall, and revealed a hidden room. The other side opened to the main hall and revealed a staircase leading upward.

Where's Scooby Doo when you need him?

At first, I wasn't even sure if the secret room had electricity. As Anna entered, she was quickly able to find a little switch on the wall near the opening.

Yellow light cast away the shadows of the room. I was able to see that the room was about the same size as the gift shop had been. I could also see that it had lots of books and artifacts that looked as old as the castle itself.

As we walked into the room, we saw that the space was mostly taken up by a large shelf filled with books. On the spines of the books, I could see words in languages ranging from Latin, Greek, and Hebrew all the way to Chinese and modern English. There were scrolls stacked on one of the shelves and display cases filled with what I could only assume were preserved biological specimens. I didn't want to know what they were.

"It's a library," Kimberly said. Curiosity had taken some of the fear out of her voice.

"How old is this?" Antoine asked. He approached the table in the middle of the room and saw a metal mechanism that I assume had something to do with astronomy. It had little metal spindles with balls that I think represented planets. At first, he reached out to touch it, but then he thought better of it.

"I think this is my time to shine," Camden said.

It really was.

"Is it demonic?" Anna asked. "What kinds of books are these?"

As if to answer a question, Camden squared himself up in front of the large shelf of books and looked them up and down, waiting for his Eureka! ability to send him information.

"Oh, here we go," he said. He grabbed a book from the shelf. It was large and leather bound. I couldn't understand the writing on the cover, but I think it was written in Latin.

"*Ars Vitae: Liber de Speculo Stellarum.*"

"What does that mean?" Antoine asked.

"I don't know," Camden answered. "I don't read Latin."

"Your power doesn't let you read other languages?" Anna asked.

"No," he answered. "I guess not."

That would probably be another Scholar trope.

"Judy might know Latin," Anna suggested, looking at me. "She knew what the phrase under the painting in the showroom meant."

She had a point. Why else would an NPC show up and demonstrate that ability if not to show the player that they can read Latin.

I wasn't sold on the idea though. "Judy could easily be a cultist or monster herself. She could also be a vampire's familiar. Let's not forget: in this story, she's the one who lured us here."

Anna clearly hadn't considered this. She took a deep breath and ran her fingers through her ponytail, as she always did when she was nervous.

"Wait," Camden said. He turned around to the shelf again and, within a few seconds, selected another book: *Munger's Latin to English Dictionary.*

He flipped through the book so quickly that you might have thought he had the pages bookmarked. His Eureka! trope told him exactly what page to go to and what line to look at. The display truly reminded me of how quickly characters read in movies. With a few quick turns, he was able to translate the title of the book.

"*The Art of Life: Treatise on the Mirror of the Stars*," he said.

Hmm.

"What's the mirror of the stars?" Kimberly asked.

"Telescope?" Anna suggested.

"I don't know," I said. The story was going in a different direction than I had thought at first.

As I was forming my new theory, Camden said, "This is going to take awhile. But I can already see the passage that we need to read." He flipped open the book to the first few pages and found what I can only assume to be an introduction. He showed it to me, but aside from recognizing some of the letters, I couldn't really make it out.

Principium est ut anima a corpore separari et in speculo stellarum collocari possit, opus est ut crystallum immaculatum et perfectum ad animae retinendam concinnatum sit. Hoc perfecte compositam artem crystallographiae requirit, sicut indicat capitulum secundum. Tunc, ad idoneum statum crystallum perducendum, ut animam in eo collocare valeat, est necessaria scientia mineralogiae, ut capitulum tertium demonstrat.

Nam, crystallum debet ad certum statum reduci, ut possit animam custodire et in suo interiori complectere, prout capitulum quintum explicat. Et postquam crystallum ad idoneum statum perductum est, anima sua virtute in eo collocanda est, quod fit per operationem magis artis quam naturae, ut capitulum sextum ostendit.

Verumtamen, anima, una ex essentiis divinis, multis mysteriis involuta est, unde opus est ad scientiam magiae, ut anima in speculo possit retineri, sicut capitulum quartum explicat. Ergo, ut anima in speculo stellarum collocetur, est opus ut artes mineralogicae, crystallographicae, et magicae perfecte exerceantur, ut in processu omni peritus sis, prout capitula prima et septima ostendunt.

Octavus capitulum tractat de solutione chemicis argenti, quae, si recte praeparatur, astralem reactionem tollere potest. Tales praecautiones necessariae sunt. Anima non vincta interiore parte corrumpitur.

Forsitan aliquando, docti artibus astralibus, habebunt mechanismum computatorium, qui eis possibilitatem praestabit calculorum et mensurarum necessariarum ad mappam plani astralis delineandam. Tunc in futurum, discriminem inter vitam et mortem tollere poterimus.

The lights flickered all at once. We looked up at the yellow bulbs and realized how foolish it was to stay in the secret room. Presumably, this was somewhere the Big Bad came to often.

"Better get to it," Anna said. "But we should definitely go back to the gift shop."

No one argued. We filed out of the room one at a time. Antoine was the last one out. He reached in to turn off the light.

As soon as the light went out, something grabbed Kimberly's arm and pulled her, not into the library that we had just left, but into the stairwell that had been revealed on the other side of the revolving door.

The door slammed shut, closing off access to the stairwell and trapping Antoine's foot as it closed. He managed to pull his leg out, leaving his shoe crushed in the door. Everything had happened in the blink of an eye.

"Kimberly!" Anna screamed. We could hear Kimberly screaming for a couple of seconds, but then all went silent. The needle on the Plot Cycle moved to First Blood.

"Kimberly!" Antoine screamed. He struggled to stand, but his foot was badly injured. It must have been broken—I couldn't tell—but at the very least, it was bloody, and he had trouble putting weight on it. Despite that, he put all his strength into getting the door to move, but it would not budge.

"It's not going to open," I said. "I've seen this in movies a dozen times. When a door slams shut like this, it's not going to open until it's too late."

I didn't need a Trope Master ability to know that.

"Shut up," Antoine said. "Help me!"

He was right. I jumped in and tried to push along with Anna and Camden, but even with the four of us, the wall didn't even shake.

"Fuck, why were we so stupid?" Anna said. "We knew that she was going to get targeted first. We should have held onto her."

"It wouldn't have mattered," I said. I knew that, and Anna probably knew that too. Kimberly had a trope that meant she would get attacked at First Blood. There was no preventing that.

"Did anybody see what took her?" Anna asked.

Everyone shook their head. The stairwell had been dark, and then it all happened so quickly that I didn't catch a glimpse of anything. I didn't even register any tropes on the red wallpaper; whatever creature had taken her had done it so quickly that it was too far away for me to use my Trope Master ability by the time I could react.

"This is supernatural," I said. "That's the only way it could be that fast."

"What about the books?" Anna asked. "The books are a clue. What do they mean? Is it some sort of cult?"

"I don't know," I answered.

There was only one way to know, and Camden was currently holding it in his hands.

CHAPTER THIRTEEN

PLEASE, DON'T BE A VAMPIRE

ow do we get upstairs?" Antoine asked. He banged his fist against the stone door.

"There's a stairway that was roped off in the showroom," Camden suggested.

"No, wait," Anna said. "We have to figure out what we're up against. We can't just go running off after them."

"It's got Kimberly," Antoine said. He began walking back toward the door separating the showroom from the main hall. His foot was out of commission, but he tried to move on it anyway. I could see the pain in his face.

I went to his side to help him move, but he pushed me away.

"I got it," he said. "Just give me a second."

Meanwhile, Camden had sat down at a table in the main hall and was busy trying to interpret the book that he had picked up from the library. He was furiously moving between pages of the Latin-to-English dictionary, interpreting the tome as quickly as he could.

"Don't read any of the Latin out loud, and you probably shouldn't read it directly translated either. Just summarize it. You don't want to trigger a magic spell or something," I offered. *Evil Dead*, anyone?

"I really don't think it's that kind of book," he said. "It reads like an academic text, even though it's complete nonsense. It presents itself as if this is science, something about creating a substance called the Mirror of Stars," Camden responded. He leafed through the dictionary; his fingers were working as quickly as they could.

"What does the Mirror of Stars do?" Anna asked. "Can you tell us that?"

"It seems to be a substance that can capture or harness a human soul," Camden answered.

"Okay, but why would you need to harness a human soul?" Anna asked.

I could answer that one.

"Communicating with the dead, using it to power magic, using it to summon a demon, or to breathe life into something," I suggested. "What can't you use a human soul for?"

Camden largely ignored our conversation as he worked. His head was shaking as he worked through it. Something about the book must have not sat right with him.

"It doesn't say what you would need a soul for, but it repeats how dangerous this process is," Camden said.

That makes sense. Separating the soul from the body is literal murder.

"Well, keep working on it. There must be something in there that will help us or else your power wouldn't have led you to it," Anna said. "Did you see any of its tropes?" she asked, turning to me.

I shook my head. "Nothing. It was there and gone too quickly," I answered, though it shamed me to say it.

"The only thing you're here to do, and you can't do it because it was too quick?" Antoine said. He gripped onto the table so hard he was liable to break it.

"Well, if I had known that the monster was going to attack at that exact moment, I might have been ready," I said. "Let's not forget that I wasn't the only one caught off guard." I gestured to his injured foot.

That was the wrong thing to say. Antoine got up as if to challenge me, but the pain in his foot brought him right back down.

"This is happening because you treated this like a game," Antoine said. "Kimberly could be dead."

"No, this is happening because you got catfished and made it our problem," I said. I'm not usually one for a fist fight, but I wasn't going to take the blame for this.

"Stop," Anna said. "This is getting us nowhere."

She got between us. "Do you have any idea what this thing is or what it might do to Kimberly?"

"Clearly, it's trying to steal her soul," I said, pointing to the book. "Could be a cult. I'm not even willing to rule out a vampire at this point because traditionally vampires practice black magic, and that book looks like black magic."

The truth was the cult angle didn't make sense. If it was a cult, then we would have met some of the members by now. It made no sense for them to be introduced this far into the story. Not to mention, Kimberly's kidnapper moved far too quickly to be a normal human.

At that moment, a scream sounded in the distance.

"Kimberly!" Antoine yelled. He jumped to his feet, ignoring the pain, and stumbled toward the sound of the scream.

"No, that wasn't Kimberly," Anna said. "That sounded like Judy."

She was right.

Antoine stopped and grabbed on to the back of a bench that was placed in the middle of the main hall. "I guess that means she's not a vampire's familiar, then, doesn't it?" Antoine asked sarcastically.

I didn't say anything, but the answer was no, it didn't really mean much. If anything, it was great misdirection that could set up a twist ending, but I wasn't going to say that out loud.

"Okay, with Kimberly gone and the NPC with three Plot Armor gone, that means I'm the next target," I said. "I have a plan, but it's going to sound crazy."

"What's your plan?" Anna asked.

I retrieved my tickets from my pocket and held up my most recent acquisition: the Oblivious Bystander. The ability was designed as a joke, I think, but its impact would be incredible if I could use it right. With this ability, monsters and killers wouldn't attack you as long as you could pretend that you had not yet noticed them. I'd seen this exact gimmick in multiple movies, sometimes used to get a laugh and other times used to heighten the tension.

A hapless character goes about their business while the monster lurks in the background. They don't get attacked until they actually see the enemy. It usually only lasts for a single scene, and the character ends up dying anyway.

But what if I could use it to make myself invincible while I scoped out the enemy tropes with my Trope Master ability?

"I just need to go off separate from the group and wait for whatever this thing is to get near me. If I can ignore it long enough, I might be able to look at its tropes and get some idea of what it is. If I see anything, I'll scream it out before it takes me," I said.

Anna looked at me. "Are you sure that will work?" she asked.

"No," I answered. But it didn't really matter. I was getting attacked no matter what; Kimberly proved that. Being in the group wasn't going to save me.

"It's up to you three," I said. "Camden, you've got to figure out why that book is important. There has to be something in there."

He nodded.

I tried to put on a brave face and sound the way I thought brave people sounded, but the truth was I had another reason for leaving the group. Ever since I got the Oblivious Bystander ticket, all I could think about was how I might be able to use it to prevent myself from getting killed.

I had one problem: if I was in a group, whenever a monster came, I couldn't ignore it no matter what direction I looked. I was still going to hear the people around me screaming and reacting to the monster's presence. There's no way I could pretend that I didn't notice the monster when everyone around me has. The best way for this gimmick to work would be for me to be off on my own.

I had visualized it in my head constantly ever since we got to Dyer's Lodge.

I needed this to work. I summoned whatever courage I had and walked away from my friends.

"Don't go too far," Anna said. "If something happens, just know that we're going to try to rescue you."

Maybe I'll be the one rescuing you, I thought. I gave her a smile and said, "Thank you," before turning out of the main hall and into the showroom.

The hidden stairway had gone upward. It seemed to me that the best direction to go to scope out our hidden enemy was also upward. Antoine had the right idea on that point. If I remembered correctly, all that was upstairs were rooms that were mostly used for storage. Guests of the museum couldn't go up there. I didn't even know if it was safe or if the floor would give out underneath me.

I got to the back of the showroom and found the large staircase that wound up and around to the upstairs. I picked up the red rope that had been used to block it off and ducked underneath.

The needle on the Plot Cycle was currently on the Rebirth phase. We were supposed to be spending this time gathering the information we needed to go on the offensive.

By that metric, everything was going according to plan. But still, my feet felt as heavy as lead. My heart was pounding out of my chest.

On my way through the showroom, I grabbed a little map of the castle. It was an essential part of my plan. I opened it up in front of me and read it by the dim yellow lights that had been installed in the castle.

I didn't actually need the map, but my thought was if my eyes were focused on the map and I could hold it out in front of me, then perhaps I could believably portray that I didn't see anything whenever the monster came for me. It's goofy, I know, but the Oblivious Bystander trope came from campy horror movies, and this strategy would work in a campy horror movie.

But what if I heard the monster first? I couldn't pretend I hadn't noticed it if it was making noise. In the silent upstairs hallway, I felt as if my ears were superhuman. Every creak and howl of the wind sounded like a footstep behind me. But I had a plan for sound too.

I started to talk to myself.

"Oh, so this is where the Halle family grew up," I said. "Sure is a nice castle. Wish I could have grown up in a castle just like this one . . ."

And I continued blathering about anything and everything I could think of because if I was talking, then I couldn't hear someone coming behind me—or at least I could pretend like I hadn't heard them. It wasn't the most elegant solution, but the Oblivious Bystander wasn't the most elegant ability.

As I was walking through the upstairs of the castle, I was passing by door after door. I didn't want to stop to try to get into any of the rooms because then I would have to let go of the map, my cover.

Truthfully, it didn't matter if I got into any of the rooms. I was only doing this to try and draw the monster to me. I wasn't trying to find it. If my theory was right, it didn't matter where I was. Our enemy would make its way to me.

I watched the needle on the Plot Cycle as it slowly moved toward Second Blood. I started to wonder why Judy's kidnapping hadn't counted as being Second Blood, but Kimberly's kidnapping did count as First Blood.

Did that mean that Kimberly had been killed, but Judy hadn't? Would my capture count as Second Blood, or would it simply be another event inside of the Rebirth phase?

Every time we asked the other players questions about how the game worked, we would get the suggestion that we would "figure it out" once we started to play. Really, I wish they had just given it to us straight. Maybe they didn't want to scare us off. Maybe the unpredictability of the game is the scariest part.

"Wow, so this door was actually not original to the castle at all," I said, muttering under my breath. Just more nonsense to give credibility to my obliviousness.

And then I saw it.

In the corner of my eye, something moved. It was impossibly fast. I could barely make it out, but I didn't need to because my power was proximity-based. I just needed to be near it. I didn't need to see it. I held the map up further, blocking my view from anything that might try to get near, and walked in the opposite direction of the figure I had just seen.

The red wallpaper started to function; a gray poster materialized in my mind. That was strange. In the corn maze, I had been able to see Benny the Haunted Scarecrow as soon as he was near, but with this creature, I couldn't.

My ability was still working otherwise though. Strangely, I could only see one trope start to appear:

Invulnerable Form	The villain cannot be affected by tropes or attacks in its current state.

So much for this plan.

At least it was a great proof of concept. The Oblivious Bystander ability was keeping the monster from attacking me, and my Trope Master ability was technically functioning, though not to great effect.

It just happened that the only trope I could see was really bad news. Invulnerable Form—what could that mean? Was it something that had to be weakened, or was it just something that had to be caught off guard? Did this trope keep me from seeing its identity?

The fact that this creature, whatever it was, had an Invulnerable Form told me that it was probably supernatural.

I tried to think about what it meant when it said "invulnerable." Did that mean the creature was literally invulnerable? Or was it rendered invulnerable by the plot?

This creature could simply be unkillable because it would not be cinematic if it died right now. You rarely see a werewolf killed unless it's in its wolf form, for example. That would be anticlimactic. Perhaps whatever my follower was, it wasn't actually indestructible but, rather, was just not meant to be killed until later. I thought to myself as I walked.

I don't mean to pretend to you that I was somehow fearless in this moment. The truth is that I was a mess. I caught myself forgetting to speak because I was so preoccupied, fretting about what was to come. It ended up not mattering because whatever this thing following me was, it did not have footsteps. I heard no sound coming from behind me; I only saw the occasional flash of a shadow in the corner of my eye.

Soon, I would have a problem because as brilliant as my plan was, it didn't take into consideration one important thing: the hallway I was in didn't go on forever. I was almost to the end. Somehow, I would have to go the other direction to get away from this thing, but how could I pretend not to see it when I turned around?

Sure, the whole muttering-fool-walking-through-the-castle-completely-unaware-he's-being-followed schtick works, but as soon as I turned and saw whatever figure was behind me, the performance would be less than convincing.

I had no choice. I had to try to find some way to turn around and get back to the stairs.

I had last seen the figure on my right, so I turned left at the last door on the hallway. I jiggled the handle and then said aloud, "Huh, it's locked."

I raised the map up as if scrutinizing something that had been written on it. I was giving the performance my all. I looked from the map to the door, back to the map.

"Oh well," I said. "Guess I'll go back downstairs."

I'll gladly accept my Oscar for that one.

I raised the map up so that I couldn't see what was in front of me and pretended to be absolutely enraptured by a description of a carving in the stone between two of the doors. I began walking back the way I had come.

I could see in the corner of my eye that the figure following me was still there. As curious as I was to see it, I willed myself not to look. The Oblivious Bystander trope was working; it wasn't attacking me.

I continued on, but my pursuer got braver. I could see it coming up behind me on my right, so I ever so gently tilted to my left. If this were a scene in a movie, I don't know if the audience would be laughing or chewing on their fingernails.

Whatever this thing was, it was agile, moving from side to side without making a single sound. I could feel the skin on my neck grow hot because the only thing I knew that moved that quickly and quietly was a vampire, and I really did not want it to be a vampire.

I trudged forward, and the creature got closer. I held the map so tight to my face that I was straining credulity. Maybe I'm just nearsighted in this story, a bumbling tourist who forgot his glasses.

The figure moved around in front of me again. I held the map up, blocking off my view. At some point in time I had stopped muttering. I was too afraid. I feared that by talking, my voice cracking would give away how not-oblivious I was.

I tried to ignore the monster in front of me and set a course that allowed me to get around it once more.

But then I slipped.

The flooring in the upper story hadn't been maintained, and my foot got bad purchase as I went to take a step. I almost fell forward but managed to catch myself just in time. I kept the map in front of my face the entire time, looking out to whichever side I knew the monster wasn't on.

It was up and to the right from where I was.

I could tell it was humanoid.

Oh, crap, it's going to be a vampire, I thought to myself.

I could tell that it was floating a few inches off the ground.

Damn it, vampires can float.

I walked forward, but it was very difficult to fight the urge to just grab a glimpse of whatever this creature was; just one quick glance, and maybe then I could make a run for it. I adjusted the paper just a slight amount and looked up and to the right.

Shit!

What I saw was a man looking right back at me. We had made eye contact. There was no pretending to be oblivious anymore.

I started to run toward the stairway, but the man was on me in a flash. It was almost hilarious how quickly he got to me.

It's funny: my status changed to Unconscious before I even felt it hit me.

As my vision grew dimmer, and I lost control of my body and fell to the ground, there was one silver lining: this man was not a vampire.

Because as I looked up at the figure looming over me, I could see right through him.

CHAPTER FOURTEEN

DEUS EX TERMINATOR

The first thing I saw upon awaking was my status on the red wallpaper:

Unscathed	Hobbled	Mutilated	Dead	Written Off	Chase Scene	Planning
Unconscious	Infected	Incapacitated	Captured (Lit)	Off Screen (Lit)	Fight Scene	Exploring

I was no longer Unscathed—the welt on the back of my head was evidence of that—but at least I wasn't Unconscious either. Instead, only two status lights were lit: "Captured" and "Off Screen." I wasn't yet sure what "Off Screen" meant, but I knew what "Captured" meant, and as I came to, I found that I was indeed captured.

I found myself restrained in a metal chair, held down by thick leather straps. The straps were tight, only giving the slightest bit of slack. I had one across each arm and then another across each leg. I wasn't going anywhere.

So much for my use-the-Oblivious-Bystander-trope-to-scout-out-the-bad-guy plan. I give myself an eight for theory and a four for execution, but maybe I'm being too generous.

If only he hadn't been able to see my eyes . . .

I didn't even manage to get any information back to my friends. Not that I had a lot of info to begin with. I would have to work on that strategy.

I took in my surroundings.

Directly in front of me was a large machine covered in dials and knobs. It had many moving parts, as well as pressure gauges reading off measurements that I wouldn't have understood even if I could see them up close. I couldn't tell you what this machine actually was, but I could tell you that, based on the turret sticking off the top, it was a weapon.

The aesthetic was something between sci-fi and steam punk. In the distance, I could see a huge computer mainframe that was out of date even for the nineties. There was a workstation with numerous shelves filled with flasks and vials, chemistry equipment, and hand tools.

"Riley?" a voice called out. Someone was in the room with me on the opposite side of the machine.

"Kimberly?" I asked. "Are you here, Kimberly?"

"I didn't know if you had woken up," she said. "I saw him bring you here. I waited for your status to change."

"I'm here. Are you okay? Are you hurt?" I asked. "Has he done anything to you?"

She was quiet at first. "No," she said. "But he's crazy. He says he's going to kill us. You have to get me out of here!" I could hear her struggling against her restraints.

"Have you been screaming?" I asked. I assumed she had, but I needed to be sure. Wherever we were, it must have been soundproof; when Kimberly disappeared, we couldn't hear her anywhere in the castle.

"We both have," she answered.

Both?

I strained my neck around to the other side of the machine and saw that there were two chairs over there. More chairs were spread out around the right side of the machine. They were empty right now. Inside one of the chairs next to Kimberly was Judy. Judy was not doing well; you could see it in her eyes.

"Just hold tight; they're coming for us," I said, but truthfully, I wasn't so sure. The only hope was if Camden could find something useful inside that book.

I looked around the room. Not all of the room was lit up; there were several corners cloaked in inky darkness, but I could see that there was a bed and some furnishings. Someone had been living down here.

"So, what kind of monster is it?" I asked. "Is it a ghost?" I had gotten one glimpse of my assailant, and he had been transparent. It didn't make sense for there to be a bed down here.

Kimberly didn't answer at first. "I don't know for sure. He's strange."

How could you not know if you were looking at a transparent apparition, I thought to myself, but I wasn't going to press her on that.

I continued looking around the room. It was large with high ceilings and a floor made of bluish stone. In fact, the floor here was made of the exact same stone that the cellar's floor had been.

The cellar! Of course! It should have seemed weird that a cellar inside a castle was that small. It's a castle; surely the basement is huge—after all, castles have dungeons. This room must have been separated from the rest of the cellar by whoever was living here. This was bad news because the others thought we were upstairs, or at least that was the theory when I left.

My eyes lifted to the ceiling as if I were looking up toward my friends.

Then I saw it.

"So that's what the Mirror of Stars is," I said aloud.

"What?" Kimberly asked.

"That up there," I said. "That must be the Mirror of Stars. From the book Camden found."

High above us, apparently growing out of the ceiling, was a large mass of dark, glowing crystals. It is difficult to describe what they looked like, but the most apt description would be that they looked like the night sky. They appeared to contain stars. Despite having what appeared to be a mirrored surface, they didn't reflect the yellow light of the basement. Whatever was inside those crystals appeared to move.

The crystals were supported there by a metal contraption, and they had all kinds of electrodes and pipes sticking out of them that wormed their way down the walls to the computer mainframe. Whoever it was that was living down here had crafted the Mirror of Stars, and whatever its purpose was, it looked like they were trying to use computer technology to perfect it.

But what were they using it for?

The weapon in front of me was connected to the Mirror of Stars by several wires, though I couldn't say for certain what the purpose of them was.

Then I decided to check the red wallpaper.

Two tropes appeared in my mind. I saw a poster of the weapon, the computer, and the Mirror of Stars.

Indestructible MacGuffin	This plot device cannot be destroyed.
Deus Ex Terminator	This object kills all targets in one blow regardless of Plot Armor.

So, it was basically the Ark of the Covenant from *Indiana Jones*.

Noted.

Immediately following that revelation, a man walked into view from another part of the basement that wasn't visible to me. I recognized him right away. I had seen a painting of him in the showroom; it was Dr. Simon Halle. Here he was in the flesh—well, mostly.

His appearance caught me off guard at first. While most of his body was very ordinary—he wore a lab coat and slacks, with shiny leather shoes—his top half was quite unusual.

His left hand was normal and swung at his side as he walked. But his right arm and his head hung limply, like a puppet whose strings had been cut; even though his right arm and his head appeared lifeless, they had been replaced. I could only describe it as if his ghost was leaking out of his body. In place of where his right arm would have been was a ghostly arm instead, and instead of a normal head, he had a transparent head.

Even though his real right arm and head hung limply in front of him, their ghostly counterparts took their places seamlessly. I watched him as he moved about his workspace, picking up tools and measuring chemicals. His face was stern and businesslike. Though his body hung limply, and his real hair was disheveled, his ghostly hair was well-groomed and his thin mustache perfectly in place.

I had heard of someone having one foot in the grave, but this took that to a whole different level.

"Ah, you're awake," he said. "I was beginning to worry I might have struck you too hard."

I didn't respond, but I did start to wonder how much time I had been out. I looked at the Plot Cycle and saw that the needle was almost to Second Blood. Dread consumed me.

"You're probably wondering why I brought you here today," he said. "Together, we're going to embark on a terrific experiment. I have a feeling that you will be the last data points I need to finish my work. The contribution that you are about to make to humankind is immeasurable."

I tried to think of something to say, some retort that might extend my lifespan, but truthfully, fear caught the words in my throat, and I couldn't dream of being clever at a time like this.

"Don't be afraid," he said. "Where you're going is a place we all must go and a place that I believe we can return from."

"Oh, shit," I said. It just slipped out.

He didn't like that. For a moment, the calm, composed scientist ghost was lost, and an enraged spirit took his place. But it was only for a moment. He recomposed himself.

"Yes, the youth of today are quite vulgar. It's distasteful, but I suppose I won't judge you too harshly. When you woke up this morning, you did not know your purpose. But now you will."

CHAPTER FIFTEEN

ASTRALIST

I saw you admiring my Mirror of Stars," Dr. Halle said. "It took decades of toil and perseverance to make the substance. You cannot manipulate the crystal with mortal hands." He raised his left hand. "Sacrifices had to be made." He lifted his ghostly right hand. "Would you like to know why I would go through the trouble?"

I was starting to get the picture but said nothing.

He tried to conceal a grin behind his stern facial expression. He continued without waiting for a response.

"When the soul leaves the body, it is jettisoned into the astral plane. The process is chaotic and difficult to measure. Who is to say where the soul goes as it leaves or how to get it back?

"Well, a Mirror of Stars lets me measure the path a soul takes on its way to the hereafter. With only a few more measurements, I believe that I will be able to map the astral plane. In doing so, I will rid the world of death. That is your purpose."

He turned and walked back to his workstation, his mind elsewhere for the moment.

He *really* loved giving this speech. I could tell. I'm sure he's given the same one to all of his victims.

I had called out loose similarities to Dr. Frankenstein pretty early on, so I wasn't exactly surprised to see that the baddie was a mad scientist. What I couldn't figure out was how he had moved so quickly when abducting Kimberly. That's why my mind had shifted toward the supernatural. Now I think I had the answer: it looked like this mad scientist had ghostly powers.

Whoever guessed "mad scientist," please take a bow. I will also accept "ghost," for half credit.

On the red wallpaper, I saw a poster appear. It was the same as the painting upstairs, except it showed Dr. Halle in his current form. His wife, Anastasia, was slumped over in this poster, her face covered by her long hair.

"*The Astralist*," the poster read. Underneath that it said, "Featuring Dr. Simon Halle as the Astralist."

Plot Armor: 12.

He was something between Dr. Frankenstein and the *Re-Animator*. Strangely, this plot was similar to the backstory of the *Casper the Friendly Ghost* movie from the nineties. Of course, this ghost wasn't so friendly.

I began looking at his tropes, but before I could focus on them, I was interrupted.

"Please let us go," Judy cried. She finally broke from her catatonic state and began weeping openly.

"I can't do that. You know that," the Astralist said. "I believe that we were meant to find a way to get our loved ones back to us. It is our purpose, *my* purpose. Observe."

He raised his ghostly right hand toward the Mirror of Stars and said, "Can't you see it? Can't you see my soul seeking hers across the astral plane?"

I looked up to the Mirror of Stars, and sure enough, I could see a streak of light taking a path across the crystalline structures—a difficult path bouncing from angle to angle but clearly emanating from where Dr. Halle stood in the room.

"What causes the Mirror of Stars to reach out to us like this? This question was pondered over by philosophers for hundreds of years, but I believe I know the answer.

"It's love. My love for my darling Anastasia is so powerful that it reaches across our universe and into the next. She waits for me there, and I can't keep her waiting much longer.

"But do not fret. Once I have mapped the astral plane, I will be able to retrieve souls from it at will. With only the pull of a lever and press of a button, I will be able to bring you back. Isn't that wonderful? Your sacrifice is only temporary. I'll be able to bring all of you back."

"All of us?" I asked. Curiosity got the better of me.

"Yes," he said. His ghostly right arm flickered like static on a dead television channel. In that very moment, a light switch flipped on the other side of the room.

All of the lights in the room turned off and back on. The equipment in the basement must have been drawing lots of power. Even turning on one light could cause them all to visibly strain. That explained the flickering lights upstairs.

A portion of the basement that had once been dark and hidden from my view now came into light.

I looked at it in horror.

In the darkened corner there were shelves upon shelves containing nothing but human corpses. There had to be three dozen bodies on those shelves. They were all fully dressed in whatever clothes they had died in. In the center of them was a table with a woman laid out in a wedding dress, her head laid upon a pillow. Even in death, I recognized her. It was Anastasia Halle.

"She was the first," he said. "She always supported my work, my effort to cure her. My machine is a thing of miracles. A body deprived of a soul through the Mirror of Stars does not decompose. Do you not find that fascinating?

"I could not tell you why this occurs, but I think that it is a sign from the heavens that I am moving in the correct direction. The bodies are virtually undamaged, and when I find a way to locate their souls, I will be able to reinvigorate them and bring them back to this life.

"So, fear not," he said, looking to the three of us.

He was being very loose with the phrase "virtually undamaged." The most generous description of these bodies was "mummified." However, it was true that there was no stench, no rotting.

Dr. Halle approached his computer mainframe and began pushing buttons and turning dials. The machine in front of me came to life, and the turret on top started to spin as the barrel of its weapon aimed at the restraining chairs placed in a half circle around it.

"Help!" Kimberly screamed.

"Help, please. Please let me go," she begged. "Please, I won't tell anyone. Just let me go."

The Astralist ignored her.

For the second time, I saw her disheveled in terror. She was not wearing as much makeup as she had when we arrived, but still, her tears created streaks through her foundation. I wanted to be able to help her, but in truth, I couldn't even get my restraints to budge more than an inch—not enough to escape. I couldn't get my voice box to make noise. The inevitability of my death was all too real.

The turret turned on its axis several times before eventually pointing at Judy. It made sense. She only had three Plot Armor. I'm not proud to say it, but I let out a breath of relief when I saw it point at her first. I just hoped that NPCs didn't feel pain. After her it would be my turn because I only had five Plot Armor.

The machine started to initiate a sequence. I could hear pressure building within it and some type of electrical capacitor charging as energy was supplied to it. There was a buzzing sound. Above, the Mirror of Stars started to glow as the machine and the crystals began communicating.

The machine fired. No laser came from the barrel, which is what I expected. Instead, it looked more like a vacuum cleaner that began to siphon glowing blue energy from the small, stout form of Judy. She screamed in agony as what I can only assume was her soul began to leave her body. She pulled against her restraints but was unsuccessful in freeing herself.

The worst was the sound. I could hear it, like the soul itself screaming.

First her feet went limp. Then her arms. Then the rest of her body drooped.

All the while, Kimberly squealed and begged to be released. The man did not even give her the courtesy of responding.

After the machine was done with Judy, the bright light that it had absorbed into the turret began rising along a metallic guy wire into the Mirror of Stars until it became one star in a constellation that shot across the entire mirror.

Dr. Halle paid close attention. He watched readouts on his computer and muttered to himself as he reviewed them.

He shut down the mainframe, and the machine started to wind down.

"My machine needs to recharge," he said. His voice was somber, like he was speaking at a funeral. "I take no joy in my duties. Nonetheless, it is the responsibility of an Astralist to map the hereafter, to connect the living with the dead, and to eliminate the difference between life and death."

CHAPTER SIXTEEN

THE CODE IN THE LIGHTS

Now, if you'll excuse me, I need to go check on my other guests," the Astralist said. He walked over to the part of the basement that held his bed and lay down. With a flicker, I saw his spirit disappear from his body. It was some form of astral projection, no doubt.

The needle on the Plot Cycle had already hit Second Blood with the death of Judy. Now we were in the initial stages of the Finale. To my understanding, we should have a small amount of time before he struck again—just enough for my friends to prepare an assault. The question was, could I help them?

I tried to push past the fear that clouded my mind and work the problem. I needed to get out of that chair, but I was strapped in. I examined the leather that was used to bind my hands and realized that the sleeve of my sweatshirt was inside my restraint.

I had an idea.

I could see my status change on the red wallpaper. The word Planning lit up.

It seemed to me that, even though the restraint was tight, part of the reason it was so snug was that my sweatshirt was taking up space. Not much, sure, but maybe enough that if I were to pull up my sleeve, I would be able to get my hand out. After all, I didn't need that much room, and I was definitely willing to hurt myself to be free.

I leaned over and grabbed my sleeve with my teeth and pulled, straining my neck to get some movement on the sleeve. The restraint was tight, and it took some effort to get the fabric rolled up, but as I tugged it on one side and then the other—pulling and struggling—eventually, I managed to get my sleeve out from inside the restraint.

Now all I had to do was use what little room that maneuver had granted me to remove my hand from the restraint and free myself.

I pulled with all my might. The leather strap was definitely looser now that I had slightly more room, but it wasn't easy to get my hand out. I felt the side of the leather cutting into my skin, and I seriously thought I was going to break a bone.

But I pulled . . .

And pulled . . .

And twisted . . .

And then I was free.

One hand down, three limbs to go. Luckily, there was no lock on the other straps. I just had to unstrap them with my free hand.

Success.

With a bloody hand, I ran across the room to Kimberly. She sat there with a terrified look upon her face. I can't imagine what it must have been like to have been right next to Judy when her life force was literally stripped from her.

"It's okay. I'm here," I said. I tried to be as gentle as possible in the way I spoke.

I quickly unlashed her hands and legs, and she jumped out of the metal chair like it was on fire.

"We have to leave," she said.

I agreed, but I didn't actually know *how* to leave. I couldn't even say which direction the cellar was or if there was a connection between the two rooms that we could use to get back into the castle.

"Did you see what direction he came from when he brought me in?" I asked.

"Over there," she said, pointing to what looked to be a solid wall.

We ran over and tried banging and pushing on it but to no avail. I didn't know whether the wall was kept shut by a lever or simply by some plot device that I was unable to see. It's possible that Kimberly and I combined just did not have a high enough Mettle stat to be able to push the door open.

I surveyed the basement. The Astralist's body still rested in his bed.

Did we dare try to kill him right there? Would that even work?

I decided that, now that I had some time, I would try to see his tropes. It might give me some idea of how to proceed, so I quickly looked to the red wallpaper in hopes that proximity to his unconscious body would be enough.

It was.

I could see all of the Astralist's tropes.

DR. SIMON HALLE	
IS	
THE ASTRALIST	
PLOT ARMOR: 12	ENEMY TYPE IMPERCEPTIBLE

Tropes	
HUMANIZING MONOLOGUE	In the final battle, the villain will attempt to gain sympathy by revealing his backstory or motives. Players who are not resilient to this will receive debuffs. Buffs villain's Moxie.
JEKYLL AND HYDE	The villain has multiple forms: Ghost (+3 Mettle, +5 Hustle), Comatose, and Possessed (+2 Mettle, +2 Grit.)
ANTICLIMAX ANTIDOTE	The villain cannot be killed in his Comatose form until the final battle.
INVULNERABLE FORM	The villain cannot be affected by tropes or attacks in his Ghost form. Except: Ghost Bane.
THE PARTING SHOT	Though the villain is defeated, he has one final trick up his sleeve: a backup plan that will terrorize the players in his absence.
HOSTAGE TAKER	The villain will not outrightly kill the player in combat until the final battle but will instead attempt to take them hostage for his specific purpose.
ALWAYS WATCHING	The villain can obtain a visual of the players at any time.
HOME LAIR ADVANTAGE	The villain can travel freely, unnoticed due to his knowledge of the setting and its pathways and secret passages.
SILVER BULLET	This monster has a weakness specific to him that renders him dead or vulnerable.

I reviewed his tropes. The Jekyll and Hyde trope was not surprising. So far, I had seen this villain in all three forms. The first was his Ghost form. Now was his Comatose form, and the final form was a merging of the two, when I saw him seemingly possessing his own body. His Ghost form was invulnerable and had a trope mentioning as much.

The Anticlimax Antidote was the sort of thing I expected to see. It would be far too easy to simply kill his body now that his spirit was gone. No, that wouldn't be allowed. I didn't know what would happen if we attacked his helpless body, but I didn't want to risk it.

What concerned me the most was the Parting Shot trope, which told me that even if we were to find victory, something else would be waiting for us.

I didn't know what his Silver Bullet was, but I hoped Camden was figuring out that information at that very moment.

"We have to get a message to the others," I said. "They obviously can't hear us or else they would have heard Judy screaming earlier."

"What do we do?" Kimberly asked. "Shouldn't we just destroy this machine?" She had a timbre of panic in her voice.

"We can't," I said. "It has a trope that makes it indestructible. That would be too easy, I guess. We also can't kill him. We have to beat him in the final battle."

I continued, "I have an idea but I'm going to need your help."

She eyed me quizzically.

"You can do something that I can't do, and I need you to figure out what that is, but I think I can only tell you a hint."

She nodded. "Okay . . ."

Kimberly had an amazing trope called Convenient Backstory. So far, she hadn't used it, but if my understanding of what it could do was correct, then it was exactly what we needed. It gave her the ability to buff herself and learn skills in the middle of a storyline simply by referencing something that happened in her past.

Have you ever seen a movie where a five-foot-four woman manages to beat up a bunch of bad guys, and then she quips about how she knew how to fight because she grew up with six brothers? How about a character who could suddenly pick a lock because they wrote a book about thieves years ago, or they had a rough life on the streets back in their past?

The Convenient Backstory was one of the strongest tropes that any of us had, but in order for it to work, it had to be convincing. You couldn't just say something and make it true. The story had to make sense. So, if my plan was going to work, I couldn't just tell her what to do. She had to figure it out on her own, and what's more, she had to tell the story all on her own.

Don't get me wrong, Kimberly was far from dim-witted—she was actually very smart with things she cared about—but she had never really engaged with the concept of playing the Game at Carousel. Not the way I had or Camden had. Anna and Antoine understood what was going on here, and they were willing to play their roles to the best of their abilities as well, but Kimberly had resisted. We could barely drag her up to the castle.

"Kimberly, every time someone turns on a light in the castle, all of the other lights in the building flicker. Did you notice that? When I was with Anna, she turned on the light to the cellar; it made all the lights turn off and back on, and just now, whenever he turned on the light to that section of the basement, the lights flickered again."

Kimberly nodded, seemingly unsure of what I was getting at.

"There's a book upstairs on Morse code. I think that if we were to flick the light in a pattern, we could communicate with our friends upstairs. We'd have to do it long enough so that they would notice it and so that Camden would have time to go to the book and interpret what we're saying, but . . ."

I looked her in the eye, and I said slowly, "One of us needs to know Morse code for that to happen, and I didn't learn it growing up."

For a moment she didn't speak, but then I saw a glint of recognition in her eye. "Lucky for you," she said, "my dad took me sailing every summer growing up. He made sure I knew Morse code so that I could signal for help if we ever got into trouble."

In an instant Kimberly's Savvy stat and Plot Armor shot up three points.

"Did it work?" I asked.

"Let's see," she said.

We ran over to the light switch, and Kimberly reached toward it, her hands shaking as she grabbed the switch.

"What do I say?" she asked.

"In cellar," I said. At the end of the day, the most important information for them to know was where we were. Nothing else I could tell them was more important than that. Anna and Camden had been in the cellar, and they would probably make the same realization that I had, that the room was far too small for a castle. Between the three of them, they had to be able to find a way to get down here.

Kimberly started flicking the light in a smooth, rhythmic motion.

"It's working!" she said. "I don't know how I'm doing it, but I just am!"

I couldn't understand Morse code myself, but it looked exactly like I had seen it done in the movies. The lights flickered in a dot and dash pattern that must have meant "In cellar."

Now all we could do was wait and see who got to us first: our friends or the Astralist.

CHAPTER SEVENTEEN

A WASTE OF A SPECIMEN

Be ready," I said. "He's a scientist, which means he's probably smart enough to figure out what we're doing with the lights. As soon as he does, he's going to be back here."

Kimberly bit her lip and nodded. I wasn't sure if I should distract her, but I didn't want her to be caught off guard.

As we waited, I mentally prepared myself for what was to come. If we succeeded, it would mean a fight. If we failed, there wouldn't be much of a fight. I reviewed Dr. Halle's stats again.

Plot Armor: 12.

My understanding was that enemies' stats worked the same way as ours did, which meant that if he had twelve Plot Armor, those twelve points were divided among his five stats. I wanted to estimate what his different stats might be so that I might be of more use when the time came.

"What's his Moxie?" I asked.

Kimberly's third trope, after Convenient Backstory and Looks Don't Last, was called Social Awareness. It let her see an enemy's Moxie stat and sense social dynamics and character relationships. She glanced at the bedridden form of Dr. Halle. Her eyebrows furrowed.

"It's zero," she said. "He has no Moxie at all."

Interesting.

That meant that all of his twelve Plot Armor points were distributed among his Mettle, Hustle, Savvy, and Grit stats.

Given that he was a scientist, I assumed a big chunk of those points would be attributed to his Savvy stat. After all, that's how Camden was distributed, and he was a Scholar archetype. I estimated his Savvy to be around five, leaving around seven points between his Hustle, Mettle, and Grit stats.

He had abducted Kimberly and injured Antoine in his Ghost form, which had heightened Mettle and Hustle. Given that both his Ghost form and Possessed form gave him a boost to Mettle, he probably didn't have much in his base form. Furthermore, he had a weapon that one-hit KO'd any target. He probably didn't need much Mettle. I figured a single point was in Mettle.

Likewise, he probably wouldn't need a high base Hustle either, given his Ghost form buffed that stat so much. I assigned it another single point, though it could be zero as well.

That left Grit.

He could easily have five or more points in Grit.

Even a boosted Antoine couldn't kill the Astralist in his Possessed form, not like that. He got two points added to Grit in that form. It would have to be Antoine and Anna working together with a boost from Anna's Who's with Me? trope. Hopefully that—plus if Camden could find his weakness—might be enough.

That could work.

I hoped my estimate was correct, and if so, that we stood a chance—especially if Camden figured out his weakness.

Now all I could hope was that I would have the chance to relay that information to my friends.

"Kimberly," I said, "I have a plan for the final battle. If I'm not around to tel—"

"Why must you always resist your greater purpose?"

My blood went cold.

I looked over to the bed where Dr. Halle had been lying. Now he sat upright. His ghostly right arm and head had returned. He must have noticed the lights.

"A clever attempt, truly. What did you think? That I wouldn't understand Morse code?"

His ghostly arm flickered, and something struck me in the chest. The wind was knocked out of me. I struggled to breathe.

"Kimberly," I tried to say, but I didn't have the ability. She needed to continue; it was our only hope. I glanced up at her. She was furiously flipping the switch in that same pattern—in cellar, in cellar, in cellar.

I needed to buy her some time.

Luckily, her Plot Armor had risen to an amazing fifteen: her original ten Plot Armor plus three Savvy, because of her successful use of her Convenient Backstory trope, and then an additional two—one to Savvy and one to Grit—thanks to yours truly.

Finally, I had actually managed to make a prediction that triggered my Cinema Seer ability. This allowed me to buff my allies by making accurate predictions about the plot. I guess the "he's going to come back as soon as he sees the lights" prediction was enough.

All the theorizing on what kind of monster we were fighting hadn't worked, but something that simple had. I'd have to make note of that for the future.

I strained to stand up.

My estimation put his current Mettle, in Possessed form, at three. It wouldn't really matter; whatever his Mettle, it was higher than my Grit.

I couldn't buff myself. I only had one thing going for me, and that was his Hostage Taker trope, which meant that until the final battle—which couldn't start without Anna—he would not try to kill me directly but would instead try to stick me back in that chair and siphon out my soul.

As soon as I was up on my feet and moving again, trying to draw his attention away from Kimberly, his arm flickered again, and this time he struck me in the shoulder. I managed to catch myself against his giant machine.

"Do not touch that," he said. "It's very sensitive."

His arm flickered again, and I was flung backward.

He was just playing with me.

"Don't you worry," he said. "I won't damage your body too much. It was true when I said that I was going to bring you back. Your death will only be temporary. Can you not see the importance of my work, how such a small sacrifice could make a meaningful impact across all of humanity? Don't be so selfish."

This ghostly arm flickered once more, and I felt it grab onto my foot. I was dragged down onto the ground as he pulled me toward one of the chairs. I was helpless to fight. After all, I was a minor character, and the best I could do was motivate my friends with my death.

"You are in luck," he said. "I think I'm close to finally mapping the astral plane. You may be revived in time to see your family for the holidays."

A knock sounded against the wall. It was loud, and I could hear wood crunching on the other side.

Camden, Anna, and Antoine had gotten the message.

They were trying to get in. Antoine's five Mettle plus Anna's three and Camden's one should equal nine total. Plus two more because of Anna's Who's with Me? trope buffing Camden and Antoine, which should be activated now since it was the Finale.

If they were all trying to get into the basement, then whatever mechanism was keeping the hidden door closed would have to withstand that. Unlike the revolving door upstairs, I couldn't think of any reason why they wouldn't be able to get through. There was a chance.

"It appears they did not want to wait their turn," Dr. Halle said. He turned and began walking toward the secret door, releasing me.

I couldn't let him harm them before they got in, so as soon as he let go of my ankle, I was on my feet and running at him.

Before he could flicker his ghostly arm, I had jumped on his back. My arms and hands went right through his ethereal shoulder and neck, and I grabbed onto his physical body.

That was a terrible idea. I was not at all spec'd for that.

He threw me off with ease, but at least his attention was on me again. The only problem was that, now that the main characters had shown up, I was sure this was the final battle. Meaning he wasn't taking hostages anymore. I lay on my back as he approached me.

"Oh, how you vie for my attention," Dr. Halle said. "But love is more important than all things, more important than *you*."

His ghostly arm reached forward and grabbed me by the neck, lifting me into the air. "You do have strength of spirit. I'll grant you that. But then, so do I."

Did he just tell a joke?

He began to choke me tighter.

Strangely, it didn't look like he enjoyed this. This was a waste of a specimen.

As I struggled, I saw Kimberly come from behind and try to beat him with a thin pipe that she had found somewhere at his workstation. It did nothing. Kimberly's Mettle was zero. I don't think she could have beat him to death if she had all day.

The room started to go dark. Here I was, just as I had feared—the character who dies. That was my true fate. I could feel tears forming in my eyes as I lost the energy to even struggle.

I watched and waited for my status to change to Unconscious. It was only a matter of time. It wouldn't stop there, I knew. The final battle must have been beginning because he wasn't trying to siphon out my soul anymore. He was simply going to kill me.

CHAPTER EIGHTEEN

THE SILVER SOLUTION

I closed my eyes as the sounds of the room grew dim.

Death was coming.

Soon, I would be jettisoned into the astral plane without Dr. Halle's big fancy GPS tracking where I went. I could feel it happening. I lamented my bad luck. I spent years putting myself in the shoes of horror movie characters.

I imagined myself living through a zombie apocalypse, outwitting maniacal serial killers and going up against unkillable monsters, yet somehow getting the better of them. In all of those idle daydreams, I always thought I would be the main character.

How ironic that it was that very hobby—watching horror movies—that would get me stuck in a world where horror movies came to life. To twist the knife even further, I was playing a minor character archetype who couldn't even win a fistfight against a sixty-year-old scientist who was already half dead.

Suddenly, I felt an intense pain in my shoulder. It was the same shoulder where the Astralist had struck me earlier, but the pain was new.

I opened my eyes. I was lying on the ground. I had landed hard on my right arm, but I was free.

I could breathe.

Air filled my lungs, and the room came back into focus.

To my left, Antoine was struggling with the Astralist. He had tackled him, and the two were now wrestling on the floor. Based on my estimate, the Astralist would have too much Grit for Antoine to win alone.

But he wasn't alone.

Anna ran up beside him with a wooden club—a table leg?—and swung down hard on the Astralist.

For the first time, the mad scientist screamed in pain. He moved his ghostly arm as fast as the eye could see and lashed out at Anna. It wasn't enough. The Final Girl had the highest Grit of all of us. If he wanted to hurt her, he would need more Mettle.

Unfortunately, he had just the trick for that. His spirit left his crumpled body on the floor and barreled full force into Anna. She flew back into the wall behind her.

Antoine struggled to get up. His foot was still messed up, and his Hustle stat was diminished to as low as mine. The Hobbled status lit up brightly on the red wallpaper under his poster. He threw the Astralist's body off of himself and moved to help Anna. I tried to warn him.

"Attack his body!"

But the words came out of my mouth too quietly. My throat was damaged from being strangled. I tried again.

"Attack his body!" I knew the Astralist's spirit form was Invulnerable. His Comatose form, however, was defenseless now that the final battle had come.

Kimberly ran to me as I lay on the ground. "What is it?" she asked. She must have seen me trying to talk.

"Destroy his body," I said. This time, more of my words got through. I looked up at her. She had a deep, bloody gash on her forehead. Luckily, her buffed Grit was enough to keep her from dying from such a wound.

You're welcome.

"Kill his body!" Kimberly yelled to Antoine, who at the time was attempting to get to Anna after getting support from one of the metal chairs in the center of the room.

Antoine's eyes went from Kimberly to me to the Astralist's body he had left on the floor. He turned, grabbed another wooden table leg—it must have come from the same table as Anna's—and performed an impressive slam into the Comatose corpse of Dr. Halle.

As I suspected, the Astralist reacted to this by returning to his Possessed form. His spirit was still dependent on his body. Even though his Possessed form was not invulnerable and had lower Mettle, he couldn't leave his body unprotected.

The Astralist rose from the ground. His mortal head dripped with blood from Antoine's attack, but his ghostly face bore a look of pure rage.

I took in a deep breath. My head ached terribly.

Getting to my feet took effort. I was dizzy. I might have even had a concussion.

As I looked to the now open revolving door that my friends had forced themselves through, Camden came running through holding the books he had picked up in the hidden library and a small bag that I couldn't identify.

"You're alive," Camden said.

"Mostly," I said. It hurt to speak.

"Listen," he said. "We need something called phlogistic gum."

"What?" I said.

"I have no idea," he said. "There's a way to reverse the reaction that lets him control his own spirit like that. We need silver powder and phlogistic gum. We've got the silver powder." He held up the sack he had been carrying. "Have you seen anything around here that looked like it might be called phlogistic gum?"

I shook my head. I said, "There are some vials over there." I pointed to the shelf by his workstation.

Camden must have made good progress during the Rebirth Phase while I was Unconscious.

I looked back to Antoine and Anna. Both of them had high Grit scores and couldn't be bullied so easily. Where he tossed me around like a rag doll, they took more effort.

Don't think that because they had high Grit stats that they weren't getting hurt. On the contrary, they were getting the shit beat out of them. Anna had a cut down her whole forearm; Antoine had an eye swollen shut and glass shards sticking out of one of his hands. I think they both had broken ribs.

Grit didn't stop you from getting hurt. It stopped the damage you took from affecting the outcome of the movie.

After all, survivors in horror movies are often in terrible shape by the end of the movie. They just take their lumps and keep going. Those same injuries to me or Camden would have us rolling on the floor, bleeding out.

Camden and I ran across the room to the shelf where Dr. Halle had kept a variety of ingredients: different powders, metals, liquids, mixtures, things I didn't recognize. I hoped that Camden, being the resident smart guy, would be able to make something out of it all.

Luckily, all of the vials were labeled, and wouldn't you know it: Camden's Eureka! ability happened to work on labels. After sifting through the vials for a few moments, he was able to grab a large container filled with a strange brown liquid.

"Give me a second," he said. He referenced the Astralist's tome. "Tertio, goculum phlogisticum gouttierei ad solutio argentea addendum est."

"What did I say about reading the Latin?"

"I think we're past that," he responded. He was flipping through his Latin-to-English dictionary. "I'm trying to understand how to combine them."

The phlogistic gum, whatever it was, looked like what I imagine honey might look like in a universe where honey was made by cockroaches instead of bees. It smelled awful whenever he took the stopper off.

"Enough!" Dr. Halle said from across the room. "Do you honestly believe that what you're doing is for the good of humanity? What I'm doing is gruesome. I don't deny it. Its morality is veiled. But sometimes, science has to be allowed to make change."

I felt a monologue coming on.

"Watch out," I said. "Don't listen to his monologue, or you will get a debuff."

Finally, I felt like I had something to contribute.

Dr. Halle ignored me.

"I watched my wife, my beautiful, vibrant, intelligent wife, turn into a husk of herself," he said. "Do you know what that is like? To see life become a curse. I tried to cure her. I tried to extend her lifespan, to treat her symptoms, but in the end, I recognized that what I was doing was worse than just letting her die.

"In the end, we told each other that we would see each other again, and when I built the Mirror of Stars, she understood. She waits for me. I must finish my machine. I must map the astral plane. Please, please, I beg of you, have some decency.

"You must understand. What could be too high a price to combat death, to eliminate the gap between the living and the dead? Do you not see the logic? Those who die will not stay dead. Their sacrifice is illusory, but what I can achieve here is real.

"The heart reaches out across the astral plane. It is a true sign that we were meant to find each other. Those we love, those who came before, they can come back. They can."

As he spoke his impassioned speech, Dr. Halle's Plot Armor increased by three. His Humanizing Monologue buffed his Moxie while attempting to debuff those who listened.

Luckily, my Moxie was already three—a tie. There was little chance of his plea working on me. Kimberly's Moxie was even higher than mine; she would be resilient as well.

However, Antoine, Anna, and Camden had most of their points divided into other stats; they were vulnerable.

"Don't listen to him," I said. I coughed. "If you listen to what he says, you'll lose Plot Armor."

It was too late.

Already, Antoine and Anna had lost points in Mettle. Anna had lost one point; Antoine had lost two. It was working.

Camden hadn't been paying attention to the speech. His stats were untouched. I imagine it's hard to read Latin and be lectured to about Halle's idea of utilitarianism at the same time.

"Camden, do you have it ready yet?" I asked.

"Almost there," he said. He had taken some of the gum into an eyedropper and was dropping it into a flask that contained dull, silvery powder.

The reaction was instant. The combination of the phlogistic gum and the silver powder created a writhing, growing mass within the flask.

"What do we do now?" I asked as the mass within the glass flask started to grow.

"Just a second," he said. He started frantically flipping through the Latin-to-English dictionary, trying to translate something from the Latin book.

"Did you not read the last instruction before combining the ingredients?"

"Shut up, I was in a hurry." He continued to read.

Antoine and Anna had returned to pummeling Dr. Halle, but his ghostly self had an insurmountable defense. With their weakened Mettle, he made it very difficult for them to harm him.

Fortunately, a tie goes to the runner; Camden was ready to enter the fight.

"Okay, we just need to put the fluid on him at the place where his spirit attaches," Camden said.

I went to grab the flask.

"Careful, it's having an exothermic reaction," he warned.

It didn't register to me what that meant the moment he said it, but I figured it out when I touched it. It was scorching hot.

"We have to throw it," Camden said. "The book says you need to stand way back."

"Accuracy is determined by the Hustle stat," I said. "And Antoine's all the way on the other side of the room, and he's currently Hobbled."

Antoine had the highest Hustle stat, but the Hobbled status lowered his score down to one. He was in no shape to come over here and help us throw the flask at Dr. Halle.

"You have to do it," I said. "Your Hustle is higher, and you'll get a Mettle bonus if you're the one wielding the weapon."

Technically Kimberly had the highest Hustle of the three of us, but Kimberly had no Mettle. I wasn't sure how that would affect things. With Camden's Right Tool for the Job trope, it made sense for him to deliver the final blow.

Camden nodded. He grabbed a rag from off the table and grabbed onto the flask.

"I hope this works," he said.

Camden ran across the room. Anna had her table leg placed against Dr. Halle's head, holding him down as his Ghost arm struck at Antoine.

As Dr. Halle looked up, his ghostly eyes saw what Camden had in his hands and he said, "No. Please, you mustn't. Everything I've worked for! If you do this to me, then they all died for no reason." He gestured back to the shelves filled with corpses.

Anna, Camden, and Antoine must not have known what he meant because at that moment, the light was still off from when Kimberly had been flipping the switch. But they got the gist.

"Get back," I yelled, forcing my hoarse voice to be loud.

Antoine and Anna backed away.

Camden ran forward and threw the flask with the concoction against the back of Dr. Halle's neck.

As soon as the flask hit his body, it shattered, and the mass within it went absolutely crazy. It was as if the concoction was reacting to Halle's exposed soul itself—like throwing gasoline on a fire. It started to grow rapidly and spat and hissed.

Dr. Halle began to scream and plead, but the solution was separating his soul from his body, severing his connection to the mortal realm. The reaction started to look almost the same as the effect of the weapon in the center of the room. I could see Dr. Halle's soul being absorbed high into the Mirror of Stars. He clung to his body with every ounce of effort his soul possessed.

As his soul was carried upward, stretched and distorted, I saw a ghostly arm flicker toward the machine. I couldn't tell what had happened, but some lights flicked on, and a process started on the computer mainframe, but I couldn't tell what.

The machine started to activate. A million dials started to whir; beeping noises, warning of something, began to go off. His soul had completely departed his body now, which lay dead on the ground. But before his spirit could enter the Mirror of Stars, something in the machine overloaded, and an explosion started from within the Mirror itself.

The Mirror of Stars shattered. The machine burst at the seams, letting off steam and sending out sparks. The lights shuddered, with only a few of the yellow bulbs remaining on.

The crystal shards disappeared upon contact with the ground. The bright energy they contained released in a hot flash.

And then there was silence.

As my friends began to celebrate, I could not.

Because I had seen his tropes, and he had one left to go.

The needle on the Plot Cycle had not yet hit The End.

Now was time for The Parting Shot.

CHAPTER NINETEEN

BLACK MAGIC REANIMATION

Is that it?" Kimberly asked. Her voice was soft, dreamy. She was nursing her head wound. Her eyes were barely open. She leaned against a wall near the computer main frame. I noticed for the first time that the Incapacitated light on her status was flickering on and off.

Whatever blow to the head she had received hadn't been enough to kill her, thanks to her three Grit, but it was enough to do real damage. I couldn't tell if it was a concussion or simply her bleeding out. She had been struck after the Astralist had ceased taking hostages, so it had been intended as a kill shot, unlike the injuries I had received before being choked.

"No," I said. "He's got a trope called The Parting Shot. It means he set a trap, and something bad is about to happen." I surveyed the room. The machine was toast. I didn't see how it could be much of a risk.

I looked to the dark corner near the hidden door.

Oh no.

"A bunch of zombies are going to come from over there," I said, pointing to where the shelves of bodies had been. It was the most logical conclusion. There's no use wasting a large supply of well-preserved corpses, not in a movie like this.

Anna, Camden, and Antoine hadn't seen the bodies. Suddenly, they weren't celebrating any more.

"We need to make for the exit," Antoine said. He was right. This was not where we wanted to be for a fight like that.

Anna grabbed her table-leg club in one hand and gestured to Camden. "Help Antoine walk."

Camden came to Antoine's side and helped him move across the room. Antoine readied his table leg in his free hand.

I went to Kimberly and grabbed her arm. "Let's go," I said.

She nodded, accepting my help.

I looked for something to defend myself with as well. I found the metal pipe that Kimberly had been attacking Dr. Halle with earlier.

"Clever, clever, clever," a voice said.

It was a woman's voice. I recognized it as Judy's, but something was strange. She was using an accent different than the one she'd been speaking with before.

She sounded like Dr. Halle.

"You think you can always be prepared for what comes?" Judy said.

Judy's body was still strapped to the chair where it had been when she was killed. Now her head was up, and her eyes were fogged over, but her mouth was very much still able to speak.

"When you killed me, it wasn't me that you wronged," Judy said. "It was them. I promised them that I would bring them back. I gave them my word that their sacrifice would not be in vain, but you destroyed everything. Now, we will never bring our loved ones back. My Anastasia . . . It is not me that you have to face for your sin. It is them."

Judy's body started to struggle against the leather straps, but she was not able to break free. In the darkness where the bodies had been kept, I heard footsteps.

"If you will not let me return their souls to their bodies," Judy/Dr. Halle said, "I'll put something else in instead."

They began to laugh.

Out of the darkness, a desiccated corpse walked upright toward us. It had been a woman wearing a sundress. After that, another left the darkness. A man wearing overalls. Then another and another, until two dozen corpses in total emerged with dull gazes.

A final zombie emerged from the darkness. It was wearing a wedding dress. Anastasia Halle, back again.

Or at least, her body.

Around me, I saw my friends' Plot Armor jump up by two—one point in Savvy and one point in Grit. My prediction of the zombies had triggered my Cinema Seer trope and buffed them.

But my ability didn't work on me.

The zombies all had three Plot Armor, which meant they weren't that big of a threat on their own, but their Plot Armor would combine when attacking together just as Antoine and Anna's had. So, if they each had one Mettle, but seven attacked you, that's seven Mettle, and none of us had a Grit score high enough to deal with that.

It turned out that Dr. Halle's Parting Shot ability was essentially Minion Maker, the same thing that Benny the Haunted Scarecrow could do. The distinction, I suppose, was how the ability played into the story.

"Run!" Anna said.

I ran for the exit, dragging Kimberly along, but we were the closest to it, and when my friends tried to follow, the zombies cut them off. They were surprisingly fast—maybe not as fast as a normal human, but far faster than a typical zombie.

They shambled after us in mindless obedience. These weren't brain-hungry zombies or virus-infected zombies. These were reanimated slaves.

They had very little Mettle or Grit and pushing through them was easy, even for me. Behind me, Antoine and Anna were sending them flying with their clubs. Compared to them, these things were made of paper.

That is, until they grouped up together.

Luckily, the secret door only opened a small amount, and while Kimberly and I were able to slip through, the zombie horde couldn't. The few that tried got tangled together in the exit, trapping themselves in the doorway. A pile-on formed, with zombie arms and legs facing every which way and none of them able to move.

That was the good news.

The bad news was that Camden, Anna, and Antoine were still inside.

"What tropes do they have?" Anna screamed over the sound of moaning zombies.

I peered at the red wallpaper in my mind and focused on the nearest zombie to me. The zombie was dressed in a Hawaiian shirt and shorts and had a pair of sunglasses hanging from his shirt pocket. No doubt they had been there whenever the machine had sucked his soul from his body.

MAGICAL ZOMBIE (CHUCK)	
PLOT ARMOR: 3	
Tropes	
BLACK MAGIC REANIMATION	Zombies resurrected by magic or spiritual methods can survive without crucial parts of their body, including the head, rendering them immune to traditional methods of dispatch. To defeat them, one must either use magic that is more powerful than the spell that animates them or destroy their body completely. Any remaining portion of their body will continue to attack relentlessly until it is destroyed.

Apparently, the technology that reanimated the zombies was more magic than science.

"You can't kill them by hitting their head," I said. At that moment, I could hear my friends struggling to kill the zombies.

"You have to destroy the whole body or destroy the spell that created them. Do you have any more of that concoction you used on Dr. Halle?" I asked Camden. I had to raise my voice to ensure I could be heard.

"No silver dust!" he yelled.

As he spoke, the zombie nearest Kimberly and I managed to break free from the knot of zombies and began rising to his feet.

"Anyone got any ideas?" Anna asked.

"Fire!" Camden answered. I couldn't see what was happening on the other side of the door, but it sounded like they were in a fistfight.

That made sense. The cool dry air of the basement had basically mummified the corpses. They would probably burn like a Yule log.

"The absinthe!" Anna screamed.

Now there was an idea. There had been several bottles of absinthe beneath the kitchen sink in the cantina. It was time to solve our problems with alcohol.

Kimberly and I were the only ones who could make it, so I said, "I'll go get it. You guys just hang in here. I'll be right back." I grabbed Kimberly's arm and guided her to the cellar stairs.

The zombie (Chuck) pursued us still. As we got to the top of the stairs, I turned and kicked him, sending him falling back down.

Kimberly could run in bursts, but then her Incapacitated status would flare up and she would need to stop altogether.

"Go without me," she said. "I'll be fine. You have to help the others."

That wasn't that bad of an idea.

"You go that way," I said. "It'll chase me because I have lower Plot Armor."

The zombie emerged from the cellar behind us and barreled straight for me. I whacked it with the thin metal pole to little effect. My Mettle had been buffed by Anna's Who's with Me? trope when the zombies emerged and the fight started, but the boost had disappeared as soon as I left the basement.

Kimberly ran off to the back of the main hall, and I went toward the court-yard where the cantina was. As predicted, the zombie followed me.

That didn't matter because I was faster than Chuck the zombie. My legs were moving faster; my *mind* was quicker. He wasn't exactly the lumbering zombie that you might see in the movies, but he wasn't fast.

But the strangest thing happened: I wasn't getting away.

As I turned the corner and started to run across the main hall toward the cantina, I looked behind me, and there the zombie was.

"Magic Zombie (Chuck)."

Plot Armor: 3.

That made no sense.

I was across the main hall in an instant. How had he gotten behind me so quickly? I continued on and wound my way around the castle until I got to the cantina, and when I looked back, there he was again right behind me as if he were keeping pace with me.

I couldn't wrap my head around how he was keeping up with me, but then I realized: he had three Plot Armor. My bet was that one of those Plot Armor was assigned to Hustle.

I also only had one point applied to Hustle.

Of course.

By the laws of Carousel, I could not outrun him. We tied in that stat. No matter how far I ran or how fast, I would always look back and see him behind me because we tied, and I had no trope to help me escape.

I made it to the cantina and quickly leapt to the cabinet underneath the sink where we had seen the absinthe. Four large, full bottles stood there waiting for me.

I grabbed one of them and quickly opened it up, just in time to turn around and see Chuck the zombie upon me.

I pushed him back and twisted off the lid. I splashed him a few times, but he quickly jumped on me. Fortunately, we were also tied in Mettle and Grit, so neither of us could really get an edge in.

Unfortunately for him, I was smarter, and I had a very flammable alcohol in my hands. A couple more splashes, not too much.

I ran to the other side of the kitchen, pushing him away from me so that I could get by. I got to the stove and turned the knob, hoping to hear a click, and sure enough, the stove came to life. When I turned, I saw that Chuck was back on me, so I grabbed him and shoved him down into the flame. His sunglasses fell from his shirt and landed on my shoe.

As soon as he caught on fire, Chuck started behaving strangely, even for a zombie.

It wasn't so much that he was in pain, but that his body was literally being eaten up by the flame. Whatever was left of his eyes could no longer see me, even with the magic that had reanimated him, and his limbs were not obeying him as the fire ate at his flesh and consumed his dry bones and skin.

Chuck crumpled onto the ground.

Those things were incredibly flammable. Before I had time to get my bearings, he was already charred black.

I needed to get that alcohol back to the others, but first, I bent down and picked up the pair of sunglasses from my shoe. I had an idea for later. I placed them inside my pocket and turned to go grab the rest of the absinthe.

I was back down in the basement in less than a minute.

The crush of zombies was still there, trying to free themselves, but were neither strong enough nor smart enough to succeed.

"Are you guys alive?" I yelled. I knew Anna would be, but I still wanted to check.

"Do you have the absinthe?" Anna screamed.

I didn't know if they were near the door. I tried peeking over the top of the zombie pile, but I couldn't make them out.

"Pass them over!" Camden screamed. I had no idea where they were.

Here goes nothing.

I lobbed one bottle over.

Crash. I heard it shatter on the other side. I hoped I at least got some on the zombies.

"Try again," Anna said.

I threw the next one. No crash.

The third one. No crash.

Fourth. A clink, but no crash.

"Got 'em?" I asked.

"Just a sec," Camden said.

Ten seconds passed.

A bottle hit the wall above the secret door. It shattered, and I could see fire rain down on the zombies through the opening of the door.

I jumped back.

The zombies lit up like tinder.

CHAPTER TWENTY

SOUVENIRS

As the bonfire of soulless corpses died down, I still heard some scuffling in the basement. The occasional voice would ring out as Camden, Anna, and Antoine took out the remaining zombies.

I took the thin pole I had been carrying and pushed the charred bodies from the door. I wasn't sure how much help I could be, but I couldn't just stand around.

The bodies had strangely fused in the fire—maybe that's something normal bodies do, I don't know. It took some poking and prying, but I got the door clear enough that I could step inside. Silently, I hoped that the zombie ash in my shoes would disappear when The End came.

As I stepped inside the secret laboratory, the source of the sounds became clear.

There were still four or five zombies running around. Antoine couldn't move well, but as the zombies came in his direction, he would give them a good smack and Anna would splash some of the remaining alcohol on them.

Of the few stragglers that remained, one of them was Anastasia Halle, dragging her wedding dress back and forth across the floor, chasing after whoever was running nearby. Her legs had been broken at some point in time, so she wasn't much of a threat. She crawled through the ash and dirt on the floor.

"Anastasia, my love, come to me," Dr. Halle said through Judy's mouth.

Anastasia, of course, ignored his pleas. She wasn't really there. Halle had to have known that; he was the one who reanimated her corpse. Still, he persisted.

"My love reaches to you across the universe," he said. "Come to me."

As soon as I had made it ten steps into the basement, all of the remaining zombies turned, stopped bothering my friends, and instead pursued me.

"Thanks," Anna said as she brought her table-leg club down on one of the zombies that had turned away from her. She pushed it to the ground and drowned it in a couple of glugs of absinthe.

Camden ran up to it holding a lit Bunsen burner. He got the flame near the absinthe fumes, and the zombie lit up.

"Works even better than I expected," he said.

He was right. These zombies burned better than they should, even after having been dried out.

"It's your Savvy," I said. "Catching them on fire was your plan, so it works really well."

Camden's Savvy was currently at nine: his original five points, plus three from his Right Tool for the Job trope activating when he used the silver solution, and an additional point from my Cinema Seer trope having buffed him when I predicted the rise of the zombies.

When he came up with the plan to burn the zombies, that plan worked even better than it should have because it was made by someone with a huge Savvy advantage.

I mean, after all, in a horror movie, even ridiculous plans work out if they are made by the main characters.

"This is the last one," Anna said as she poured the remaining absinthe on Anastasia Halle's crawling body.

"Not the last one," a voice said from the door. It was Kimberly. She had come back down. Her wound had stopped bleeding, but she was pale and sickly. Her Incapacitated status still blinked on and off sporadically.

"What?" Anna asked. "Oh, right."

Judy/Dr. Halle still sat in the metal chair, bound and unable to move.

"Release me," they said. "Anastasia, darling . . ."

"What do we do about them?" Anna asked.

Camden approached Anastasia Halle and lit her up with the Bunsen burner. "Leave them," he said. "We can't burn them."

Dr. Halle screamed in agony at the sight of his wife's corpse igniting.

Camden was right. As we all stared at the pitiful form of Judy possessed by Dr. Halle's spirit, we had the same realization that Camden had.

"Won't burn," he said. "Won't die."

Judy's body was fresh—for lack of a better term. It wasn't dried out and mummified like the others. It would not burn even if there was more absinthe. Even with Camden's elevated Savvy, a plan had to be plausible, and this wasn't.

"If the machine was still working, we could probably use it on them," I said, "but . . ."

The machine was completely out of commission. There were parts of it lying on the floor all over the lab. There would be no Deus Ex Terminator for Dr. Halle.

"So, we go?" Anna asked.

We all looked at each other, but no one said anything. We all turned to leave.

This time, I helped Antoine to walk. Lord knows he had put his injured foot through enough already today. Anna helped to guide Kimberly.

As we walked from the castle, I could still hear Dr. Halle's mournful cries in the basement. No one spoke as we each watched the needle on the Plot Cycle tick forward. When we stepped out onto the cloudy courtyard, it happened.

The End.

Finally.

My head and shoulder instantly ceased aching. A look at Kimberly showed that she was back to being runway ready. Antoine's foot was healed. He even had his shoe back.

I reached my hand into my pocket. Success. The sunglasses I had snatched from the Hawaiian-shirt-clad zombie, Chuck, were still there.

Try seeing my eyes next time.

If a monster couldn't see where I was looking, how could it know that *I* had seen *it*? These sunglasses breathed new life into the Oblivious Bystander trope strategy.

I started to laugh. Everyone joined me.

We had done it. We had squared off against a mad scientist with ghost powers and come out on top. Not to mention, we killed a *lot* of zombies.

"Morse code in the lights?" Camden exclaimed. "That was so clutch!"

"It was Riley's idea," Kimberly said. "He noticed that the lights flickered whenever a new one was turned on."

Aww, shucks.

"I couldn't have done it without you," I said. "You were the one who actually knew how to do Morse code."

"Not really," Kimberly said. "I've already forgotten—"

"Step right up!" a voice said from the center of the courtyard. "You've won a ticket!"

Of course, Silas the Showman was there. He moved his mechanical limbs and opened and closed his mechanical mouth. His lights flashed into the dark, overcast sky.

We looked to each other.

"Let's do it," Anna said.

We each took turns pressing the red button, but when we did, something strange happened. You see, up until that point, all we had gotten from Silas the Showman were archetype tickets and tropes, but this time when we pressed the button, we got some surprises.

As we lined up one after another, we were each given two normal-sized tickets and two tickets that were much smaller, more like raffle tickets.

We also got money. Around twenty bucks each in coins. They looked like the little commemorative coins you might get at Disneyland except with scary creatures on them. We hadn't needed money up until then, but we knew there were places you could spend it, as we heard people at the lodge talk about buying things all the time.

After I got over the excitement of getting paid, I examined the small tickets because I had never seen those before.

"Claim this ticket for a boost in one stat: Moxie, Hustle, Mettle, Savvy, or Grit. Just say it aloud and give it a rip," Silas said, answering the question we all had.

That explained a lot. Up until that point, we didn't actually know how to increase our stats. We just knew that our allies back at Dyer's Lodge had way more Plot Armor than we did.

"Hey, we leveled up!" I said. "Twice!"

"Oh, thank God," Camden said.

We took turns discussing what we would like to improve. For the most part, everybody ended up getting the stats that they felt they were missing during the Astralist storyline.

I wanted to improve Moxie and Hustle. The Oblivious Bystander trope used the Moxie stat, and a little extra Hustle would put me in a better position to pull it off as well. At the end of the day, if the strategy failed, I needed to be able to run back to the group and report what I had learned.

I grabbed the two smallest tickets. "Moxie," I said, and I ripped one. Just like that, my Moxie stat went up by one, and my total Plot Armor jumped up to twelve.

"Hustle," I said. I ripped the second ticket. Success! I now had thirteen Plot Armor, and with a little extra Hustle, I might actually be able to maneuver.

"Still want to try the oblivious thing?" Camden asked. He must have put together what my stat choices meant.

I nodded my head. I had been worried about how the others would react after the strategy failed the first time.

There was a silence in the group for a moment. I thought there was about to be an argument. To them, I just disappeared without a word. They might not have seen the potential.

Or maybe they did.

"Better get it working," Anna said. She gave me a reassuring smile. "If they can't kill you, they can't kill the rest of us."

I nodded my head again.

After a little discussion, we all used our stat tickets. Here were the changes to everyone's stats:

Player Stats					
	Riley	Antoine	Anna	Kimberly	Camden
Archetype	Film Buff	Athlete	Final Girl	Eye Candy	Scholar
Plot Armor	13	14	16	12	13
Mettle	1	4	3 + 1	0 + 1	1 + 1
Moxie	3 + 1	1	2 + 1	4	2
Hustle	1 + 1	3 + 1	2	3	2
Savvy	5	0 + 1	2	1	5 + 1
Grit	1	4	5	2 + 1	1

Next, we each reviewed our new trope cards. We had each received one new trope except for Kimberly, who got two. I've listed those below.

Anna received a green ticket:

Let's Not Fight
Type: Buff
Archetype: Any
Aspect: Any
Stat Used: Moxie+

When two players get too hotheaded and forget to play as a team, it takes someone else to remind them what's at stake and to keep them on track.
When this ticket is equipped and a player breaks up an argument or fight, all those involved receive a boost to their Savvy.
The success of this trope relies on the Moxie not only of the player using it but of all those involved in the fight. If the fight isn't believable, this trope will fail.

Antoine received a white ticket:

Just Walk It Off
Type: Healing
Archetype: Any
Aspect: Any
Stat Used: Grit

In the movies, you'll see a character get terribly injured and not be able to stand or walk, but then a few scenes later, it's like they never even received that injury, or the severity of that injury has somehow lessened considerably. When this ticket is equipped, a player can heal the Hobbled status simply by continuing to walk. The higher the player's Grit, the fewer steps are needed.

Camden received a green ticket:

<table>
<tr><td>

Zippos Are Cheap
Type: Buff
Archetype: Any
Aspect: Any
Stat Used: Savvy

</td></tr>
<tr><td>

Why is it that when a character in a movie needs to start a fire, they always choose to throw a lit Zippo lighter to do it? Why can't they light the fire and just walk away instead of wasting a perfectly good lighter?
When this ticket is equipped, the player will receive a large bonus to Savvy for any plan that involves lighting a fire by throwing or otherwise sacrificing a lit Zippo lighter.

</td></tr>
</table>

Kimberly received two blue tickets:

<table>
<tr><td>

Get a Room!
Type: Rule
Archetype: Eye Candy
Aspect: Beauty
Stat Used: Moxie

</td></tr>
<tr><td>

The Party is the main exploration phase of a story, and it is often during this phase that characters try to do some "exploring" with a love interest, only to be interrupted by the discovery of some important plot element.
With this ticket equipped, a player has a heightened chance of finding important plot information during the Party phase if they explore the setting with a love interest.

</td></tr>
</table>

<table>
<tr><td>

A Hopeless Plea
Type: Action
Archetype: Any
Aspect: Any
Stat Used: Moxie

</td></tr>
<tr><td>

It makes your heart hurt to see a character beg for mercy when you know their captor will never relent. It must be dreadful to continuously plead for release, only to have your jailer ignore your pleas.
With this ticket equipped, a player who begs for release must be verbally denied by their captor. If the captor does not verbally deny mercy, persuasion may still be possible.

</td></tr>
</table>

I got a green ticket:

<table>
<tr><td>

Escape Artist
Type: Buff
Archetype: Any
Aspect: Any
Stat Used: Savvy

</td></tr>
<tr><td>

The first step of a great escape is a solid escape plan. The player who equips this tactic will be rewarded for their clever escape strategies.
If the plan is plausible based on the player's Savvy, they will receive a boost to Hustle to help execute it. This tactic can only be activated while captured or during a chase sequence.

</td></tr>
</table>

No doubt, this was an award for escaping the metal chair in the basement. That could be useful.

We must have worked well as a team because we each received eight stars except for Camden, who got nine. We had each also received an additional ticket that, by their size, looked like tropes, but we had not seen anything like them before.

I received:

<table>
<tr><td>

Magically Reanimated Zombie
Chuck

</td></tr>
<tr><td>

Chuck Treglio was coasting through life on his third gap year, just trying to "chill" and "take it easy." However, his noble pursuits were cut short when he encountered the Astralist at Halle Castle.

</td></tr>
</table>

Instead of having a player trope or even an archetype, it simply had the image, name, and description of the zombie I had killed. I got Chuck, complete with an image of the Hawaiian-shirt-wearing zombie I had burned to a crisp earlier.

Anna and Antoine each got one zombie. I suppose you only got one of each type of creature you killed, because they killed way more than that.

Anna got Anastasia Halle:

<table>
<tr><td>

Magically Reanimated Zombie
Anastasia

</td></tr>
<tr><td>

Anastasia Halle was a brilliant mind and a beautiful woman, with a heart full of kindness and compassion. Her life was cut short by an incurable illness, leaving her husband, Dr. Simon Halle, devastated. Determined to save his beloved wife at any cost, he delved into the dark arts of astral science, seeking a way to restore her to life.

</td></tr>
</table>

Antoine's ticket was exactly like mine except with a guy named Wilbur wearing a sweater vest:

<table>
<tr><td>Magically Reanimated Zombie
Wilbur</td></tr>
<tr><td>Wilbur Jenkins was Dr. Simon Halle's accountant, responsible for managing the books of the Halle estate and Halle's research facility. He was a congenial and hardworking man, dedicated to his job and his family. However, his life was tragically cut short when Halle began experimenting with astral science and made the family accountant his first experiment.</td></tr>
</table>

Camden, however, received something far more interesting:

<table>
<tr><td>The Astralist
Dr. Simon Halle</td></tr>
<tr><td>Dr. Simon Halle sought a way to bring back his beloved wife, Anastasia, even to the point of killing dozens of innocents. Using astral science, he modified his body to allow himself to manipulate his own soul, at the cost of his sanity. Now, hidden in the darkest dungeon of his family's former castle, he awaits unsuspecting victims to help him realize his ghastly vision.</td></tr>
</table>

"What are these?" Anna asked.

"I have no idea," I said. No one at Dyer's Lodge had told us about these. "Collectibles?"

"We'll have to ask," she said.

With that, we left Halle Castle behind.

CHAPTER TWENTY-ONE

AN OUTSIDER

The trek back to Dyer's Lodge presented a new challenge. We didn't have Todd to guide us this time, but we had the next best thing: a cocktail napkin with scribbles on it.

Before we left for Halle Castle, Todd had opened up a gigantic binder filled with information players had gathered over the years. Adeline, our leader, called it the Carousel Atlas. Everyone else called it the Survivor's Bible. Todd had thumbed through it and scribbled down some instructions on the napkin that could guide us back.

The instructions were extremely helpful. They included such gems as "don't talk to the lady with the dog," "don't take the mirror," "don't help the guy change his tire," and, my favorite, "avoid the fog on Calumet Ave." Each of these, I assume, was designed to prevent us from unwittingly entering a difficult storyline.

As we walked back, we found the lady walking a very excited Great Pyrenees who kept pulling on its leash and lunging at passersby. "He never does this, I swear," the woman would say to everyone he lunged at.

As instructed, we ignored her, much to the pup's dismay.

On Pyre Street, a disheveled young woman left her Victorian-style house crying, bleeding from her wrists and nose. She didn't stay outside long but was out just long enough to hurl a large silver mirror into an open trashcan near the street. It landed just perfectly to be in view of those on the sidewalk.

"That's a really pretty mirror," Kimberly said softly as we passed, entranced by the jewels affixed to its frame. She stopped to admire it, reaching a finger out to touch it.

Anna took her by the shoulders. "Let's get out of here, girl. We have mirrors at the lodge."

As we walked off, Kimberly shook her head. "What just happened?"

Unfortunately, we didn't see a guy who needed help with his tire, but by the time we got to Lake Line Road—where the Omen was supposed to show—we weren't really seeing anyone at all. The route did pass Calumet Avenue, but it was so far away I didn't get to see the fog. How disappointing.

By the time we saw another building or person after that, we had made it to the lake, to Camp Dyer. As we arrived at the sign for the camp, we saw a large moving truck backed up to the entrance as far as it could go. We had to squeeze past it just to get through the fence.

"This is new," Camden said.

The moving truck was one of those you can rent from a national chain, except it was a fictional, Carousel version called GET OUT OF TOWN MOV-ERS. The driver was gone, and there was nothing in the back.

"Maybe there are some new players?" Antoine offered.

That didn't make sense. It was usually years between new arrivals, according to Antoine's brother Chris.

"They must have had a lot of luggage," I said.

As we circled the truck to get by, Anna said, "Look at the back."

I followed her eyes to the pull-down door on the back; it had a bloody hand-print on it. This couldn't be good. For a moment, we all looked at each other, unsure of what to do. The Plot Cycle didn't show us that an Omen was nearby. What else could it have been if not that?

"Let's go," Anna said.

As we set out on the path, everything appeared normal. The birds were chirp-ing, and the creepy happy campers were flitting about.

"Will you help me find Cindy?" a little girl asked me as we walked the trail to Dyer's Lodge. "I think she went over by the abandoned cabin."

The camper pointed over to the dark, boarded-up cabin far away from all the others, around the bend of the lake. "Girls Cabin 14" was the off-limits cabin.

"Go away," I said. The little girl ran off teary-eyed as my friends laughed behind me.

"Why is it always me they talk to?" I asked.

"Aww," Camden said. "You're their favorite camp counselor."

Finally, we made it back to Dyer's Lodge.

As we arrived, we figured out what the moving truck had been for. Four men carried a large pool table up the stairs to the lodge's entrance. Both doors had been propped open to get the table in.

One of the men was Bobby, the married guy who had arrived in Carousel at the same time we had. He was looking pale and had blood on his face.

Lots of players had gathered around to watch the men deliver the table. Most had bemused smiles on their faces. Many sported the red plastic cups that you might see at any gathering of free adults. In Carousel, alcohol was in great supply, after all.

A few players clapped as they left their rooms to see what the commotion was about and saw the pool table.

Someone in the crowd, I don't know who, asked, "Is that from Solomon's Tavern?"

Travis, one of the players we had met on our first night at camp, said, "Sure is. The bad news is we only have three good pool cues. We had to use the others to kill the vamps." This elicited some chuckles. I didn't know much about this guy.

"Travis Haley!" a voice rang out from within the lodge. It was Adeline. She marched through the still-open doors and stopped in front of the men carrying the table. "What the hell are you doing with that?"

The four men set the table down on the deck, unable to move forward.

"Addie!" Travis said. He smiled his white-toothed smile and put on the charm. "Just thought the place needed some billiards is all. There's room. You want the first game?"

Adeline ignored him. "Where did you get that?"

"Solomon's Tavern. No worries. They won't miss it," he said. "We've got it under control."

Adeline was not having it. She may have been short, but for most people, there was no question who had seniority. Travis wasn't most people.

"Did you finish the storyline?" she asked.

I hadn't realized that the four men who had been carrying the table were, indeed, roughed up badly. Bobby, the Wallflower, was in worse shape than the rest. He leaned against the table for support. I couldn't tell where he was bleeding from, but he was bleeding. If they had finished the storyline they got the pool table from, all of that would have been healed.

"We couldn't do that yet," Travis said. "But we've got it figured out. You see, if we kill the vampire queen before we get the table, the tavern explodes. Can't get the table if that happens. So, our plan was to rush in, get the table, deliver it, go back, and then kill the queen. See, we've thought of everything. We're going back later tonight and killing her. Won't be a problem."

Adeline's gaze would have killed a lesser man. "And what part of the plan was it to bring back an infected player, let alone an infected *new* player?"

I hadn't seen it before. Bobby's status revealed that he was Infected. He wasn't just sickly; he was becoming a vampire as we sat there watching. I had never seen that status light up before. I hadn't thought to look.

"That wasn't part of the plan," Travis said. "It was more of a loose improvisation, if you will." He was apparently hoping to get a chuckle from the crowd but failing.

"Go kill the queen," Adeline said. "And take him with you!"

Travis turned to his party-mates. "Unless you want us to set the table up first."

"Now!" Adeline said. That was that. She went back inside.

Travis waved the other three men back. "I guess we're going to have to go kill the queen. Who knows, she might wake from her hundred-year sleep sometime in the next hour."

"He always like that?" I asked Todd later, after we had managed to get inside the lodge.

"Travis? Yep. His brother Vernon was the big guy helping him carry the table. Travis's archetype is Outsider, in case you didn't see it. They are damn useful, but they tend to develop an attitude," Todd said. "Kind of like Comedians."

Todd and Valerie were busy working up a route for my friends and I to go on. They had a special storyline in mind for us. One that would help us get more accustomed to town.

"Don't worry about him," Todd said. "He gets restless sometimes, but hey, we all do." He lifted a sheet of paper from the table he had been working on. "Here you all go. Directions to the university, for when your next storyline is up. Explore campus and downtown between scenes if you want. Remember, though, if you wander into a monster's den, it will still kill you even if you aren't a part of its story."

We had just learned that you couldn't trigger a storyline if you were already in one in Adeline's tutorial. This, we were told, gave a player limited means to travel about the town. Whatever this story we were about to do was, it had several scenes that were hours apart, giving us time to explore.

After asking around, no one knew what the enemy cards were for exactly. From what I understood, they mostly just traded them and used them for clout. I doubted my little zombie card was good for either.

CHAPTER TWENTY-TWO

THE FAR SIDE OF THE MOUNTAIN

The very next time the five of us were back on the couches in the common room together, Antoine stood up and spoke to us like a lawyer arguing his case to the jury.

"We have been handed an ordeal that no one on this planet should ever have to deal with," he said. It was funny he said no one on this planet because I wasn't even sure we were on Earth anymore, but I listened instead of making a joke. "I think that this situation we are in is more difficult for some people than it is for others. What's more, I think some of us have been dealt a hand that is worse than what others have been."

He coughed and looked back at Kimberly.

"Kimberly has been given a trope that is inarguably very powerful, but it isn't fair, and she's not dealing with it well. I don't mean that to be mean," he added. "I would hate that trope too. We all would. I say that we should allow Kimberly to go into storylines without Looks Don't Last equipped. I think that we are good enough as players that we don't have to rely on something that causes so much distress for one of our teammates. It isn't fair to ask that she always die."

He took a deep breath. He knew how big of an ask this was.

"Think about it. Kimberly doesn't have any tropes to help her survive long enough to get any meaningful debuff on the enemy, so all this trope is actually doing is stressing her out and taking her out of the game." He looked like he was about to say more than that, but then he just kind of did a nod or a bow of some sort and sat down on the couch next to Kimberly.

It felt like he really didn't want to have to ask that of us. He knew that if she didn't use Looks Don't Last, that meant the rest of us could be killed instead. More specifically, it meant I would be killed instead.

Anna was the next to speak. "Kimberly, if you don't want to use that trope, I understand. I can't sit here and say that you should have to die when I don't have to."

So, it was decided.

Camden probably didn't agree with the decision. Looks Don't Last was a very useful trope, even if we didn't get a good debuff, but I don't think Camden was going to cause an argument here when we were already outvoted. It was three to two at best.

I said nothing for the same reason, although a dark feeling grew in the pit of my stomach. I tried not to let my disappointment show; I'm not sure I was successful, but no one said anything.

Days after we returned from the Astralist, we found ourselves out on the pavilion, sitting around a table for our next lesson from Adeline. That day's lesson was short and sweet. Adeline explained that the Astralist storyline we experienced was a shorter, easier version. Unlocking the harder version meant bringing different archetypes or aspects into the storyline. She went over a few different variations and then asked us to rate ourselves.

We all got eight stars, so we couldn't have done that bad. Still, I felt like I could have done far better, and I explained why. Adeline didn't seem sold on my Oblivious Bystander strategy and didn't seem surprised when it failed. That hurt to hear.

Ever since it was decided that Kimberly wouldn't have to use Looks Don't Last, her mood had improved dramatically. I couldn't blame her.

The days after that were like those that came before the storyline. We woke up, explored the camp, sat at a bonfire into the night, and then went to bed.

One night, a few nights before our next storyline, I had just drifted off to sleep when there was a knock at my door. Camden was the first to get up and open it.

It was Todd, there to wake us up. I didn't know what could be so important as to drag us from our beds, but I did notice that there was a purple shade of light coming in from the window.

As I blinked myself awake, we were brought out onto the back deck, underneath the overhang on the right side of the lodge. Chairs had been brought out and pointed in the direction of the lake.

It was pretty clear to see why we had been summoned. It was overcast, and there was water in the air; it would start raining soon. In the distance, the rain had already started; we could see it causing splashes on the other side of the lake.

But that wasn't what we were there to look at.

The thing that was notable was that in the distance—on the other side of the lake, perhaps seven or eight miles away from us—was a mountain. It wasn't a particularly large mountain in the grand scheme of things, but it did have one peculiar quality: it was glowing. Or perhaps a better way of putting it was that something on the other side of the mountain was glowing.

As the storm raged, a fog grew around the mountain, and a light on the other side was caught in the fog, creating a glowing aura that was so visible that we could see it on the other side of the lake. It was a bright purplish hue with violet low lights.

I could see why they brought us out there; it was quite beautiful. I wondered what sort of storyline was causing something like that.

We sat with the veterans and waited for the storm to get to us.

Adeline was there; she turned to us and said, "That's it," pointing to the mountain. "The far side of the mountain. That's the way out."

"What?" Antoine said. "That's the way out? How do you know that?"

"You'll see," Adeline said with a smile.

We waited to find out what it was that the veterans knew that we didn't. While the mountain was beautiful, I could see no indication that it was the way out of Carousel. In fact, it was in the exact opposite direction that we had come from when we entered.

"When I was your age, that was the reason the veterans in charge first came to Lake Dyer, before we moved the whole group here," she said. "With any luck, you'll figure it out soon enough."

As we watched and waited, the storm grew, and the purple lights lit it up beautifully. And then I saw what it was that Adeline wanted us to know. Lightning struck on the other side of the mountain, and I wasn't sure at first. By the time the second bolt struck, I was certain.

I had not just seen the lightning with my eyes.

I saw it somewhere else—on the red wallpaper.

When I describe the red wallpaper that way, it's because even though it is in your mind, it still feels like you're looking at an actual ornate wall that you might find in a very old building. It looked like high-quality, textured wallpaper in varying shades of red.

When the lightning struck, a flash appeared on the red wallpaper, casting shadows against the wall. For the first time, I could see the red wallpaper in three-dimensional space as the shadows bounced off of it.

"Oh my God," Kimberly said.

"The red wallpaper is over there?" I asked.

"That's the theory," Adeline said. "We think the red wallpaper isn't just in our heads. What do you think?"

"It's on the other side of the mountain," I answered.

Another lightning bolt, and again I saw shadows as if the red wallpaper were on a wall right against a window, and when the lightning struck down, it was casting light into the building that the red wallpaper was in.

I didn't know what to think of it, but I finally understood why the veterans were so moved by the purple lights. If the red wallpaper had a connection to something on the other side of the mountain, that was a very strong argument that the way out was over there.

But how were we supposed to get over there? We had learned over and over again that the strongest storylines, the most dangerous Omens, were west of us as you tried to get around or over the lake. There was even a highway over there that was impassable because of some nightmarish being called the Highwayman.

I now understood the obsession with moving west.

I watched until the storm faded, and as I went back to bed, I tilted my head in the direction of the window until the fog had lifted, and the purple lights were no longer visible.

CHAPTER TWENTY-THREE

DELTA EPSILON DELTA

*I*f there is one thing that Carousel has plenty of, it's college students.

As we followed the final instructions Todd and Valerie had given us to lead us safely to Delta Epsilon Delta, we arrived on Traditions Boulevard, the street that held most of the Greek-life houses at the University of Carousel.

We got there just as the sun was going down, which is funny because it was only a quarter after three in the afternoon. It must have always been sundown on that street. Throngs of NPC students joined us as we walked down the street. They were all divided into groups, each with a unique destination in some storyline or another.

The atmosphere was electric as the students spoke excitedly of tomorrow night's game—in fact, several told Antoine "Good luck." Of course, they were also excited about whatever parties, mixers, and get-togethers they were going to that night.

Delta Epsilon Delta was separated from the road by a huge row of hedges; it was set a ways back from the road. The driveway to the house was cobblestone, and the house was large, white, and adorned with columns in the Greek-life aesthetic you might see at any college in the US. This one only had one thing that set it apart.

A man was hanging from the balcony.

Not a real man, as far as I could tell. It was a mascot costume of some sort. The costume consisted of a flat-brimmed cowboy hat, a pair of leather chaps, and a poncho. The letters "SMU" were emblazoned on the front of the poncho and on the hat. The mascot's face was stuck in an ambiguous stare that might have been a cartoonish glare or grimace; I couldn't tell because his entire lower face was covered in a bandana. His outfit was charcoal black with accents of midnight blue. He sported a large foam machete in his belt.

A noose was around his neck—a rival team's mascot hung in effigy.

As we stared at it, the needle on the Plot Cycle jumped to Omen.

"We ready?" Anna asked.

We all looked at each other and nodded.

Loud music blared from inside the house. As we reached the front steps and Antoine knocked on the door, the needle on the Plot Cycle moved from Omen to Choice to Party.

We had made our choice.

"Now *this* is a party," Kimberly said as the door opened and revealed a house full of lively, drunken college students. She was right. In this storyline, the Party phase actually was a party.

It made sense that Kimberly was happy. "We" had decided that Kimberly would not bring her Looks Don't Last ticket on this storyline. "We" were relying on my Oblivious Bystander strategy, so why would we need it? Without her trope, the bad guys would target me first instead of her. Really it was Anna's decision, and no one argued.

It felt like all of the pressure was on me now.

It was time to explore.

"Anna!" the guy who answered the door said as he caught sight of her. It was an NPC named Evan. He was a handsome trust fund kid from what I could tell. Probably intelligent and funny too. I disliked him immediately.

"Evan!" she said back, not missing a beat.

"I didn't think you were going to show," Evan said. "Come on in." He looked at the rest of us and gave us a quick smile. "Hey, Antoine. Kimberly. Camden."

He skipped me. It seemed strange at the time.

As the night wore on, more and more NPCs would pop out of the woodwork and greet one of my friends.

Antoine was greeted by some football players. "You ready to hand SMU their asses tomorrow night!?" They peeled him away from us to talk about the game.

Kimberly was shepherded over to a gaggle of pretty sorority girls from Epsilon Epsilon Kappa.

"Early admission, U of C School of Medicine!" some guy yelled at Camden with a hug and chest bump.

These were what Antoine's brother Chris called "scripted interactions" or "roles."

In some storylines, every player was assigned a role based on their archetype. Anna was the likable main character that everyone seemed to know—and some guy named Evan had a crush on. Kimberly was a sorority girl at Delta Epsilon Delta's sister house. Antoine was an athlete playing in the big game. Camden was some overachiever.

I . . . was sitting on the couch with a big bowl of popcorn in my lap watching the whole thing go down.

An hour into the party, I had not had a single scripted interaction. Everyone else was laughing and talking about school. They were singing and dancing along to a song that sounded like Nickelback from a parallel dimension.

A bunch of the guys had spikey hair with frosted tips and cargo pants. The girls wore skinny jeans and straight, bottle-blonde hair. The guys were dressed like Justin Timberlake, and the girls were dressed like Paris Hilton. It was the early 2000s in this storyline, apparently.

That explained the huge, outdated TV in the living room.

I took it upon myself to explore the house. Odds were, we would be trying to fight a killer there soon. I moved from room to room checking drawers and closets. All I found were a bunch of staring strangers. Nothing useful.

I didn't know what determined your luck in finding important information during the Party phase. Whatever it was, I didn't have much of it. My theory was that total Plot Armor was the determining factor because I had almost none of that.

As I moved through the kitchen, I saw that the backyard pool was surrounded by chairs. They were mostly empty. I decided to go outside and take a seat while I waited for one of the NPCs to come and tell me what my role was.

Just as I sat down, I heard a squeal of tires out front, and a bunch of the NPCs went that way, so I followed. An old orange farm truck had just pulled into the driveway. From the look of it, it narrowly avoided missing the front porch of the building. The driver opened the door and stepped out.

"Torsos!" he screamed.

Everyone else screamed, "Torsos!" back.

It was a strange interaction.

"Ruck, you idiot. You're drunk as hell," Evan said. He and Anna had come outside after the commotion. "What are you doing driving?"

Evan appeared to know this Ruck character. Anna, Evan, Camden, and the guy who chest-bumped him gathered around Ruck and started talking to him. The passenger in Ruck's truck came around too. His name was Nathan. I returned to my seat in the back. I can't explain it; it would have felt like I was spying to stay there with them. That wasn't my "role."

Ruck was an interesting guy, if only because he was the first NPC I had seen so far with a last name—Johnson. He was a heavyset fellow with a backward cap and a patch of whiskers on his chin.

Every once in a while, Ruck would scream, "Torsos!" and the whole house of people would respond, "Torsos!" back at him.

My luck eventually turned around. Anna, Ruck, Camden, and the rest eventually made it back around the pool area where I was. I think Anna might have had something to do with that.

Just as Ruck was about to lie back in a deck chair a few seats away from me, some chick in a tube top named Amber showed up and shoved him back into the seat.

"You asshole!" she screamed.

Ruck landed hard. "Hey, what did I do?"

"You told Robin Roeper that I slept with you on winter break," she yelled. "Do you know how embarrassing that is?"

Ruck was drunk as a skunk but was not too far gone to respond. "I didn't tell her you slept with me," he said in his best peacekeeper tone. "I told her you slept with every guy at the resort. She must have misunderstood."

Amber screamed an animalistic scream and yelled at him for five more minutes before leaving in a huff. She had caused quite a scene.

"What was her name again?" Ruck asked as she left.

Anna scolded him in a disapproving tone. She snuck a look up at me, one of those "are you getting all this?" looks. She had sensed, as I had, that this storyline was going to have something to do with everything we were seeing right now. Anna was the main character of this story. If the story brought her here, it was probably important.

The stereo played four or five knock-off Backstreet Boys songs after that before something else happened. Three enraged men arrived. One, named Kevin, was fuming. His ire was directed at none other than Ruck.

"You son of a bitch!" Kevin said. His black hair hung in his face, and an SMU college T-shirt told me what he was mad about.

"Did I tell people you slept with me too?" Ruck asked.

"What? Our mascot," Kevin said. "You're the one who stole it."

"You got no proof of that," Ruck said with a grin.

"It's hanging from your balcony, you idiot," Kevin said. "And I know you were the one who dumped that huge pile of cow shit on our field before our game last week. I saw some in the back of that crap truck you drive."

"The pile of shit on your field last week was your offensive line," Ruck said. "Now get the hell out of here."

"We're talking to your dean," Kevin said.

"Don't do that. I can prove it wasn't me."

"And how's that?" Kevin asked, incredulous.

"Look," Ruck said, putting his hand into his back pocket. He took his hand out of his pocket and smacked Kevin in the face, sending him reeling back into the pool. Kevin's meathead friends tried to throttle Ruck for that, but the ruckus had attracted a crowd, including Antoine and his NPC teammates. Kevin's friends looked tough, but Antoine and the other football players easily separated them from Ruck.

Kevin quickly pulled himself from the pool and gestured for his lackeys to leave with him, but as he left, he gave Ruck the middle finger and cursed up a storm.

As Ruck lay back on the lounging chair, he looked over to me and said, "I'm going to pay for that, aren't I?"

That was the first line an NPC had spoken to me all night. What's more, it was true. I knew then that whatever involvement Ruck had in this storyline, he wasn't going to like it.

"Torsos!" Ruck cried. Again, everyone yelled, "Torsos!" back.

It was strange. In movies, scenes were always cut up so that the character interactions and motives were layered and mysterious. As I sat off-screen and watched it all play out at once, it sure looked like people were just lining up to air their grievances against Ruck one after another.

The night moved on after that. Evan asked Anna to dance; she was very flattered and took up his offer. Camden had settled into a chair near me, and we struck up a conversation about what we had seen so far. Antoine and Kimberly disappeared for a bit. I didn't see them again until they opened the door to the back balcony that overlooked the pool. Everyone outside looked up and screamed different things to the effect of, "Don't go out there, the balcony is broken."

Sure enough, the support beams looked rotten even from the ground.

A discussion broke out about what everyone was doing after college.

"I'd really like to go to Harvard," Anna said. "They have a program there for my field of study and I know some of the faculty, actually."

"What kind of school is Harvard?" Evan asked.

That might have been the first thing Evan said all night that caught her off-guard. They must not have had the Ivy Leagues here in Carousel.

"It's a private school," she answered.

"Hmm," Evan responded.

Evan was staying on at U of C for his MBA. The guy that had been Ruck's passenger in his truck, Nathan, said that he wanted to be a doctor. He was pre-med. He and Anna talked about how much work that line of study would take. The guy must have been passionate because he got teary-eyed as he talked. That might have been the beer though.

I finally figured out what the whole "torsos" thing was about. "The Torsos" was the school's team: the University of Carousel Fighting Torsos.

How artful.

I knew this because Ruck had a theory that the Torso was the toughest college mascot.

"What about the Tigers?" Evan asked.

"No. Torso wins. Tigers instinctually go for the throat. The Torso has no throat. Tiger gets confused and, during its confusion, the Torso strikes."

"All right, buddy," Evan said. "You've had enough to drink."

That explained why some of the students wore shirts with cartoon mutilated torsos on them.

As the night began wrapping up, some guy wearing a University of Carousel T-shirt ran back into the backyard hollering about how someone was "tearing up the field" and to "come quick!"

It was like everyone in the house was scripted to leave as soon as possible at that very moment. They all got up and followed the guy back toward the field, wherever it was. The house was abandoned in the blink of an eye. Everyone was gone. Even my friends. I ran to follow behind, but I noticed that one person was still in the backyard: Ruck. He had fallen asleep in the lounging chair.

The needle on the Plot Cycle neared First Blood.

The only question was, did I stay at the frat house, or did I follow the crowd?

CHAPTER TWENTY-FOUR

RANGER DANGER

I was nearly to the street when I stopped to gather myself and make a decision. I knew that I had to leave the backyard. Ruck was about to get killed, of that I was certain. We had been shown suspects, but none of them stood out to me.

Plot Armor: 3.

No enemy tropes. As far as I knew, I couldn't see the tropes of NPCs, though I suspected they had some.

The crowd was quickly moving on down the street. As I watched them go, a realization dawned on me: I didn't recognize any of them. Not only were my friends nowhere to be found, but every other person I had seen at the party had somehow vanished into the crowd. It made absolutely no sense. I had just seen these people leave the Delta Epsilon Delta house, but I couldn't pick out one person I recognized.

A chill went down my spine as I realized that a trope had appeared on the red wallpaper in my mind. I couldn't see the bad guy, but I could see one of their tropes. It was like how I knew the Astralist was spying on us and that Benny the Scarecrow could change his corn maze at will.

I read the trope:

EVERYONE IS A SUSPECT	No characters or players will have an alibi for the murders occurring before the Finale.

It took me a moment to understand why I was seeing that, but then I figured it out. Every single named character had gotten lost in the crowd, including my friends. None of us would be able to vouch for the location of any of the suspects.

Of course.

This was a whodunit. We had all been split up so that none of us could act as an alibi for anyone. It made the mystery more difficult. On the bright side, that meant Anna and Evan had been separated too.

I looked back at the house. The SMU mascot costume was no longer hanging from a noose. Had Kevin and the SMU guys retrieved it? It had seemed like they left too quickly for that.

If I went to the field with everyone else, I probably wouldn't be able to meet up with my friends until after the murder; might as well stick around and put Oblivious Bystander to work. I returned to the house and entered through the front door. Ruck was out back, so I figured the killer would be too.

I retrieved the sunglasses I had taken from the Astralist storyline. With them on, my eyes were mostly covered. I could still see pretty much everything, but covering my eyes gave me the plausible deniability needed to make the Oblivious Bystander strategy work.

Soon, I was trying my best to stay casual while walking through the house. I had no defense if the killer just stepped out in front of me, but truthfully, I didn't think that was going to happen. When I had used this trope at Halle Castle, the Astralist had kind of . . . gone along with it. His Ghost form had simply followed behind me, only attempting to reveal himself when he could do so without interrupting me. The whole point of the trope would go down the drain if the bad guys could just tap me on the shoulder, after all. I wasn't sure that would always be the case. It was time to find out.

The kitchen had a great view of the backyard, so that was where I went. As soon as I walked into the small dinette area, I looked through the window in the back door. There Ruck was, lying out on the lounging chair just as he had been when I left.

Someone was standing over him while wearing the SMU mascot's costume. In a gloved hand, they were brandishing a large kitchen knife.

When the costume had been hanging on the roof, it had not occurred to me how similar the outfit was to well-known slasher getups. The rubber mask, the soulless, hollow eyes. It reminded me of The Shape's mask in the *Halloween* franchise. If Michael Myers had worn a bandana and flat-brimmed cowboy hat, that is.

I quickly jumped into the kitchen to try to be out of the line of sight. I crouched down behind the counter and my mind went blank.

What was my plan again?

Oh yeah. I was going to act like the really scary thing wasn't happening.

But *how*?

I looked around the kitchen and saw that cereal boxes were lined up on top of the refrigerator. I quickly grabbed one. I started pretending to read the back of it . . . Was that enough though?

I know, I'll pour a bowl, I thought.

This was so ridiculous. A killer was looming over an overweight frat guy twenty feet from me, and I was searching through the cabinets for a bowl and spoon so that I could eat some healthy delicious Icy Flakes.

Next, I needed to put the cereal in the bowl. Did I need to pour quietly? Yes and no. I didn't want to attract the killer's attention, but I was supposed to be pretending not to see the killer.

I held my breath and poured. Every little ding in the bowl sounded like a bomb going off in my ears. Was my hand shaking? *Stop it.*

I turned to get some milk out of the fridge. Should I chance a glance at the killer so that I could read their tropes?

Yes.

I peeked quickly and turned my eyes back toward my meal.

That was too quick. I didn't see anything. *Come on, keep it together.*

I poured the milk into the bowl and put the carton back in the fridge. Now I needed somewhere to eat this. Should I sit at the kitchen bar or the table? Or should I eat it over the sink like a true bachelor? I couldn't eat it over the sink, I realized; there was a window that pointed straight into the backyard. I would see too much to pretend I was oblivious.

The needle on the Plot Cycle touched First Blood.

Shit, I was missing it.

I casually walked over to the table and sat down with my cereal and the box. Having the box there gave me extra cover. Plus, there was a word search on the back.

I was positioned in such a way that I could just barely see the backyard without turning my head. I had to strain my peripheral vision. If I turned any more, I would have had my back to the killer. It was the best I could do.

With the deftness of a world-class spy, I looked out the window. The cowboy mascot, or whatever he was supposed to be, was pulling the blade from Ruck's corpse.

Part of me felt guilty for not trying to save him, but I knew that I wouldn't have been able to do anything. Carousel was where horror movies came to life, not superhero movies. He was scripted to die and so he did. If I got in the way, it would just be both of us dead. My friends and I could only survive by getting to the end of the story. Part of that story had Ruck getting killed.

I casually lapped up spoonful after spoonful of the off-brand Frosted Flakes as I watched the killer stare at Ruck's lifeless body. Ruck had never even woken up.

I peered into the red wallpaper:

RANGER DANGER	
PLOT ARMOR: 15	
TROPES	
QUICK CHANGE ARTIST	This villain can change into and out of their disguise without being seen or getting caught.
HIDDEN IN PLAIN SIGHT	The villain will appear as an ordinary NPC until they don their disguise.
THEY'LL NEVER BELIEVE YOU	When tangling with this villain, the authorities will not believe or take seriously anything the players tell them.
PATTERN KILLER	Before the final battle, the villain will only kill victims chosen according to a pre-established motive.
NO NEIGHBORHOOD WATCH	The villain will not be seen by NPC witnesses when off-screen.
EVERYONE IS A SUSPECT	No characters or players will have an alibi for the murders occurring before the Finale.
THE IMMORTAL MASK	This villain cannot be defeated, captured, or unmasked until their identity and motive have been deduced.

My first question was, "What the hell is 'Ranger Danger'?"

Then I realized it was probably the name of the SMU mascot. What were they, the SMU Rangers? Knowing Carousel, they could just as easily have been the SMU Dangers.

Plot Armor: 15.

That made sense. With my Plot Armor of thirteen, we were roughly similar in level.

These tropes spelled out a very specific set of rules for this storyline. As I had thought, this was a whodunit. Scoping out the guests at the party had been useless. Because of the Hidden in Plain Sight trope, he could have been any of them. Apparently, that ability trumped my Trope Master ticket because I had seen nothing but a bunch of level-three NPCs. I meant to ask my friends if they had seen anything but didn't get a chance.

The killer dressed as Ranger Danger had ceased staring at Ruck and now had moved away from Ruck's body. He was walking toward me.

Quick, how does a normal person eat?

As I munched on my processed-corn cereal, the killer approached the window behind me. For some reason, I didn't feel very protected by that glass. But

I kept eating. I stared at the cereal box and tried to make out some of the words in the word search: "Dead," "Execution," "Assassination." Dang. No wonder the kids in Carousel were so creepy, with games on the backs of cereal boxes that dark.

I became acutely aware that the light on my Off Screen status had flicked off. That made sense. Antoine's brother Chris had explained that the Off Screen status was an indicator of whether you were "on camera" in the sense that the scene you were in was important.

I had concluded that I was rarely doing anything important. I was off-screen for most of the Party phase. As I understood it, some cool tropes could only be used off-screen. Some others could only be used on-screen.

Right now, I was finally in an important scene.

Whenever you see the Oblivious Bystander trope in a horror movie, the camera will always cut or zoom in to reveal the killer posing in a scary way while the oblivious bystander is none the wiser. This would be accompanied by that deep scary sound effect that every horror movie has.

That's what this was.

This was a scene used to build tension in a horror movie. It might even get a laugh. The hapless cereal eater has no idea that a murder was just committed outside the window. How close did he come to death without knowing it?

I took one last look at the killer out of the corner of my eye before he disappeared. I committed his tropes to memory. The next time I saw him, I would need to be prepared.

At that moment, I needed to get out of the house. I didn't want to be caught with the dead body.

I wasn't the main character, so I might not have important information that would help me deduce the killer's identity. I needed to meet up with the others to go over everything.

After I had waited a few minutes for the needle on the Plot Cycle to move firmly out of First Blood, I put my cereal bowl in the sink and left the house.

With that, the game was afoot.

CHAPTER TWENTY-FIVE

END OF SCENE

First, I found Camden a few blocks away by the field.

"What just happened?" Camden asked. "I was right next to Mark, but then suddenly he was gone." Mark was the name of the guy that had chest-bumped Camden when we got to the party.

I explained the Everyone Is a Suspect trope to him. Everyone got separated from everyone else. I didn't get a chance to explain what I had seen on my first successful use of my Oblivious Bystander strategy because we were surrounded by NPCs.

"That explains why I can't find the others . . . It was Ruck, right?" Camden asked quietly.

I nodded as I scanned the crowd. NPCs as far as the eye could see. Any one of them could have been Ranger Danger. There would be no way to know.

"I didn't get anything," Camden said. "None of my abilities are helpful with this one."

It was true. Camden could find information from books and got a bonus when using a Zippo lighter or when exploiting an enemy's mortal weakness. Ranger Danger didn't have a weakness in that way. He (or she) was just a human.

"I guess you could light something on fire," I suggested.

Camden smiled. "I'll see what I can do."

Antoine and Anna found each other after the crowd died down. They had found a place in the stands to survey the damage on the field. We joined them and kept an eye out for Kimberly.

"Evan disappeared as soon as we started running off," Anna informed me. Did she suspect him? I think she might have. I was tempted to let her believe that his disappearance was suspicious, but I couldn't. If there was anyone that needed all of the available information, it was Anna. I told her about the Everyone Is a Suspect trope.

The field had a twenty-yard streak starting at one of the endzones. Someone had wrapped a chain around one of the goalposts, pulled it down, and dragged it until it had caught in the ground and the chain broke.

"Suspect still unknown," a campus policeman said after the crowd started asking for details. He looked absolutely overwhelmed by the situation and kept a whistle in his mouth to blow every time someone even looked like they were going to walk onto the field to inspect the damage.

His name was Officer Ricky on the red wallpaper. His Plot Armor was three.

The veteran players had told us that all the storylines share one police force and that we would get to know the cops pretty well in our time at Carousel. This was the first one I had met. Given how jumpy he already was, I wondered how he'd handle it when they found the body. As I was watching the panicking policeman, I heard a familiar voice.

"Look who I found."

It was Evan. He had found Kimberly and helped her find us. Then he plopped down on the bleacher right next to Anna.

With him there, we couldn't talk shop, so we spent twenty minutes trying to talk about the classes we were taking and other fictitious nonsense. I say "we"; I didn't do any talking. Evan didn't seem too interested in what I thought. We were soon joined by Nathan and Mark. They didn't seem interested in talking to me either.

It was uncanny. Don't get me wrong, I've been on the outer orbit of a friend group before, but they weren't even making eye contact with me.

As I contemplated their strange behavior, a line of police cars approached in the distance.

"Whoa. Looks like they're taking this seriously," Mark said.

However, the line of police cruisers kept going past the stadium.

Down on the ground, Officer Ricky got a message on his radio that made him grow pale. Everyone was moving down the stands after the police passed.

"What happened?" Evan asked over the roar of the crowd.

Officer Ricky was backing away toward his security golf cart parked near the field entrance. He seemed to be weighing priorities between guarding the field and going along with the other officers. Eventually, he had a burst of clarity.

"They found a body," he squeaked out as he turned on his cart and drove away with the sound of a high-pitched *wee woo wee woo.*

"A body?" Nathan asked. He had sobered up a bit on the jog over.

"Wait, where's Ruck?" Evan asked.

Everyone in the area suddenly showed great concern. They all looked around. Of course, everyone's favorite frat dude was nowhere to be seen. I tried reading their faces to see if any of them were acting weird, but they all had the worried, frantic energy to them that I would expect.

We took off down the road to the scene of the crime.

By the time we got there, the scene had been cordoned off by the police. No one could get in or out of Delta Epsilon Delta. It was a good thing I left when I did.

Just as we arrived, a large body with a sheet covering it was being loaded into the back of an ambulance. I assume that the timing of it was scripted because it was too perfect.

All that could be seen from the body was one large arm dangling out of the sheet.

"Ruck!" Evan screamed as soon as he saw the body and attempted to cross under the police tape.

An officer grabbed hold of him and stopped him from getting there. "We cannot allow you near the crime scene. You have to understand. I'm sorry, son."

We weren't the only ones to arrive at the scene. Several news crews arrived just after we did and began asking bystanders questions about what had happened.

As the ambulance closed its doors and took away Ruck's remains, a woman's wailing could be heard from on the property. It was coming from the backyard.

"Who is that?" Kimberly asked.

"Was someone else hurt?" Anna asked. She glanced over at me as she said it, almost as if she was asking me whether there was another victim. I didn't dare answer her, not in front of the NPCs.

As we watched, an officer appeared from behind the house escorting a young woman. The woman was crying with her makeup smeared and her face contorted into a caricature of its natural form. Her face, hands, and much of her tube top were covered in blood.

It was Amber, Ruck's maybe girlfriend who had yelled at him earlier.

Officer Ricky passed by us on the other side of the tape, clearly trying to stay as far away from the blood in the backyard as possible.

"Ricky," Evan said. He leaned as far over the tape as he could without breaking it.

"I really can't talk to you right now," Officer Ricky said.

Anna joined in. "What is she doing here?" she asked.

Officer Ricky looked at Anna and there was a glint of recognition, as if he knew whatever character she was portraying. "Anna," he said, "that's police business."

"Come on, Ricky," Kimberly joined in. Kimberly had a higher Moxie, so her efforts must have worked even better.

"Girls, Evan . . ." Ricky said, closing his eyes as he spoke. "Okay, fine, but you can't tell anyone. I don't want to get in trouble . . . She found Ruck Johnson's body. Ran out into the street and flagged down campus police."

"Oh my God," Nathan said. "Is it really Ruck?"

Officer Ricky's eyes opened wide. "Oh, shoot. I wasn't supposed to tell you that."

Nathan kneeled over and put his hands on his knees. "Oh, fuck. Oh, fuck," he said.

Anna instinctually put a hand on his back. "Let's go sit down over here," she said, gesturing toward the curb on the other side of the street.

"They seemed pretty close," Antoine observed.

Mark nodded. "Ruck and Nathan have been friends forever. Nate was his tutor, chauffeur, wingman, and everything else Ruck needed."

The group migrated across the street to where Anna and Nathan were.

"If I hadn't been drinking, this wouldn't have happened," Nathan said through tears.

"You don't know that," Anna said. "We all left Ruck behind. It's all our faults—"

"No," Evan interrupted. "It's the fault of whoever killed him."

Anna shook her head. "You know what I meant."

Evan ignored her. "And whenever I find out who did it, they're going to pay."

Maybe I was imagining it, but when he said that I thought he glanced at me.

Not long after that, people started to clear away from the Delta Epsilon Delta house. The news crews, rubberneckers, students, and even the police all found somewhere else to be. Even Mark, Evan, Nathan, and the other stragglers we had gotten to know from the party made excuses and left.

For the first time in a long time, every one of my friends had their Off Screen statuses lit. Mine was usually on because I was a minor character, but Anna's only turned on for a few minutes at a time.

"Does this mean we're between scenes?" Kimberly asked.

I shrugged.

The veteran players had told us about this. The storyline we were in was composed of multiple scenes. From what Todd and Valerie had said, our next scene didn't start for hours. Until then, we were free to roam Carousel—within reason. We couldn't trigger another storyline until this one was over. As long as we didn't walk into a monster's territory, we would be fine.

Town square was a known safe zone, so that's where we headed.

"I've been dying to just go somewhere," Kimberly said. "Anywhere where we don't have to deal with this horrifying stuff."

As we turned into town square, three women who looked like 1950s housewives walked by us. They had impeccable hair and makeup and wore big, lipstick-clad smiles.

"You're so pretty," the first one said to Kimberly in a high-pitched, cheery voice. She wore all purple.

"So pretty," the second one said in a matching tone. She wore all yellow.

"Very pretty," the third said. She wore all red.

Then they continued walking, only turning their heads away from Kimberly once they were fifteen feet away.

They never blinked.

"What the fuck was that?" Antoine asked as they moved into the distance.

I had no idea. We would deal with them when their storyline came up.

"I hate this place," Kimberly said, moving back to the center of the pack.

Town square looked . . . normal. Like a real town square. There were stores and cheery townsfolk. The square was well lit, and the nightlife here was bustling. Sure, the occasional odd character would show their head, but mostly it was normal. But maybe that was because we couldn't trigger any Omens.

We found a malt shop and took a seat. The prices were incredibly low. A malt for fifty cents. We indulged, except for Antoine, who kept looking at ours like he expected something to crawl out of it.

I told them everything I had seen and explained Ranger Danger's tropes as I remembered them.

"Wow," Camden said. "That's a lot of rules."

"The basic concept is that you have to figure out who the killer is to win."

Anna pursed her lips. "It could be any of them. I assume we can cross out Amber?"

"Maybe?" Antoine said. "Just because she called in the body doesn't mean it wasn't her."

That was true.

"We may not have all of the information we need yet. It's still really early in the Rebirth phase," Camden said. In fact, the needle hadn't moved much at all since I left my bowl of cereal after First Blood. There was still a lot of story to go.

"Ranger Danger is a pattern killer," I said. "It said so right in his tropes. He kills according to a pattern."

"And?" Kimberly asked.

Anna looked me in the eye and nodded. She understood. "You need more than one body to form a pattern," she said.

CHAPTER TWENTY-SIX

THE PUBLIC ACCUSATION

Antoine said that the party was mostly a bust for him. None of the other players he had met had any connection to Ruck that he could find. He was starting to think that he would have to play in the game tomorrow. That was only a problem because he didn't know what position he played or even what plays this team ran. All he knew was that they liked to run the ball and that SMU had a good defense but a weak offense.

I wasn't sure how that information was going to come in handy.

Kimberly had even less useful information. All the sorority girls had talked about were great places to shop around town, boys, and things that were happening in their classes. She spent most of the evening with Antoine.

Anna described everything that had happened to her from her perspective. "Ruck drank and drove to the party because Nathan was far too gone to drive anymore. Evan told me he had recently gotten broken up with because of accusations of infidelity last year. He wanted me to know he would *never* do that. Basic boy stuff. We went to the back and saw a lineup of suspects arrive and yell at Ruck. Then someone, probably the SMU guys, started tearing up the field. You know the rest. Anything else, Camden?"

"Not much. Mark is just really happy to have gotten into medical school. No drama," Camden answered.

"Evan's really into you," Kimberly said to Anna.

Anna laughed. "I prefer guys with free will."

"But not, like, too much free will, right?" Kimberly asked.

We all laughed at that.

I estimated the time to be around eleven at night, but this world ran on "movie time," which never made too much sense. As we sat, we noticed a lot of

NPCs had begun walking toward the college. It started to rain gently. NPCs took out umbrellas and trudged forward.

"Next scene?" Anna asked.

I nodded cautiously. The others agreed.

A lot of shoppers and shopkeepers alike left where they were to follow the crowds.

Soon enough we saw a familiar face among them.

"Nathan," Anna said, holding up her hand and drawing his attention.

He looked far more somber than he had earlier that night and a great deal soberer. He walked slowly over to us.

"Ruck thought of you as a friend," Nathan said, speaking to Anna. "We're doing a candlelight vigil at the football stadium. I thought you would want to come."

"Of course," Anna replied. "How did you manage to get this together so quickly?"

Nathan looked around at the people solemnly walking toward the football field. "It was Evan. He can do anything if he puts his mind to it. You know, it's funny. Ruck never would have thought that people would mourn him. I guess he never knew how much people cared."

Talk about a sudden shift in tone.

We walked in silence. I had never been to a candlelight vigil before. Many of the people who attended appeared to have just woken up out of bed, gotten changed, and come out. They looked tired, but they played the part of the heartbroken community very well.

I had never really thought about the lives of NPCs. Did they just wait around all day for the script to tell them to do something? Were they just lying at home asleep only to wake up and realize they had to get dressed and go to a memorial service for another NPC?

Some of them I recognized from being at the party, but others were clearly just filler. You could say they were *extras*. Never meant to be looked at too closely.

By the time we got to the stadium, the stands were almost full, and a temporary stage had been erected on the part of the field that had not been torn up.

The students started to pile into the remainder of the field—even the part that had been damaged by the goalpost. Officer Ricky tried to stop them at first but gave up after he got overwhelmed. He tucked his whistle in his pocket.

Everyone stood watching the stage.

There was a line of chairs on the stage accompanied by some NPCs, most of which had titles to go along with their names on the red wallpaper. They were affiliated with the school for the most part except for the sheriff and a couple of deputies. There was a psychologist there, probably acting as a mental health advocate after the tragic loss of a student. Like all of the other NPCs, these had three Plot Armor.

Evan was up there too. He stood next to an older man with a pronounced bald spot and big, horn-rimmed glasses whose name was Dean Lewinsky. "Dean" as in the title for a person who runs a college, I imagine. I doubt his name was also Dean.

Dean Lewinsky was the first to speak. He stood in front of a wooden podium with an attached microphone. He read a short speech off of a piece of paper in his hand.

"Dear members of the University of Carousel community," he said, adjusting the microphone in front of him so that it caught his voice better. "It is with a heavy heart that I stand before you today to address the tragic and untimely death of one of our students, Russel 'Ruck' Johnson, only hours ago. Ruck was a beloved member of our community, a student who was loved by his peers and respected by his professors.

"Unfortunately, we have lost Ruck in an act of senseless violence that has left us all shaken and heartbroken. As we mourn the loss of this bright and promising young man, we must also come together to support his family, friends, and loved ones during this difficult time.

"We do not yet know all of the details surrounding Ruck's death, but we are working closely with law enforcement to ensure that those responsible are brought to justice. Our thoughts and prayers are with Ruck's family and friends as they navigate this painful and difficult time.

"As we come together to mourn Ruck's passing, let us also remember the many contributions he made to our community during his time with us. Let us honor his memory by continuing to work towards creating a safe and inclusive community where all students can thrive and reach their full potential. Thank you."

From the sound of it, I doubted that Dean Lewinsky had ever actually met Ruck.

After reading his speech, Dean Lewinsky adjusted his glasses and stored the piece of paper inside a coat pocket. It would probably stay there until he needed to read it for the next dead student. I wondered if he was one of the characters that was shared between storylines.

"Some of Ruck's friends have elected to speak tonight," Dean Lewinsky said. He looked over to Evan.

Evan got up and leaned into the microphone and asked, "Nathan, would you like to go first?"

Nathan walked up to the stage and took his spot in front of the podium.

"I can't even believe it. When they told me Ruck was really dead, I . . . I just thought this couldn't be real. I thought I must have been imagining it, but unfortunately . . ." He trailed off for a bit as the emotion overwhelmed him.

After a moment, he continued.

"When I told Ruck that I always wanted to be a surgeon, he told me that was great because he always wanted to live in a surgeon's pool house." He paused as the crowd let out a nervous laugh. "That was when I knew that we would always be friends. That was who Ruck was. He was someone that you always wanted to be around. I wish that I could be around him right now. It's ironic that this is the exact type of social gathering that Ruck was so good at making bearable. I'm still going to try to be a surgeon. And the first life I save, I'll do it for him."

Nathan could barely get out the last part of his speech before he began to cry and left the stage abruptly.

"I guess it's my turn," Evan said. "Ruck . . ."

The name caught in his throat. I could see that he was struggling with the death of his friend. "He was a great guy. And a great friend. He would do anything for those he loved." He looked away for a moment, taking a deep breath before continuing.

"I've known Ruck for a long time. You know, freshman year he was actually shy. He was afraid to pledge to a fraternity. It's crazy to think now, but that's what people do—they grow, and they mature. It's hard to wrap your mind around the idea that one day, people might just stop moving forward, that their growth might be taken from them. We'll never know what kind of man Ruck would have become, but I think I would have liked him."

Evan used the podium for support; he was having difficulty standing. "What's so hard about this is that I know who he was before and who he became, and I think I had an idea of who he was going to be, but that's not what anybody is talking about. All they're talking about is that a frat guy got killed at a party like it's some sort of punchline. I heard what the news reporters were saying."

He took a deep breath.

"Ruck doesn't deserve that. What Ruck deserves is justice. And what we deserve is answers. And I think I know how to get both."

After he said this, the crowd erupted in whispers. Curious faces looked from side to side to see if anyone knew what he was talking about. Anna looked over at me, an eyebrow raised, but I had no answers. I didn't know where Evan was going with this.

"Because I think I know who did it. He's standing here today at the memorial service like he cares about Ruck, but he doesn't. He didn't leave the Delta Epsilon Delta house when everyone else did. People saw. He got to the field later than everyone else too. I can't think of any good reason for a person to stay behind like that and not tell anybody. I'm going to ask the police to investigate what that reason is."

The sheriff walked across the stage toward Evan and whispered something in his ear, a question.

Evan looked directly at me.

"It was Riley Lawrence," he said. He pointed his finger at me, and everyone in the crowd turned to look at me.

The crowd's whispers turned into full gasps as people stared at me in horror.

"Why did you do it?" Evan asked me directly, his voice echoing over the stadium. "What were you even doing at the house? No one invited you; I asked around."

He turned his attention back to the crowd. Tears formed in his eyes as a look of absolute hatred appeared on his face. "He's a freak. He sits around all day watching horror movies. He's obsessed with death and gore. Maybe even snuff films. He's probably involved in the occult—a devil worshipper or something. I think that's why he did it."

"Oh, shit," I said.

Suddenly, so much of what had happened in this storyline started to make sense. How no one at the party was talking to me and anyone who acknowledged me just stared. Evan, Mark, and Nathan basically just ignored me because they couldn't be friendly with me. It was against the script.

All this time I thought that I was being treated that way because I didn't have any scripted interactions—because I didn't have a role to play. I was a minor character.

But I did have a role.

I was a *suspect*.

CHAPTER TWENTY-SEVEN

THE USUAL SUSPECT

I sat alone in the interrogation room where the sheriff's deputies had left me. Shortly after Evan accused me of murdering Ruck, the scene ended. The NPCs were filing out of the stadium as I was being asked "nicely" to come with the cops.

The interrogation room was a small sterile chamber with stark white walls and a single fluorescent light fixture hanging from the ceiling. The only furniture in the room was a metal table and two chairs, one for the suspect and one for the interrogator. The table was bolted to the floor, and the chairs were made of hard plastic with no padding, designed to be uncomfortable and unwelcoming.

There were no windows, no decorations, no distractions of any kind. I don't know if the room was soundproof or if the characters outside were just silent because they weren't on-screen.

A two-way mirror on one wall allowed observers to watch the interrogation without being seen. I wondered if they were watching me right then.

They had not handcuffed me, so technically I should have been free to go, but this world went off movie rules, not actual constitutional law. This was a scripted scene. My status was Captured. I wasn't going anywhere.

As I sat there all I could think about was how Evan knew that I had been at the frat house at the time of the murder. If I understood the tropes and timeline at play, then the only person who should have known I was there was Ranger Danger.

It was true that Evan had been antagonistic to me, but I didn't know if that was because I was typecast as a loner with a frightening and scary hobby, or if it was because he was the bad guy. Was this whole thing an attempt to frame me for his crime?

The needle on the Plot Cycle was nearly vertical. Given my understanding of how the Rebirth phase worked, soon we would receive a revelation that would allow us to go on the offensive and start hunting down the bad guy. In the Astralist storyline, that revelation had likely been the discovery of Dr. Halle's weakness. I didn't know what it was going to be in this story.

All I could hope was that soon we would find some information to either prove Evan's guilt and motive or to rule him out altogether.

Soon, my status changed. I was still Captured, but the Off Screen status flicked off. The "camera" was rolling.

The only door to the room opened and a man entered. His name was Detective Marcus Blackwood. He was an NPC. His Plot Armor was fifty. That was the highest I had seen for an NPC, but that was not the thing that concerned me the most about Detective Blackwood.

He had enemy tropes. Or at least it looked like it.

Normally, I didn't know if an NPC had tropes because my ability only worked on enemies. But Trope Master did work on Detective Blackwood. The problem was I couldn't actually see what his tropes were. With fifty Plot Armor, he had enough Savvy to drown out my measly five points. Due to the level mismatch, I had no idea what his tropes were. To my eyes, they were just grayed-out posters on the red wallpaper.

Detective Marcus Blackwood was a tall, lean man with a commanding presence. He stood at about six foot two and had a chiseled, angular face with piercing blue eyes that seemed to scrutinize everything around him. His salt-and-pepper hair was kept short and neat, and he sported a well-groomed mustache. He wore a tailored suit, which emphasized his sharp features and gave him a professional air. Despite his intimidating demeanor, he moved with a grace and fluidity that hinted at some trace of athleticism despite being in his fifties.

"Good morning," he said. "I hate that we have to meet this way, but the circumstances demand it."

Was it morning already? I didn't respond.

"We thought it was best to get you out of there," Detective Blackwood said. "We were worried that the crowd might take things into their own hands if we didn't."

He flashed a weak smile.

Again, I said nothing. I'd like to tell you that I was just being a hard-ass but truthfully there was something about Detective Blackwood's presence that took away my ability to think. All I could do was hope that the direction this scene was taking wasn't going to get me locked away in prison.

"We'll get right to it then," he said. "What were you doing at the Delta Epsilon Delta house? Your accuser said that you were not invited. Is that true?"

"I went there with my friends," I said. Truthfully, I thought that I was a member of the frat, but apparently my character was just crashing the party. How embarrassing. I was playing a loner. Not a far stretch for me.

"Your friends?" Detective Blackwood asked. "I see. We'll get to them later. How do you know Russell Johnson?"

I didn't know what my character was supposed to know. I didn't know my backstory. "I met him at the party."

"The party that no one invited you to?" Detective Blackwood asked.

"I told you I went there with my friends."

Blackwood ignored me.

"Russell Johnson. Twenty-two years old. Sports medicine major. Numerous parking violations, a suspended driver's license, and DUIs, but nothing recent. A list of grievances from other students a mile long. Russell was a bit of a trouble-maker, wasn't he? But I don't see anywhere that he'd had a run-in with you until last night." Detective Blackwood watched me with his piercing gaze.

"What run-in? We barely talked to each other. Ruck might have said five words to me last night in total."

"Did he ask you why you were at the party?" Detective Blackwood asked. What was this guy's deal?

"I went to the party with my friends. It's a perfectly normal thing to do."

"And how many college parties would you say you've attended?"

Truthfully, after three years in college, that was my first one. I know, lame.

"Not many," I said.

Blackwood interlaced his fingers and leaned forward on the table. "So what made you decide to go to this particular party?"

"I told you I just went there with my friends. They were going, and I went with them. It's not that complicated." I was getting worked up. Was that the effect of one of his unseen tropes, or was I just irritable?

Suddenly, my Moxie dropped by one point.

Guess it *was* a trope. Did he debuff me by asking me a question repeatedly?

For a moment, he didn't ask any more questions. He just stopped and stared at me with his piercing blue eyes.

He said, "I've asked around. I know all about you and your . . . friends."

The way he said friends at the end . . . It was like he was calling into question whether they really were my friends.

"I see here that you went to high school with both Camden Tran and Anna Reed."

I nodded my head. Was this interrogation about my character or was it about me?

"However, I can't find any evidence that you maintained any relationship with them into college. You had no classes together; you were in no clubs together."

He paused to let me respond. I didn't.

"You don't share a major, and I can't find anyone who remembers seeing you at any party or event that they've been to before this one."

He wasn't just talking about my character. He was talking about me. Real-life me.

"Look, Anna was my neighbor; we grew up next to each other. Camden was my best friend."

"Was?" Detective Blackwood asked. "I thought he invited you to the party?"

"I didn't say that he invited me to the party. I said that we went to the party together."

"So, you went to the party with Anna Reed—who was your neighbor as a child—and your former best friend from high school? Or was it middle school?"

What did this guy know? How did he know it?

Camden and I had been best friends in middle school, but when high school came, he got popular, and I didn't. It happens. When we went to college, we didn't really hang out until he reached out to me a week before we came to Carousel and asked if I still liked scary movies. Apparently, that's what I was known for.

Anna had been my crush since I was a little kid, but I wasn't about to talk to this guy about it. I didn't care what tropes he had or how high his Moxie was.

"So, you tag along to a Delta Epsilon Delta party with Camden Tran and Antoine Stone, who are actual members of Delta Epsilon Delta, and Anna Reed and Kimberly Madison, who are members of the sister sorority Epsilon Epsilon Kappa?"

He leaned back in his chair.

"Are Antoine and Kimberly old friends too?"

"No," I said. "Recent friends."

That was close enough to the truth.

I don't know what debuffs this guy had, but as he dug into my past and friendship insecurities, my Moxie, Savvy, and Grit all dropped by one point again. It took everything I had just to concentrate.

"So, you used some old 'friendships' as a way to get into the party, and then what? What did you do once you got there?"

"Nothing," I said. What was I supposed to tell him? That I spent the whole time looking for a killer? That I combed the house over for information that I might need in the final battle?

"You didn't talk to anyone?"

"Yes, I talked to people."

"I thought you said you did nothing?"

I couldn't even answer; I was growing so frustrated. I couldn't form the words.

"Who did you speak to? Because I asked around, and the other partygoers said that you were a loner."

That was false. "I talked to my friends."

"There you are calling them your friends again. Do you think that they will appreciate that term when we haul them in here for questioning? Or do you think that when we turn up the pressure, they're going to tell us the truth: that you weren't actually invited?"

I didn't respond. Luckily this threat was empty given the circumstances. Anna, Camden, Antoine, and Kimberly weren't going to play along. He was just trying to antagonize me. He knew my insecurities. Probably figured them out with an insight trope.

Suddenly I realized what this character actually was. He was a secondary antagonist. He wasn't the bad guy that went around killing people, but he did cause problems for the heroes. Well, he caused problems for me at least. Scary movies were full of cops like this.

"If you were there for innocent reasons, I have to wonder why you didn't leave when every other person at the party did. You didn't care that the field was being torn up? Or were you—"

The door to the interrogation room opened. A low-level NPC police officer walked in and said, "We've got a match to the paint found at the crime scene up on Turn Around Road." He produced a manila file folder and handed it to Detective Blackwood.

"Thank you, Officer Peters," Blackwood said. He gave the man a warm smile.

The officer left and closed the door. Blackwood turned to me; his smile disappeared instantly.

"Did you kill Russell Johnson?" he asked.

"No," I said.

"But you were around him at the time he died, and no one else was. You didn't see anyone else, did you?"

How was I supposed to navigate this? If I said no, then I'm admitting that I was alone with the victim at the time of the murder. If I say yes, then I have a lot of explaining to do as to why I hadn't said anything before.

"I saw Ruck arguing with a chick named Amber. He also argued with some guys from SMU. Have you brought them in?"

Detective Blackwood shook his head. "I'm aware of those altercations. Those occurred long before Mr. Johnson was murdered. Amber Terry weighs a hundred pounds at most. She could never have subdued Russell."

I almost said, *But he was asleep when he was killed*, but somehow held my tongue. I think Blackwood set that trap on purpose. He would have known there was no struggle.

"I'll ask again. Was anyone else there with you around the time Russell Johnson was killed?"

"No, it was just me. I didn't even know that Ruck was in the backyard. I thought he had gone up with everyone else to the field. I was just . . . eating cereal."

I expected him to home in on my weak alibi, but he didn't. Detective Blackwood said nothing. He just stared at me. The silence was louder than any question. I was certain that he was employing a trope against me.

It was the strangest thing. The longer the silence lasted, the stronger my desire to confess grew. Not to confess to the murder of course. I hadn't done it.

Words started to well up in my throat that I *had* to say. Detective Blackwood had already debuffed my Moxie by two points—not that he needed to. There was no way that Detective Blackwood, with fifty Plot Armor, had less than four Moxie. I was powerless. He had me beat.

"Ranger Danger," I said. I couldn't help it.

"Excuse me?"

Now that I had said the words that his trope had forced me to, it was like I couldn't stop. I just had to avoid saying too much. "Someone dressed in the Ranger Danger costume was at the house."

"You're telling me that the mascot for SMU murdered Russell Johnson?" He looked away from me up toward the mirror on the wall. No doubt whoever was up there was having a good laugh. Detective Blackwood himself couldn't conceal a smile.

"I didn't say that Ranger Danger killed him. I said someone dressed as Ranger Danger was at the house. Ruck stole the costume and they had it hanging from the balcony when I got to the party. Someone had taken it down and was wearing it when I left."

"The jury is going to love that," Detective Blackwood said.

"You've got to believe me," I said, with every bit of sincerity I could muster. Now that was a cliche line. I wondered if I said it because I wanted to or because of Ranger Danger's They'll Never Believe You trope.

"I did not kill Ruck. I had nothing to do with it."

The pressure to be seen as innocent was so strong even though I knew that Detective Blackwood would never believe me.

All I had to do was hold on until the end of the scene.

The entire time we had been talking, my Off Screen status had flicked on and off. Much of this conversation had been on-screen, but now, the light stayed lit. I was free. The scene change was coming on.

Apparently, Detective Blackwood wasn't as interested in my horror-movie-watching hobby as Evan had been because he didn't even ask about it. I think the entire point of the scene was to establish that I was an untrustworthy loner and force me to confess to having seen Ranger Danger. I wondered how that was going to come into play down the line.

The next thing I knew I was being walked out of the station.

Detective Blackwood kept close to me. When we left the station—a large building only a few blocks from campus—my friends were there, eating sub sandwiches. I guess for them it was a break, and they used it to grab a bite to eat. Good for them.

"Oh, look," I said. "My friends are here to pick me up."

Detective Blackwood didn't say anything.

Suddenly, we were on-screen again.

"We're going to have some more questions for you," he said. "Don't leave town."

Very funny.

The steps up to the police station were very large. It was surrounded by benches and well-kept greenery. There was a set of steps down to the street. A man stood at the bottom.

"Detective Blackwood!" he said. He was a man in his late forties or early fifties. He wore a plaid shirt and jeans along with some very well-worn boots with dirt clinging to the sides and stuck in the treads. He wore a green cap on his head that reminded me of the ones that would say "John Deere" in the real world.

"How come you got the whole police force out looking for someone who killed some drunkard, but you ain't sent but one squad car over to find out what happened to my Nelly?"

Detective Blackwood recognized this man. "Mr. Birch, that's simply not true. We are investigating your daughter's death with every resource available to us. In fact, I am working on her case right now."

He held out the manila file folder he had been given during my interrogation as if it were proof of how hard they were working.

Mr. Birch wasn't having it. He reached out and attempted to grab the file but only succeeded in knocking it to the ground right in front of Anna. It opened, revealing a ghastly picture of what remained of Nelly Birch, some papers with biographical information and witness statements, and a small baggie filled with little orange specks.

"How come this frat kid gets a candlelight vigil with news crews? You all couldn't pay attention to her for more than a few hours before some other kid becomes more important? She was a student too! She was taking business classes. Why didn't she get a candlelight vigil? Why didn't you say anything at all?"

"Mr. Birch, we are doing everything we can to find out what happened to your daughter. The vigil was something that the university put on. A student dying on campus from cold-blooded murder got people worried. They needed reassurance."

Camden gently nudged Anna out of the way and bent down to pick up the file, glancing at it for only a few seconds. He held it out for the detective.

Detective Blackwood quickly retrieved the file folder and continued talking with Mr. Birch, leading him away from us as he did.

"So, are you going to prison?" Antoine asked.

"At first, I thought I was. But then the scene was over, and suddenly he just wanted to get me out of there." I would fill them in on the interrogation later.

"So did you see anything important in that file?" I asked Camden. He had only seen it for a few seconds, but his Eureka! ability would have shown him everything important.

Camden seemed to be working something over in his mind.

"Yeah," he said. "That girl who died . . ."

He paused, thinking.

"What about her?" Anna asked.

"I think Ruck killed her."

CHAPTER TWENTY-EIGHT

A PATTERN EMERGES

What do you mean that Ruck killed her?" Anna asked.

None of us had been prepared for that curveball.

"She was killed in a hit-and-run sometime yesterday evening before the party. Witness statements said that it was an orange pickup truck. The description sounded just like the one that Ruck was driving. They had paint chips from the scene," Camden said.

"Oh . . ."

"In real life, it would be a coincidence, but . . . I doubt it is here," Camden said.

"Okay, but what does this have to do with him getting murdered?" Kimberly asked.

None of us knew.

Was it possible that someone from the party knew this girl? If so, how would they have known that Ruck was responsible?

"He did almost hit the house when he pulled into the driveway," Anna said. "He had been drinking."

"But who would have known so quickly?" I asked. "It doesn't make sense."

The murder victim in a whodunit having a dark secret is not unusual. However, this was really late in the movie to find out about it. I couldn't figure out how this fit into the larger puzzle.

"In any case," I said, "we have to look into Evan. Only one person could have known that I was at the house at the time of the murder, and that's the killer. Either he is Ranger Danger, or Ranger Danger told him that I was there."

Evan was the best suspect so far, even if we didn't know the motive.

"I'm not going to be able to do that," Antoine said. "The game is today, so unless this story ends before then I'm probably going to get forced into playing."

It hit me.

"You will be forced into playing," I said. "Think of it. We're being hunted by someone dressed as a football team's mascot. I'll bet anything that he's there."

"He'll blend right in," Anna said.

"Exactly."

With Second Blood approaching, these were our stats and abilities:

Player Stats and Tropes					
	Riley	Antoine	Anna	Kimberly	Camden
Archetype	Film Buff	Athlete	Final Girl	Eye Candy	Scholar
Plot Armor	13 / 2	14 + 2	16	12	13
Mettle	1	4 + 1	4	1	2
Moxie	4	1	3	4	2
Hustle	2	4 + 1	2	3	2
Savvy	5	1	2	1	6
Grit	1	4	5	3	1
	TROPE MASTER Type: Insight Stat: Savvy Effect: Sees enemy tropes. Lose half of PA.	IT'S PART OF THE UNIFORM Type: Buff Stat: --- Effect: Higher Mettle when attacking with sports equipment.	LAST ONE ALIVE Type: Rule Stat: --- Effect: Cannot die until the party is killed.	CONVENIENT BACKSTORY Type: Buff Stat: Moxie Effect: Can change backstory to assist with the current task.	EUREKA! Type: Insight Stat: Savvy Effect: Helps find important information within text.
	CINEMA SEER Type: Buff Stat: Savvy Effect: Buffs Savvy and Grit of allies by predicting plot elements.	GYM RAT Type: Buff Stat: Moxie Effect: Buffs Mettle and Hustle by revealing athletic backstory.	WHO'S WITH ME? Type: Buff Stat: Moxie Effect: In Finale,	SOCIAL AWARENESS Type: Insight Stat: Moxie Effect: Can see the Moxie stat of all characters	RIGHT TOOL FOR THE JOB Type: Buff Stat: Savvy Effect: Buffs Savvy and

			allies gain a buff to relevant stat when assist- ing the player.	and enemies. Can intuit social dynamics.	Mettle when fighting an enemy with their weakness.
	THE OBLIVIOUS BYSTANDER Type: Rule Stat: Moxie Effect: Cannot be targeted while convincingly acting oblivi- ous to the enemy.	JUST WALK IT OFF Type: Healing Stat: Grit Effect: Heals Hobbled status by walking.	LET'S NOT FIGHT Type: Buff Stat: Moxie Effect: Stopping infight- ing buffs Savvy.	LOOKS DON'T LAST (Not brought into the storyline)	ZIPPOS ARE CHEAP Type: Buff Stat: Savvy Effect: Boosts Savvy for plans that expend Zippo lighter.
	ESCAPE ARTIST Type: Buff Stat: Savvy Effect: Plau- sible escape plans boost Hustle.			GET A ROOM! Type: Rule Stat: Moxie Effect: Explora- tion with love interest during the Party boosts the odds of important discoveries.	

				A HOPE-LESS PLEA Type: Rule Stat: Moxie Effect: Asking to be released forces the captor to explicitly deny the release.	

As you might imagine, Antoine found it easy in this storyline to talk about how he plays sports and works out. I hadn't been around when he did it, but it didn't really matter. He got the bonus to both Hustle and Mettle that his Gym Rat trope afforded him.

Not long after our conversation about the hit-and-run, a group of university students and football players came to get Antoine for the big game. The rest of us were dragged right along with him.

Even having seen the University of Carousel stadium twice, I wasn't prepared to see it on a game night. The entire place came alive. The stadium was not the biggest football stadium I had ever been to. In fact, it wasn't even as big as the one back at my real college. However, it was still large.

The stands were in the shape of a horseshoe. On the left of the entrance was the section for the away team. It was sparsely populated by SMU fans. I wouldn't want to go to Carousel for a football game either.

On the right was the home-team side, filled to the brim with cheering fans of the Fighting Torsos. In the curvy part of the horseshoe was the student section along with food vendors.

The stands were built on a large concrete-enclosed base. I didn't know what was under there. I assumed it was storage or locker rooms. With the many entrances and exits to the area, it was difficult to navigate or track the people coming in and out of the stadium.

The field had been repaired between scenes. The only reason you could tell that something had happened to it was the slightly off-color sod that had been used to repair the grass. The goalpost had been put back in its proper place, but it still bore nicks from the chain that had pulled it down.

The roar of the crowd made talking difficult.

"Kimberly and I will go to the student section," Anna said. "You two go to the home section. Find Evan. He's either going to give us a lead to Ranger Danger's identity or he's going to incriminate himself. Either way, if you guys find him, I think Camden should be the one to talk to him." That was probably a good idea. Evan wasn't going to be happy to see me not in jail.

The previous scene had been early morning. This scene was getting darker as nighttime approached. The stadium lights turned on. The game was about to begin.

Camden and I rushed to the home section of the stadium. Moving around there was difficult. The stands were really packed, even more so than they had been at the candlelight vigil. Maybe I was being paranoid, but I got the impression that a lot of the traffic was scripted. Perhaps we were being held up, delayed.

"Do you see anything?" I asked Camden. I practically had to yell.

"Nothing!" Camden answered back.

I looked all around the stadium. I needed to find Evan. Heck, if I could lay eyes on Ranger Danger, at least that would be something. Both were no-shows. In fact, I didn't know where any of the NPCs were. Mark, Nathan, Amber, the SMU guy that had yelled at Ruck. They were in the wind.

"Look, it's Anna," Camden yelled at me. He pointed over to the student section.

I could barely see what he was pointing at, but then I saw her waving her arms trying to get our attention. She and Kimberly were pointing toward something beneath us down on the field. We were up in the stands, so we couldn't easily access the field, but we quickly walked down to the guardrail and peered down at what she was pointing at.

It was Evan. He was standing amongst other students in what I can only assume was the tunnel that the team was about to come out of. He was far closer to us than he was to her.

"Let's go," I said.

I didn't know how Camden would go about trying to pry him for information, but we were running out of time. When the Finale came, we would not be able to find any new plot information to help us solve the mystery.

If we couldn't find the killer's identity and motive, then we would just slowly get picked off until we all died in the final battle. Ranger Danger's Immortal Mask trope would make him unbeatable without this information.

It was now or never.

It was just as difficult to get back down from the stands as it was to get up there. We could only hope that Evan would still be near the tunnel when we finally made it. Everyone walking along the pathways and ramps leading up to the stands was trying to go up. We were the only two trying to go down.

After what seemed like an eternity, we finally got down to ground level and ran around the outside of the stands near the field. We ran as fast as we could to the tunnel where we had seen Evan standing.

We were in luck. He was still there talking to some other NPCs.

I stayed back in hopes that he wouldn't see me. Camden walked forward and crossed over the side of the tunnel to where Evan was.

And then the bad news came. A poster appeared on the red wallpaper with the name of one of Ranger Danger's tropes: Everyone Is a Suspect.

It was like Carousel had waited for that very moment. We weren't just playing against the story. It was playing against us.

Just as Camden made it to the other side, the band started to play, and football players, coaches, and cheerleaders started to pour out of the tunnel that Camden had just crossed over.

We were being separated again, just like we had been at the frat party. I tried to keep an eye on Camden. I saw him and Evan moving closer toward the mouth of the tunnel as the emerging players caused a surge in the crowd. After a few players had passed, I couldn't see Camden anymore.

Did they go in the tunnel? Was this scripted?

The needle on the Plot Cycle was nearly to Second Blood. If that wasn't enough, the Everyone Is a Suspect trope only activated when a murder was about to take place.

Now, I know what you're going to say: "Don't go into the tunnel with a killer around."

But I didn't have a choice. I didn't know if I would be able to find Camden, or if the same trope that separated us would keep us apart. However, I knew there were limits to the trope's power. After all, the trope didn't stop me from witnessing a murder.

Would it stop me from preventing one?

I pushed forward into the tunnel, fighting against the stragglers who were running out. By the time I got through, I didn't see Camden or Evan. I wondered how long it would be before I could find either one of them.

I raced through the labyrinthine tunnels. That place was massive and confusing. There was no sign of either of them. There was no sign of anyone at all. There were so many doors and paths under there that I could have passed right by them without even knowing it.

Those same doors could also have concealed a killer.

I quickly raised my hood over my head and put on my sunglasses. They made traveling through the dimly lit tunnels under the stadium difficult, but they also bolstered my Oblivious Bystander trope.

Maybe I was pushing my luck, hoping to survive another run-in with Ranger Danger using only Oblivious Bystander as a shield, but I had no choice.

The only sounds that could be heard were the faint whispers of the wind and the distant roar of the crowds above, echoing down through the concrete corridors. I could feel the vibration of thousands of feet stomping along to a fight song.

There were dim yellow lights placed along the tunnels, along with some shafts of light from the stands above where bolt holes and seams in the metal had not been covered, allowing the stadium lights to shine through.

Footsteps.

I heard them behind me; they made a distinct soft echo. They were quiet enough that I would not have noticed them if I had not been listening for them. I was being followed. I couldn't turn to look and see who it was, but given the circumstances, I had one guess, and he was wearing a flat-brimmed cowboy hat.

Did I just keep walking deeper into the tunnels, or did I try to find a way to turn around and get back out toward the entrance? Going forward was easier than turning around if I wanted to keep Oblivious Bystander active.

I moved forward at an even pace trying to act like I was supposed to be there. The footsteps followed. I noticed that my Chase Scene status had turned on. That was all the confirmation I needed. Ranger Danger was ten feet behind me.

After a long hallway, I started to doubt that Camden would have gone this far. Unlike me, he wouldn't have had any way of protecting himself. Of course, he may not have had a choice.

Heck, for all I knew he could have been hiding out behind one of the doors I had passed.

As I moved forward, I noticed that the hallway had begun to turn left. I must have been approaching the turn in the horseshoe shape of the stadium.

When I got there, I was going to bend over to tie my shoe in hopes that I could get a peek at the person behind me while doing it. If I angled it right, I could kneel down facing the corner, and Ranger Danger would stand directly behind me. I could then find a way to stand back up, turning back the way I came instead of farther down the tunnel.

Then, I would lead him back out to the entrance of the tunnel and make my escape, while leading him away from anywhere Camden might be.

My Hustle stat increased by one point.

I had almost forgotten.

I had been awarded the Escape Artist trope for completing the Astralist story-line. I got the trope as a reward for coming up with a clever way of escaping my restraints. It gave me a boost to Hustle whenever I had a plausible escape plan. But the trope didn't just work when I was captured—it also worked when I was being pursued.

Not only did that boost my ability to get away, but by awarding me a point for having a good plan, it also confirmed for me that the plan could theoretically work, which was arguably a more useful perk.

Now it was all down to execution.

Maybe that's a poor choice of words.

As I walked up to the corner where the two abandoned tunnels met, I casually bent down and pivoted my body to be pointed directly at the corner. With my sunglasses and hoodie, I thought it was completely believable that I wouldn't be able to see whoever it was behind me.

Have you ever tried to tie your shoes while a knife-wielding murderer walked behind you? I was so nervous that I nearly forgot how.

Ranger Danger stood behind me and paused. I didn't get a chance to look at him, but I was confident that it was the same masked figure I had seen before.

And then he kept walking.

At first, a wave of relief poured over me, but then confusion set in. To my understanding, he shouldn't have been walking away from me. If I was his target, he should continue to pursue me until I eventually saw him and he could strike. That's how it worked with the Astralist. When I talked to Adeline about my plan, she confirmed it. My low Plot Armor should force the bad guy to continue to pursue me.

Why was he walking away then?

Instead of turning left and going back in the direction I came from, I waited for a moment and turned right. I was going to follow him.

It was him all right. He paid me no mind.

I had spent hours mentally preparing myself to use the Oblivious Bystander trope to avoid enemies, but I had not yet considered whether I might be able to use it to follow them. I wasn't prepared. But I needed to see where he was going.

I had a sinking feeling in my stomach.

I waited until he cleared around the next corner before I followed him. At this point, the tunnels stopped being straight and started curving in multiple directions. I imagine that these smaller tunnels were for vendors, as this was the location in the stadium where all of the food kiosks were set up.

I wish I had brought a book or a newspaper, something to hold in front of me to make it look like I might not have seen Ranger Danger. Instead, I was just going to have to keep my distance and hope that he wouldn't turn around to look at me.

The crowd overhead suddenly burst into cheers. Somebody must have gotten a touchdown. Another scream joined in with them. It wasn't coming from the stands above; it was coming from a small tunnel offshoot of the large pathway. Ranger Danger had just entered there.

"Help!" Camden screamed.

Ranger Danger must have been chasing Camden when I finally made it back into the tunnels after fighting through the crowd. He wouldn't need a special trope to find him; a Chase Scene is resolved by a simple comparison of Hustle stats unless a trope contradicts it. If the killer's Hustle is higher, they will catch you. It's that simple.

Camden only had two Hustle.

No wonder my Escape Artist trope activated successfully. I wasn't the real target. His chasing me was just him playing along with my Oblivious Bystander trope.

I took off my glasses and pulled back my hood as I ran to catch up with Ranger Danger. It didn't matter anymore if I was oblivious.

I burst into a room that held an exit door with crates of sports equipment stacked in front of it. Camden was trying to squeeze behind the crates, hoping to keep away from Ranger Danger. No doubt Camden had come in here seeking a way out. There was no way out because his Hustle score was too low; the story would not let him get away.

"Stop!" I screamed.

Ranger Danger did stop. He turned and looked at me. He waited for a moment as if he was taking time to consider whether to attack me or not. He decided that he would.

He lunged. I turned to run, hoping that my boost to Hustle would be enough to get away from him, to lead him away from Camden.

But it wasn't.

I wasn't ten steps away from the door before I felt the knife. He grabbed me from behind, brought the knife around, and drove it into my stomach. The blade pierced right through my hoodie and sank into my flesh.

The pain was unbearable. My status changed. Now I was scathed, and the Incapacitated light began turning on for long stretches of time every time I took a breath. Whenever it did, the pain was so unbearable that I could barely move. I had seen how this status had affected Kimberly, and now I understood.

I was on the ground without even feeling the fall. I expected the finishing blow to come any second. But it didn't.

Ranger Danger was gone.

I was in shock, having trouble figuring out what was going on.

I heard Camden scream.

I resolved to get to him even if I had to crawl. That was all I could do while Incapacitated. I forced myself to move across the floor. You never notice how often you flex your abs until someone stabs you there. Every movement shot pain throughout my body.

Eventually, I made it to the door.

Ranger Danger was standing over Camden.

Camden wasn't unconscious. He wasn't Incapacitated. He was bloody. He was dead.

"Why?" I asked. It just came out.

Why had he only wounded me but killed Camden? I couldn't take my eyes off my childhood friend lying on the ground. I didn't know how many times he'd been stabbed, but it had been more than enough. This wasn't like one of the NPCs, whose deaths were so easy to accept because they weren't real.

My Unconscious status started to flicker on the red wallpaper.

This time I screamed, "Why?"

Tears streamed from my eyes.

Ranger Danger gave no answer. Instead, he pushed on the same crates that Camden had been trying to push; he apparently had much higher Mettle, because he was able to move them just enough to squeeze through to the exit door. He left.

The room started to go dark. I could see Camden's status as being Dead but that wasn't enough. I crawled closer to him even as my own consciousness started to wane. Blood soaked my clothes and the floor underneath me.

I remembered us being kids and pretending to fight zombies. Most of what we did back then revolved around my strange interest in scary movies. His parents never let him watch them. When we played as kids, our characters always lived no matter who we fought against, whether it was vampires or Lord Voldemort.

But against Ranger Danger—against Carousel itself—Camden had died.

Why had I been spared?

I had suspected what was going on from the moment Ranger Danger passed me in the hall instead of attacking me.

Pattern Killer	Before the Finale, the villain will only kill victims chosen according to a pre-established motive.

He couldn't kill me.

We finally had our pattern for the killer's motive.

And I wasn't a part of it.

CHAPTER TWENTY-NINE

ONE LAST GUESS

Single penetrating wound to the abdomen . . .”

“. . . bleeding has stopped . . .”

“. . . prepping for transport . . .”

I came to as I was being placed on a stretcher. The pain in my abdomen echoed all over my body. I was thirsty, and even just moving my muscles hurt from fatigue. A paramedic was holding a wad of blood-soaked fabric against my wound.

My shirt was ripped open. My hoodie was gone. Sunglasses missing.

The first thing I noticed before looking around was my status on the red wallpaper:

Unscathed	Hobbled	Mutilated (Flickering)	Dead	Written Off (Flickering)	Chase Scene	Planning
Unconscious	Infected	Incapacitated (Flickering)	Captured	Off Screen (Lit)	Fight Scene	Exploring

Several lights were turning off and on: Mutilated, Incapacitated, Written Off. Written Off?

Was I done? Had I been taken out of the story? It couldn’t be over.

I looked around. I was outside of the stadium. A crowd of NPCs had gathered around to watch as the paramedics and police tried to sort out the situation. Flashing lights from the ambulance and the police cruisers colored the night red and blue.

There was a murmur among the crowd as they watched. I imagine that many of these were the same NPCs that had seen me publicly accused. Now it was their job to cry and watch as I got loaded into the back of an ambulance.

In the distance, I saw Officer Ricky. He had blood on his hands. He sat on a curb near his parked police golf cart on the edge of the parking lot. His hands were shaking, and his eyes were fixated forward, staring, lost in a dark thought.

Was that blood mine? Had Officer Ricky been the one to find me?

It was strange to see that the NPCs still put in so much effort when they were off-screen. Not only were we off-screen, but I was about to be Written Off. I knew only the basics of what that status condition meant, but the gist was it took you out of the story. Effectively it was like dying except you don't die. You go to jail. You get hospitalized. Your death is left ambiguous. Several things could get you counted as Written Off. Whatever the case, if you were Written Off, you could not complete the story. If your team lost, you lost.

The status was flickering though. Did that mean I had a choice?

I could hear a familiar voice sharper than the blade that had cut me.

Detective Blackwood.

I didn't know where he was; I think he was on the other side of the ambulance talking to some other police officers. But I did hear what he said.

"We must have missed something."

No kidding.

"Spree killer?" one of the police officers asked him.

"I believe that all of these incidents are interconnected," Detective Blackwood said. "There's a pattern here. The victims were acquainted with each other, and there are multiple crime scenes. It seems that the killer is attempting to cover their tracks. I need to have a word with the survivor before the paramedics take him away."

Attempting to cover their tracks? How would killing Camden . . .

Just thinking of his name sent waves of intense dread through my body.

. . . How would killing Camden cover up the death of Ruck? So many clues pointed to different motives for Ruck's death. Which ones also explained Camden?

One of the police officers spoke, bringing me back to reality. "He must have seen something. He was found next to one of the stiffs."

Stiffs? Plural? There was more than one body? Panic set in as I tried to figure out who the other victim could be.

I immediately thought of Anna. I know it makes no sense because Anna's Last One Alive trope would have ensured that she survived much longer, but I had to know for sure.

I tried to sit up.

And failed.

It wasn't going to happen. Every time I flexed my abdominal muscles, my Incapacitated status would flare up and I would go limp.

I was on a stretcher, and the EMTs were messing with some stuff up in the cabin, preparing to bring me with them, but I couldn't let them.

"Wait!" I screamed.

They seemed alarmed that I was awake. "Hold still, kid, we'll get you to the hospital," one of the EMTs said.

"No," I said.

I fought to pull myself off the side of the stretcher. They were designed to prevent that sort of thing, but I was adamant.

"Where's Camden?" I asked. "Show me!"

The paramedics ignored me. The script said that they were going to take me to the hospital. That's what they were going to do.

"Did my friends come to see me? Did they say anything?"

One paramedic looked at the other. "They'll come to see you in the hospital. Just get back in—"

I pulled away from the paramedics as they tried to restrain me. Incapacitation and even mutilation don't impede your Hustle stat. Only the Hobbled status does. When my Incapacitated status flared, I wouldn't be able to move for a few seconds and I might fall over. But technically, I still had Hustle. Theoretically, that is all that should matter.

The EMTs stabilized my wound and secured it with a big wad of gauze and tape. It would have to be enough. I needed to see who else was killed.

Mutilation affected Grit and overall Plot Armor; it reduced my Grit down to zero. My Plot Armor was now a measly three. That was okay; it wasn't like I was using either of those anyway.

I had two points of Hustle going into the storyline. I got a third point because of the successful use of the Escape Artist trope in the tunnels. A lot of good it did me down there. The EMTs only had one point in Hustle like all basic NPCs.

I rushed away from the stretcher trying not to breathe. Breathing made my wound hurt more and triggered my Incapacitated status. I did a quick burst away from the stretcher and caught myself against a cop car nearby. I didn't have long. I just needed to look around and find where they had put Camden's body. It would be the same place as the other victim. I had to know who it was.

I quickly turned around to look at the ambulance and the area around it.

I spotted them. There were two more ambulances parked on the other side of the one I was being loaded into. In front of them were two stretchers, both of which held a deceased body covered in a white sheet, just like Ruck's had been.

I ran to the first. The paramedics gave chase, but I was launching myself forward as quickly as I could and using the vehicles in between us to hold myself up if necessary. Running is hard when you know that your body can give out on you at any second.

But I persisted.

The first body was small, just shorter than me. Someone with a thin, wiry frame, as if they spent more time in the library than at the gym. I couldn't bear the thought of seeing him lying there like that, so I lifted the side of the sheet until I could see his hand. It was Camden, just as I had expected.

His stats on the red wallpaper were still visible. He had gotten a boost in Savvy and Grit from my Cinema Seer ability. I had predicted that Ranger Danger would strike at the football game. Not that it had helped anyone.

But who was under the other sheet?

This one was larger. It was a man, based on the general shape. Not big enough to be Antoine, but bigger than me.

I reached out for the sheet, and just as the paramedics were getting to me, I pulled it off.

It was Evan.

I didn't want it to be him. I was hoping it had been Mark or Nathan. I thought Evan would be Ranger Danger. So many things in the story seemed to point to him; how could he not be the killer?

The paramedics started to pull me back toward the ambulance. I didn't give them a fight.

Evan had been the one to notice that Ruck was missing. Evan had known Ruck was dead just from seeing a hulking figure under a sheet being loaded into an ambulance.

Nelly Birch took business classes; Evan was trying to get his Master of Business Administration. Maybe they had classes together? A stronger connection never appeared.

Evan's girlfriend had broken up with him because of a rumor of cheating. Ruck had started a rumor that Amber had slept with a bunch of guys. I was certain that I would eventually find that those two facts were related, but I never did.

Most suspicious of all, Evan somehow knew that I was at the house when everyone else had left. If he wasn't Ranger Danger that meant that the real killer had told him. We had tried to ask him. Alas, that knowledge died with him.

Evan was a red herring. He was too perfect in every way except the ones that mattered. He had no motive, and all we knew about the killer was that Ranger Danger *did* have a motive.

I thought back to what Detective Blackwood had said.

Someone was trying to cover their tracks.

Why didn't I see it before?

The paramedics got me back to the stretcher, but before they could load me, I struggled forward and caught myself against the ambulance door before pivoting away and running again. I would never be able to keep away from them for long, even with my higher Hustle. My Incapacitated status would kill that advantage eventually.

The Finale had been going on for a while in my absence. It was nearly time for the final battle. I had a hunch about where it was going to be. We were going back to where this whole thing started: Delta Epsilon Delta.

The reason is kind of funny. I'll give you a chance to guess before I tell you.

But how did I get back there?

No matter what I did, I would eventually become Incapacitated, and they would catch me because of that. There wouldn't be cars that I could hold myself up on, like there were in this parking lot. And I was losing energy. Endurance is determined by Grit. I had none.

How could I escape?

My eyes scanned the area, and I saw Officer Ricky again.

Ricky was having a very hard time with what he had seen that day. He was a gentle soul; anyone could see it. I almost felt bad for what I was about to do, but I had a feeling he would forget about it by morning.

Behind Officer Ricky was the police golf cart that he drove. It was designed to be driven around campus. An idea formed in my mind of how I could get away from the paramedics.

My Hustle stat increased by one: Escape Artist had activated again. That was all the confirmation I needed.

I booked it.

I had to make it to the golf cart all on one breath or else my Incapacitated status would take over and I would face-plant onto the concrete.

I raced over to the parking lot and jumped the curb, barely catching myself against the cart as I finally took a breath. Officer Ricky was more shell-shocked than I expected because he barely even registered that I had run past him.

I jumped into the seat of his cart and reached down under the seat to where the ignition switch was. I flicked it on. My foot found the gas, and I was immediately shocked by how much giddy-up this thing had. It was enough that just the shift of my body weight triggered my Incapacitated status, but it didn't matter because I was sitting down, and the golf cart kept going even if I couldn't.

I circled the parking lot. The paramedics had no chance of catching me on this thing, not unless they wanted to hop in their ambulances and follow.

By all means, let them. We were probably going to need them.

I raced back toward the Delta Epsilon Delta house.

As I drove, I saw Detective Blackwood. I swear he had an amused smirk on his face.

There was only one person who had a motive not only to kill Ruck but also to kill Camden and Evan to try and cover it up.

And I knew who it was.

CHAPTER THIRTY

THE IMMORTAL MASK IS BROKEN

I didn't know whether the police would follow me. If they did, they wouldn't get there in time to do anything. This was a movie, after all. I was sure that the cops would probably get there just in time to deal with the dead bodies.

The walk between the stadium and the frat house had been five to seven minutes, if memory serves. The electric golf cart got me there in two minutes max. I rolled it right up to the front porch and parked it next to Ruck's orange farm truck, which was still in the driveway from the night before.

As I arrived, I surveyed the house. The front door was open. At first, I didn't know how I was going to find my friends, but that part turned out to be easy. They were upstairs in the room that led off to the balcony, where the mascot outfit had been hung from.

Kimberly had her back to the window. Antoine and Anna were pressed up against the door, trying to keep it shut. They must not have figured out the whole motive yet.

They didn't see me.

I could hear something upstairs. Wood cracking. Loud footsteps. Muffled talking. They were stuck in that room. Who knows how long they had been fighting? Kimberly was alive. She had the lowest Plot Armor of them. If she was still around, I wasn't too late.

How could I get to them?

It was the final battle, so Ranger Danger could kill any of us now. That should mean he would target me when I got close.

After all, I was down to, what, three Plot Armor? Four maybe?

No sunglasses.

No hood.

To get Oblivious Bystander to work this time, I needed to play a very specific character. I needed to be someone in the throes of such raw delirium that they wouldn't even notice the killer. Luckily, I had a huge advantage in that department courtesy of Ranger Danger himself: I had an ambiguous abdominal wound.

It was bad, but I needed to pretend like it was *very* bad. I needed to pretend that I was on death's doorstep using the last of my life to get to my friends.

I put one hand on the temporary bandage that the medics had placed on my stomach. The other I used to catch myself on every door frame and stair rail that I came across on my way upstairs. I needed the "audience" to see how out of it I was as I laboriously tried to climb the stairs.

The whole time I would be screaming out everything I knew. Getting the truth out there was all that mattered now. Anna had all of the important clues; she must not have put it together. Can't blame her.

"Anna!" I screamed. "Anna, is that you? I figured out who the killer is."

It felt weird to be talking so loudly while trying to be oblivious. I held my wound, and I bent over in pain. I dressed every word with anguish.

"I know what happened!"

I never let my eyes focus on anything, not the ceiling, not the floor. They mostly stayed closed, wincing with my pain. I only opened them to see the stairs in front of me as I clung to the rail.

It was time to give a summation. A hallmark of the mystery genre. Time to put all the pieces into place for the audience.

"It was Nathan!"

They might have already figured that part out just by process of elimination, but seeing as they were still trapped upstairs, I figured that they didn't know why Nathan had done it—why he had killed Ruck, why he had killed Camden and Evan.

Why he was going to kill them.

Specifically, why he was going to kill *Anna*. If my theory was right, Antoine and Kimberly weren't on the hit list. They were only in danger because this was the final battle, and Ranger Danger was finally allowed to kill anyone—even people he didn't have the motive to kill.

"Here's what happened," I said. I climbed the stairs slowly, struggling with each step. Some of the struggle was my real Incapacitated status flaring up constantly, but I held firm against the railing. I was getting all of my Moxie's worth with this one.

"Yesterday afternoon Nathan was driving Ruck's truck. He often drove it around. In fact, he did it so often that Mark called him Ruck's chauffeur." I took a moment to struggle with my ascent up the stairs.

"What kind of description of a friendship is that? A chauffeur? But Ruck needed Nathan to drive him. Ruck had a suspended driver's license and drunk driving arrests. Ruck wasn't allowed to drive himself around. Remember how surprised Evan had been to see Ruck driving drunk? He didn't do that every day. Not anymore, at least."

I took a moment to breathe. I held myself up against the railing.

"Detective Blackwood said that none of Ruck's charges were recent. I think that was because Nathan was driving him. The only reason Ruck drove to the party was that Nathan was too drunk to drive that night.

"Nathan killed Nelly Birch while driving Ruck's truck. Maybe he was drunk. Maybe getting drunk was just an excuse to get Ruck to drive. I don't know if Ruck was even in the car.

"Nathan had a problem. If he was ever connected to the crime, his chances of getting into medical school were out the window. He had to act fast. He got Ruck to drive him to the party.

"Nathan knew that Ruck could tie him to the hit-and-run. Either Ruck witnessed it, or he was at least aware that Nathan had been driving his truck and would tell the police that whenever they questioned him. Nathan did what he thought he had to for his future. He grabbed the Ranger Danger costume and killed Ruck at the first opportunity.

"I don't know how real his drunkenness was at the party; he may have just been pretending, but we can never know for sure. At some point, he remembered something Ruck had said when they arrived, something I wasn't around to hear.

"But you were around to hear it, Anna. You and Camden." My voice cracked when I said Camden's name. That wasn't acting. "You, Camden, Evan, and Mark. You were all around Ruck's truck when they showed up. It was the only time that all the victims were in the same place while I wasn't with them.

"Nathan had to cover his tracks. Ruck had said something to you all that would have put Nathan in the driver's seat at the time of the hit-and-run.

"Anna, you said it earlier. When we were in town square. You said Nathan was too drunk to drive *anymore*. You didn't say he was too drunk to drive at all. The difference is crucial. That's what Ruck told you, isn't it? That Nathan had been driving earlier that day. That Ruck took over because Nathan couldn't anymore. The four of you could lead the police to Nathan. It may not be enough to prove that Nathan had killed Nelly, but it would be a cloud over him forever.

"That's why he killed Camden and Evan. He may have even killed Mark already. That's why he's here tonight to kill you. Because you can tie him to the hit-and-run, even if you don't know it. That's why he didn't kill me: because I wasn't around for that conversation, he had no motive to kill me.

"That's what this has all been about: Nathan is trying to save his future. Don't you remember what he said outside when they were taking Ruck's body away? He said, 'If I didn't drink, this wouldn't have happened.' He confessed right to our faces!"

I stood at the landing at the top of the stairs. That was it—that was every-thing I knew. If I was right about everything, then that meant Ranger Danger was vulnerable now. If I was wrong, we were screwed.

Either way, I had drained everything going up the stairs. I staggered back to the railing over the landing to support myself. I kept my eyes down the same as ever. I heard the footsteps again. They didn't echo as they had under the tunnel. Instead, they creaked on the floorboards of the house.

It was Ranger Danger.

I didn't know if I could continue to pretend that I didn't see him. I had no sunglasses, no cover. Hopefully, it wouldn't matter. Anna and the others had surely heard me. My part was done.

With his shoes in my view, I was certain that Oblivious Bystander was bro-ken. How could I claim not to have seen him now?

I lifted my head.

His hollow eyes stared back at me.

What happened now? Did he kill me? Did he monologue?

For a moment there was silence.

And then he spoke.

"I should have killed you when I had the chance," Nathan said. I could hear his anger and frustration in every word.

He reached up to grab the bandana that surrounded the rubber mask and pulled the entire thing off, hat and all.

The Immortal Mask was broken.

Now the real fight began.

CHAPTER THIRTY-ONE

CHEKHOV'S BALCONY

The Ranger Danger outfit wasn't nearly as intimidating without the mask and hat.

But now I could see that crazed look in Nathan's eyes as he edged toward me with his knife. He was being cautious, as if I could hurt him. Did he not remember what happened in the tunnels?

As he prepared himself to slice, I thought that would be the end for me. I had played my part already. I would be in a morgue somewhere soon, surely.

But then I spotted the football player.

Antoine was still wearing much of the football uniform he had been given for the game. He had ditched the shoulder pads, but he still wore the leg pads and the cleats, and in his hand was a football helmet.

He had managed to sneak out of the room they had been holed up in. He was trying to walk on the hallway runner so that his cleats wouldn't make a noise against the hardwood.

I needed to distract Nathan.

My main advantage in that pursuit was that he wanted to kill me. From that perspective, distracting him should have been easy. The disadvantage was that he could kill me very quickly. I needed to draw it out to give Antoine time to get into a better position.

"You told Evan that I was at the house when you killed Ruck," I said. By now it was obvious, but I needed to get a reaction out of him. Hopefully, I could get him to monologue, to talk about his big killing plan.

"Uh-huh," he said. He continued to creep closer.

So much for that. He wasn't going to talk to me. Up until that point we hadn't had any dialogue with each other that I remembered. There was nothing to discuss. No unsettled issues between us.

"The police are on their way right now," I said.

I saw a glint of fear in his eyes. The walls were closing in.

"Then I better be quick."

So that was the wrong thing to say. Now he was coming faster.

He lunged at me, but Antoine was close enough now that just as Nathan managed to get his hands on me, Antoine hammered him in the back of the head with his helmet.

That must have done a lot of damage.

Antoine not only had a high Mettle to begin with, but he had boosted it using his Gym Rat ability earlier in the storyline. Add on to that another buff he got from using a sports implement as a weapon, and that attack was enough to make Nathan nearly crumple to the ground. He caught himself and backed away from both of us, readying his knife to deal with the new threat.

Nathan was bleeding now. A cut had opened up on the top of his head. I wondered if enemies could have status ailments the same way we could; if so, it shouldn't take too many hits like that to make Nathan Incapacitated.

Shortly after the scuffle, Anna emerged from the room they had been in, holding a small nightstand as a weapon. Now that they were working together, Anna's Who's with Me? trope boosted Antoine's Mettle even further. He had a total of seven. I don't know which tropes were responsible for which buffs, but at our level, seven Mettle was huge.

I could only guess what Nathan's stat distribution was. He probably had significant points in Grit, Hustle, and Mettle, but I know he had to have at least some Savvy and Moxie in order to pull off his deception. With a total Plot Armor of fifteen, there was no way that his Grit was higher than Antoine's Mettle.

The problem was just because Antoine could take him out didn't mean Nathan couldn't kill him right back. It was all a matter of who got enough hits in against the other.

Antoine had a lot of Hustle, but using the football helmet as a weapon wasn't exactly something you could do swiftly. He had to put a lot of power into it and swing it in a high arc.

Nathan's knife, however, was quick, and every time Antoine would draw near, Nathan would have his blade out slicing at the air.

They were at an impasse.

I had an opportunity to get out of there. I had no place in the middle of a fight like that. I crawled on my hands and knees past the brawling trio toward the back of the house. On my way, I saw the door that they had barricaded to keep Ranger Danger out.

I assumed that Kimberly was somewhere in there, hiding off-screen. In the room, I saw a mannequin laid out on the ground. That must have been dressed in the Ranger Danger costume when it was hanging from the front balcony.

Luckily, Kimberly had already done her job. Thanks to her, I had a pretty good idea of where this fight needed to go: the back of the house.

I heard Nathan start to monologue. It almost hurt my feelings how quickly he went into it with the right audience.

"Don't you understand, Anna?" he pleaded.

"How could I understand killing people? Killing your—our—friends?" Anna was furious at him. She had lost a real friend in this storyline.

Nathan let out a frustrated cry. "I'm going to be a surgeon. I can't have everything I've worked on for my entire life wasted because of one mistake. I am going to save lives. I'm going to save one life for the girl. Then I'll save a life for . . . ," he choked up for a moment, "Ruck. Then one for Mark, one for Evan, one for Camden . . ."

I stood up in the hallway so that I could move faster. I used the wall to hold myself up, and every door frame I came across was a fingerhold. To the audience, it must have looked like I was panicking and trying to get away. I was actually trying to get somewhere specific.

I got to the back of the hallway where two glass doors opened up onto the back balcony. As I opened them, I put all the effort I could into turning the handle loudly and opening the doors with a bang as I fell against them.

". . . and then when I've done that, I'm going to save a few more for all of you."

With that, Nathan turned away from Anna and Antoine and rushed down the hallway at me. Now that he was done monologuing, I was the target again. And an easy target at that, as I could barely hold myself up against the back doors.

He got to me quickly. He grabbed me, and he moved his knife into my ribs. The pain was even worse than the one in my stomach as his knife scraped along my ribs. He pulled out the blade. He repositioned it to plunge it into my heart. This time he was going for the kill.

Just as he was about to plunge his knife into me, Antoine caught up to him and tackled him out through the open doors onto the back balcony.

The same exact back balcony that Kimberly and Antoine had found yesterday at the party.

Do you remember that hunch that I had but didn't tell you about yet? This was it. When Kimberly and Antoine had found it, an obviously scripted response occurred. Everyone told them that the back balcony was rotten and not to go out there. It was so obvious that even my friends had picked up on it.

The Party phase is the exploration phase and, thanks to her new Get a Room! trope, Kimberly had an increased chance of finding useful plot elements when exploring the setting with a romantic interest. Antoine was happy to fill that role, I'm sure.

There was only one thing that having NPCs point out a rotten back balcony could mean in a movie like this: it meant that somebody was going to fall through it. That's how I knew that the Finale would happen at Delta Epsilon Delta.

There was only one reason Kimberly would have been able to find something like this. When you're watching a movie and you see a character put a gun into their waistband, you can expect that that gun's going to go off by the end of the movie.

The same idea applies to unsafe balconies.

This decrepit balcony was a weapon in our hands as much as any gun would be. We just had to find a way to use it.

As soon as Antoine tackled him onto the balcony, the entire thing gave way and fell off the back of the house. There was a crunch of wood and dust that flew into the air as Antoine, Nathan, and about ten thousand termites fell to the ground below.

I had no way of knowing how much damage that fall would do to Nathan. I knew that in a movie like this, that fall would be a great ending blow. I leaned over so that I could see down to where they had fallen. Antoine lay sprawled out, reeling in pain. Nathan lay next to him completely still.

Not that I trusted that. We already knew that he had a lot of Moxie. He could be faking.

Anna had taken the stairs and had to run around the side of the house. She quickly grabbed Antoine and helped him to his feet. He was clearly dazed, and I could see that his Incapacitated status was going on occasionally, but otherwise, he just had the wind knocked out of him.

Then she approached Nathan and kicked him to turn him over.

His knife was sticking out of his sternum. Even he didn't have enough Moxie to fake that.

He was breathing hard, but I saw a rage within him as he screamed.

"I was going to make up for it!"

He struggled, attempting to get to his feet. When he didn't manage to do that, he got on his knees and crawled toward Anna. She backed away. Still, he persisted.

I could tell he wanted to say something, but now he was the one that was bleeding out. He was losing the energy to hold himself up. He made one last attempt to lunge at Anna, but she struck him with the nightstand, sending him falling sideways into the backyard pool.

The needle on the Plot Cycle was nearly to The End as the pool grew murky with blood.

In the distance, police sirens could be heard.

They came just in time to deal with the body.

* * *

When the needle struck The End, I felt myself taking an involuntary deep breath. It didn't hurt this time. I reached toward my abdomen. No wound. No ripped shirt. No blood.

I even had my hoodie and sunglasses back.

Quickly, the four of us left Delta Epsilon Delta. We ran down the road toward the stadium. I didn't know if we had to pick up Camden from the hospital or if he'd be right where I left him.

Even though the storyline had ended I could tell that things were still not back to normal. Some police cruisers were still in the parking lot of the stadium along with one ambulance. But the people were gone.

As we approached, we saw Camden walking slowly toward us. His eyes were wide in shock.

We ran to him and piled onto him in a hug.

At that moment all I wanted to do was apologize for not being able to save him. I also wanted to ask him what it was like. Was he aware that he was dead? Was he watching us?

I didn't do any of those things. I was just glad to have him back.

The group hug might have lasted longer, but we were interrupted.

"Step right up," Silas the Showman said. "You've won a ticket!"

The fortune-telling machine was in the middle of the street. Its lights were drowned out by those of the ambulance and police cars, but it was still hard to miss the little animatronic man and his silver flashlight clicking off and on.

You know the drill. Here's what we got:

My friends got ten stars, but I got eleven. I wasn't sure if it was worth getting stabbed.

Each of us received two stat tickets. Our Plot Armor wasn't going to grow this fast forever. Eventually, it would level off and then the grind would begin. For now, we were flush with stat points.

I put one into Moxie and one into Savvy to make sure that my Trope Master ability stayed up to snuff. So far, my Oblivious Bystander scouting strategy was working. At least there were promising signs. It wasn't perfect yet—I wasn't perfect at it yet—but I wasn't going to give up on it if it helped me get to the end of the story to help my friends.

Here are our stat changes:

Player Stats					
	Riley	Antoine	Anna	Kimberly	Camden
Archetype	Film Buff	Athlete	Final Girl	Eye Candy	Scholar
Plot Armor	15	16	18	14	15
Mettle	1	4	4	1	2

Moxie	4 + 1	1 + 1	3 + 1	4 + 1	2
Hustle	2	4 + 1	2 + 1	3	2
Savvy	5 + 1	1	2	1	6
Grit	1	4	5	3 + 1	1 + 2

Each of us was just trying to make up for what we felt we lacked. Antoine wanted more Moxie so that he could scale his Gym Rat ability. Camden, as could be expected, wanted more Grit, so he put both points into it. And so on and so forth.

Antoine got the Ranger Danger card. Well deserved. I mean, really it was a team effort. Kimberly found the rotten balcony. I lured Nathan into position. Anna pushed him into the pool, where he sank to his ambiguous demise. But it was Antoine that took the fall, activating the rotten balcony plot device, so he got the win.

Ranger Danger
???
Someone is out to kill Ruck Johnson. Donning a grim uniform stolen from a rival school, they become a killer who is unstoppable until they are unmasked. Armed with a knife and deception, Ranger Danger sets out to kill all those on their list.

Each of us also received a trope except for Kimberly. I suppose it was fair; she was already ahead.

Anna got a blue ticket:

A Kind Face
Type: Insight
Archetype: Final Girl
Aspect: Girl Next Door
Stat Used: Moxie
Perhaps the most significant advantage that a Final Girl has is that everyone seems to trust them. As they seek information in order to survive, even strangers will go the extra mile to help them out.
When this ticket is equipped, NPCs will be more likely to share important plot information with the player during the Party phase.

Antoine got a blue ticket:

The Playbook
Type: Insight
Archetype: Athlete
Aspect: Sport
Stat Used: Grit

Unspoken communication is an important skill set for any survivor. Skills and teamwork learned on the field can apply in a fight.
When this ticket is equipped, the player will be able to perceive whenever the time to perform their role in a pre-planned strategy has come, even without communication from a teammate.

Camden got a purple ticket:

Hide and Seek
Type: Rule
Archetype: Any
Aspect: Any
Stat Used: Savvy

Sometimes you can't run, but you can hide. In a movie, the right hiding spot can mean the difference between life and death.
Normally, when being chased, the player's Hustle will be compared to the pursuer's Hustle to determine whether the player is caught. When this ticket is equipped, a player who plans to hide during a chase scene will be able to pit their Savvy against the opponent's Savvy instead, even before the player has chosen a hiding spot.
Beware, however: this effect will not last.

I received a blue ticket:

Casting Director
Type: Insight
Archetype: Film Buff
Aspect: Filmmaker
Stat Used: Savvy

The Film Buff can recognize the role that a character will play in a movie just from watching the trailer.
During the Party phase, the player will perceive information about their team's roles in the storyline.

We had always talked about coming up with a strategy that would keep us from getting killed, even as the veterans told us that it was impossible. They told us death was part of the game; avoiding it would be like beating Monopoly without passing "Go."

We still decided that we would be different, that we would find a way. But Camden had been killed right in front of me. As happy as I was that he was still up and walking around, the memory of his death was still fresh. He wasn't talking to anyone. I didn't know the words to comfort him.

When we went back to our room, I tried to ask him how he was, but the words caught in my throat. Because how stupid of a question is that? So instead I just said, "Goodnight, see you in the morning."

He didn't say anything back.

My injuries had healed before the adrenaline even wore off. I could still remember being stabbed, and I could remember the pain of trying to struggle through it. The instant it was healed, much of the trauma that I associated with it was gone.

There was no such convenience for Camden; he had the hollow, gaunt look on his face that I recognized from when Bobby and Janet had gotten killed.

The only person who seemed to have taken it well was Dina.

The next night, at dinner, Adeline prepared a plate for Janet and brought it to her room. As I understood it, the strategy was to try to talk Janet into going on a storyline, an easy one.

A few moments later, we heard screaming.

Janet slammed the door and yelled something to the effect of, "I am never going anywhere with you people! Bobby! Bobby!" she screamed.

The veterans looked at each other; they were at their wits' end.

CHAPTER THIRTY-TWO

TO THE ATTENTION OF JANET GILL

The day the package arrived started like any other day at Camp Dyer.

It was the day after we had finished the Delta Epsilon Delta storyline. I awoke to someone tapping on the large glass window that dominated a whole wall in my room. It was the NPC campers again. No surprise there. I lifted my head and glared at them, and they giggled and ran away. Most of the players had gotten used to these kids, but I found it very difficult.

Camden had remained quiet ever since dying in the last storyline. He insisted that he was fine, and he just needed some time.

"Everyone takes death differently," Valerie had warned us. "Just give him his space."

So, I did. I left him to sleep on his bunk as I went and got ready for the day.

Mornings at Dyer Lodge could be hectic if you were inside. Over fifty people were clamoring to get breakfast, and even though the accommodations of the lodge were very good, the kitchen was not large enough for everyone to move about.

Many players had taken to the tradition of eating breakfast outside a few times a month. The weather was always nice, after all. Camp Dyer had several campsites close to the lodge with large grills that could be used by the players. Grace, of course, was in charge of the cookout.

What she cooked varied wildly. Food was never hard to find at Camp Dyer. The veteran players would make food runs into town. There was a large wholesale store somewhere in Carousel where players could stock up on anything that they needed with only a moderate risk of triggering a storyline.

Today's brunch was fish. When she was cooking, I could see many of the same qualities that probably made her a good teammate in a storyline: very well organized, very well spoken, and incredibly bossy—I mean a good leader.

She had to be bossy. She was the leader of the group that was called The Bowlers because they had a habit of going to Carousel's bowling alley and clearing it of storylines so that they could spend the day throwing back beers and playing.

They were one of several teams that didn't have a Final Girl. The Bowlers consisted of three—yes, three—Bruiser archetypes. A Bruiser is usually a heavy-set character with high Mettle and Grit but little Hustle or Savvy.

I'll repeat, Grace's team had three of them.

In a movie, a Bruiser is usually going to be a biker or prisoner or maybe the husky kid at high school who gets picked on. Additionally, they had an Outsider named Jesse. Jesse was a long-haired, hippie type of guy. I got the impression that Jesse and Grace used to date, but now they were strictly platonic.

It's kind of a funny story.

One of the Bruisers, Reggie, was Grace's brother. A few years after Grace and Jesse got lured to Carousel, Reggie started getting letters in the mail that he believed were from Grace. Those letters are what eventually drew him and his Bruiser buddies here.

How did Carousel trick him? It had "Grace" promise to make him some paprikash.

It's funnier when Grace tells the story.

To make myself useful, I decided to go help Lee with the fish. Lake Dyer was surprisingly bountiful for existing in a nightmarish reality. You could angle fish from it all day long.

Lee, a Wallflower, would spend hours every day out on the dock near the lodge doing nothing but fishing. Lee did not have a team that he belonged to. He used to though. I don't know what happened to them.

He was an old greybeard. Mid-sixties. He was the oldest player here, though he only had a Plot Armor of thirty-three, and he was far from the most experienced, having only arrived ten years ago.

"Now the trick to fishing," Lee would say, "is that you got to reel up what you catch right to the water's surface, but don't pull it out until you make sure it's a fish."

The first time we spoke to him, Anna was with me. "What else could it be?" she had asked.

"Could be lots of things," Lee said. "A cursed ring, a magical conch, anything. You just got to cut the line if it's not a fish. Because if you reel it in, you'll wish you hadn't."

That morning, he had brought in a large haul. I arrived just in time to help him bring it back to Grace.

Antoine, his brother Chris, and a whole host of other players had started playing catch with a frisbee. As they played, Antoine regaled them with tales of his football heroics the night before.

"I was running back," he said. "I hadn't played football since high school, so I thought I was about to get creamed by these guys, but then I realized these are all NPCs with one Mettle. So as soon as I get the ball, I run right through them like they're not even there. As soon as I touch them, they fly back and land on their asses. Felt like I was Superman."

Chris and the others were laughing at his story as he talked about scoring touchdowns and trying to run up the scoreboard before the scene ended.

"The announcer was losing his shit," Antoine said. "It was like he'd never seen anything like it."

I sat at a table where I could keep an eye on everything that was going on. I laughed along with Antoine as I tried to get to know the other players.

Anna was talking to Grace and the Femme Fatale, Roxy. A Femme Fatale was an advanced archetype that often played a more morally gray role than a straightforward protagonist. Her base archetype was Eye Candy. Her teammate Lara was a Psychic archetype, one of the archetypes that I was most eager to learn about but hadn't gotten the chance to.

They were talking about our performance in the Delta Epsilon Delta storyline.

"So, who killed Ruck?" Grace asked.

I hadn't considered until that moment that there might be more than one version of the mystery. That explained why the Ranger Danger ticket hadn't included Nathan's name.

"Nathan," Anna had answered. "We figured it out when he was the only one left alive. I knew why he had killed Ruck, but I couldn't figure out why he was killing everyone else. Luckily, Riley figured it out."

"Nathan? Isn't that Ruck's friend?" Roxy said. "Haven't had him before."

They also apparently hadn't been arrested when they'd played. Most of them never even made it to the football game.

"I've done it three times," Grace said. "Twice it was Evan. Once it was one of the football players."

As they were talking, I noticed that a commotion had broken out near the lodge. Something had sent all of the players away. They weren't just walking, they were running.

"Oh my God," Lara was exclaiming over and over again. She wasn't looking over in the direction of the lodge but was instead staring off into the distance. I recognized this look; she was looking at the red wallpaper. One of her Psychic tropes must have been activating.

I tried to get a closer look at what was causing the commotion. As I moved toward the lodge, I got warnings from various players that I passed. They told me to get back. Whatever they had seen must have put them on edge.

I wasn't going to get too close.

As I got closer, what I saw was a man holding a large cardboard box. The box was rectangular. It was sealed shut sloppily with more tape than would be necessary. At first, it wasn't the box that drew my attention.

The man was clearly in disarray. He was an NPC. He had nothing out of the ordinary in terms of Plot Armor, nor did I see that he had any enemy tropes. His name was Donald.

His hair was uncombed, and the shirt he wore didn't fit. As he stood there, he would occasionally try to pull down the sleeves to cover up what appeared to be large circular bite marks on his arms. They might have been from a dog, I wasn't sure. Some wounds were fresh. Others were scabbed over. He also appeared to have one on his left ankle. Moreover, he was missing a finger on his left hand, which had been hastily bandaged.

"I have a delivery for Janet Gill," he said. He spoke loudly; his voice cracked as if he were afraid of something. His entire manner was devoid of sanity.

He appeared to be desperate in his search for Janet.

That was incredibly strange to me.

Janet had exemplified her archetype better than any person I had met. She had refused to leave the lodge at all. While my friends and I had been out playing through storylines at the demand of the veteran players, no one had been able to successfully pry her out of her room.

The idea that an NPC would be looking for Janet was very strange. She had not interacted with anyone. Up until this point the only time I had seen NPCs acknowledge players in any meaningful way had been whenever you were in a storyline with them. Whenever you had a scripted role to play, the NPCs would speak to you as if you were an old friend or an employee, or whatever relationship the script said you had.

Even at Camp Dyer the NPCs didn't talk to us in any substantive way; they mostly just scurried about. There was this implication that we were counselors at the camp, but none of the NPCs had had any scripted interactions with us in that regard because we were not in a storyline with them.

This man, though, was certain that he needed to speak to Janet Gill.

"Please, I have to give this to her. Have you seen her?"

The needle on the Plot Cycle was at Omen.

The veteran players were very attuned to ignoring NPCs who were acting strange, so up until that moment no one had actually spoken to this guy, nor had they gotten close enough to come anywhere near the package.

Donald stood on the back deck trying to get into the lodge, but someone had had the foresight to lock the door. He knocked furiously at the back door almost to the point that I was afraid that he would try to break it down, but he never did.

So far, Omens had not gone out of their way to make it out to Camp Dyer. Not in this way at least. Camp Dyer had its own Omens related to the abandoned cabin and, of course, whatever it was Lee was dredging up from the lake along with our breakfast.

However, NPCs going out of their way to try and trick you into a storyline? It had not happened here yet. That's why this location was chosen by the veteran players.

"Please, you don't understand," Donald implored those few players who dared stay within twenty yards of him.

No one took the bait.

Behind me, I could hear some of the more experienced players start to form a plan.

"We need Arthur and Adeline," Grace said. "Are they at the diner?"

Those around her nodded in agreement.

"Jesse," she said, looking at her Outsider teammate. "Go get them. Be quick."

Jesse nodded his head and started running down a path toward the main road, being sure to give the lodge and the deranged NPC a wide berth.

"What's happening?" Antoine asked. No one answered him, but he quickly surveyed the situation and realized what was going on. "Kimberly's in there!"

"Don't worry," Chris said. "He's not getting in. He's not going to break down the door."

I turned back to the NPC. He was staring down at the box in his hands. It almost looked like he was listening to it.

"I'm trying," he said desperately.

He looked around hoping some player would be willing to take the box, but none offered. Eventually, he decided to just leave it. He propped the box up against the back door and backed away, unsure of whether this was acceptable.

He tugged at his sleeves, still trying to hide the bites on his arms.

He looked like he was about to cry.

"I'm sorry," he said as he turned tail and started to run away from the lodge, leaving the box for us to take care of.

With the NPC gone, I felt a little braver about getting close. Some of the other players must have felt the same way because we started to close in to look more closely at the parcel.

As we got closer there was a succession of gasps as each of us was able to see something on the red wallpaper.

"Grotesque."

Plot Armor: 43.

But I was able to see more because of my Trope Master ability. I could only see two of its tropes, but I could tell that there were more. Whatever this thing was it must have had at least enough Savvy to counter my six and limit Trope Master.

GROTESQUE	
PLOT ARMOR: 43	
TROPES	
PROGENITOR	This creature has the ability to create duplicate offspring.
JEKYLL AND HYDE	This villain has multiple forms. Stone: Grit = 0, Living: Grit = 20.

As I got close, I could see that there was something written on the box: "To the Attention of Janet Gill."

CHAPTER THIRTY-THREE

THE GROTESQUE LOTTERY

We waited for the longest time.

I felt like I was twelve years old again and hiding out in the cellar with my grandparents as the storm of the century raged above. I had felt like I was just waiting to find out whether that was how I would die.

When I asked my grandpa whether we were going to be okay, he answered, "We will or we won't."

That was that.

My grandmother was much better in a crisis and comforted me and said that no matter what happened, she would be there with me.

It wasn't that my grandfather was cold. No, he just had a different outlook. Even when cancer put him on his deathbed, he still had this slight grin on his face like he was amused that death would finally show its face to him after all these years. When speaking of his potential demise, he would say again, "I will, or I won't."

Of course, he would have to have a pretty strange outlook on life to get his young grandson hooked on horror movies.

I must have gotten a lot of my personality from him because even as the players around me scrambled, all I could wonder was, is this how I die? I'm not saying that I'm particularly brave or unafraid of death, but I am more curious than I am scared.

Anna, on the other hand, was far more interested in being prepared. She immediately started asking around about whether things like this had happened before and what to do about them. Should we run? *Can* we run?

Grace, under pressure, continued to cook. I could see that she was frazzled, which wasn't normal for her.

"This hasn't happened in years," she told Anna. She took a cleaver and chopped the heads off of the fish that Lee had caught. "And never like this."

I wasn't sure what she meant by "like this."

Her hands were shaking. She really shouldn't have been holding that cleaver, but I wasn't going to say that to her.

"Why is no one leaving?" Anna asked, hoping one of the veteran players would let her in on whatever secret it was that they knew.

Roxy, who had immediately found the front entrance to the lodge and gone to her room to change into attire more appropriate for a storyline, had mercy on Anna and explained it to us.

"Everyone who has seen that Omen can be chosen. It doesn't matter which team actually picks it up. It doesn't matter if everyone else runs to the other side of Carousel. All we know for sure is that Janet will be on the team. What's going to happen is there's going to be a short debate and then Arthur is going to pick up the Omen. Then the lucky winners will march off to complete the storyline."

"Can't we just . . . not touch it?" Anna asked.

Roxy smirked. "This one? Maybe. The next one? Probably not."

I noticed that she had changed her tropes around. She was no longer a Femme Fatale; she had downgraded back to Eye Candy.

When I asked her why that was, she explained that it was bad practice to have multiple advanced archetypes on a single team. Advanced archetypes tend to take over storylines and much of the plot will become focused on them. If you have more than one, it can be pretty convoluted and difficult to discern how to proceed.

"When whatever a 'Grotesque' is starts killing us, I want it to be Arthur's responsibility, not mine," she said.

She then started helping Grace shuck corn.

Todd, who had the foresight to lock both doors whenever he saw a strange NPC coming, had emerged from the lodge ready for a fight. While the Comedian archetype was not a combat class, Todd had something called a background trope, named Recently Home from the War.

A background trope allowed you to modify your character's past. In doing so, it made a variety of tropes—centered around a theme—equippable to players that normally wouldn't be able to use them. It was the closest thing to multiclassing that you could do in Carousel. Most of the veteran players had their favorites.

His Recently Home from the War trope gave him access to four or five other tropes, mostly related to combat and firearms. His small collection of weapons consisted of two sidearms and a large knife.

After thirty minutes or so, Arthur and Adeline finally arrived.

They had run the entire way.

I barely had time to tell them about the Grotesque's tropes before they locked themselves away to plan a response. As Roxy had predicted, they spent ten to fifteen minutes debating what they were going to do with some of the higher-level players. When they emerged, they decided that Arthur would activate the Omen.

Adeline gathered everyone up outside. "Go in through the front door and get whatever tropes you think will help you assist Arthur's Monster Hunter. Players who have sacrificial builds, please prepare them."

Even she seemed concerned over this Omen. I thought that was strange because her Plot Armor should have put her well out of range to worry about something like this. Both she and Arthur had twenty Plot Armor on this creature.

"We thought that we would have another month at least before something like this happened," she said. "Some players have a difficult time adjusting to Carousel. Others take to it very intuitively. We cannot blame Janet. We're just going to have to do our best to react and overcome this."

Even as every player who had been in the vicinity of the Omen was prepping for the apocalypse, no one had managed to get Janet out of her room yet. No one had seen her husband because he was out doing a storyline with Travis.

My friends and I had found our own place amidst the chaos. Unlike everyone else, we really didn't have much preparation to do. We didn't have enough tropes yet that we had to create builds. We just had to use what we had.

Carousel "didn't like it" when high-level players lent tropes to low-level play-ers. I didn't know what that meant exactly, but I could use my imagination.

My friends and I tried to comfort each other.

"It's not going to be you," Antoine said to Kimberly. He held her in his arms, showing a rare moment of public affection. "That thing is way too high a level. It's going to pick somebody else."

He didn't know that. After all, Carousel had just sent a level forty-three Omen after Janet, who only had nine Plot Armor. I wasn't going to correct him.

Camden was doing his best to stay calm. This couldn't have been a good thing to wake up to after what he had just gone through.

"You know Arthur's going to activate the Omen, and he's a Monster Hunter. That's just an advanced Scholar archetype, and they probably don't need two Scholars," I said to him. It made sense to me, but I didn't know if that would be a factor at all.

"Thanks," he said softly. I could tell that he was afraid. Anna gave him a hug.

Anna was far more concerned with making sure that each of us was okay. She was made for situations like this, in a way.

I wanted to ask Kimberly how much Moxie the thing in the box had. I knew I shouldn't, not with how she was handling things.

It would have been useful information to have. I knew it didn't have a ton of Savvy because my Trope Master ability worked on it. If I could get an idea of its other stats, I might feel like it was less of a threat. Being able to create duplicate offspring was such a scary prospect. Even Arthur couldn't withstand getting surrounded by a lot of creatures of this level.

As I considered this, I realized that that might be the reason that even the high-level players were so concerned. Even though Adeline and Arthur were in their low sixties, that didn't mean they had enough Grit to protect them from whatever a Grotesque was. If this creature had a particularly high Mettle, enough of them could probably kill everyone at camp.

An hour after the package had arrived, Lara, the Psychic archetype, publicly declared that we needed to take it before nightfall.

She had several tropes that could give her information about storylines that she wasn't a part of and Omens that had not yet been activated. Tropes with names like Soothsayer and Harbinger. I wasn't sure which one she used to make this prediction.

As if they had been waiting for such a sign, Adeline and Arthur got everyone to arrange themselves by Plot Armor. They acted as if proximity to the Omen might play a role in choosing the team, so they wanted the strongest players closest. I couldn't say if that was something they knew to be fact or if it was just a theory.

The air was tense as Arthur, who had packed a large duffel with all of his monster hunting gear, got near the parcel.

There was nothing left but the luck of the draw.

Just looking at the package I could see that the needle on the Plot Cycle was at Omen. For some of us, maybe even all of us, it was about to change.

He reached down and grabbed the package. He took a knife from his belt and opened it up slowly as the surrounding players watched, many with their hands on their holsters.

From within the package, Arthur retrieved a stone statue about the size of a border collie. The statue was hideous. It had the body of a dog, the tail of a lion, the face of a man screaming in agony, and teeth like something out of Hell. Two curved horns grew from its head.

I finally figured out what a Grotesque was. It was a gargoyle, and not the Saturday morning cartoon version.

He started looking around at the crowd of players. "Who do we got?"

Three hands raised into the air. There was Reggie, a Bruiser with Plot Armor thirty-eight. Valerie, a Final Girl with Plot Armor fifty-eight. And Roxy, the Eye Candy, who smiled like she was expecting it. Plot Armor of forty.

Arthur—Monster Hunter, Plot Armor sixty-four—was also part of the party.

Of course, Janet the Hysteric, Plot Armor nine, would be as well.

"Anyone else?" Arthur asked.

There was someone else . . .

Me.

I raised my hand.

"Oh no," Anna said. She hugged me.

I was numb. I couldn't even hug her back.

Arthur cursed.

"Carousel can't resist a Film Buff," Roxy said with a laugh.

"You're going to be okay," Anna said. It was more of a question than a statement.

"I will, or I won't," I said under my breath.

When the veterans built their teams—when they had a choice—they always created charts of the players with the stats and tropes they were bringing into a storyline. With enough scouting and enough planning they always felt that they had the power to choose their fate.

For the Grotesque storyline, our team, stats, and tropes were not ideal.

To start with, there was me:

I had fifteen Plot Armor, but when the story started that would be divided by two and rounded down. My Mettle and Grit were both one, so I was pretty much useless in a fight. My Hustle wasn't much better, so I wasn't going to be able to run away without any help. Even my highest stats, Moxie and Savvy, were way underpowered for this storyline, but they were the best I had going for me at five and six points respectively.

Riley	
Film Buff	
Plot Armor:	15
Mettle:	1
Moxie:	5
Hustle:	2
Savvy:	6
Grit:	1

My tropes were not coordinated yet because I didn't have enough to actually create a loadout. I was just going to bring in all the tropes I had. Trope Master let me see enemy tropes—a useful skill that I had all but exhausted already. Cinema Seer would help me boost my allies' Grit and Savvy by predicting important story elements. Escape Artist would help me escape captivity or get away in a chase by boosting my Hustle if I could come up with a plausible escape plan. My newest trope, Casting Director, would help me know the role that my allies and I were supposed to play in the story, so that I could hopefully avoid the confusion that occurred in the last storyline. Finally, Oblivious Bystander could, with a little finessing, prevent enemies from attacking me as long as I pretended that I didn't know they were there.

These were a lot of cool tropes, but I wasn't sure how much use they'd be against a high-level threat.

Ability	Type	Archetype	Aspect	Stat	Effect
TROPE MASTER	Insight	Film Buff	---	Savvy	Sees enemy tropes. Lose half of PA.
CINEMA SEER	Buff	Film Buff	---	Savvy	Buffs Savvy and Grit of allies by predicting plot elements.
OBLIVIOUS BYSTANDER	Rule	Any Minor Archetype	---	Moxie	Cannot be targeted while convincingly acting oblivious to the enemy.
ESCAPE ARTIST	Buff	Any	---	Savvy	Plausible escape plans boost Hustle.
CASTING DIRECTOR	Insight	Film Buff	Filmmaker	Savvy	Insight into player roles in storylines.

Roxy was a lot more experienced and had a much better set of stats and tropes. She had forty Plot Armor. Most of it went into Hustle and Moxie, and she gave herself a slightly elevated Savvy, but even for her level she was not spec'd as a fighter, with her Mettle and Grit scores.

Roxy	
Eye Candy	
Plot Armor:	40
Mettle:	5

Moxie:	10
Hustle:	11
Savvy:	8
Grit:	6

Roxy's entire loadout revolved around the trope that Kimberly was so afraid of, Looks Don't Last. To complement that she had an interesting trope called The Red Mist, which ensured her an instant, painless death, and the trope Tragic Beauty, which gave a buff to other players when she died.

She had the same basic Eye Candy exploration trope Kimberly did: Get a Room!. And she got a buff to Hustle because she was wearing heels, using the trope I Run Better in Heels. She had access to unlimited money to spend in the storyline because of Daddy's Credit Card, though her purchases would disappear after the end.

The rest of her tropes were devoted to the idea of controlling the on-screen/off-screen function of the storyline. A Scream in the Distance sent her off-screen and put an ally on-screen as they heard her in the distance. Call Sheet allowed her to know when she was about to go back on-screen. Complementing both of those, and also giving her additional Hustle, was her Mystifying Geography trope, which allowed her to move faster when she was off-screen.

I wasn't sure how all of these would play out, but it did look like they coordinated together well, and Roxy assured me that she knew her part and she was ready to play it.

Ability	Type	Arche-type	Aspect	Stat	Effect
LOOKS DON'T LAST	Debuff	Eye Candy	Beauty	---	Debuff stats of all enemies by 1% for each minute survived, up to 15%.
A SCREAM IN THE DIS-TANCE	Action	Any	---	Moxie	Screaming loudly causes the player to go off-screen as camera cuts to a teammate.

THE RED MIST	Perk	Any	---	---	Lowers PA by 10%. Guarantees instant, painless death.
GET A ROOM!	Rule	Eye Candy	Beauty	Moxie	Exploration with a love interest boosts odds of important discoveries during Party.
I RUN BETTER IN HEELS	Buff	Eye Candy	Beauty	Moxie	Buffs Hustle while wearing heels.
DADDY'S CREDIT CARD	Perk	Eye Candy	Socialite	---	Gives player infinite money to spend in-story. Purchases disappear after.
TRAGIC BEAUTY	Buff	Eye Candy	Beauty	Moxie	Buffs allies' highest stat upon the player's tragic demise.
CALL SHEET	Insight	Any	---	Savvy	Insight into whether the player will be on-screen soon.
MYSTIFYING GEOGRAPHY	Buff	Any	---	---	Buffs Hustle of player and nearby allies when traveling while off-screen.

I had only spoken with Reggie a few times at camp. I wasn't sure what types of tropes he would bring into the storyline, but I certainly wasn't expecting the ones he did.

His Mettle and Grit stats were very coordinated toward a melee build, and his Hustle and Savvy were pitiful at three and one, respectively, though he did put a few points into Moxie. It was easy to see what kind of gameplay Reggie was prepared for.

Reggie	
Bruiser	
Plot Armor:	38
Mettle:	14
Moxie:	7
Hustle:	3
Savvy:	1
Grit:	13

Reggie's loadout consisted of tropes devoted to gaining benefits because of his body shape and gaining benefits from movie tropes related to drinking, along with a few Bruiser standards. Brawn over Brain gave him a boost to Mettle the lower his Savvy was, which explained his stat distribution. Anything Can Club helped him find club-like weapons in a storyline. I'm Just Big-Boned buffed his Mettle when responding to insults based on his weight.

Further along that line, Extra Padding and It's Mostly Muscle buffed his Grit and Mettle, respectively, based on his size alone. To cap it all off, he also had a trope that allowed him to go off-screen at will, as long as he acted winded, called I Need a Breather.

His alcohol-based tropes started with Liquid Courage, which buffed his Grit and Moxie with a swig of alcohol. Hair of the Dog helped provide a mental and emotional boost through drinking. Self-Medication could heal pain and non-visible injuries. And finally, Totally Wasted allowed him to manually lower his Plot Armor by getting really drunk.

One thing I'll say about his collection of tropes is that they were consistent.

Ability	Type	Arche-type	Aspect	Stat	Effect
BRAWN OVER BRAIN	Buff	Bruiser	Brute	Mettle	Gives buff to Mettle based on the difference between the player's innate Mettle and Savvy.
ANYTHING CAN CLUB	Rule	Bruiser	Brute	Moxie	Can find a suitable club weapon in any scene with lots of items.

I'M JUST BIG BONED	Buff	Bruiser	Bully	Moxie+	Once in Party phase, player gets a buff to Mettle when responding to weight-related insults.
LIQUID COURAGE	Buff	Any	---	Moxie	Temporary buff to Grit and Moxie when taking a swig of alcohol before the relevant action.
HAIR OF THE DOG	Perk	Any	---	Moxie	Drinking alcohol and pretending it soothes a hangover provides a mental and emotional boost.
EXTRA PADDING	Buff	Bruiser	---	---	Gives Grit buff to players with extra weight.
IT'S MOSTLY MUSCLE	Buff	Bruiser	---	---	Gives Mettle buff to players with extra weight.
SELF-MEDICATION	Healing	Any	---	Moxie	Drinking alcohol or similar vice temporarily heals pain and non-visible injuries.
TOTALLY WASTED	Action	Bruiser	Gentle Giant	Moxie	Drinking excessively and acting inebriated lowers the player's Plot Armor.

I NEED A BREATHER	Action	Bruiser	Gentle Giant	Moxie	Acting winded and requesting a break causes the player and nearby allies to go off-screen during travel or work.

Valerie was a Final Girl. I had seen some of her tropes on the very first day we arrived in Carousel. She had used them to calm down all of the new players and get us to comply with what they needed us to do. I was eager to see which tropes she would pick when going into battle.

Valerie's stats were strangely evenly distributed, which told me that normally she relied on tropes to gain an edge. Most veterans had extremely specialized stat distributions. Perhaps when you were guaranteed to survive to the end of the story, specialization wasn't as important.

Valerie	
Final Girl	
Plot Armor:	58
Mettle:	13
Moxie:	11
Hustle:	13
Savvy:	9
Grit:	12

To start off with, Valerie had Last One Alive—the signature Final Girl ability—which ensured that she could not be killed until the rest of her party was. She had a background trope called Actually, I'm a Veterinarian, which gave her access to some healing tropes. Fluent in Medical Jargon allowed her to play down the severity of an injury by using medical-related words or prognoses. If You Can't See It, It Won't Bleed allowed her to temporarily heal mutilation and hobbling simply by covering up the wound. Her final medical trope, This Is for the Pain, allowed her to administer pills that could ease pain and cure incapacitation.

Better than the Boys gave her a buff when she was competing with a male player. Better Make It Count increased her Hustle and Mettle when firing her last round of ammunition for a weapon. A Kind Face helped her get information from NPCs during the Party phase. Who's with Me? buffed allies who assisted her in the Finale, and All Roads Lead to the Climax increased the odds that her allies would arrive to assist her in the final battle. Finally, A Girl's Got to Know How to Protect Herself allowed her to bring simple self-defense items into a storyline.

Ability	Type	Archetype	Aspect	Stat	Effect
LAST ONE ALIVE	Rule	Final Girl	---	---	Cannot die until the party is killed.
ACTUALLY, I'M A VETERINARIAN	Background	Any	---	---	Background as an animal doctor. Can now equip: - Fluent in Medical Jargon (Doctor) - Animal Whisperer (Adventurer) - If You Can't See It, It Won't Bleed (Soldier) - This Is for the Pain (Doctor) - Always the Right Dose (Doctor)
FLUENT IN MEDICAL JARGON	Healing	Doctor	---	Savvy/ Moxie	Understand medical jargon, diagnose and treat wounds with varying severity.
IF YOU CAN'T SEE IT, IT WON'T BLEED	Healing	Soldier	GI	Moxie	Dressing hides wounds temporarily, healing Mutilated and Hobbled statuses.
THIS IS FOR THE PAIN	Healing	Doctor	Medic	Moxie	Medication eases pain, healing Incapacitated status from pain.

BETTER THAN THE BOYS	Buff	Any	---	Moxie	Female player buffs when acting competitively with male characters.
BETTER MAKE IT COUNT	Rule	Any	---	---	Last ammunition round is more accurate and powerful.
A KIND FACE	Insight	Final Girl	Girl Next Door	Moxie	NPCs more inclined to share plot information during Party phase.
IMPORTANT CHARACTER STUFF	Action	Any Major	---	Moxie	Player reveals important character arc info, goes on-screen.
WHO'S WITH ME?	Buff	Final Girl	Team Leader	Moxie	In Finale, allies gain buff when assisting the player.
A GIRL'S GOT TO KNOW HOW TO PROTECT HERSELF	Rule	Any	---	---	Female players can bring self-defense weapons into the storyline.
ALL ROADS LEAD TO THE CLIMAX	Rule	Final Girl	Team Leader	---	Surviving allies converge on climax location as final battle approaches.

Arthur's tropes were the ones that I was most interested in seeing. His Plot Armor was sixty-four—the highest I had seen on any player.

Arthur	
Monster Hunter	
Plot Armor:	64
Mettle:	11
Moxie:	4
Hustle:	10
Savvy:	21
Grit:	18

Arthur kept a few of the Scholar tropes leftover from before he started using his advanced archetype.

His Monster Hunter tropes were quite interesting. Legacy Hunter's Journal allowed him to bring a prop journal into a storyline and intuit important lore information that had supposedly been stored inside. Know Thy Enemy helped in identifying creatures, monsters, and other paranormal entities. They Went That Way allowed him to track enemy movements via their footprints. Mind over Monster explained why his Savvy was so high and his Mettle so low because when fighting creatures, monsters, or paranormal entities, Arthur could use his Savvy in place of his Mettle stat. Finally, his Hunter's Arsenal allowed him to bring in an array of weaponry for killing monsters.

Reload After Cut allowed him to intentionally go off-screen by reloading his weapon. Mercy Kill buffed his Grit when he killed an ally who was severely injured and begging for death. Cut the Head off the Snake changed the win condition so that all you had to do was kill the Leader of the enemy horde in order to win. Extended Arming Sequence allowed the player and allies peace to prepare for the Finale. And finally, Master and Apprentice allowed him to temporarily share one of his tropes with any player whom he was mentoring.

Ability	Type	Archetype	Aspect	Stat	Effect
RIGHT TOOL FOR THE JOB	Buff	Scholar	---	Savvy	Buffs Savvy and Mettle when fighting an enemy with their weakness.

LEGACY HUNTER'S JOURNAL	Insight	Monster Hunter	---	Savvy	Player can research enemies in a journal brought into the storyline during the Party.
EUREKA!	Insight	Scholar	Researcher	Savvy	Helps find important information within text.
RELOAD AFTER CUT	Action	Any	---	Moxie	Reloading a gun makes the player go off-screen.
MERCY KILL	Buff	Any	---	Mettle	Killing dying or severely injured team-mates who beg for death buffs Grit.
KNOW THY ENEMY	Insight	Monster Hunter	---	Savvy	Can identify creatures, monsters, and paranormal entities and assess their Mettle.
THEY WENT THAT WAY	Insight	Monster Hunter/ Adventurer	---	Savvy	Allows a player to track enemies who leave even the faintest evidence.

MIND OVER MONSTER	Buff	Monster Hunter	---	Savvy	Swaps player's Savvy and Mettle when fighting a creature, monster, or paranormal entity.
CUT THE HEAD OFF THE SNAKE	Rule	Any	---	---	Changes win condition of a storyline that requires the elimination of all enemies.
EXTENDED ARMING SEQUENCE	Rule	Any	---	---	Gives the player extra time between Rebirth and Second Blood to prepare weapons and traps.
MASTER AND APPREN-TICE	Rule	Any	---	Moxie+	Allows player to share a "teachable" ability with an ally through mentorship.
HUNTER'S ARSENAL	Rule	Monster Hunter	---	---	Player can bring monster-hunting equip-ment into the storyline.

Finally—sadly—there was Janet.

Janet still had her starter stats. By stats, she was the worst off of the group—though, technically, she did have a higher Plot Armor than I would once we got in the storyline.

Janet	
Hysteric	
Plot Armor:	10
Mettle:	0
Moxie:	4
Hustle:	3
Savvy:	2
Grit:	1

She only had two tropes: I Don't Like It Here . . . and Will Someone Shut Them Up? The first allowed her to detect Omens and gain information about activating them. The second made her invulnerable when she screamed in a shrill or annoying tone but reduced her Plot Armor with every scream.

Ability	Type	Archetype	Aspect	Stat	Effect
I DON'T LIKE IT HERE . . .	Insight	Hysteric	Craven	Savvy	Gives player insight into the location of Omens and how to avoid activating them.
WILL SOME-ONE SHUT THEM UP?	Action	Hysteric	Craven	Moxie	Player is invulnerable while screaming in a shrill or annoying tone. Lowers Plot Armor with each use.

CHAPTER THIRTY-FOUR

A FAMILY IN CRISIS

*Y*ou would probably be surprised to hear that once we explained to Janet everything that had happened and how important it was that she accompany us on this storyline, she immediately had a change of heart and became a team player.

You *would* be surprised to hear that.

But you're not going to hear that.

Because it didn't happen.

Luckily, I wasn't part of the group that had to get her on board. Arthur and Valerie took up that task. Not that they were quick about it. It took them thirty minutes to get her out of her room, and they only managed that because Arthur implied that he would pick her up and carry her if she didn't walk.

After all the trouble they had had getting Janet to leave her room, watching her step out of the lodge and take a look at the gargoyle felt like a huge win. However, the battle was far from over because they had to convince her to go on the storyline with us.

Adeline and all the other players who weren't involved in the storyline stayed in the back. They were all refusing to be involved in any capacity. As soon as we were chosen, it almost felt as if we were lepers and that if they spoke to us too much or interacted with us, they might catch what we had.

It occurred to me that I never asked Kimberly what the creature's Moxie was. I wondered if I were to go around back where the other players were, would they let me talk to her? I asked Roxy about it while Valerie and Arthur tried their best not to scream at Janet.

"Normally, I'd say go for it," she said. "But with this one, you probably should have done that before the storyline started. Might not want to risk it."

"What's the difference?" I asked. I had the feeling ever since I arrived at

Dyer's Lodge that there was something the veteran players didn't want to tell us. A secret. Even now, as Roxy contemplated her answer to my question, I could see that—despite her intentionally cool demeanor—there was something she wasn't telling me. Something that scared her.

When she didn't respond immediately, I asked, "What is it that you know?"

I could see on her lips that she was debating telling me something.

She must have decided against it.

"You know I have a theory on Janet," she said. She ran her fingers through her long, dark hair. "I don't think she's supposed to be here."

"Well, neither am I," I said with a smirk.

"No, I don't mean like that." She got close like she was telling me a secret. "Most people who come here figure out really quickly that you have to follow the rules. Intuitively. Don't you find it weird that most of us manage not to break the rules even though they are not written down anywhere?"

Truthfully, I don't know if she was right. I don't like the idea that I was somehow compatible with Carousel. I just followed the rules because I wanted to survive.

"Well, some of us just played a lot of role-playing games growing up," I said.

"And watched horror movies," she added with a smile.

"That too."

Arthur and Valerie seemed to have finally been making progress. As the day wore on, our need to get a move on increased exponentially.

In the end, Janet's terms were this: she would not go near the gargoyle statue; she would not be asked to fight anything; Arthur would force her husband to stop going on storylines with Travis; she wouldn't talk to any NPCs because they freaked her out; and, finally, Arthur promised to protect her, even if it meant dying.

Arthur swore up and down to everything that she required. Eventually, she swayed. Of course, I didn't believe him at all. I think at that point he would have said anything to get her on board.

Upon examining the box that the Grotesque had come in, Arthur found that it had been reused. It originally had a shipping label on it with an address: 665 Toother Street.

Arthur grabbed his duffel bag; Valerie had a large purse. I wasn't sure what was inside either of them. Reggie carried the Grotesque. I'm glad he was willing—I didn't want to touch it.

I thought we needed to steal some bicycles or a car or something. The long trek to and from Camp Dyer may have kept us safe from most Omens—current storyline excluded—but it made getting around Carousel very time consuming.

For most of the walk we were off-screen, so we discussed what we knew about the little gargoyle so far. As it turned out, many of the veteran players had been using their insight tropes to learn what they could about the monster before the storyline started. After all, the more they knew, the better they could prepare their builds and strategies.

Like me, they had all shared this information with Arthur before he activated the storyline.

Arthur had a trope that let him determine the creature's Mettle. It was nineteen. None of us were safe against that. Chris, Antoine's older brother, had an Athlete trope that told him about the creature's Hustle, which was eleven. Grace had a trope that would have let her determine the creature's Savvy, but it would have involved interacting with it, which she couldn't do because she didn't want to touch it.

My Trope Master ability allowed me to tell that this creature had no Grit while in stone form but would get twenty Grit when it came to life.

While contemplating this, I had a sudden realization.

"When this thing comes to life, does that mean its Plot Armor is going to be sixty-three?" I asked.

"Don't ask me," Arthur said. "I left all my math tropes behind."

Apparently, Arthur did have a sense of humor.

"No, I mean is that how it works?"

The Astralist had a similar gimmick, but I hadn't remembered whether his Plot Armor changed between forms because I was busy getting the crap knocked out of me around the time I should have looked.

He nodded.

I had felt safe in the knowledge that I was with higher-level players. Even though they seemed panicked, I had assumed that was exaggerated. All I knew was that we had better be able to defeat this thing in its stone form before it came to life.

It wasn't like we could just break it right then, either. First, that wouldn't make sense for our characters to do because they didn't have the information we had. Second, breaking it might be the very thing that made it come to life, so we couldn't risk it until we knew.

So far, the needle on the Plot Cycle had remained at Choice. That was very fortunate because we wasted a lot of time getting Janet.

When we got to 665 Toother Street, the needle nudged over to Party.

Toother Street was in a neighborhood with lots of large old homes. Most of the homes had gardens. Almost all of the homes had nosy NPCs that watched us as we walked up the street.

The house in question was a fairly nice place. Stylistically, it looked like it was out of the seventies. The lawn could have used a mow, which I'm sure annoyed the NPCs in the homeowners' association.

The walkway up to the door had a great variety of lawn ornaments. River rocks surrounded the stepping stones, and wind chimes were hung from little stands. On the left side was a pedestal with a lion statue on top; on the right side there was a matching pedestal but with a vase of flowers on it.

As I understood it, Arthur's Monster Hunter archetype would help steer the plot. However, Valerie was still the protagonist. If she wasn't here, Arthur probably wouldn't have been either.

I decided to try out my new Casting Director trope to determine what roles each of us would play. The information appeared on a small brass plate underneath our archetype posters on the red wallpaper.

Arthur played an aging, world-weary paranormal investigator taking a case like nothing he'd ever seen before. Janet was his client, desperately seeking help after having been mailed a strange statue that she believed to be cursed.

Valerie was Arthur's longtime monster-hunting partner. Roxy and Reggie were their employees. Reggie was only characterized as being loyal. Roxy was supposed to be Arthur's younger sister. My role, which I didn't quite understand, was a cocky, young protege with a mysterious gift.

I informed the group of this dynamic. Arthur said that most of his roles went something like that. I'm not sure how they would have learned some of those details if I hadn't told them, but I suppose some of those details might not have been there if I wasn't there to see them.

I don't know what my "mysterious gift" was, but I don't think it was talking about my ability to throw playing cards into drywall like Gambit from the X-Men.

"Remember, I'm not talking to anyone," Janet said.

"We know," Arthur said.

Valerie knocked on the door.

Moments later, the door was opened by a middle-aged woman in a pink robe. Her name was Sally. Behind her was a young girl, maybe seven years old. Her name was Jocelyn. They were both run-of-the-mill NPCs. Plot Armor three.

"Hello?" she asked cautiously as she opened the door. She scanned the group of strangers that had just arrived at her home.

Before Valerie could answer, Sally saw the gargoyle Reggie was carrying.

"I told him I don't want that anywhere near this house," she said. She slammed the door. She looked genuinely afraid.

"Reggie, why don't you and Janet go wait for us near the street," Valerie said.

Reggie nodded. The two of them headed off away from the house. Janet was careful not to be anywhere near the gargoyle.

It took more knocking and pleading through the door to get Sally to open it again. Eventually, she relented. We were in the Party phase and Valerie had her A Kind Face trope doing the heavy lifting, coaxing information. Sally was very hesitant to talk to us. Eventually, she invited us into her dining room, where we all took seats around the table. Valerie sat closest to Sally.

"Look, everything in my life was perfect before Donald got the job at the church," she said. "Is that where you got the statue? Did Donald give it to you?"

"Did you see that woman that was with us at the door?" Valerie said. "She received the statue in the mail a few days ago, and like you, she just wants her life to be normal again. We're hoping that you can help us make that happen for her."

Valerie was giving the audience backstory. It wasn't what actually happened, but that didn't matter. The audience didn't see the package delivered to Dyer's Lodge. Valerie was helping Carousel tell the story.

Sally began to cry.

Valerie was good at this part. Maybe she was experienced, maybe she was just an empathetic person. She put her hand on Sally's and said, "This is exactly the kind of thing that we do. We can fix this. We just need to hear your side of it."

Sally wiped tears from her eyes with a cloth napkin that had been on the table.

"I did everything I know to do," Sally said. "It's just . . . he's obsessed."

"Who's obsessed, Sally?"

"Donald. Donald, my husband. Or at least he's supposed to be," she said. The tears began returning to her eyes.

"Do you think Donald is the one that sent this package?" Valerie asked.

Sally nodded.

"Do you know why he would do that?"

Sally shook her head, desperately seeking some explanation but finding none. "I'm sorry. He's explained it so much, but nothing he said made sense. Donald is an art restorer. He's been working at the church over near Culling Creek Junction. That's where he found that . . . *thing*."

"Mommy," her little girl's voice sounded from the living room where she had been sent while the grownups talked.

"Just a second, pumpkin," Sally said.

She continued. "Ever since he brought it home, he's been different." Her voice got quiet. "I hear him talking to it sometimes when he thinks I'm not around."

For the first time, Arthur interjected, "Does it talk back?"

Sally seemed surprised at the question. "Well, of course not. It's made of rock."

Despite having sixty-four Plot Armor, Arthur only had four Moxie. And it showed.

Valerie took over again. "Do you remember the types of things he would say to it?"

"Well yes, he would say—"

"Mommy!" Jocelyn said from the living room.

"What, honey? I'm talking to our guests."

The little girl entered the room. She was nervous.

"It's just . . ." She must have suddenly gotten shy.

"What is it?" Valerie asked gently.

The little girl pointed at the wall toward where the street would be on the other side. "That's not Daddy's statue," she said. "Daddy's statue had wings."

CHAPTER THIRTY-FIVE

THE HARBINGER

In the course of the interview we learned sparse new details. Sally had kicked out her husband, Donald, once his obsession grew too . . . rabid. She believed that he was staying at the church where he was currently working. She didn't know for sure.

The interview went on until eventually everyone in the house was off-screen. This must have been a signal to Valerie that she had obtained about as much information as she was going to.

Then the screaming outside started.

"Arthur!" Janet screamed. "Get out here!"

Arthur leaped up from the table and ran to the front door. As soon as he got there and opened it, I could see him roll his eyes.

The rest of us filed out to see what the commotion was.

Janet was standing next to a tall woman wearing a body-length coat. She might have been in her mid-forties. Most of her attire was muted except for her hair, which had been adorned with beads and jeweled broaches. She carried a large umbrella that she was currently using as a walking stick. Her eyes were lightly shadowed with purple makeup.

On the red wallpaper, I saw that her name was Madam Celia Dane, "Proprietor—Ethereal Emporium: Antiques and Spiritual Readings. NPC. Plot Armor: 50."

"You said I didn't have to interact with these people," Janet said.

The woman, Celia Dane, looked downright offended. "You'd be a bit kinder if you knew what the spirits were saying about you, missy."

She turned to Arthur. "Arthur! My dear friend. I got your message. I thought I might come over here and see if my gift could be of service."

Arthur didn't miss a beat.

"Thank you, but the kid's got that covered," he said.

"Why, I'm sure he does," she said. "After all, I am the one who recommended him to you, aren't I."

"I remember."

"And aren't I also the one who sent this case to you?"

"You are."

"It just seemed so strange. Days ago, this woman appeared in my shop asking for help with that vile statue. Now she won't even look me in the eye. I just thought it was odd that she was staying out here, when the answers to what plagues her might be in there."

Madam Celia turned to Janet. "Don't you want to know what has brought this curse down on you?"

Janet froze. She had a look on her face between disgust and fear. You might have thought that a slug had just spoken to her.

"I'm sure she does," Arthur interjected.

It was only then that I realized that we were on-screen again. This entire interaction had been on-screen. When we had left Camp Dyer, Arthur made Janet promise that she would not break character unless the Off Screen status was lit. She didn't seem too keen on keeping that promise.

"Well, come on then," Celia said. "Let's get you in there. You might find a way to ease your fate."

"Madam Celia," Valerie said. "I think this poor woman has had enough." She gestured back over her shoulder toward Sally, the NPC. "I think we have a lead. We really should pursue it. Thank you for offering to help, but we have it from here."

"Maybe so. It seems to me that your client might have every incentive to seek the truth. After all, receiving an evil thing like this is a terrible . . . omen. She must want to get to the bottom of it, is all I mean."

"I'm sure she does," Valerie said. "And we're going to help her do that."

Madam Celia turned back to Janet. "I hope so. But is she willing to steer the wheel of fate herself?"

For a while, Celia stared at Janet. She shook her head.

With the flick of a light, we were off-screen.

Madam Celia began walking away using her umbrella as a walking stick. Like most NPCs, she was quick to exit after a scene was over.

But then she stopped.

She cast an eye toward me.

"So, Arthur, how is the new recruit doing?"

He was slightly taken aback at the question.

"Still reserving my judgment on that," he answered, raising his eyebrow.

Celia smiled. "That's good. Sometimes it takes time for the gifted to assert themselves, but I assure you, he does have the gift you . . . need."

"I'm sure he does." Arthur reached out and patted my shoulder. He began walking down the street, beckoning us to follow.

Madam Celia continued, "I am certain that in time, he will find his place in the scheme of things, wouldn't you say?"

Arthur stopped short. He turned and looked at her. "I . . . would."

"It is very important that we all find our place in the scheme of things, wouldn't you say?"

Arthur bided his time answering. I couldn't read his face—he was too emotionally closed off for such a thing—but if I had to guess, I would say he was confused.

"I would."

"Good," she said. With that, she began walking down the street. The enigmatic harbinger left as quickly and mysteriously as she had come.

When Madam Celia was gone, Valerie asked, "You find that strange?"

Arthur didn't answer at first.

When he did, he spoke to Janet. "You have to go along with us now. We can't do this whole thing for you anymore. We need to play a clean game. You have to play your character."

"You said I didn't have to," Janet protested.

"And Carousel said otherwise."

He began walking away, hauling his large duffel with a quick gait. Valerie ran to catch him. She started asking him questions in a hushed tone.

The rest of us followed.

When we were a good distance from the house, Roxy found me and said, "I've never seen Carousel do this much handholding before."

I thought it odd that she would phrase it that way. "You think sticking her in a storyline way out of her league is handholding?" I asked.

Roxy didn't answer right away. She looked like she was considering exactly what to say and how to say it. It was that familiar face that some of the veterans were so quick to wear. The do-I-tell-him face.

"She could have just disappeared."

I wondered if I could get Roxy to tell me more. "Is that why so many players are missing? Do they just disappear? You didn't think we would notice that some players outlived their teammates? How exactly is that possible? I thought it was everyone dies, or no one does."

But she didn't tell me more. Instead, she looked ahead of us and said, "Look at that!"

I suddenly noticed that we were not anywhere near the neighborhood we had just left. Roxy's Mystifying Geography ability was just that: mystifying. I had no idea how far we had traveled in only five or ten minutes.

The thing that Roxy had been pointing at was an old-fashioned Ferris wheel. We were approaching some fairgrounds. As we passed by, I read the phrase "Carousel Arts and Crafts Fair."

Behind that, there was a giant limestone statue of a man. He was wearing an evening coat with an ascot. He was posed as you might see a statue of a founding father.

"That," Roxy said, "is Bartholomew Geist, founder of Carousel. You can learn about him in a bunch of different storylines."

Up until that point, I had never learned much about the canonical backstory of Carousel. It made sense that it would have one. Every storyline we had been in so far had its own backstory, so why shouldn't Carousel itself?

"When you say founder . . . Do you mean like a character who is part of Carousel's fictional history, or is that the actual person who made this place that we're stuck in?"

"I have no idea," Roxy said with a laugh.

The church we were headed to was another five-minute walk from the fairgrounds. I don't know how far away it was in terms of actual distance with Roxy's geography trope active.

The church was a tall, lonely building in the middle of a large graveyard. The architecture was old. I'm not an art historian, but I think the style of the building was called "Covered in Gargoyles." Needless to say, I knew we were in the right place.

The sun was just starting to set as we approached.

We were on-screen again.

Arthur turned around before we were too far along in the graveyard.

"You got anything?" he asked.

At first, I didn't know what he meant, but then I figured it out. He meant "psychic readings," or whatever my character was supposed to have. The best we figured it, my character's abilities were just an in-story explanation for my Film Buff tropes.

He knew to ask me because even though he couldn't see the tropes of enemy characters, he still had access to the red wallpaper and was still able to see much of what I was seeing when I looked around the church and graveyard.

There were Grotesques spread everywhere. They blended in with the normal gargoyle statues. I didn't know which was a Grotesque and which was just a statue. Perhaps there were two dozen enemies. I couldn't give a real count because it was hard to tell where they actually were. But no matter which direction we looked we could see them.

I did have some insight, though. The trouble was I had to filter it through what my character should have known.

"This place is overwhelming," I said.

I knew how to play a psychic in a horror movie. All you have to do is struggle with every word. You have to pretend like your intestines are being pulled out through your belly button and that the spirits are attacking your very presence because they know you're a threat.

"There are too many," I continued. I started to breathe hard. I gazed around the graveyard like I was seeing the very ghosts that rested there, like I felt their pain. "Some like this one." I gestured toward the statue that Reggie was carrying.

I winced.

"Most are different. They don't seek to spread the curse. They are the curse. They seek . . . violence."

I tried to make my performance convincing. Or at least passable. I don't know how Lara, or any Psychic archetype, kept that up full time. Their tropes were usually Moxie-based. They had to pretend to be seeing into the ethereal distance all the time.

I breathed out deeply to signal I was done. I would fill them in on the real details off-screen.

Arthur nodded his head.

What we both understood was that many of the Grotesques around us were of a lower level than the one that we carried. Everyone could see that. What only I knew was that only the strongest ones had the Progenitor ability.

The weakest didn't even have a high enough Savvy to stop me from reading their tropes; they had three:

Grotesque	
PLOT ARMOR: VARIES	
TROPES	
IT PLAYS WITH ITS FOOD	This creature spends time toying with its victims. Often, it enjoys the playing more than the killing.
WHERE'S THE GOAT?	This creature can sneak up on players with implausible stealth but may not attack until the players notice some seemingly innocuous clue to its presence.
JEKYLL AND HYDE	This villain has multiple forms. Stone: Grit = 0, Living: Grit = 20.

"Maybe a place like this isn't somewhere you should be. What with your gift and all," Arthur said. "Roxy, help him out while we go investigate inside. If we need you, we'll holler."

"Don't worry, big bro," she said. "I'll take care of him."

I almost forgot that Roxy and Arthur's characters were siblings in this story.

Roxy and I started to walk back down the path we had entered from. We were still early in the Party phase. We shouldn't run into danger for quite a while.

"You want to go check out the fairgrounds?" she asked. She grabbed me by the hand and started pulling me along. If I didn't know any better, I would have thought she was flirting with me.

But I did know better.

She just needed a "love interest" to make her Get a Room! trope work. I wasn't going to object. That Ferris wheel did look enticing, as much as I wanted to see the inside of the creepy church.

It was time to go exploring.

CHAPTER THIRTY-SIX

THE GROTESQUE KISS

The way Roxy explained it, she knew that the fairgrounds were a place we needed to explore because she had never seen the arts and crafts fair before. The fairgrounds were a blank canvas. Much like the football game for Delta Epsilon Delta, this entire scene seemed to have been handcrafted for this storyline.

The arts and crafts fair was very lively. There were dozens and dozens of NPCs looking at all the booths, playing the carnival games, and riding the rides. We spent time walking around all the booths and engaging in idle chitchat while we waited for the Off Screen indicator to go off.

We had to be ready any time that we were on-screen.

While we admired a half-size terracotta warrior that had been set up as a display for a booth that was filled with clay figurines, an elderly NPC approached us. He had a pronounced hunch and a long wispy beard.

We were on-screen.

The NPC didn't have a name. Instead, he only had the title Sculptor.

Plot Armor: 3.

"What a beautiful young lady we have here," the man said. He got really close to me and said in a feigned whisper, "You know if you buy her one of my figurines, she'll have something to remember you by."

Roxy let out a polite laugh.

"You want one?" I asked.

She moved over to the shopkeeper's table and began perusing the figurines. There were a large variety of subjects on the table. Everything from ballet dancers to reindeer.

Roxy made her selection. It was a small figurine of a frog. The frog's mouth was spread into a cartoonish smile. The whole thing was about the size of a baseball.

"This one," she said.

I hated to waste what little money I had for a short romantic bit in a storyline, instead of actually spending it on myself, but I reached into my pocket anyway. I began fishing out some of the larger denominations of the demented Chuck E. Cheese tokens that Carousel gave out as money.

"No," Roxy said. "I'm going to buy it for *you*."

She withdrew a small coin purse that she had stowed in a hidden pocket at her waist and withdrew a handful of coins.

"Oh," the shopkeeper said, pretending to blush. "It sounds like she wants you to have something to remember her by."

She handed me the small figurine. I stared at it.

"Thanks . . . for the frog." I laughed.

Roxy giggled. "If you kiss a frog, it will transform into a handsome prince."

She grabbed my hand and pulled me along toward the Ferris wheel.

Suddenly, we were off-screen again.

"Wait, was I the frog in that metaphor?" I asked with a laugh.

She laughed back. "I don't know. We'll have to see what you turn into when I kiss you."

She turned and ran to join the line for the Ferris wheel.

Oh shit. How did I watch so many scary movies and so few romcoms?

We were loaded onto the Ferris wheel. I gripped the bar tightly. My character was going to be afraid of heights because I was.

"It's going to be okay," she said.

I gave her a smile. "I'm just a little nervous," I said.

She squinted. "You've been with a woman before, right?"

"Not about that," I said. "I'm afraid of falling."

"After one date?"

I laughed. "I'm afraid of falling *off the ride*."

At some point during our exchange, we went on-screen again.

I had thought up some talking points for what I was going to say. She was Arthur's younger sister in the storyline; I thought I'd play off that.

"Do you think . . . Do you think Arthur will be upset about this?" I asked.

She took her hand off me and turned away.

"He's not my father. I know you can't tell that because of how he orders me around, but I am a grown woman."

"I know that," I said. I reached to grab her hands again.

She gave a slight tease of resistance but just for show.

"Do you know what I'm thinking right now?" she asked.

She wanted me to play psychic again.

I closed my eyes and focused. Was my character supposed to be telepathic? Who cares. I shook my head and smiled playfully.

Before I could say anything, she leaned over and kissed me. My heart didn't seem to know that it was a pretend kiss, because it nearly leaped from my chest. I don't know if she intended to keep kissing me because as soon as our lips touched, a bright light blinded me from down below. It got her too. We both recoiled awkwardly.

The sun was almost set. The fairground crew had just hauled in trailer-mounted spotlights that were powered by generators. They waved back and forth in the sky, announcing to the world that something was happening at the fairgrounds.

I cleared my throat.

We leaned away from each other for a moment.

Suddenly, we were off-screen again.

"We won't be on-screen for another fifteen minutes," Roxy said. She was all business. She had a trope that allowed her to know the next time she would be on-screen. It made sense for her build. "That means this scene is probably done. We should get back before dark."

As we crested the top of the wheel one last time, I looked in the distance toward the gothic church. It was about five miles away. It was the last place in Carousel I wanted to go to at that moment, but I felt like that a lot here.

We didn't quite manage to make it back before dark.

The crimson-red vapors of sunset had just disappeared as we made our way to the church. Luckily the night was clear, and we could see well enough by starlight alone. Just as I was debating whether or not my sunglasses would make things too dark to see, or whether I would need them at all if I could feign night blindness, Roxy said something that spelled our doom.

"Didn't the church have more gargoyles on it than that?"

As if to answer her question, a large creature emerged from behind a nearby gravestone.

It was a Grotesque. In the flesh.

It wasn't the same one that Janet had been sent. Nor did it have wings. But it did have the Progenitor ability. Its tail was like that of a fish. Its body was like a bobcat's. As with the other Grotesque, its head was human, and its face was distorted into an expression of anguish. Its teeth were like needles.

Perhaps the most disturbing aspect of this creature was that it made no noise except for the sound of its teeth scraping against each other. It didn't breathe; it didn't growl.

As soon as we saw it, I could hear Roxy taking a breath. She was preparing to use her A Scream in the Distance ability to take us off-screen. I still wasn't clear what the advantage of going off-screen was, but apparently, it was important because several of the veterans in the party had tropes equipped that allowed them to go off-screen at will.

I expected to hear her scream and for the Off Screen light to flicker on. Neither happened.

Because this creature was not targeting her like it should have been. It was looking at me.

"What's happening?" Roxy yelled. It wasn't just her character that was confused.

The creature walked awkwardly but quickly. It was coming right for me. I tried to run, but my Hustle stat paled in comparison to its. I might as well have been standing still.

As I turned to run, it tackled me from behind. I was on the ground in seconds. I had no Grit at all; any attack from this thing would likely be lethal. I turned over to try and push it off.

The creature raised one paw and slashed at my stomach. Its claws dug into my flesh and ripped a long gash into me. A familiar pain spiked in my abdomen.

In a last-moment burst of desperation, I searched the red wallpaper for some explanation for why this creature had attacked me instead of Roxy. I found none. It had the same exact tropes as the one Janet had been sent. It had many tropes that I couldn't see.

One of those must have been responsible.

Roxy approached the beast and kicked it. The creature gave no sign of being injured, but the kick was enough to send it a few feet to the left. This did little good, as it was right back on top of me before she could do anything about it.

I wondered why she didn't try to go off-screen right away, but then I saw something on the red wallpaper that shook me to my core. The needle on the Plot Cycle was nowhere near First Blood. This thing should not have been attacking anyone right then.

I pushed back against the creature with my hands, and its needle-like teeth bit into my fingers. This was not an animal attack. It was not trying to eat me. It wasn't even trying to kill me. Its bites were ungraceful and uncoordinated. Its claws failed to hit their mark most of the time.

I realized that like the lower-level versions of the Grotesques, this creature must have had It Plays with Its Food. Benny the Scarecrow had the same trope, but for him, it meant that he made you run around his corn maze scared out of your mind.

For this creature, playing with its food was its only option. It had no killing instinct. It had no throat, no stomach. When its needle-like teeth sank into my hands as I tried to push it away, it didn't clamp down and try to pull my fingers off as a dog might. It just opened its jaw and bit again.

"Run!" I screamed. Roxy didn't have the build to defend me right now. Still, she tried her best.

It raised its feline claws again, and this time I knew the end was coming. There was no way I could survive one more cut to my abdomen.

But it didn't cut me—it wrapped its sharp claws in the fabric of my hoodie. If I didn't know any better, I'd think it was trying to get something from my pocket. Upon this realization, I quickly unzipped my hoodie and pulled myself out of it as the creature clamped its teeth around one of the sleeves.

The gash in my stomach wasn't as deep as it felt; this creature wasn't trying to kill me, I realized.

It was after something else.

Soon enough, it had torn my hoodie to shreds, along with my sunglasses, until all that remained was . . .

The frog figurine.

Soon enough, the little statue had fallen out of what remained of my hoodie pocket. The Grotesque threw my shredded clothing aside and focused solely on the small clay statuette. Then, in a complete departure from its previous uncoordinated behavior, it slowly bent down and touched its teeth to the smiling little frog.

At first, nothing happened.

Then I heard a cracking noise.

The frog had started to twitch. Horns started to grow out of its head, and its smiling amphibian face chipped away to reveal the ghastly face of a human under torture.

Now a new poster appeared on the red wallpaper:

"Grotesque."

Plot Armor: 15.

CHAPTER THIRTY-SEVEN

A PLAN INTERRUPTED

Roxy screamed.

We went off-screen. She started to run, and I followed. Due to the effects of her Mystifying Geography trope, my Hustle was on par with hers. With her boost to Hustle, we were fast enough to escape the Grotesque pretty easily.

"Roxy!" Arthur yelled from somewhere in the darkness.

I could see a flashlight moving back and forth in the distance. It wasn't coming from the church. No, it was coming from out in the graveyard. In the distance, I could see Arthur and Janet running toward us. Janet appeared none too pleased to be running toward danger.

Now that we had joined up with Arthur, we were back on-screen again. Roxy's A Scream in the Distance trope had passed the camera to him, apparently.

"What happened?" Arthur screamed.

I almost said that we saw a live Grotesque, but before I did, I realized that my character didn't know what a Grotesque was yet. That word hadn't been established within the narrative.

"It was a . . . ," I gave myself a moment for my character to come to terms with what he had just seen, "a gargoyle."

"No," Arthur said, "it was something else." He produced a large leather-bound journal with tons of bookmarks, dog-ears, and inserts. "It's called a Grotesque."

Arthur's Legacy Hunter's Journal trope allowed him to bring his own source for researching monsters into a storyline.

Arthur hugged Roxy. She was his baby sister in this story, after all.

"Come on. We found a shed over on the outskirts of the graveyard. We'll be safe there for a while," Arthur said.

The Grotesque we had seen on the path toward the church had not continued to pursue us. That made sense. It wasn't First Blood yet.

Arthur led us across the graveyard through rows of mausoleums and monuments. Every shadow made my heart jump. Every cherub statue looked like it could come to life at any moment.

"Valerie is following a lead at the church," he said. "We're trying to figure out where these creatures are coming from."

Roxy shook her head. "They aren't coming from anywhere," she said. "It looks like they can infect other statues."

"Infect?"

Roxy explained what we had just seen.

"Then we are in bigger trouble than we thought," Arthur said. "Come on."

Arthur opened the door to the shed that he had been leading us toward. It was a sparsely decorated, windowless building. It had nothing but some crates and a table in the middle. Arthur retrieved a small electric lamp from inside his duffel. He sat it on the table and turned it on. Next, he began thumbing through his hunter's journal.

"At first, I thought the statue was a garden-variety cursed object. But then Reggie said it had come to life and run off. I went through Riker's journal. He wrote about these things," he said.

Riker was the fictional person who had given him the journal within the narrative.

"Possessed statues. Towns completely destroyed in a matter of days. He said that they follow a pattern. They wake, they spread, and then they hibernate. Sometimes for decades."

He started thumbing through the hunter's journal and showing Roxy and me the entries. They were blank. Or rather, they were nonsense. His journal was comprised of a bunch of random reading materials stuck together to make it look like a real journal. It was just a prop. He must have been getting the real information on the red wallpaper.

"People found a way to shield themselves from them centuries ago," he said. "They would carve their own gargoyles onto their buildings. The theory was that the Grotesques would see the gargoyles and think that the curse had already been spread there. Supposedly it worked."

"Why isn't it working here?" Roxy asked. "That church was covered in gargoyles."

Arthur shook his head. "I don't know."

"Okay, well, how do we kill them?" I asked.

Arthur continued flipping through the pages. "It says here that fire has some effect. I can't tell you more than that."

"Why is it we always just end up burning things to death?" Roxy asked.

"If it ain't broke . . ." Arthur said as he unzipped his duffel to reveal that he had brought supplies for a variety of hunts. Most relevant to this story, he had brought a lighter, a flare gun, and supplies to make Molotov cocktails.

Once we were off-screen, Arthur started to relay the plan to me. When First Blood approached, I would stick with Roxy in order to help her survive as long as possible after she was attacked. Not that I could be that helpful. When she died, I would take a huge bonus to Savvy because of her Tragic Beauty trope. In fact, we would all get bonuses.

Once I had a lot of Savvy, I would regroup with Arthur, then he would use his Master and Apprentice trope to teach me to temporarily use Mind over Monster. After that, I might actually be a threat against these things.

Seemed straightforward to me. Except for the part where Roxy was supposed to survive for fifteen minutes against these creatures. I wasn't sure how that was going to happen.

While we planned, Janet sat on a crate not saying anything. None of the plans involved her. She had insisted on it.

Somewhere, Valerie was exploring. She had Reggie as backup. Not that she would need him. We didn't know what she was seeing, but we had some idea of when something important was happening because of the Off Screen indicator flicking on and off, likely swapping between our two groups.

The needle was nearly to First Blood.

I could hardly sit still because of the nerves. I wasn't sure if I'd even get to use Oblivious Bystander in this scenario. That had been my security blanket up until this point.

There was a rustle outside.

The Grotesques' Where's the Goat? trope made them ideal sneak attackers. The question was, would they attempt to use that trope? Or would they consider a more direct approach because of the fact that we couldn't see outside?

We were on-screen.

Thump.

Something hit the side of the shed. Direct attack it was.

Thump. It was there again.

If this were real life, barricading ourselves inside the shed would have been a bad idea, but this wasn't real life. We were here to give Roxy her best shot at getting a maximum survival time for her Looks Don't Last ability.

The next part was tricky. We needed Roxy to be attacked; the timer didn't start until then.

Arthur retrieved a shotgun from his duffel. He aimed it at the door, and Roxy moved to open it.

"Shoot anything you see," she said to Arthur. Her character didn't know that Arthur's shells would only do marginal damage. He had twenty-one Savvy. With his Mind over Monster trope, those points would replace his Mettle in damage calculation against the Grotesques. Even with a one-point advantage, Arthur would not be able to get a clean kill fast enough to prevent the creature from attacking.

She opened the door up just an inch.

Crash!

One of them tackled the door just as she opened it. Roxy was knocked back into the table. The door opened wide, revealing several Grotesques clamoring to get in. Arthur fired on the closest one. It clearly felt the blow, but only for a moment. It would take more.

"Molotov," Arthur said.

I grabbed one of the cocktails and lit the rag that we had placed into it as a wick. I handed it to Arthur. He needed to be the one to throw it. His tropes would give him stat advantages for it.

He threw the Molotov at the three Grotesques nearest the door, and they lit up in flame. I could hear a crackling noise coming from them. The beasts appeared to be partially immobilized. They struggled to move. It took a moment to notice why.

Parts of them had been turned to stone.

Arthur aimed his shotgun again. He fired. One of the gargoyles' heads broke into cracked pieces of rubble. White dust rose from the wound. Arthur let off two more shots. One shot split a smaller gargoyle in half. The other shot appeared to miss its mark and hit living flesh.

"Reload," Arthur said. He started pumping more shells into his shotgun.

We were off-screen again.

Roxy closed the door, and she and I moved a couple of crates in front of the door.

"That do it?" Arthur asked.

"Yep," Roxy said.

She had been attacked. Her Looks Don't Last timer started. Fifteen minutes to go.

A barrage of banging started to surround the shed from all directions. The shed wouldn't hold up to it. One of the walls was already buckling under the weight.

"Once they break through, exit out the door and make a run for it," Arthur said.

Roxy and I nodded.

Arthur retrieved a pistol from his duffel and handed it to me. It wouldn't be very useful in my hands—not unless we lit more of them on fire—but it made sense for me to be armed.

"Make it stop!" Janet screamed.

Arthur gave her a fierce look. "We're fine. We'll be okay."

He had to be careful of what he said to her because we were on-screen.

"Make it stop. You said you would protect me!"

"And I will. We just have to follow the plan."

Janet wasn't having it. "Why did we even come here? We should have stayed at the church. We would have been safe."

Of course, we weren't *trying* to be safe.

"We'll be okay. We do this sort of thing all the time."

The wall that had buckled was starting to splinter. They would be through any second. Roxy and I got close to the door to make a run for it.

"I don't want to play this 'game' anymore!"

Arthur cursed. He tried to regain his composure. He had to stay in character. "I'm not playing with you. We can handle this!"

It was like she couldn't even hear him. Some part of her refused to believe that Arthur didn't have some power to end all of this.

"I don't want to do this anymore! Bobby! Bobby! Please!" Tears streamed down her face as pure, unstoppable panic took control. "Bobby! Please, help me, Bobby. I quit. I quit the game."

The first thing I noticed was the Plot Cycle. Normally it ticked forward at a slow, if inconsistent, speed. Suddenly it started to move backward. At first I thought I was just imagining things, but then it was clear.

It was moving backward.

Not a whole lot but just enough that First Blood started to move further and further away from the tip of the needle.

Then I noticed the light through the cracks in the wooden planks that made up the shed. The sun was coming back up. As it rose, the Grotesques that had surrounded the shed went quiet. I could only assume that they had turned back to stone.

I will never forget the look I saw on Arthur's face. Normally Arthur didn't display any emotion. But I could see that something affected him tremendously. He got really quiet. He dropped his gun onto the table.

"What's happening?" I asked.

No one answered.

"I knew it," Roxy said.

"You knew what?" I asked.

Again, no answer.

Arthur began placing all of the items that he had taken out of his duffel bag back inside of it. Roxy went and unbarricaded the door.

"We need to go," Arthur said. He put the strap of his duffel bag over his shoulder, opened the door to the shed, and began walking out.

Was the storyline over? Had we failed?

Roxy followed behind Arthur. I followed her. For a moment, Janet stayed in the shed, but after we had walked fifteen yards or so from the entrance, she ran to catch up with us.

"Is it over?" Janet asked.

"Don't take another step," Arthur said. "You're on your own now. You didn't want to play. We've done everything we could for you." He tried to sound firm and strict, but in the end he tacked on, "I'm truly sorry. I wish we could have helped you."

Janet looked totally taken aback by what he had just said.

"You told me that you would protect me."

Hearing that appeared to sting him, but he didn't respond. He, Roxy, and I continued walking.

"Why are we leaving her?" I asked in a rushed whisper to Roxy. She looked at me with a mournful expression on her face. Suddenly, a look of fear replaced it.

"Hope you like keeping secrets," Roxy said. I followed her gaze, but I didn't see anything.

And then I looked behind us.

I heard a loud pop. I could feel hot liquid start to gush from my ear canal. I put my finger to it. It was blood.

Arthur and Roxy turned to look in the same direction. For the first time since coming to Carousel, I saw actual fear on Arthur and Roxy's faces.

Standing on the other side of the field was a man.

A chill ran up my spine.

I tried to figure out who he was. I looked at the red wallpaper.

He wasn't an enemy.

He wasn't an NPC.

He wasn't a player.

He had no presence whatsoever on the red wallpaper.

Despite this, I recognized him. I had seen him hundreds of times since arriving—every time I looked at a fellow player.

On the red wallpaper, every player archetype is represented by a movie poster. Camden's had a picture of him studying in a library. Mine depicted me eating popcorn and sitting on a couch watching a movie. Anna's had her running with a flashlight. They all had one thing in common, however. Standing behind us in each of those posters was a figure.

It was a man wearing a dark cloak carrying an axe.

That's who I saw on the other side of the field. I could hear him breathing even though he was hundreds of yards away.

He started to walk toward us.

CHAPTER THIRTY-EIGHT

THE RULEKEEPER

I could hear his footsteps. It was like they were right behind me. His breathing got louder as he walked toward us. Why did it sound like he was so close? What was going on?

"Come on," Arthur said. "To the church."

We started to run. I couldn't believe that we were really going to leave her behind. It occurred to me that Janet had the exact same Hustle stat as me, so if she ran with us, how could I outrun her?

Yet, somehow, I did.

We were off-screen and Roxy's Mystifying Geography ability was boosting my Hustle up to the same as hers. However, it wasn't boosting Janet's. That ability was supposed to work on all allies.

Was Janet not an ally anymore?

As we fled, I did not want to look behind and see what was happening, but I felt like I needed to. When people asked me what happened to Janet, I needed to be able to give them a definitive answer. So much of what the veterans had told us at that point had been vague and useless information. Was that because they always ran whenever danger came around?

"Can you shoot him?" I asked.

"Don't shoot him!" Arthur said. His reaction was visceral. I'd forgotten he had given me a gun.

We zigzagged through the gravestones and stone planters between us and the church.

I could hear Janet screaming behind us. Yelling for us. Pleading for us to return. I remembered back in the corn maze when I had seen Janet killed by Benny the Scarecrow. I had done nothing to help her. When that happened, I was truly disappointed in myself. Yet here I was, not helping her again.

I tried to push those thoughts out of my mind.

As we raced to the church, I heard a louder scream from far behind us. I turned to look. If I couldn't help her, I would at least be a witness. Not that she would appreciate that. She was out of my line of sight, so I turned and climbed up on a stone bench to get a better view.

In the distance, I saw that the man with the axe had caught up to her. She had not done a remarkable job in evading him. I had seen her survival instincts in the corn maze; she wasn't a fighter. She wasn't even the type to flee. She froze.

She screamed loudly and shrilly.

That should have made her invincible. It was one of the few tropes she had; her scream should have protected her, if only for a moment. But it didn't.

He cleaved her at her collarbone, slicing her torso in half all the way from her shoulder down to her waist with one swing.

Oh, fuck.

With that one swing of an axe, Janet disappeared from the red wallpaper. Her status wasn't Dead or Mutilated or Written Off. She was just gone.

The last thing I saw as we rushed into the church was the axe murderer lifting her body over his shoulder and turning to walk away.

In a way, she got what she wanted.

She had found a way to quit the game.

"Why would she do that?" I screamed as soon as we entered the church and found a room where we could talk privately.

Roxy and Arthur didn't answer me at first. They appeared to be listening for something. I paused and listened too. I could hear footsteps walking away from us. Faint breathing.

I could still hear the axe murderer.

"Why can I hear him?" I asked.

Roxy and Arthur looked at each other.

Roxy spoke up. "Everyone who sees him can hear when he's around. And sometimes when he's not."

"Everyone who's seen him?" I asked.

Roxy nodded.

"The higher-level players? Who? Who knows about him?"

Arthur gestured toward a chair and said, "Sit."

I wasn't going to argue.

"Who all knows? Is it everyone but me and my friends? Because I know you guys are keeping secrets from us. Why would you not tell us what would happen if we broke the rules?"

"It's just under a dozen of us," Arthur said. "The others . . . They *understand,* but they don't really know."

"They don't know that you get butchered just for breaking character?" I asked. Janet's death had freaked me out. It was so terrifyingly final. In the Astralist storyline, Kimberly had freaked out too. How close was she to getting killed?

"No," Arthur said. "It's not just breaking character. It's not just breaking the rules. Everybody does that, especially in the beginning. Carousel can be pretty forgiving with that stuff. It's about doing it on purpose. That's what matters the most."

"Why are you keeping this a secret?" I asked. "If Janet had known that this was going to happen, she would never . . ."

I lost my words. I had just seen a death. A real death.

"We couldn't. We've tried. She knew what would happen. Even if she didn't know how. We made sure of that."

"What do you mean you've tried? Does Adeline know? Valerie? Reggie?"

Arthur took a deep breath. "You have to be careful how you phrase things. When you try to talk about him, it sounds like he's right behind you. Like he's watching what you say . . ."

At that moment I could still hear the axe murderer faintly in the distance. Would I always be able to hear him?

"We just say that players disappear. We can't acknowledge that we know anything more than that. Believe me, we've tried."

I wasn't in a state of mind to really think about any of that.

"Adeline doesn't know. Reggie and Valerie do," Roxy said.

Wait . . .

"Every single veteran player on this team knows about . . . him?"

What were the odds of that?

"We call him the Rulekeeper," Roxy said.

"No, we don't," Arthur said.

"We call ourselves the Secret Keepers."

"No, we don't."

Had this whole thing been a setup? What were the odds that every veteran player chosen for this storyline just happened to be one of the few players that knew about the axe murderer? Why was I there?

"Well, you don't have any excuse now," I said. "Tell me everything you know about *him*."

Arthur didn't put up a fight. I suppose on some level he thought I deserved to know. Now that he could tell me, he was willing.

"Few years after I got here, some of the folks noticed something out west, past the lake. There's a small mountain. You know the one?"

I nodded. "The mountain and the lights."

Arthur was having a tough time telling me this. I could see it on his face. He had clearly spent years keeping so much of this a secret.

"That's it," he said. "Well, at that time it was the only lead we had. We started devoting all our efforts to getting over there. But that was a huge problem; the farther west you go, the harder the storylines get. If you get just halfway around the lake, even I would be under-leveled there.

"So, we tried to get clever. We tried to sneak over there in between scenes from other storylines. Can't trigger a storyline if you're already in one. We'd start up one of the easier stories, and then as soon as it was time for a scene to end, we would steal a car and head west. That was the plan at least. Three of our group tried it. They were just supposed to go scout things out and come back. They never did."

Arthur took a moment to compose himself.

"Whenever a group dies in a storyline, a missing poster appears on the bulletin board outside the diner. But for the players that tried to sneak out west, no missing poster appeared. We had no idea what happened to them. Don't get me wrong, we'd had players go missing, players that never got posters on the bulletin board. We never knew why.

"So, we gave up on that plan. We decided that if we couldn't sneak over that direction, we would just have to level up so high that we could beat any storyline they threw at us. There's a road south of the lake with a trolley track built into it. Never seen the trolley, but the road seemed to go right in the direction we needed. We figured that's the right route to take. If you go over the lake, there are all types of water monster storylines that you can trigger just by being in the water out that far. The forests are just as bad, but that road seemed like our best bet. More manageable, maybe.

"The question was: How were we going to level up enough to get over there? Took us years to find an answer. There used to be these things called rescue tropes. They were these marigold-yellow tickets you could get. If you had one of those, you could grab somebody's missing poster from the bulletin board, and you could go rescue them from whatever storyline they had died in.

"All the archetypes had their own tropes that worked in different situations. I had one called Trail of the Monster. There were all kinds. That used to be how things worked: if a team ever died, another team would go rescue them. The trouble is a rescue storyline is always more difficult than the base storyline. At least on paper.

"The truth is, in some situations, the rescue storylines were actually easier because they were more straightforward. And the thing about rescue storylines is that they paid off way bigger than normal storylines. You'd get ten times the cash, a handful of tropes, and far more stat boosts than you would normally expect.

"We got greedy. We would have teams purposefully fail storylines. What did it matter? We had died hundreds of times before at that point. What was one more death? Then another team would come to rescue them. Once we started this, we leveled up as much in six months as we had in the five years before that.

Felt like we had found a loophole that could get us out of this place. Finally had momentum.

"One day we were doing a rescue run. My team drew the short straw. We were going to die, and one of the other teams that was with us at the time would come to rescue us. Only after they rescued us, the axe murderer showed up. It was the first time I saw him. He killed that whole team like it was nothing. Ripped right through them.

"After that, our rescue tropes disappeared, and Silas stopped handing them out. In fact, most of the players here today don't even know they existed. This would have been about twelve years ago. Without being able to rescue each other, leveling is slow-going—especially once you get up to around my level. My Plot Armor hasn't gone up in nearly two years. We should have known better. We cheated the game."

I couldn't believe what I was hearing. There had been a way to rescue dead players, and they had gotten it taken away?

Roxy took over. "I met him on my first day in Carousel. Arthur and the others didn't manage to intercept us when my friends and I got here. Some NPCs ended up herding us into some type of tutorial. It was a nightmare. Three storylines back-to-back. Almost no explanation for what was going on. It was like they thought we should know certain things already. My friends quit before the third storyline was finished. Then the Rulekeeper showed up and killed them right in front of me."

A tear dripped down her face.

"Truth is, I didn't keep playing because I was smart or brave. I kept playing because I was too afraid to stop."

Losing all of her friends on the first day . . . I couldn't imagine that.

"A tutorial?" was all I could think to ask. On our first day in Adeline's class, Todd had jokingly called it "Adeline's tutorial." Was that the joke? That there was an actual tutorial that the veteran didn't want us to know about?

"That's why we take you to *The Final Straw II*. Benny's got a gentle touch by comparison. Anyone who tries to quit the game, he ends up killing them before the guy with the axe shows up," Arthur said.

It made sense. Benny killed anyone who tried to cut through the walls of his corn maze. Any player that tried to quit would get turned into one of his minions before they had the chance to leave the story.

"We've seen the axe murderer off and on throughout the years since," Arthur said. "He kills rule breakers. Disappears. Won't bother you if you play the game."

"The other players speculate about what happens to them," Roxy said. "They understand that the missing players are dead, but not the details."

For a while, I just sat in silence as I absorbed everything they had just told me. They did have a plan to get out of here. They just gave it up a long time ago.

We weren't working toward anything anymore. We were just trying to stay alive. But for what?

For all they knew about the axe murderer, they didn't really know much at all. Who was he? What was he? Where did he go? Why did he do these things?

"I don't understand one thing," I said. That was a lie; there were a dozen things I didn't understand. "Did she think that she would really be able to get out of this just by quitting? How is that rational?"

I didn't want to blame what happened on her. Ever since I had gotten to Carousel, the goal of staying alive had been so clear. Every single action I had taken had been motivated by trying to stay alive, living long enough to figure out what was going on. To figure out what the veterans knew. To find a way out.

I couldn't imagine giving that up soon.

"You think we're the rational ones? We have to die over and over," Arthur said.

"Dozens of temporary deaths have to be better than one permanent death," I said.

"Get back to me when you've died dozens of times," Roxy said.

Arthur shook his head. "In a few years, when you've died a hundred painful, terrifying, pointless deaths, and you're no closer to getting out of here . . . then we can debate about whether playing the game is the right decision. I'm not saying she thought it through. She was probably just scared . . ."

I imagine Arthur and Roxy had put a lot of thought into this very thing.

"It's just . . . Not everyone wants to survive at any cost. Some of us really take to Carousel. Others don't. I'm not sure which group is the sane one," Arthur said.

Janet had been scared. That was true. You could hear it in her voice. But she had refused to adapt to the situation. I didn't think I would ever understand that.

"Did you know this was going to happen?" I asked.

Roxy had implied as much when the Rulekeeper showed up.

They didn't answer for a moment. Arthur appeared to be choosing his words carefully, but Roxy spoke up before he could.

"We did know this was going to happen. Ever since she first refused to go out on a storyline. We could tell. She was going to get the axe. The only question is, what's with the theatrics? Was this whole Grotesque thing just a trick to get her away from the lodge? Or was it really trying to give her a second chance?"

"This wasn't just about her," Arthur said. "It's also about him."

"Me?" I asked. "How?"

"Because Carousel is always trying to bring in Film Buffs. One out of every ten players that have lived at Camp Dyer over the years were failed Film Buffs. Like Bobby. He was invited here because of his horror interest, wasn't he? Only half a dozen have actually gotten the archetype. Since you did, I think it wanted you to know the stakes."

"Wait . . . There are no other Film Buffs," I said. I hadn't seen any other Film Buffs at Dyer's Lodge, let alone half a dozen. I had wondered since the day I got there why I was the only one. Sure, there were minor archetypes that were pretty rare, but the Film Buff was the only one with just one player.

"That's the thing about Film Buffs," Arthur said. "They . . . disappear."

CHAPTER THIRTY-NINE

THE RED MIST

They disappear . . ." I repeated in a whisper. "He got them? All of them?"

"Not exactly all of them," Arthur said. "A couple took the easy way out. Triggered storylines way out of their league. Wasn't such an uncommon thing back when there were rescue tropes. Not just Film Buffs either. Some people just get tired of dying over and over again. Figured they'd pick a short easy death and wait till the day we escaped to be rescued. But the rest disappeared without a trace. The only thing I know that could have happened is the axe. No missing posters. No clues."

I stared ahead for a moment. Was there something about Film Buffs that made us more likely to break the rules? Or was there something else going on? And would I be ready the day I figured out what it was?

"That's enough of the campfire stories for now. We still have a storyline to finish," Arthur said.

I broke out of my mental fog upon hearing that.

"Wait, how are we supposed to finish the storyline without Janet? Isn't she a major character?"

"You always have to finish the storyline," Roxy said. "Carousel's not going to let some little thing like one of the actors getting murdered in the middle of the show change that."

Arthur put his duffel on his shoulder and said, "Given where we are on the Plot Cycle, I think I need to go reshoot some of the scenes that I had. I'm going to go find Reggie and Valerie. I'm sure they've already figured out what happened, but we need to coordinate. I figure we won't have to redo anything that happened at the house. You probably don't need to do any of your scenes again because Janet wasn't in them."

He left the room.

"So, what do we do?" I asked.

"We're going to have to wait until it gets dark again then reshoot the scene where we find Arthur after running from the gargoyle that transformed the frog. After that, Arthur is probably going to have to explain the whole lore behind the Grotesques again. Then I get to die just like we planned."

I wondered how many times it took for them to figure this out. What did the other veterans do when this happened, the ones who didn't know about the axe murderer? Did they just go along with it?

Roxy gestured toward the door. We started exiting the church. For the first time, I actually looked around the building. The entire thing was under renovation. There were several larger statues covered in big white sheets spread around the sanctuary. I didn't know what was under them. They might have been saints or angels, I couldn't tell.

"We're going to have to fight those," I said.

"I'm not."

I guess that much was true. Maybe being First Blood wasn't all bad.

Waiting around for our next scene was strange. Technically, all the gargoyles that had been on the sides of the church were already gone, so we didn't have to worry about them attacking us as the sun went down. Despite that, it was incredibly unnerving to just sit there and wait, knowing that as soon as darkness spread across the sky, monsters were going to start waking up around me.

To look at Roxy you would have thought we were just waiting for our shift at work to start. She wasn't exactly happy to be there, but at the same time, she wasn't distressed either.

"Did you know any of the Film Buffs?" I asked.

She nodded her head but didn't offer any more information.

"So did they all just break the rules or something?" I asked. If she knew something, why not tell me?

Roxy considered her answer. "The guy I knew just started taking things too far. Thought he was seeing patterns everywhere. He thought Carousel was secretly talking to him, leaving him messages. That's what Arthur didn't want you to know. I'm not sure what happened in the end. I assume he got the axe."

As she told me this, she watched my face like she was looking for a reaction. I didn't give her one. I wasn't sure why it was such a crazy thing to think that Carousel was communicating with us. Wasn't my very presence in this storyline a form of communication?

"We've got a minute and a half. Come on," she said. It must have been incredibly convenient to know when you were about to be on-screen.

We walked down the path toward the place we had been when the gargoyle first approached us. It was dark again. It wasn't quite First Blood yet, so we didn't have to worry about getting attacked. I didn't have a frog figurine in my pocket either.

As we stood there and waited for our cue to run, I rifled through the scraps of my hoodie that lay on the ground. My sunglasses were unsalvageable. It would have been expecting too much to hope that they had made it out unscathed.

Roxy held up three fingers. Then two. Then one.

Action.

We raced across the graveyard. In the distance, we saw two figures running toward us. One of them carried a flashlight, and the other figure lumbered behind far more slowly. It was Arthur and Reggie.

"Roxy!" Arthur screamed. "What happened?"

He wrapped Roxy in a hug.

"It was . . . a gargoyle," I said. "It was alive!"

Arthur shook his head. "Not a gargoyle," he said. He produced his leather-bound hunter's journal. "It was a Grotesque. Come on."

Arthur led us across the graveyard. At the boundary where the graveyard met the forest was a small shack. It was the exact same shack that we had just been in. The gargoyles that had surrounded it were gone now. The damage they had done to it had also been reversed. I wasn't sure when that had happened.

Arthur led us into the small windowless building; it had nothing but stacks of crates and a dusty table in the middle. Arthur went through his spiel about the lore of Grotesques. It was the same as the last time, give or take a few choice words. Long story short: Grotesques were demonic hibernating statues that gargoyles were designed to protect against. Fire weakened them.

"Why is it we always end up just burning things to death?" Roxy asked.

"If it ain't broke . . ."

Arthur opened his duffel bag and produced the supplies to create Molotov cocktails, a lighter, and a flare gun.

"Want a swallow?" he asked Reggie as he unscrewed the lid from a bottle of spirits.

Reggie shook his head. "I brought my own. I don't drink that cheap shit."

He pulled one of the biggest flasks I have ever seen out of his pocket, unscrewed the cap, and took a swig.

His Moxie and Grit rose because of his Liquid Courage trope.

He held out the flask toward me.

I grabbed the flask and turned it up. I could use all the buffs I could get.

The taste surprised me so much that I almost choked.

"That'll put some hair on your chest," Reggie said.

I wasn't surprised because it was hard liquor; I was expecting hard liquor.

I was surprised because it was peach tea. Reggie's flask was just another prop, like Arthur's hunter's journal. It worked though; I got the buff.

After that, we went off-screen.

"Okay, the plan this time," Arthur said. "Everything's the same except you guys are taking Reggie with you. He can help get you off-screen. After you leave, I'm going to run over to the church, so I can be around Valerie. That should be enough to set up the cartwheel."

"Ten seconds," Roxy said.

We all took our places and then . . .

On-screen.

Thump.

Something hit the side of the building.

Thump.

It happened again. Roxy moved to open the door just a crack.

Crash!

One of the creatures tackled the door, slamming Roxy back against the table. With the door open, three gargoyles were revealed in living flesh. Arthur took a shot at one of them.

It barely did anything.

I grabbed one of the Molotov cocktails and lit the wick. I handed it to Arthur. He threw it at the gargoyles, engulfing all of them in bright orange flames.

Bang. One of the gargoyles was decapitated as the slug from Arthur's shotgun made contact with its now stone face.

Bang. Another gargoyle was almost torn in half as one of its arms got blown off along with much of its torso. The remainder of its living flesh struggled to maintain some semblance of life, writhing and attempting to stand, before returning completely to stone.

Bang. The top of the remaining gargoyle's head popped right off.

He got all three this time. Practice makes perfect.

Roxy closed the door and Reggie moved a stack of crates in front of it. Now, we waited.

The gargoyles started to tackle the shed from all around us. It wasn't any less scary the second time. Every time they threw their bodies against the building, I thought they were going to come through. Reggie was poised to remove the crate so that we could leave through the door. Roxy and I stood behind him, prepared to make our exit. Arthur started to reload his shotgun.

Off-screen.

"Nice shootin', Tex," Reggie said.

Arthur nodded his head graciously.

On-screen.

The Grotesques surrounding the shed were back at it. They were throwing their bodies against the walls, digging their claws into the wood. We could see little traces of them through the holes in the slats.

Crack.

One of the walls started to buckle; I could hear the wood being torn apart. Any second, they would be through.

Finally, a hole appeared in the side of the building. One demented gargoyle's claw reached through and tore the wooden plank siding off the wall, widening a gap almost big enough for it to fit through.

Reggie pushed the crates out of the way and opened the door.

Roxy was the first out, followed by me and Reggie. As we left the shed, gargoyles started to approach us from the other sides. Roxy screamed loudly.

Off-screen.

"Seventy-two seconds," Roxy cried out.

Now that we were off-screen, we easily outran the Grotesques. Arthur stayed behind, but that didn't matter much because we had distracted them, and they were chasing us. Whichever unlucky ones chose to remain probably wouldn't last long. I saw a flash of fire behind us, and a few more shotgun blasts rang out.

We ran along a different path than we had before. I thought we were headed back to the church but along a more twisted and winding path. The audience wouldn't be able to tell.

"Ten seconds," Roxy said. "Get ready, Reg."

"I got you," Reggie replied. For such a big guy he was putting up with running pretty well. That made sense in a way. In Carousel, Grit covers endurance and Reggie had plenty of Grit.

On-screen.

We ran for a few moments before Roxy stopped and looked behind her.

"I think we lost them," she said.

Reggie started to wheeze and double over. "I need a break. Just a minute."

Roxy nodded.

"Over here," she said, taking us to a secluded area between two mausoleums.

Off-screen.

Reggie stood back up straight. He took out his flask and had another drink of peach tea. I think that one was actually just to quench his thirst.

"Two and a half minutes," Roxy said.

I was starting to understand the strategy. I had wondered why they were so insistent on going off-screen all the time. Characters can die off-screen, after all. But they can't die without context—not a main character, at least. Roxy was a main character. The camera couldn't just cut to Roxy being killed. There had to be a setup, a cinematic kill sequence.

We were interrupting it.

In the distance, I could hear the Grotesques closing in. Still, we waited.

"Twenty seconds," Roxy said. "It's out of our hands now."

She waved us forward. We continued to run along the path she had chosen.

On-screen.

The gargoyles started to pour out from all around us. It was like they'd been hiding behind the gravestones waiting for the moment to emerge and kill Roxy.

One got close to her. I reached for the gun in my pocket that Arthur had given me, but as my fingers touched the fabric of my jeans, I realized it wasn't there.

We had forgotten it.

I didn't have a trope that would allow me to bring a gun into a storyline. I had to get one from Arthur. We had forgotten to reestablish that he had handed it to me when we reshot the shack scene, so now I didn't have it.

Shit.

The gargoyle closest to her tried to wrap up her legs. She easily dodged it. She moved with the grace of a ballerina through a sea of gargoyles that lunged and jumped at her. None of the gargoyles could get her because this was her kill sequence. They couldn't simply hurt her. They had to kill her all in one hit because of her Red Mist trope. These creatures were so inelegant and stupid that they were having a difficult time finding a way to trap her without injuring her.

Reggie and I piled behind her as she ran. Reggie was strong enough that he could throw the gargoyles. He picked one up in front of me and swung it down on another that was about to tackle Roxy. They collided with a *thud*, and both tumbled across the ground.

I didn't know how long we could do this. We couldn't dodge them all day. We needed to go off-screen, but I got the sense that none of the techniques they had used so far could be repeated—not so soon, not within the same sequence.

But then, suddenly, we were off-screen again.

Valerie.

Valerie had the ability to force herself on-screen by having a character moment. I don't know what that would have been, but it had succeeded.

We continued to run. The Grotesques still chased us, but you could tell that they weren't going for the kill. A proper kill sequence had not been set up yet.

"Three minutes," Roxy said.

Whatever character moment Valerie was having, it must have been pretty heavy for that kind of screen time.

We continued to run. After a minute or two we were finally able to make some distance between us and the Grotesques.

"This will be it," Roxy said. "I think this is as far as it'll take us. Should be almost thirteen minutes between everything. I was really hoping to get the full fifteen."

"You can still make it," I said. "Those things can't kill you in one hit. You should be able to survive the rest of the movie."

Roxy laughed. "I thought you were supposed to be an expert," she said. "Nothing good is free."

I didn't know what she meant.

"Look at the stars," she said.

I looked up. I couldn't see anything at first. Then I noticed that a dark shape was flying around above us. It had wings so big that it blocked out the starlight everywhere it flew.

I guess you don't get anything good for free.

We still ran.

"Fifteen seconds," she said. "I think Rebirth is at the church. But the arming sequence needs to take place at the fairgrounds. There were artisanal spirits and all kinds of hand tools there. I'm sure you remember the spotlights."

Roxy was a lot more observant than me. While I was distracted by the statues, the NPCs, the festivities, and the pretty girl, Roxy had been scoping out weapons.

"Five seconds," she said.

I wasn't ready.

On-screen.

The thing in the sky swooped down above us. We slowed down and ducked so that it couldn't hurt us. It was a gargoyle—a big one, nearly twice the size of the others. Its wingspan was as long as a bus.

"Run!" I screamed.

We were running. It didn't matter.

The creature swooped by us again. If we didn't go off-screen soon . . .

It was too late. This was a kill sequence.

The flying creature was clearly after Roxy. It swooped by her and let out a claw that almost grazed her head.

"Tell Arthur I—"

The creature landed on top of her. Her status flicked to Dead in an instant.

CHAPTER FORTY

WHISPERS IN THE DARK

I froze.

The Grotesque wasn't facing me, but even then, its hideous features were terrifying. Its wings were big and leathery like a bat, and as it turned its head, I could see its long, jagged, needle-like teeth sticking out of its human face. I could only imagine what this thing had been before it got infected by the Grotesque curse.

With the death of Roxy, my Savvy shot up eleven points. Reggie's highest stat rose a few points as well. I don't know if I had a bigger jump because my character was closer to her or because I was at such a low level. Whatever the case, the Grotesque in front of us had its own change in Plot Armor with the death of Roxy.

This one's Plot Armor had been sixty-one. As soon as it landed, it dropped down to fifty-three. The 13 percent or so drop across all of its stats affected its Savvy to such a degree that, between my buff and its debuff, I was able to see a few more of its tropes.

GROTESQUE		
PLOT ARMOR: 53		
TROPES		
PROGENITOR	This creature has the ability to create duplicate offspring.	
WHISPERS IN THE DARK	This creature can sense a player's or NPC's vulnerabilities and manipulate them via impulsive thoughts that are perceived as whispers.	

HEAD OF THE SNAKE	The creature with the Head of the Snake trope is the Leader for the scene.
IT PLAYS WITH ITS FOOD	This creature spends time to toy with its victims. Often, it enjoys the playing more than the killing.
WHERE'S THE GOAT?	This creature can sneak up on players with implausible stealth but may not attack until the players notice some seemingly innocuous clue to its presence.
JEKYLL AND HYDE	This villain has multiple forms. Stone: Grit = 0, Living: Grit = 20.

One of the newly revealed tropes was called Whispers in the Dark. That explained how the NPC Donald had gotten wrapped up in all this. When he had dropped off the box at the lodge, he was speaking to the Grotesque. I was wondering how the Grotesque had been speaking to him if it was made of stone.

I had my answer.

The creature reared up and appeared to be howling, but of course, it couldn't speak and made no noise other than its poorly formed teeth grinding against each other as its mouth moved.

I took one last glance, trying to memorize the other new trope that this creature bore: Head of the Snake. That one must have been given to it because of Arthur's own trope, Cut the Head off the Snake. But the description had me concerned. It almost sounded like the Leader would be able to change in this story.

That's when it turned around and looked right at me.

Riley.

I heard my own name in my head. A whisper.

While I was transfixed, Reggie was far more prepared. He grabbed me and started to drag me backward across the graveyard. Eventually, I snapped out of whatever fear or fascination had afflicted me and turned to run with him.

Without Roxy, our movement was slow. Fortunately, the period just after First Blood is relatively safe. There needs to be a lull in action so that the characters can react to what has just happened.

It was also fortunate that, even though we had run what felt like miles across the cemetery, we were never that far from the church. Our entire chase scene occurred within walking distance of it. Carousel wouldn't care about that. It just needed good footage.

We ran back to the church. The flying Grotesque took back to the skies, but it didn't attack us. Pretty soon after we started running, we were off-screen again.

When we made it back to the church, I half expected it to be overwhelmed by Grotesques. However, as soon as we got there and opened the door, I could hear Arthur and Valerie talking. They were off-screen too. We must have been in between scenes.

As far as I could tell, they were planning out Valerie's character arc. For whatever reason, they were whispering. They stood at the back of the church where the priest would normally go. When they heard us come in, Arthur acknowledged us with a glance and Valerie waved.

I kept expecting us to go on-screen so that we could have an emotional reveal of Roxy's death, but it didn't happen. Even when we got all the way across the building to them, we were still off-screen.

"The next scene is in there," Valerie said when we approached, as if she had seen the confusion on my face. "I found Donald down there. You can hear him yelling."

Down where? I followed her gaze. There was a door at the back of the church. It had been covered up by a curtain, but the curtain had been moved back, and now I could see light flickering under the door frame. I could also hear Donald speaking faintly. It sounded like he was talking to himself.

"Where does that lead?" I asked.

"Catacombs," Valerie answered.

"I saw a couple more of the high-level Grotesque tropes," I said.

Arthur looked at me expectantly.

"It can talk to you in your mind and tempt you to do things."

"Well, that explains a little bit what's going on down there," he said.

"Probably a Savvy check?" Valerie said with a high inflection at the end, like she was looking for Arthur's input.

"Probably."

"There was also another trope," I said. "Head of the Snake. It said that the creature with that trope was the Leader for that scene. Is that how your Cut the Head off the Snake trope normally works?"

"For the scene?" Arthur looked away for a moment.

I think that threw him for a loop. It certainly had thrown me.

"No, that's not how it normally works," Arthur said. "That explains why Carousel's got you having a mysterious gift in this storyline. You have to identify which one is the Leader. Normally there's an obvious Leader, and killing it will end the story or open up an opportunity for you to escape, or something like that. Seems like Carousel had a different game in mind."

That made sense. It hadn't been clear exactly why my character needed on-screen psychic powers. By making me—one of the weakest players—a character that has to make it to the Finale, was I designed to be a burden to the rest of the team?

"Be ready to run up to us as you come on-screen," Valerie said.

"I know, I know," I said back.

Valerie and Arthur had their guns cocked and ready. Arthur opened the door to the catacombs and Valerie entered. Soon they were both down the stairs, and all I could hear were the echoes of their footsteps mixed with the whispers of Donald somewhere deep in the catacombs.

I sat and chatted with Reggie for a bit. He was explaining the technique they used to clear the bowling alley. Apparently, his sister Grace had come up with it. They had everything timed and planned out so that they could divert most of the Omens that come nearer the alley and easily clear any remaining storylines. He said that he would show us sometime.

Eventually, I heard loud voices coming up from the catacombs. I had trouble picturing exactly how big the underground must have been for it to have taken so long. Must have had a lot of rooms down there.

As time passed, I could hear Donald talking louder and louder.

"No, don't do it!" Donald screamed.

I could only imagine what he was asking Arthur and Valerie not to do.

"I have to finish. You don't understand! I have to finish."

Valerie and Arthur burst from the door with Donald hogtied. Arthur was carrying the man over his shoulder.

"My family shouldn't have to die too!" Donald screamed. "Don't you understand? There is no escaping."

Just as the door had started to open, we had shifted on-screen.

We ran toward Arthur and Valerie as if we had just burst into the church looking for them.

"Arthur!" I screamed. He glanced over at us; he was preoccupied with handling Donald.

He glanced back again.

"Where's Roxy?" he asked.

I couldn't find the words. Not just my character—I personally couldn't. How would you act in a situation like that?

"She . . ."

Arthur abandoned Donald and walked toward us. "Where is she?"

Reggie and I looked at each other.

"She was killed," I said.

Arthur didn't say anything at first. He walked to the nearest pew, and just as I thought he was about to turn and sit down, he kicked it, sending it flying backward and toppling.

"Why didn't you look after her?" he screamed. I didn't know if he was talking to me or Reggie. I suppose it didn't matter; it was for the audience.

Arthur was breathing heavily, and I could see him trying to cover up his tears—or cover up his lack thereof.

"Where is she?" he asked. He walked over to where he had left his duffel bag and started to unzip it to retrieve a firearm.

"Arthur," I said, "she's gone."

Still, he persisted, grabbing for a shotgun. He walked over to me and got in my face and asked, "Wasn't this the kind of thing we had you around for? To make sure things like this didn't happen?"

I had no answer.

"Arthur," Valerie said. She walked to him and hugged him. While they had their character moment, I didn't know what to do.

After a beat, Arthur calmed down.

"We have to finish this," he said resolutely. "That asshole has been manufacturing gargoyle statues down there. Hundreds." He looked over at Donald lying delirious on the floor. He was on him in a second. He lifted Donald up by his shirt collar and said, "Now you tell us everything. These things just killed the person I care about the most in the world. I don't have to tell you what happens if you don't talk."

Donald didn't react fully to what Arthur said, but talking was not a hard thing to get him to do. In fact, after a while, I was wondering if we could get him to shut up.

If I were to distill down everything that he said, most of which he repeated over and over again, this is it:

"If you know the world's ending—if you know the bad guy is going to win— doesn't it make sense to be on the winning side? Conventional notions of morality are for peacetime. But they have a war coming. They're going to kill us all. But if I help them, they'll spare me and my family. It wasn't an easy decision to make.

"When I first found the statue buried beneath the catacombs, I knew I had found something spectacular. I tried to resist. I really did. I tried burying it back, but then it wound up on my porch the next morning. I tried smashing it, but then it would show up again in a different statue. It even took over one of the statues on my front lawn. There was no escape. I had to help it."

"Why did it need your help?" Arthur asked. "If it can just infect new statues, what did it need you for?"

Donald didn't answer at first but instead grew a ghastly smile. For a moment, his sanity seemed to show through and a look of horror replaced the smile.

"Most of them are just too dumb," he said. "Vicious, terrible things." He raised his arms and showed the bite marks that littered them to emphasize his point. "They were too noticeable. The biggest weakness of the Grotesque."

What could that mean? The biggest weak—

And then I understood.

"Oh my God," I said.

Donald started to laugh.

"What?" Valerie asked.

"Motherfucker," Arthur said. He understood too.

"He's been helping to breed only smart ones," I said. "Culling all of the dumb ones before they can go attract attention."

"It was hopeless. We would all have died either way. At least this way those that will remain will be able to be lenient," Donald said. "To some."

Arthur punched him in the face, sending him flying backward onto the ground.

If you were to ask what the biggest weakness of a Grotesque was, the obvious answer would be the fact that it was completely vulnerable during the day in its stone form. A less obvious, but perhaps more intelligent, answer would be that Grotesques were weak because most of them were stupid. Most of the creatures I had seen so far on the red wallpaper had such low Savvy that I could see all their tropes. That low Savvy translated to being unintelligent, belligerent, and dangerous. That was good for killing a bunch of people, but it wasn't good in the long run. The stupid ones would attract attention from humans, and they would all be wiped out before they could ever have a chance to actually create the apocalypse they so clearly desired.

After all, only the smart ones had Progenitor—the ability to spread the curse.

Donald had been helping kill the ones that were too stupid so that all that would be left, at least initially, would be an army of intelligent Grotesques. All capable of spreading their curse, all intelligent enough to be discreet and to strike without detection. We must have stumbled onto this late in the game because they had already started spreading their curse en masse.

Noises started to come from outside. Skittering and scratching. I could hear the grinding of stones.

Donald didn't react all that much to being punched. In fact, he was smiling. As if he'd just been vindicated in his decision to join the Grotesques.

"He's here."

CHAPTER FORTY-ONE

EXTENDED ARMING SEQUENCE

We need to get out of here," Valerie said, grabbing Arthur's duffel and handing it to him. Arthur didn't put up a fight.

The four of us ran as fast as we could out of the church. We left Donald tied up. His Grotesque friends would need to rescue him. When we got to the door, Arthur had a shotgun up in case anything tried to stop us, but nothing did.

As we ran out into the courtyard of the church, we saw what had made the noise. The large, winged creature that had killed Roxy was up on the roof. It didn't attack us as we left. It probably didn't want to bring down a fight at that moment. It had to go in and spread its curse to all of the statues that Donald had been manufacturing in the basement.

Off-screen.

"The fairgrounds," I said. "Roxy said that the arming sequence should happen at the fairgrounds."

"Roxy would know," Arthur said.

The trip back to the fairgrounds took far longer without Roxy there with her Mystifying Geography trope. When we eventually started to get close, I noticed that something was wrong. Something was different. It was too quiet. The Ferris wheel was still running, but I couldn't tell if anyone was inside the seats.

The Grotesques had been here.

As we arrived, we were back on-screen.

"Oh my God," Valerie said. She raised her hands over her mouth and nose, evidence of the horror that she saw before her.

It had been a massacre.

Many of the festival goers had been able to escape but plenty hadn't. What remained of them was strewn about the fairgrounds.

"Just focus on the mission," Arthur said. "The entire town is going to be like this if we don't stop them."

"Arthur," I said, "I don't think we have to kill all of them. I think we only have to kill the Leader."

Arthur turned to me, "You think, or you know?"

I nodded my head slightly as if reassuring myself. "I know. When he killed . . . When we first saw him, I made a connection. I can't really explain it, but I saw his weakness. We kill him, they all die."

I had just made Arthur's Cut the Head off the Snake trope canon. The audience needed to know.

Off-screen.

"We'll set up over here by the spotlight," Arthur said. "Reggie, drag a table over here."

The spotlights were attached to their own unique trailer so that they could be hauled to different locations. They had a logo for a rental company, the same one the moving truck Travis had stolen had. They were powered by portable generators that stood next to them on the ground and ran on gasoline. A little boxy pickup truck was hooked up to one of the spotlights.

"Found the keys," Valerie said, after having fished them out of the pocket of one of the poor NPCs lying around us. The entire fairground smelled of blood.

"How long do we have till they're back?" Reggie asked.

Arthur shook his head. "Not long. It's too early for us to do the arming sequence, but we can still prep for it. We're probably going to have a wave of them here soon. I see you've got a weapon."

He was referring to the sledgehammer that Reggie had found.

"I also found these," he said, tossing three smaller hammers onto the table that he had just hauled over near the spotlight.

"During the arming sequence, we have to go see if we can find some supplies. Riley, grab that hammer and help me with this real quick," Arthur said.

On-screen.

"When I lift this up, I need you to break that bracket there," Arthur said. He hoisted the spotlight up. I took the hammer and, to the best of my ability, smashed a small metal bracket that was designed to keep the spotlight from swiveling independently of its motor.

"These things are weak to sunlight. I bet they're probably even weakened by the lights at the fairgrounds. This thing has got to do some damage. We're about to bet our lives on it. When they come, you have to aim for the stone portions of their skin. If you hit living flesh, you aren't going to do much, but the stone parts will crack."

He reached into his duffel and pulled out a handgun. He spun it around and then handed it to me, handle first.

"You think this is going to do anything against those big statues underneath the sheets at the church? You know those things are going to be alive the next time we see them," I said.

I had been waiting for some on-screen moment to make that prediction. I couldn't have done it when I told him that Roxy was dead; that wouldn't have made sense for my character to do at that moment.

"Try hitting that sign over there," he said, "right in the letter 'O.' Let us worry about the big ones."

I looked at where he was pointing. The sign read "staff only."

I took the gun.

Arthur started to instruct me. Don't hold the gun so tight but still hold it firm. Breathe out before you pull the trigger. Keep track of how it shoots so that you can adjust for the next shot. Always count how many shots you've taken, so you know when you have to reload.

This was intercut with me taking shots at the sign and missing most of them, but in the end, I actually managed to hit right in the middle of the O.

"You'll do fine," Arthur said.

Off-screen.

Before I knew it, I noticed that something new had appeared under my poster on the red wallpaper. I had a trope called Mind over Monster. Arthur had just taught it to me temporarily. That must have been how the Master and Apprentice trope worked.

"We're coming up on an attack," Valerie said. "I can feel it."

Arthur nodded. "Okay, none of us have to die here. We're still in the Rebirth phase. We just play this thing right, and we'll be fine." He talked like he was talking to everyone, but really, I think he was just talking to me.

I didn't know if they were going to try to sneak up on us all at once. They certainly had the tropes they needed to get that done, and so far, they hadn't used it very often. Maybe just knowing that they could sneak up on you was more unnerving than them actually doing it.

We had liberated another of the spotlights so that it could be aimed independently of its motor. Arthur was going to aim one; I would aim another. Valerie would have our backs with a shotgun.

And then there was Reggie. Reggie stood out in the middle of a clearing holding a sledgehammer in one hand and his flask in another.

On-screen.

It was time.

At first, all I heard were scratches. Then I heard thumps; they were knocking into things as they came from deeper in the fairgrounds where they had run chasing their victims.

And then they emerged.

"On the left!" Valerie cried out.

With all my might, I pivoted the spotlight over so that it shined to Reggie's left. The spotlight was so bright that it created a visible beam, a shaft of light that stood between him and anything that approached from the left. On his far side, he was protected by a brick building that might have been used for storage. On his right, he was protected by Arthur's spotlight.

The first gargoyle emerged. It was a small one that ran right through my beam of light, turned to stone, bounced off of Reggie's chest, and landed on the ground with a *crack*. Reggie was quick to bring down his sledgehammer and shatter it to pieces.

"Right!" Valerie said.

Another one, bigger this time, approached on the right. It jumped and nearly cleared the beam, but luckily, Arthur raised his light just in time to turn the gargoyle to stone.

Smash.

"Wooo!" Reggie screamed.

Again on the left, then on the right.

By the time the creatures could get to him, either all or most of their bodies had been turned to stone, and all Reggie had to do was shatter them. This was our plan to conserve ammunition, the one finite resource we had.

Even when one slipped through, hiding in the shadows of their stony brethren, Reggie's hammer was powerful enough to smack them back into a beam and then shatter them to dust.

Technically, the Grotesques were after me. I had the lowest Plot Armor. But they would have to get through Reggie in order to get to me the way we had set up our defense. Arthur made it clear that I had to survive to the Finale, so they had planned everything in order to make that possible.

"Up top!" Valerie screamed.

It was the terracotta soldier that Roxy and I had seen when we were here earlier.

The statue had originally had swords, but now those swords had fused into its arms. What's worse, this one was high level; it was one of the smart ones.

It jumped down from the roof right on top of Reggie.

I tried to move the spotlight fast enough to hit it before it got to him, but I just couldn't get the large light to budge in time.

Arthur was quicker. He got his light to move, but the damn thing was so smart it stayed on the other side of Reggie, using him as a shield.

Luckily, Reggie had designed his build around buffing his Mettle. Even with this thing's high level, Reggie was able to send it flying backward into the brick building with one swing of his sledgehammer. It was quick to return back to him, running at full speed, its blade arms ready for a strike, and its sharp teeth ready to tear into him.

And then Reggie did something that was far cleverer than his archetype would have you believe he was capable of.

He turned sideways.

He was a big guy, big enough to block out the light and keep the terracotta Grotesque from turning to stone. But once he turned sideways, both of the monster's arms got caught in the light and were unable to deliver the killing blow once it got to him.

As it neared, he grabbed onto it and snapped its arms off. He then swung his hammer and knocked it out into my beam of light. One more swing, and it broke to pieces. After that, the waves of Grotesques slowed down.

Eventually, the arming sequence started.

"We need some of that homemade liquor that you were telling us about," Valerie said.

I didn't exactly see where it was, but I was familiar enough with the area to be able to find it.

We got to work.

The Extended Arming Sequence trope that Arthur brought with him was a game-changer. An arming sequence can't get interrupted typically, so we spent the next forty minutes or so assembling Molotov cocktails and preparing for our assault on the church.

As the needle on the Plot Cycle tipped closer and closer toward Second Blood, Arthur and Reggie would make regular eye contact. Reggie seemed to be asking him a question nonverbally. Arthur would signal him, "Not yet."

I knew what they were talking about.

It was time for another sacrifice play.

When my friends and I had played through our storylines, we always just accepted whatever First or Second Blood came to us. The veterans went out of their way to choose when, where, and how First and Second Blood would occur.

One last time, Reggie looked at Arthur asking his silent question. This time, Arthur nodded.

Reggie took out his flask and swallowed a drink.

On-screen.

"I'm going to go see if there's a concession stand," he said. "My blood sugar's getting low."

"Stay close," Arthur said.

Reggie took a drink out of his flask and raised his other hand into a thumbs-up. He started walking away from the rest of us, drinking excessively as he went. He started to stumble as he walked, to lean on things.

As he got farther away, I could see his Plot Armor had started to drop.

* * *

We worked in silence finishing up our preparations and loading them into the back of the truck. Then it was time.

On-screen.

"Where's Reggie?" Valerie asked. "Have you guys seen him?"

As if right on cue, a scream echoed through the fairgrounds.

We all grabbed our guns and ran toward the sound. When we got there, I was horrified by what I saw.

The figurines from the shop where Roxy had bought me the frog had all been transformed. They, plus a few regular-sized Grotesques, had managed to take down Reggie. However, they hadn't killed him. They just continued to bite and claw at him without any clear strategy to end his suffering.

I didn't have to fake the horrified look on my face.

When Reggie saw us, he yelled, "Help me!"

But it was too late to help.

Arthur removed his gun from his belt. Reggie saw.

"Just do it," he struggled to say.

Arthur aimed the gun at his head and shot him. Valerie threw a Molotov at the creatures. They were all doused. We spent a few minutes destroying them with hammers off-screen.

In the story, Reggie's character had gotten so drunk that the creatures had been able to get the drop on him. In real life, Reggie had pretended to be so drunk that his Totally Wasted trope activated, and his Plot Armor dropped down below mine. He pretended to be so wasted he couldn't help himself when attacked. What kind of self-control must it have taken to do that?

It really did take a special kind of person to survive in Carousel.

With that, Second Blood had been spilled.

Reggie's flask lay next to his body. It had been shredded open and its remaining contents leaked out onto the concrete next to him.

As I stared at it, I noticed something strange. I could see little ripples being created in the peach tea that had puddled up. Little concentric circles appeared rhythmically in the liquid.

Pound. Ripple. *Pound.* Ripple.

CHAPTER FORTY-TWO

GO. FASTER.

Valerie must have followed my gaze and seen the ripples in the puddle.

"We have to get out of here now," she said. "Run!"

We started running before we even knew what was chasing us. By the time we were halfway back to the truck, that had become clear.

I glanced back over my shoulder and saw booths and carnival games flying through the air behind us. As the dust settled, I tried to make sense of the chaos around me. My eyes were drawn to a towering figure in the distance.

It had been a thirty-foot-tall statue of a man, but now it was something else entirely—a monstrous gargoyle, with malformed wings that stretched outwards as if trying to attain flight, if only they were able. I could see the pain etched into its human face, twisted into an agonized grimace. Its long, pointed teeth gleamed menacingly in the low light, and its claws were too long for its hands. It moved like it was roaring, but no sound came out.

It was the statue of Bartholomew Geist, Carousel's supposed founder, in the flesh.

Now a Grotesque. Plot Armor: 48.

As I watched in horror, the Grotesque stepped forward, its massive form casting a shadow in the starlight. Its eyes seemed to glow with an otherworldly fire, and I could feel the ground tremble beneath my feet as it moved. The stench of death and decay filled my nostrils as the creature flapped its useless wings. I could feel my heart pounding in my chest.

In the face of such a monster, I felt powerless.

As I watched it destroy everything in its path, I couldn't help but wonder if there was anything that could stop it. All I could do was hope that we would survive long enough to figure it out. Survival was possible—only just—thanks to

Reggie's sacrifice. Second Blood had passed. None of us *had* to die in this scene . . . But how would we get away?

Valerie tried to light another of the Molotov cocktails. She handed it to Arthur in hopes that he would be able to do more with it than she could. As the creature approached us, its thunderous footsteps and the claws that had replaced its hands created chasms in the earth.

The Molotov cocktail landed on one of its feet. Arthur fired his gun and managed to chip off a section of stone on its foot that had been solidified. He might as well have done nothing. The giant statue didn't notice.

"Drive," Valerie said, tossing me the keys that she had found.

As we approached the spotlight and truck, Arthur said to Valerie, "Help me get the generator in the back of the truck."

I jumped into the driver's seat. I wasn't a good choice to drive, but I was a bad choice for any part of this story.

Valerie and Arthur hoisted the generator up into the back of the truck. Valerie got up in the back with it and started rifling through Arthur's guns before finding his large shotgun. I waited to see where Arthur was going to ride, but he never came around to the cab, nor did he jump up in the back of the truck before Valerie smacked the roof and yelled, "Go! Go! Go!"

I floored it.

The little truck was not designed to go fast. I tried to coax every single ounce of speed out of it as I guided the truck up onto the road. I still didn't know where Arthur was.

Until I heard him screaming.

I saw the spotlight moving around behind us. Arthur was lying down on the small trailer that the spotlight was attached to. He was aiming the light.

It took only seconds for the creature to catch us. If you watched it move, it looked like it was very slowly lumbering about. However, it was moving at an incredible speed because of its long limbs. It started chasing us down the road.

It was hard to focus on driving when I was so concerned about that thing following us. I floored the little truck, but this wasn't a performance model. It was designed to be fuel efficient.

In the bed of the truck, Valerie was letting off shots left and right. Every time Arthur would turn part of the creature to stone, she would try to get a hit in. At first, I thought she was wasting ammo, but then I realized she had a plan.

The road between the fairgrounds and the church was curvy. Getting a straight shot on the creature was therefore very difficult because as we went around a curve, Arthur had to try to steer the light and keep it on the creature.

As fast as I could drive, the Grotesque was gaining on us.

"Go. Faster," Arthur said very loudly and very sternly from behind me.

The creature was reaching out to the spotlight trailer, coming within mere feet of destroying it, right along with Arthur.

"It doesn't go faster!" I yelled back.

After a moment or two to think, Arthur responded, "Slow down."

Why the fuck would I want to do that?

But I did. He had a high Savvy, and if he had a plan, I was more than willing to see if it could work out. I slowed down a hair. I tried to keep an eye in the rearview mirror to see what it was he was doing. Previously, he had kept shining the light in the creature's face, hoping to blind it or, at the very least, keep it from biting into us.

Now he was aiming for the legs.

Genius.

I slowed down even more. The limbs were a tough target.

Boom. Boom. Boom.

Its footsteps were louder and louder as I slowed down. Arthur's plan had better work.

Arthur was trying to get the large spotlight trained on the Grotesque's legs. He was focusing on its calves and feet. It was taking too long; the creature was moving its limbs so fast that the light couldn't rest on them long enough for the entire limb to turn to stone.

Arthur needed to get the timing right.

We were careening around corners. Arthur was trying to keep the light on target. I tried keeping the truck as steady as possible for him, but there wasn't much I could do. As we rounded a large curve, Arthur managed to keep the light on the creature's left leg for two, three seconds. Then five seconds.

The creature lumbered after us, swiping its long claws forward.

Seven seconds.

Crack.

Arthur must have successfully turned one of its legs to stone because I heard something break, followed by a sound that I could only describe as "unscheduled demolition of building."

The creature had fallen.

In my rearview mirror, I saw that one of its legs had snapped off.

Turning it to stone and shooting it wouldn't easily work on something this size, but if you could turn one of its limbs to stone and then wait for it to try to put weight on it, you could use the creature's own weight against it, causing it to break itself.

The creature pursued us now on all fours—well, threes—trying to compensate for its broken limb. It would be harder for that tactic to work again now that its weight was more evenly distributed among its three limbs and one partial leg.

Still, Arthur kept at it.

Crack.

Three of the creature's fingers broke off. Somehow, with the pressure that was placed on them, one of them actually jumped into the air and overtook the car, landing on the road in front of me.

Meanwhile, Valerie had spent at least ten shots. I wasn't sure how much ammo she even had for that gun. I got the sense that she was trying to get down to the last bullet.

We had a huge advantage when cornering now because of its destroyed limbs. I took the initiative and sped up a little, hoping to give us a little time for the next tactic. After a few more bends, the church was right up ahead; we only had a few hundred more yards before we had to turn. I didn't know what would happen if this thing was still alive when we got to the church, but I had a feeling it would tear the place down looking for us.

Eventually, Valerie announced the phrase that I'd been waiting for her to say for most of the drive.

"I've only got one slug left!" she said.

I slowed down. It might not have been enough for the audience to tell, but I'm sure that Arthur and Valerie could. In the rearview mirror, I saw Arthur aiming his spotlight up at the creature's face.

"Better make it count!" he yelled.

As the creature's face turned to stone, Valerie took aim and fired her last shotgun shell. The round entered the creature's mouth and exited out the back of its neck, creating a profound crack and an explosion. The remaining tissue was not strong enough to hold up the weight of the head. It snapped off and fell to the ground, smashing against the concrete. The giant's body convulsed and twitched as it lay on the ground, but it was killed.

Valerie's Better Make It Count trope had given her a critical hit with her final round.

After the worst drive of my life, I turned at the church's entrance. Behind me, Arthur had somehow managed to turn the spotlight around and aim it up ahead at the top of the church.

The large, winged creature that had been there was gone.

Before we got too close to the church, I spun the wheel so that I could turn the entire truck around and have the spotlight in range to aim at the door of the building. As we arrived, dozens of Grotesques burst from the door ready to come for us. The spotlight created a roadblock. As much as they struggled to come forward, they could never push beyond the pile of petrified gargoyles that built up in front of them.

That wasn't a huge relief.

Because we were about to go into that building.

CHAPTER FORTY-THREE

NOT-SO-DIVINE HEALING

The very moment we stepped out of the truck we were in a fight.

Even with the spotlight aimed at the door to prevent the Grotesques inside from pouring out, there were still those coming from the graveyard around us. There were dozens of them.

I had a hammer in each hand. My gun wouldn't do me much good here. I needed to make every hit count because even with the buffs I had gotten, and even with Arthur sharing his Mind over Monster trope, I had to hit them in just the right spot to get them to go down. If I hit living flesh, they wouldn't even react. And that's not even to mention that my abysmal Hustle meant I couldn't hit anything that wasn't at point-blank range.

Arthur and Valerie stuck with guns.

With Arthur's shotgun depleted of ammo, they were down to handguns and one semiautomatic rifle, but they were both capable shots. They also still had the flare gun, but that wasn't much good in a brawl like this.

The beam of light from the spotlight created a safe pathway for us as we ran to the church. Arthur carried his duffel full of Molotovs and guns. The trouble was we were standing in the very light that kept the horde from pouring out of the building toward us. Fortunately, it took longer for the gargoyles to reanimate than it did for them to turn to stone in the first place. We had a window of seconds to kill them before they could kill us.

As we were attacked from the sides, we would wait until the creatures got close enough to us to start to solidify.

A small gargoyle attacked me from the left.

Smack.

No good. I hit living flesh.

Crack.

My second hammer found stone and smashed it to pieces.

Luckily whenever Donald was mass producing these things, he had created them to be quite small. That made sense: he didn't want to create a bunch of large, powerful, stupid ones. It was more logical for him to create lots of small ones. The small, intelligent ones would still be able to spread the Grotesque curse. Most of them were only about the size of a terrier or a bobcat.

The thing was these weren't the intelligent ones. In fact, I hadn't seen any intelligent Grotesques since we had pulled up. One or two of the creatures were almost human-sized. Luckily, intelligence didn't appear to correlate with size. Some of the big ones were so stupid they would step right into the light just to get mowed down with a single shot or strike from my hammer.

None of the creatures thought to attack the light.

"Move!" Arthur said. We needed to make our way to the door. Though that was the last place I wanted to be.

When we finally got to the building, it was like shooting fish in a barrel, as most of the gargoyles in this area had been frozen to stone by the spotlight and then had gotten tangled up with each other as they struggled to get through the door.

Shattering them was easy. As soon as they were moved out of the way, more would come out, get turned to stone, and get shattered.

We still hadn't found the smart ones. They must have been in the catacombs where we were heading. If only we could have taken the spotlight with us. We almost made it inside without a single injury. I didn't even see where the Grotesque came from.

I felt it though.

Its long, thin, jagged fangs sank into my right leg. I could feel its teeth against my bone, crushing, crunching.

I was down and screaming before I even knew what got me.

"Arthur," Valerie said. "Watch my back."

She pulled out a small hammer. She got right down next to me and lifted my leg up so that the creature attached to me would be exposed to the spotlight. Then she brought the hammer down on its head.

That was the most excruciating pain I had ever been in in my life. When she broke its head open, the force of the blow sank the creature's teeth back into the wounds they had just created, nearly causing me to faint. Its teeth were thin and snapped off when she struck it.

She retrieved a first aid kit from her purse. She began wrapping my leg in gauze or fabric, or whatever the stuff was called. Some type of field dressing or bandage.

"You're lucky none of these were deep," she said. "We need to leave them in there, so you don't bleed out. You should have full mobility for now."

Bullshit. One of her tropes allowed her to partially heal an injury by down-playing how serious it was to the audience.

She grabbed a small, round, pill-sized object from her purse and handed it to me. "This will help with the pain."

I dropped it in my mouth. It was a candy-coated piece of chocolate.

Regardless, the pain did ease almost immediately. I was able to move my leg again. I could even stand. Valerie's collection of healing tropes allowed us to just pretend I wasn't horrifically injured. Despite the damage, I didn't even have a Hobbled status. And yet I knew that under those bandages, my leg was irreparably destroyed and my bone snapped.

Healing magic was very weird in Carousel.

Something else haunted me about this. I knew that all of the healing tropes Valerie had just used on me were temporary. Soon I would be feeling the full effects of the injury I had just received. That fact was on my mind with every step.

Even with me out of commission, Valerie and Arthur were able to clear the Grotesques coming from the cemetery around us.

"This isn't enough," Arthur said. "There should be more of them."

We were on-screen, so I didn't know if that was his character talking or Arthur himself, but either way I agreed. The way they talked about it, Donald had been down below in the catacombs making hundreds of these creatures. Thousands.

Was it really possible that he had destroyed so many in his quest to create intelligent Grotesques that we were only met with a few dozen?

"We didn't explore the whole catacombs," Valerie suggested. She had begun trying to break away the now lifeless stone limbs of the Grotesques that blocked the doorway. I did my best to help. Walking on a leg that was destroyed and held together with only a bandage and magic was very difficult to get used to.

Arthur scanned the skies, hoping that he could find some explanation for the hundreds of missing gargoyles by looking there. They weren't there either.

"Where are the smart ones?" he pondered aloud.

After a couple of minutes, we broke through the barricade and were back in the church. It looked like my prediction about the statues underneath the white sheet was right. They were long gone.

"Oh, God," Valerie said. She was looking up ahead toward the back of the church. At first, I couldn't tell what it was she was looking at, but then I saw him.

We had left Donald tied up; we hadn't really had time to untie him the last time we were here. He was still lying on his stomach, hands and feet bound.

What was left of him, at least.

It turned out that the Grotesques he had helped to create hadn't been so keen on sparing him after all. As we approached cautiously, we noted that

Donald's arms, legs, and much of his torso had been attacked viciously with tooth and claw. I couldn't even make out distinct bite marks, there were so many of them.

As we got close, Arthur nudged him with his foot.

He let out a painful groan.

He was still alive.

Arthur bent down next to him and tried turning him over onto his side so that he could look at him. The man was in terrible shape.

"Where's the army?" Arthur asked. "Where are all these intelligent Grotesques that you helped make? Where's the fight?"

I could see Donald's lips moving like he was trying to talk. Whatever was left of his consciousness was fading quickly.

Arthur grabbed him by the hair and pulled him upward.

"Where is this apocalypse you were talking about?"

Donald said something, but it was too quiet for me to hear. Arthur put his ear close so that he could try to make out what it was Donald was saying.

"He's saying . . . 'everywhere.'"

Arthur dropped the man back down.

"We have to find that main Grotesque that you were talking about," he said.

"Why? What does 'everywhere' mean?" Valerie asked.

The truth was that Valerie already knew. We all did. We just had to tell the audience.

"He already sent them out," I said.

Arthur made eye contact with me with a subtle nod, confirming my suspicion.

Donald had already sent out all of the intelligent Grotesques. They were probably in similar packaging to what Janet had received. That was the plan. There weren't going to be huge swarms of intelligent Grotesques at the church. He had mailed them out—hundreds of them.

"You mean . . . ," Valerie said.

"People are dying right now. Everywhere he sent those things," Arthur said. He looked at me. "You better be right about this."

I nodded.

At that moment I received an urge that was becoming all too familiar. The story was putting words in my mouth. There was something I needed to say as much as I dreaded to say it.

"Those statues under the white sheets are gone," I said quietly. We had noticed at the moment we got there, but our characters hadn't.

There was a noise above us. The high ceilings of the church were perfect for concealing the types of enemies we faced—the ones that could fly. Through their Where's the Goat? trope, they had remained hidden from us until I noticed that the statues were gone.

Above us, half a dozen flying Grotesques—from the size of a dog, all the way up to bigger than a man—began gliding down in a swarm of teeth and claws.

"Into the catacombs," Arthur commanded.

We ran back to the door that had once been concealed behind a large curtain. Valerie opened it and Arthur beckoned me forward. I ran as fast as I could.

Not fast enough.

A Grotesque tackled me before I could make it through the door. Unlike the first one I had dealt with earlier that day, this one was actually trying to kill *me*. In a matter of seconds, its claws had dug into my stomach and my chest, up near where my collarbone was. The pain was immeasurable.

I wasn't able to look down. I thought my collarbone was broken, maybe even downright slashed in two, and that movement was too painful for my body to let me do it. If I were to guess, I would say that the injury was severe. Fatal.

Arthur was quick to pounce on the Grotesque. He drove it off of me with the heel of his boot and then fired a few good shots at it. Even in its living flesh form, it couldn't take that many shots from Arthur at such a close range. It jumped back into the air and flew off.

I couldn't move.

Arthur grabbed my hand and began pulling me back toward the door to the catacombs.

I'm not proud to say it, but in my panic and pain, I looked up at Arthur and said, "Do it. Finish me." I gestured toward his firearm. My speech was slurred, difficult. Every movement of my jaw sent shockwaves down into my chest. I was bleeding profusely.

In my defense, I think that his Mercy Kill trope influenced me to say that. I was fatally wounded and in great pain. The words just came out.

Arthur looked down at me. I think I saw pity in his eyes for a moment. Only a moment.

"Can't let you go yet. Still need your gift."

He dragged me through the door, and Valerie pulled it shut behind him.

CHAPTER FORTY-FOUR

THE GROTESQUE ANGEL

Barely missed an artery," Valerie said. She was trying her best to pretend that the injury I had just sustained wasn't going to kill me. "You'll need to take it easy. Looks like you're not going to be a part of this fight. I can patch you up, but you're going to need stitches after this. A whole lot of stitches."

Her voice shook a couple of times during that speech. Her trope required her to pretend that my prognosis was good. That, combined with covering up the injuries, allowed me to continue. It's the same thing that happened with my leg outside. She used up the rest of the bandage material just trying to hide my enormous gashes from view.

Arthur watched on with a gun raised, ready to fight anything that broke through the door and followed us, but the door held. Eventually, we stopped hearing bangs against it. The Grotesques on the other side must have found something else to distract themselves with.

Maybe it was Donald.

"You should be able to stand, but don't run. Don't want to get your blood pressure up. I really don't want to do this because you just had one, but what the hell," Valerie said, handing me another one of her pretend pain relievers.

I swallowed it whole.

As before, it worked. It took the edge off my pain.

Off-screen.

"You don't have long," Valerie said. "Even at my best, I can't hold off a fatal wound for more than a scene or two."

Arthur sprang into action. He reached down and grabbed me by the arm and pulled me up onto my feet.

"We need you to identify this creature on-screen, and then you can die," he said.

The way he said it was like he thought I actually wanted to die, but he wasn't going to let me until my shift was over. Standing there—broken leg, broken collarbone—I think I had been disemboweled and was bleeding out. And yet none of that was true because the audience was told it hadn't happened. I felt like I needed to throw up. This was unnatural.

"Let's go," I said.

The catacombs were massive. The chamber that we walked into when we went down the stairs was at least the same size as the church above. Tunnels branched off in multiple directions. It wasn't clear which way we needed to go. The place was dark and damp. Arthur had brought a flashlight in his duffel; he aimed it around the room.

The place was littered with molds for casting statues. Donald had used them to build new Grotesques. He must have been at this for weeks. Hundreds of bags of concrete lay empty and strewn about. Around them, hundreds upon hundreds of shattered Grotesques were stacked up in the corners of the room. Donald must have just smashed them with a hammer any time they came out stupid and violent instead of smart and cunning.

On-screen.

"So, this is where he made them?" I asked. My character was the only one that hadn't been down here.

"Ground zero of the apocalypse," Arthur responded.

We walked around the room getting a sense of things, allowing the camera to get shots of us taking everything in.

With every step I took, I knew I was on borrowed time. We needed to get to the final battle soon. Luckily the needle on the Plot Cycle seemed to be on our side. It was coming fast.

"Stay here. Be careful. Wait for us to come back," Arthur said. He pulled another flashlight from his duffel and held it out toward me.

I shook my head. "Give it to Valerie. She needs it more."

We made eye contact, and I think he understood.

I was safer in the dark. I was safer when I couldn't see what was trying to get me.

Valerie and Arthur went off to separate tunnels stating that they would go for five minutes and then turn around. That way they could systematically check every tunnel. If one of them didn't come back, the other would go searching.

I would just kind of stand there and try not to die until I had told one of them which Grotesque was the Leader.

Fortunately, whenever we got attacked in the church, I had been able to buff both Valerie and Arthur because of my prediction that the creatures underneath the white sheets would come to life. It wasn't much, but a little Grit and Savvy could go a long way in their hands.

When they left, I stayed on-screen. That had to be the most ominous thing possible. I kept expecting to go off-screen as the camera watched them explore.

It didn't happen.

I had leaned myself against the wall. Given what I thought was about to happen, I started to walk around and examine the room more in the dim lighting that seeped in under the door upstairs.

As my eyes adjusted, I saw them. They came creeping out of one of the tunnels one at a time. I hadn't used Oblivious Bystander in near darkness like this.

As I walked around, six or seven Grotesques of various shapes and sizes started to disperse around the room. I needed to stay oblivious to all of them. I spread out my hands to help me guide myself. I blinked my eyes in an exaggerated way to show exactly how blind I was. I even tried to incorporate a little of the "I'm in so much pain that I can't tell what's going on" thing that I did with Ranger Danger.

The Grotesques moved around, crossing my path, following me. They were silent for the most part, only making the faintest trace of noise.

I started to breathe loudly; I gave myself a cough—anything to explain why I couldn't hear the scratches on the ground around me. Coughing felt excruciating, even with Valerie's magic pain pill.

Still, I powered through.

I only had to wait five minutes. If I knew movies, and I did know movies, the tunnel that these creatures had just come out of would be the one we needed to go down. I needed to relay that information to Arthur.

As I walked along, I was heading straight for a table that Donald had been working at. There was a row of busted Grotesques on that table. At the far end of that row, one of the small live Grotesques had crawled into place next to the broken ones.

Dammit. Carousel wanted *that* scene.

Everything was lined up. Part of the price of using Oblivious Bystander was that I had to make it entertaining. It was strange using a mostly comedic trope so near the climax of an action movie like this, but here we were. I had almost thought that Carousel wouldn't give me a chance to use it at all.

I walked along the desk, my hand feeling among the broken Grotesques. I made my way slowly. As I went along, I could almost feel the camera following me, the tension rising in the audience as they thought I was about to touch one of the living Grotesques.

There were seven broken Grotesques ending in an eighth that was alive. I made my way past the first, the second, all the way on to the fifth and sixth.

Just as I got to the end of the table, and was almost to the live Grotesque, I stopped. I had heard a noise coming from the tunnel that Arthur had entered. I could see a faint flash of light.

I looked behind myself. "Arthur?"

When I turned back, the creature wasn't there anymore.

How would my character react to this? It was the setup for their Where's the Goat? trope. Could I be oblivious to it? Or did I need to react to be realistic?

As was my way, I ignored it.

I could hear Arthur and Valerie coming back into the main room. I turned to greet them, knowing full well that the creature was somewhere behind me.

Bang!

Arthur had drawn his gun and shot something behind me. I turned to look. It was the Grotesque that had been trying to jump-scare me. The point goes to the Oblivious Bystander.

"Didn't I tell you to be careful?" Arthur said.

"I could have taken him," I responded.

Arthur rolled his eyes; he shone the flashlight around the room just in time to watch the gargoyles that had entered slink back into the tunnel they had come from.

Arthur had the same idea I did.

"Let's go get them," he said.

As we followed them along the tunnel, the temporary part of Valerie's temporary healing job was starting to rear its ugly head. Not only were my bandages literally starting to come off, but I could feel the pain starting to return. We couldn't exactly run; we needed to be cautious. Even still, every time my right foot hit the ground, I wondered if my leg was going to snap.

As we moved forward, Arthur handed me the duffel bag. It wasn't ideal, but he needed to be ready to fight, and I wasn't going to be able to do that.

"When we need fire," he said, "light one of the Molotovs and hand it to us."

The duffel was heavy. We had managed to make fifteen or so of the fire-bombs. I only hoped that it would be enough.

Eventually, the tunnel broke out into another large room, even bigger than the first one.

Riley, you came back. I didn't take you for brave.

The Leader was back in my mind. Whispering in the dark.

"He's talking to me," I said.

"I assume he's not surrendering," Arthur said.

"No luck there."

You're too late. My children have spread to the far shores. My brothers will rise. For millennia we have tried and now we succeed. Lay down your arms, and you will be spared. I promise.

He must have thought I was really gullible. He had somehow forgotten to spare Donald for all of his efforts. Perhaps he just didn't have control over his more violent offspring.

I didn't know where the voice was coming from at first, but then I heard the swish of air above us. I saw the starlight. The room's roof was raw stone like you might see in a cavern. There was a small opening at the top. Just a pinprick really. The Grotesques that could fly were up there scraping at the hole trying to form an exit.

I looked around the room as my eyes adjusted to the starlight.

Down a set of steps from where we were standing were dozens and dozens of stone statues. These ones were larger than the ones we had seen. They all had wings.

One of the Grotesques was going along the lines and awakening the statues with his awkward, terrifying kiss. The statue would come to life with a *crack* of stone, as its features deformed and became more demonic. It would take flight and join those up above.

I looked for the Leader. Eventually, I saw him. He was flying in the air, a part of the swarm above us. It wasn't the exact same gargoyle that I had seen earlier. That one had been more animalistic. The statue that he inhabited now was far more humanoid. In fact, I think it had once been an angel.

"He's the one with the feathered wings," I said. The rest had bat-like wings; the one who had Head of the Snake as a trope didn't.

Arthur came over to me and unzipped his duffel. He retrieved from it the flare gun that he had brought, along with three extra cartridges. The Molotov cocktails wouldn't do us much good unless we could get these things on the ground fighting us.

He held out his hand. I grabbed one of the Molotov cocktails and lit it. He threw it out onto the floor on the level beneath us. He hit the Grotesque that had been waking the statues.

After it was on fire, Valerie was able to get a few clean shots off and break off a large portion of its head. She was also able to kill the statue that had just woken up, which had also gotten covered in fire.

With that, the fight was on.

Not for me. Blood had started to rise up in my throat. I spit it out on the ground. Valerie's healing trope was about spent. I dropped to the ground, more because sitting down was too difficult than because I couldn't stand.

The seams were starting to come apart, fast. I leaned up against a wall near the entrance.

Arthur shot a flare at one of the flying gargoyles. As soon as it hit, one of the creature's wings turned to stone, and it fell to the ground with a crash. It stopped moving, so I assumed that was a kill shot.

With that, a couple of the flying Grotesques came down to swipe at them.

"Molotov," Arthur said. When I wasn't there to hand it to him, he looked back and saw what kind of shape I was in. He ran over and grabbed his bag and dragged it away from me so that he would have access to it. In the process, several of the bottles of alcohol rolled out onto the ground.

I had to stay alive. As long as I was alive the Grotesques would attack me, giving Valerie and Arthur the chance to finish this.

Arthur lit a Molotov and doused one of the flying Grotesques as it approached him from the air. It suffered a similar fate as the one before, losing the ability to fly and careening into a stone wall before shattering.

Pointless. All pointless.

The voice of the Leader echoed in my head. He might be right. The gargoyles up at the top were carving their way through to the outside world. Once they escaped, that was it. We would lose.

Arthur took another shot with the flare. This time he missed, only turning one of the gargoyle's arms to stone. Not enough.

Just under a dozen creatures remained, unless one of them wanted to go down and start waking up the statues beneath. Those that weren't clawing their way through the opening were swarming around like wasps in a huge circle. It wasn't that there were a ton of them, but they were moving so quickly that it was hard to tell which one was the Leader, even though he looked different.

You cannot resist me. I can see your heart's desire. You do not want to be here.

No shit.

Arthur fired off one more round from the flare gun. This one hit one of the Grotesques near the Leader. It went down.

"One flare left," Arthur said. He handed the flare gun to Valerie. "Better make it count."

Then, after having attempted to evade for so long, the circling Grotesques changed tactics. They started to attack.

One after another, they divebombed Arthur and Valerie, preventing Valerie from getting a critical hit against the Leader because of her Better Make It Count trope.

Arthur did his best to hit them with a Molotov and break them when they got close. It was made difficult because after burning one, he had to get ready for the next before he could take the first one out.

All the while, the Leader hid behind his brethren.

The Leader of the Grotesques was a terrifying creature. I didn't know if there was normally a Leader for this storyline, or if this creature had been crafted specifically because Arthur had brought his Cut the Head off the Snake trope.

What I can say is that this creature did have one defining weakness, even at night when it was living flesh and virtually unstoppable. It hated being ignored.

It had been speaking to me off and on all fight. I had mostly not been paying attention. Part of that was because I was dying. The other part was because enemy monologues do start to all sound alike.

Ever since it began whispering to me, I could feel an urgency pick up in its voice. The longer I went without responding, the more frustrated the voice became. At first, it was like he was trying to be friends with me, but now I could feel his rage.

Humans believe that they are superior. They build altars for gods. But whose image do they adorn them with? Mine. Could there be any greater evidence of what you truly fear? Come now. Join me, serve me, and I will spare you.

A monster with a god complex. I thought only humans could have one of those.

I will not be ignored. Pledge your service to me or face my wrath.

Riley, the Leader continued, *take your weapon and kill your comrades and you will live. You were always better off alone. Would you even be in this hellish place if you hadn't been dragged here by those who claimed to care for you?*

The joke was on him. I wasn't even sure that I could kill Arthur and Valerie with my gun. I didn't know how the stat matchup worked with friendly fire. I assumed that the audience could hear him tempting me, so I had to play it up as if it might be working.

I kept a hand on my gun and held it out, though not all the way toward Arthur—I needed to show that I was struggling with the decision. In a way I was. I could feel the temptation to succumb, to betray those around me. It was just so distant behind the pain.

I dropped the gun and let it rest on the ground.

Even as Arthur and Valerie were shooting them in the sky, I could see the Leader continuously trying to look at me. I was the target, after all—my low Plot Armor demanded it.

At that moment, I realized that Arthur and Valerie had a real chance to lose. The way they were fighting, they were attempting to keep me alive in case the Head of the Snake was passed to a different Grotesque. They had all worked to keep me alive. Not because I deserved it, or because they cared about me living, but because the way the story was set up, me being alive was the only way to get to the end.

I thought about Roxy, who had died first, and Reggie, who had voluntarily lowered his Plot Armor so that he would be targeted instead of me.

For so long, all I could think about was finding a way to live until the end of the story. I didn't want to die. That was the motivation that steered every action I took.

As I lay there, a plan started to form in my mind. A plan that could help Arthur and Valerie end the story. But it would only work if I was taken out of the picture.

"I will not help you!" I screamed defiantly. Blood choked me as I spoke, but I screamed through it.

That did it. I had its attention.

The Grotesque Leader stopped flitting around in the air with his brethren and made a beeline for me. He pounced on me, landing on my leg and crushing my knee. He drove one claw into my stomach—undoing whatever positive effect Valerie's healing had done—releasing my wounds from their bandages and putting me further on my path toward death.

If I was going to die, I would die executing one last plan. Roxy had died to buff my Savvy, after all. Seemed a shame to waste it. I only hoped that my death would be a good death, that it would give Arthur and Valerie a shot.

I reached out toward the Molotov cocktails that had fallen out of the duffel and grabbed one of the bottles. I grabbed onto one of the creature's horns and drove the bottle over his head, smashing the glass. Flammable liquor poured over his torso and flooded down onto me.

After that, I was done. I had nothing left in my body to fight with.

Pop!

I heard a noise to my right, like a firework.

In the corner of my eye, I saw a bright-orange fireball.

My entire body erupted in pain. I hadn't thought that I could be any more injured, but this agony was something new. I wasn't numb to it.

I was on fire.

But so was the Grotesque.

Bang! Bang!

Gunfire continued to ring out, this time much closer to me. I couldn't tell if they had managed to kill the Grotesque. I was too preoccupied with my own hellish existence.

You fool! You worthless—

The Grotesque was speaking to me, but I couldn't hear most of what it was saying. It sounded like it was in pain too.

All I could think about was hoping that my pain would end.

After what felt like an eternity, it finally did.

Bang.

The pain stopped. All went dark. I died.

CHAPTER FORTY-FIVE

REWARDS TO DIE FOR

I opened my eyes.

It was daylight outside. Late evening perhaps. I could see the sun poking down through the hole at the top of the cavern.

I raised my head. I was alone. Arthur and Valerie were gone. The giant Grotesque Leader wasn't there either, though I suspect that I saw pieces of him lying here and there.

I looked down at my body. No bandages, no wounds. I was wearing my hoodie again. My sunglasses were in my pocket.

I tried to stand up, but my body shook. I could still feel the fire on my skin. I wondered if I'd ever forget.

It took me a few minutes to bring myself to a standing position. I tried to remember how it was we had gotten here and where I needed to be at that very moment.

It was then that I realized that the Plot Cycle was stuck at The End. We had succeeded. They had succeeded—Valerie and Arthur. Had I even made it to the end?

I suspected not.

All I remembered was intense pain. Then a gunshot, and it was over. I shuddered to even think about it.

Once I had gathered my nerve, and the shakes had stopped, I remembered how we had entered this room and made my way to leave it. The tunnel seemed farther now. When I had entered it before I was in really bad shape. Now I was better. I've tried not to think about what happened between those two points in time.

The path took me to the room where Donald had created so many of the Grotesques. Then, I found the stairs up to the doorway to the church.

As I opened it, I heard voices.

Roxy, Valerie, Arthur, and even Reggie had all made it out and were wait-ing for me in the pews. Roxy stood closest to me, so I looked to her for some explanation.

"We made it?" I asked. My voice cracked like I hadn't spoken in days.

Roxy smiled. "How else would I be here?" she asked.

I know that she was making a joke, but at that moment, I couldn't really focus on it to laugh or respond.

"You did a good job," Valerie said.

"Thanks . . . ," I said.

When she said that, Arthur nodded, which I think is the same as him saying it too.

I couldn't think of anything to say or ask. I was pretty sure that I had just died. I felt like I needed to throw up. Luckily the church was pretty much wrecked at that point, so I found a secluded bench and dry-heaved behind it.

In the distance, I heard someone talking. It was a familiar voice by that point.

"Congratulations! You won a ticket!" Silas the Showman said. His carnival music played in that slightly off-key way and filled the church with its crooked echoes.

The others were a bit less shaken up than me. I imagine they had each died plenty of times, save Valerie perhaps, who might not have even died once.

Valerie was the first to press Silas's red button. This storyline had actually been a little over her level, so she got rewarded pretty well. I don't know what tropes she got; the veterans didn't share the same little ritual of showing each other what tickets Silas had given them. I saw that she got some tropes and one stat ticket, which was probably pretty impressive at her level.

She also received something else she was very excited about.

"Arthur, look," she said, holding out the ticket.

Arthur looked at it and a smile grew on his face. "Looks like we're in busi-ness," he said.

I got close enough to look at what they were talking about.

Her ticket read, "One Free Voucher for any group of six or fewer aboard Carousel's own Excursion Train! Any included destination, any time. Ticket is valid for a round trip, assuming you make it out alive."

An excursion train? To get to destinations presumably outside of Carousel? That sounded huge. What kind of places could you go?

"What destinations are there?" I asked. I felt numb inside and out, but this sounded important.

"All around," Valerie said. "They're for storylines that can't take place in Car-ousel. We've been trying to get another ticket for a while."

I thought about what she was telling me.

"Any destinations to the west?" I asked.

Arthur smiled. "In fact, there are."

For years they had tried to go directly west. Now they were going to try and take a train west instead. Maybe they would have an easier time getting to the mountain with the lights that way. I wondered if that could work. Would Carousel see that as cheating?

"It's worth a shot," Valerie said. "I guess they told you . . ."

"He knows," Roxy said.

I smiled faintly. I was now one of the few who knew about the Rulekeeper and the veterans' attempts to make it west. I still didn't completely understand why it was a big secret, but it was nice to know.

Arthur got tropes. No level up.

Reggie got two stat tickets and five or so tropes.

Roxy got the same.

They all got a handful of coins.

Then it was my turn. I pressed the red button and . . . It was like I had won the jackpot.

Coins and tickets started to pour out of Silas's receptacle. In the end, I got around two hundred dollars, five stat tickets, and thirteen tropes. I even got a monster ticket, though only for one of the smaller Grotesques that I had killed with a hammer. I guess I didn't get the kill for the big one.

My star rating? Twenty-seven stars. That's what being really under-leveled got me.

I decided not to use the stat tickets until I had time to clear my head. The tropes I received fell out of the machine in two batches.

With the first batch, Silas said, "It's a shame to waste a good plan. Luckily, in Carousel, we recycle."

I wasn't sure what he meant at first.

Awarded tropes:

Raised by Television
Type: Buff
Archetype: Film Buff
Aspect: Fanatic
Stat Used: Moxie

The Film Buff has spent their entire life on the sidelines watching heroes of
the silver screen. Though in most of the story, they are a minor character,
they can achieve great things by referencing their fictional heroes and trying
to emulate them.

When this ticket is equipped, the Film Buff will receive a buff in whichever stat allows them to take a heroic or otherwise larger-than-life action. However, after this action is taken, the player's status as a minor character will catch up to them, often leading to disastrous results.

I must have gotten that for my self-immolation stunt.

My Grandmother Had the Gift . . .
Type: Background
Archetype: Any
Aspect: Any
Stat Used: ---

In movies, characters that have strong intuitions, but not explicit psychic powers, often explain their abilities by referencing a relative who had "the gift." A player who equips this background ticket will be able to work this explanation into their backstory to explain their otherworldly instincts.

The player may now equip:
Animal Whisperer (Adventurer)
He Has a Tell (Detective)
Like a Magnet for Evil (Psychic)
I Don't Like It Here . . . (Hysteric)
I Had a Feeling About You Two (Eye Candy)
We're Being Hunted . . . (Monster Hunter)
Don't Go in There! (Film Buff)

I Don't Like It Here . . .
Type: Insight
Archetype: Hysteric
Aspect: Craven
Stat Used: Savvy

The Hysteric has a keen sense of the ominous and strong self-preservation instincts. Using these abilities, they can ferret out Omens and help guide their group out of potentially tricky situations.

That was Janet's trope. What kind of sick joke was that? Giving me a fallen player's trope? I couldn't even think. I needed to clear my mind.

The second batch of tropes came out after I had already grabbed the first three. There were ten, and I couldn't equip any of them. I didn't know what to think of that.

When I asked Arthur about it, he said it happens sometimes, though not usually in that quantity. He told me to take the ones I didn't want to the pawn shop in the town square. He said the guy there would take them in trade for all kinds of things.

Still, it was confusing.

The tropes were as follows:

<table>
<tr><td>

A Glitch in the Matrix
Type: Insight
Archetype: Hysteric
Aspect: Defiant
Stat Used: Savvy

</td></tr>
<tr><td>

In a supernatural story, characters can often become paranoid as events start to unfold in a way that cannot be explained by natural law. During the Party and Rebirth phases, the player that equips this trope will continue to see events that do not line up with reality and that hint at the true nature of the evil that surrounds them.
Or maybe you're just paranoid . . .

</td></tr>
</table>

<table>
<tr><td>

A Story within a Story
Type: Rule
Archetype: Artist
Aspect: ---
Stat Used: Savvy

</td></tr>
<tr><td>

Horror writers are common protagonists in horror movies. Often, the stories that they write have a way of reflecting or predicting the main storyline. With this ticket equipped, the Artist will be able to bring a book or work-in-progress prop into the storyline. By intelligently relaying the events and themes of their story in the Party phase, they can manipulate larger events and themes of the storyline. This trope takes much practice to control.

</td></tr>
</table>

<table>
<tr><td>

Watching over You . . .
Type: Buff
Archetype: Departed
Aspect: ---
Stat Used: Moxie

</td></tr>
<tr><td>

In films that touch on departed loved ones sticking around on earth, their presence is often felt by those around them, even if it is only a vague emotional embrace. The player who equips this ticket can buff their still-living teammates' Grit simply by following them around after death. The stronger the characters' relationships on-screen before the death of the player, the stronger the buff.

</td></tr>
</table>

Who You Truly Are . . .
Type: Rule
Archetype: Outsider
Aspect: Newcomer
Stat Used: Moxie

A character often begins a storyline believing their troubled history will define their future, only for circumstances to arise that allow them to overcome their past.

A player with this ticket equipped will slowly gain Plot Armor boosts, and their role will increase as the storyline progresses, moving them from a minor character at the beginning to a major one at the end. The player must perform the role as it is assigned to receive the associated buffs and increased screen time. Must begin the story with a lower Plot Armor than other major characters.

Everybody loves a comeback story.

Friends in High Places
Type: Action
Archetype: Soldier
Aspect: Agent
Stat Used: Moxie/Savvy

In movies, cops and soldiers are often able to act like complete mavericks and ignore all rules without consequences. One excuse for why they can get away with this is because they have a friend high up in command who will cover for them.

When this ticket is equipped, the player will be able to invoke favor from some fictional character that has direct authority over the situation. Creativity and conviction are required to make this trope function. This ability can be used to gain access to restricted areas, get out of trouble, or simply to make some quality-of-life adjustments for the players.

"Any minute now your phone is about to ring, someone's going to yell at you, and then you're going to apologize to me . . ."

This Is Going to Sting a Bit . . .
Type: Healing
Archetype: Doctor
Aspect: Medic
Stat Used: Moxie

Some injuries are so severe that healing them at all would completely destroy the suspension of disbelief. However, there is a cure for that as well. When this trope is equipped, the player can heal their teammates with heightened effectiveness as long as they play up how painful the procedure is.

Making the cure painful can keep the suspension of disbelief intact. However, both the player and the teammate being healed must consistently act as if the procedure is painful. Sometimes, they'll need to do more than just pretend.

Accidentally Captured on Film
Type: Insight
Archetype: Artist
Aspect: ---
Stat Used: Moxie

If an important character is taking pictures on-screen in a horror, thriller, or mystery film, there is an 87% chance that those pictures will not only eventually appear on-screen, but will contain some clue that will allow the character insight into the story. Equipping this trope allows the player to carry a camera into a storyline. Any pictures that they take during the Party phase have an increased chance of revealing useful information that was not readily apparent at the time.

Stick to the Plan
Type: Rule
Archetype: Final Girl
Aspect: Team Leader
Stat Used: Moxie

The job of a good leader is to continue to move the team forward even when all hope is lost. Often in a movie, the survivors' plan will be in shambles, and yet they'll continue forward. When equipped, this trope will allow the player to get even an apparently failed plan back on track, simply by convincing the audience that there is still a chance through a late-game rallying speech.

Back to Where It All Started . . .
Type: Rule
Archetype: Detective
Aspect: ---
Stat Used: Savvy

Mysteries often have themes about the past affecting the future. The sins long-since forgotten reach forward to strangle us. When this ticket is equipped, the player will be able to change the setting of the final battle to one of the settings either from the beginning of the storyline or from something that occurred in the past, by using a well-spoken and well-reasoned argument for why the plot "will" go in that direction. If successful, the players will get a brief reprieve in order to scout out and explore the setting before the final battle arrives. This will function as a miniature second Party phase wherein most believable exploration tropes will be temporarily reactivated. You may not be able to change the past, but sometimes you can reexplore it.

The Intrepid Guide Who Knows the Way
Type: Rule
Archetype: Adventurer
Aspect: ---
Stat Used: Moxie

What do you need when you need to find a lost ancient tomb? Who will take you deep into shark-infested waters when no one else is brave enough? Who can take you into the most dangerous jungle and then bring you back out again? An adventure guide.

When exploring places uncharted or long forgotten, the players will have the option to either hire or invite an NPC guide who has been to their destination before. Beware, the relationship you have with your guide may make the difference between life and death.

This guide will provide you with assistance and insights. But if they die, you may not be able to find your way home.

I didn't know what to make of these new tropes. I pocketed them and soon left the church with the others. I wasn't looking forward to what we were going to say about Janet.

What would we tell her husband?

CHAPTER FORTY-SIX

KEEPING SECRETS

On the return to Camp Dyer, Carousel was like a new place. Janet's I Don't Like It Here . . . trope was transformative. I could see Omens everywhere; no wonder she was freaked out all the time. I even saw things that Arthur didn't mention as he guided us back.

When I looked at something that was an Omen, I would see a brass display sign on the red wallpaper with the word "Warning."

Sometimes, I would get a whole lot more information than that. I occasionally got entire posters, with storyline titles, vague suggestions of difficulty level, specific actions needed to trigger the Omen, everything. The determining factor appeared to be my Savvy. Low-level storylines I knew everything about. For high-level storylines, I only got "Warning."

There was a storyline called *The Look Back* that could be triggered by walking through an alleyway and . . . looking behind you. The poster just showed a man carrying groceries with a look of horror on his face. Its difficulty level was "Get to the car now!"

Whatever that meant.

I saw another storyline called *Just Deserts* that took place at a sweets shop called Just Desserts. It was triggered by ordering something and not appreciating it. I'm not sure what that meant exactly. Its difficulty level was "I'm fairly alarmed."

Very informative.

Most storylines gave much less information than that, but it was amazing to see beyond the veil, if only a little. If I was in a better state of mind, I might have enjoyed looking around at all the stuff. That may just be me though.

As we moved past town toward Camp Dyer, I got less and less information. Things really did get tougher out this way.

* * *

Once we got back to camp, the tension in the air choked any conversation that could start. No one was looking forward to telling people what had happened to Janet. Arthur had assured us that he would be the one to tell everyone. Apparently, that had been something that he and Adeline had done many times over the years.

As we approached the lodge, we were greeted by a sea of curious players. What had happened that day was everyone's business. I didn't see Bobby among them. I really didn't want to.

Adeline greeted us on the trail before we got to the lodge. We stopped to talk to her.

"Janet?" she asked.

Arthur shook his head. "Disappeared."

Adeline nodded. I could tell from her face that she understood what that meant. They had told me that she didn't actually know about the axe murderer, and yet I got the sense that she knew enough. As far as I knew, Arthur and Adeline had been in Carousel for nearly twenty years.

How had Arthur kept the secret from someone he had known for so long?

Did he even have a choice?

As we approached the lodge, Adeline was quick to gently get the word out to those outside about what had happened to Janet. Her "disappearance" was taken very well. The reaction was somber, but none of the veteran players seemed to be surprised.

My friends, however, looked horrified. I couldn't blame them. They didn't have the *understanding* yet.

This was clearly a big event. Even Dina, who only socialized to go out on storylines every once in a while, had stuck around awaiting our return. As soon as we got back, her eyes zoned in on me. It looked like she was reading about me on the red wallpaper.

It was only when we got inside, and everyone had gathered around to hear a rundown of what had happened, that Bobby Gill, husband of the deceased, made his presence known.

"Where is Janet?" he asked. He had been worried. You could tell he was a bundle of stress. He was standing with Travis and company—ironically, the exact people Janet had not wanted him to be around.

"Look, Bobby, maybe we should go outside," Arthur said.

Travis shook his head, having apparently already figured out the bad news. "I knew it."

"Knew what?" Bobby asked. "Where's Janet?"

Adeline intervened. "Let's go outside, Bobby."

"Why? What happened to Janet?" he asked. "Tell me what happened to Janet!"

"She disappeared," Arthur said.

Whispers echoed throughout the crowd from those who had not already heard. I couldn't tell what they were saying, but I knew they didn't sound surprised either.

"Disappeared?" Bobby asked. "Where? How?"

"On the storyline we went on," Arthur answered. "She didn't show up at The End."

Bobby didn't get it. "I was telling them she wouldn't have gone on a storyline. She has anxiety problems. Why would she be on a storyline?"

He must have been told she went out on a storyline. He was still deep in denial over it.

"Just take a seat," Adeline said. "Come here."

She gestured for him to sit on one of the couches. When he didn't move, she gently placed a hand on his back, guiding him in that direction.

"No!" he said. He pulled away from her. "Why was she on a storyline? We need to go find her."

I could only imagine what was going through his mind at that moment. When you hear the word "disappeared" you don't think "dead." You think that there's some hope out there. That was the flaw in using that term as a euphemism for death.

And yet, it appeared that everyone else *did* understand. They knew what "disappeared" meant. They probably even knew why she was gone, more or less. They just didn't know about the Rulekeeper.

"People go missing sometimes," Adeline said. "They disappear without a trace. I'm so sorry."

"No," Bobby said. "She would never have gone on a storyline. We talked about it; she was going to wait until I could go with her."

Adeline explained everything that had happened. She talked about how the box had been delivered specifically for Janet and that there was no way we could have avoided sending her on that storyline.

She said everything short of "Your wife died because she broke the rules," presumably out of some desire to treat Bobby delicately, as she was so hellbent on doing with new players. It might have been better if she had just come out with it, instead of relying on subtlety and tact.

"She wouldn't have gone!" he yelled. "Not without telling me."

At that point, many of the others who had been there to witness what had happened tried explaining that she had gone on the storyline. Unfortunately, so many people were talking at once that they may have actually made things worse.

"Who forced her to do this?" Bobby yelled.

"Carousel," Arthur said. "We had no choice."

The outsider, Travis, looked livid. "We don't know that," he said. "We're taking your word on that. I heard about what happened. What if you had just left the package there? It could have been gone in a few days. Why is it that in this place we are constantly struck by situations we have never seen before, and yet we're supposed to trust that you know the right way to handle them?"

"Now is not the time for this," Arthur said through gritted teeth.

Travis laughed. "In Carousel, all we have is time, and yet there's never enough time to discuss things that you don't want to talk about."

At that point, the argument ended. Not amicably, but because Reggie had grabbed Travis and started to haul him out of the lodge.

"You want answers to your questions, Bobby," Travis said as he was being hauled away. "Ask why the kid has her trope."

Everyone in the room, including my friends—including Adeline herself— turned to look at me. Even the teammates that I had just taken on the Grotesque storyline with hadn't realized that I had gotten Janet's trope.

Every eye in the building was on me.

"I got it as a reward," I said. I must have sounded really nervous at the time. "From Silas."

I hadn't really thought about the implication of wrongdoing. I thought it was just another example of Carousel mocking us. Give the new guy the dead person's old ticket. That sort of thing.

"What happened to Janet?" Bobby asked in a raised voice.

I panicked. I wasn't prepared to answer that question. When Arthur had said that he would tell everyone, I had stopped thinking about it. Most of the people I spent time with came with a pause and rewind button.

I actually did attempt to tell them what had happened. But when it came down to it, right as I was about to speak, I heard *him*.

I heard his breath in my ear. The axe murderer. The Rulekeeper. It was so loud that I jerked around to look behind me.

"I don't know," I stammered out.

No one said anything.

"She . . ." How was I supposed to word this in a way that wouldn't upset the entity that had apparently taken root in my brain? "She didn't . . ."

Fortunately, it only took a few moments for Adeline to get her feet back under her after the reveal that I had been awarded Janet's trope.

"It doesn't matter. Carousel does things all the time to twist the knife," she said. "I'm sure this was just part of that."

I felt a hand on my shoulder. I turned to look at who it was. It was Roxy.

"Don't worry about it. Travis is an asshole; no one's going to take him seriously."

I hoped that she was right, but with the day's events—the stress of meeting the Rulekeeper, the stress of dying—I was in no shape to think clearly.

As embarrassing as it is to admit, it felt like I was about to tear up. Exactly no part of my personality would allow me to show emotion like that in front of people. I had spent decades building walls to prevent that exact thing.

I pushed my way through the crowd to the little room I shared with Camden and shut the door.

As I closed the door, I could hear Valerie explaining that I had died for the first time that day.

I stayed there for hours. As silly as it was, I contemplated breaking the window so that I could leave the room without having to go back out through the crowds of people outside.

I lay on my bed hoping that sleep would give me a break from all of this, but it was hard to sleep until the sun went down—because of the westward-facing window and because I had a million things on my mind.

How were we going to escape?

What was the story behind the axe murderer?

Why had I been given Janet's old trope?

I thought about what Silas had said when he gave it to me. "It's a shame to waste a good plan. Luckily, in Carousel, we recycle."

Was that just Silas saying some canned joke, or did it mean something . . . more?

As I thought about that, there was a knock at the door. I really didn't want to answer, but if it was Camden, I couldn't keep him out of his own room.

When I opened it, I was greeted by my friends. What was I going to say to them?

"Riley," Anna said, "we didn't get a chance to talk. Do you mind if we come in?"

I wasn't sure if I was in a headspace to talk, but I waved them into the little closet Camden and I called home.

I didn't know what to say, so I just let them speak.

"I'm sorry you had to go through that," Antoine said. "I'll make it up to you and Camden. Everyone."

Antoine still blamed himself for everything.

"Are you okay?" Anna asked. "It must have been terrifying."

I nodded. "At parts."

"You know you can talk to us about stuff," she said.

"Nothing to talk about."

There was an awkward silence for a beat.

"You get any good loot?" Camden asked. He hadn't spoken much since having died himself. But I guess it was his turn to hold the support baton.

I hadn't thought much about the awards I had gotten. A spark of excitement ignited in my mind because that was something I could talk about. It was something I could distract myself with.

I reached into my pocket. It was strange. Even though I had a big stack of tickets now, I hadn't noticed how inconvenient it was to carry them around until I went to grab them. It was almost like they weren't even there until you reached for them. Strange.

Whatever the case, I took out the tickets and started to show them around. Most of them were useless to me. I showed Anna the Final Girl trope I had gotten, Stick to the Plan, and promised to give it to her. I explained how useful it could be. She conveyed interest, but I think her mind was on something else.

I showed them the monster ticket with a high-level Grotesque on it. I told them about the pawn shop Arthur had spoken about. I theorized we might be able to trade the monster tickets there.

Camden was amazed at how many tropes I had gotten, not to mention the stat tickets, which would put my Plot Armor well above his once I used them.

I read off the array of useless tropes I had gotten.

Then I told them about on-screen/off-screen manipulation, and how we had been able to keep Roxy alive long enough for a 13 percent debuff on all the creatures.

Of course, geeking out could only last so long.

"Was Janet . . . gone already when that happened?" Antoine asked. "We're just curious."

Kimberly and Anna gave him a scolding look.

I couldn't blame him. No matter what I said, the question that they would most want answered was what had happened to Janet. In my explanation of our exploits in the storyline, I had left her out altogether. She had been gone by the time most of the interesting stuff started.

I nodded quickly. I held my breath, wondering if that simple answer would summon the phantom presence of the Rulekeeper. Luckily, I heard nothing.

I took out the I Don't Like It Here . . . trope ticket and showed it to them.

"Do you . . . Do you know what happened to her?" Camden asked.

After having died, nothing felt real. I felt like I was sleepwalking. Nothing felt important or urgent, not even the dire circumstances of my captivity here in Carousel. But as soon as I contemplated telling my friends about the axe murderer, suddenly everything felt real.

My heart was beating faster than it had been when fighting the Grotesques.

I could hear him as if he were right behind me. I could hear his feet shifting on the ground, his breath in my ear.

Still, these were my friends, and keeping him a secret felt wrong. It felt like they deserved to know. I'd learned that day that everyone basically knew what happened to the people who "disappeared," but nobody knew the specifics. They also knew why it happened. No one had to be told why Janet had been singled out. Even then, telling them that there's an actual entity enforcing the rules around here felt important.

And yet I was afraid.

I was afraid that I would be endangering them by telling them. I was afraid that I was endangering myself.

"She just . . . disappeared," I said, with a deep sense of shame I couldn't shake.

And as I scanned their faces—Anna, who was so trusting; Camden, whom I had shared my secrets with as a child; Kimberly, a sweet and honest soul; and Antoine, who might have had the strength to be honest if he were in my shoes . . .

I could tell that they knew I was hiding something.

I had never felt so alone.

ABOUT THE AUTHOR

Rob M. Lastrel is the author of the Game at Carousel series, originally released on Royal Road. Fascinated by the eerie and unknown, he writes weird, otherworldly escapism. When he isn't writing, he spends his time hiking and hopes to one day visit every national park in the United States.

DISCOVER
STORIES UNBOUND

PodiumAudio.com